Also by Kathleen Shoop

The Last Letter

My Dear Frank

(The letters that inspired, The Last Letter, edited by Shoop and Jacobs)

A Novel

AFTER

The

FOG

KATHLEEN SHOOP

To the people of Donora—past and present

"Many people from Donora were immigrants or their parents were. Things were bad where they came from and they had nothing. Many of them had lived in lands of kings. Life in Donora was good—no one could tell them what to do because they weren't born into a certain family. And, they weren't going to mess that up because of a little bit of fog."

Dr. Charles Stacey—2008

[discussing the perspective of some Donorans at the time of the killing smog]

"These men stormed the beaches of Normandy—what's a little smoke to them?"

Harry Loftus—2008

[discussing the way some Donorans viewed the daily smoke/smog]

Author's Note

During the week of October 24th, 1948, Donora, Pennsylvania experienced an environmental disaster that drew the nation's attention. The events of that week brought tragedy to the great steel town and transformed the way the world viewed industrial pollution and its effect on the environment and public health. Although the characters and their plotlines in this novel are fictional, the disaster is not.

Chapter 1

Tuesday, October 26th, 1948
Donora, Pennsylvania

Inside the Greshecky home, Rose pressed the light switch but knew it wouldn't work. Ian appeared, his form outlined by the paltry light slipping through a gap in the wood siding. Even in darkness his complexion—white as the smoky plumes billowing from the zinc mill—told Rose things were not well with his Aunt. He opened his mouth, but Rose grasped his shoulders and shoved the twelve-year-old toward the kitchen before Ian could form a single word.

"Heat the water. Get the clean towels we hid away for the birth."

Ian looked at his feet, but didn't move.

"Go on. You remember," Rose said.

Ian nodded.

Isabella's screech from the back of the house summoned Rose toward the bedroom. She groped the walls trying to remember the placement of the furniture. The last thing she needed was to trip and fall. She stepped where the wood floor dropped a few inches into an unfinished dirt path, stumbled and twisted her knee. She grimaced and fell back against the wall, bent over, grasping her throbbing leg. Nothing felt out of place. Another wail. Rose pushed off the wall and limped down the hall toward Isabella. She slammed open the bedroom door, tearing it from its hinge.

In the middle of the shadowy room, Isabella squatted as though urinating, her nightgown splashed with blackened blood, its thick iron odor choking the air. Rose hooked Isabella under the arms and hauled her toward the window, and the mattress on the ground. Rose dug her heels in; thankful traction was the one good attribute of having a mud floor.

She gritted her teeth, wanting to reassure Isabella, to remind her of the slew of births Rose had assisted over the years. But Isabella's awkward two hundred pounds consumed the energy Rose might have spent on reassuring words.

Isabella groaned and bucked forward. Rose knelt in front of her on the mattress, praying for the moon to move a sliver to the right and illuminate the shadowy room. Rose needed to assess why there was so much blood; Ian was spooked enough to forget the candles she had requested, and his uncle, the baby's father, was on shift at the mill.

Rose gripped Isabella's knees and tried to wrench them apart. "It's all right, you can let go. It's okay, Isabella. Baby's coming." Isabella's legs gave way and fell open as she dropped back onto the mattress, gasping. Rose felt between the woman's legs to the baby's crowned head. She felt a surge of panic at Isabella's sudden silence, but pushed her fear away.

Rose supported the baby's head and reached for Isabella's hand. She squinted, trying to gauge if Isabella's nails had blued from lack of oxygen, but it was too dark.

"Isabella? You all right? Baby's here. Prop yourself up, you don't even need to push, he's coming, he's—"

The baby slid out, bringing the usual tumble of cording, but so much more Rose thought she was witnessing the birth of triplets. So much flesh falling through her fingers in the darkness. The rush of blood warmed Rose's knees, saturating her nurse's uniform as if it were consuming it.

Her breath tripped and sputtered as she fumbled through the mass of expelled tissue and peeled the baby away. She flipped the body over, whacking its back. Part of Rose understood what she was experiencing, but in the darkness, she could pretend.

"It's a girl, Isabella. Your baby girl's here. Just like you wanted. A girl to stay by your side." Rose worked quickly, firmly opening the baby's airway and bracing her against her chest, warming her back to life. The baby was definitely full-term, but too thin, and not breathing, heart stilled. Rose cursed herself for not forcing Isabella to take the labor inducement, but the woman thought God alone had the right to induce anything.

"Auntie Bella?"

Rose snapped around. She hadn't heard anyone come into the room. Behind her stood Ian, a nearly invisible form holding fresh bleached towels that glowed in the twilight. The image of a happy birth flashed through Rose's mind, a plump, pink baby and healthy mother. Rose's heart heaved with desolation at what Ian was about to understand.

She waved Ian to her. "I need you to hold this little princess while I tend to your aunt. And, get the scissors from my bag."

He nodded, handing over the downy towels and dashed to Rose's bag. She didn't have time to tell him how to be sanitary when handling them, too busy toweling the blood and fluid from the baby's eyes, her own burning from the emotion she was stuffing away.

Ian dashed back with the scissors, thrusting them under Rose's nose.

"She's okay, right? Both of them?"

Rose lay the baby on the towel, not saying a word, and cut the infant's cord. Next she swaddled the baby and handed her to Ian. She shuffled him toward the chair across the room and ordered him to sit; fearful he might pass out, afraid if he wasn't in the room, she might.

3

Rose resumed her attempts to stop Isabella's bleeding and rouse her with soft words, knowing the woman died with the birth of her daughter. Even without surgical lighting, Rose saw the woman's uterus had been expelled with the baby and even in a hospital, it was unlikely she would have survived.

"Sweet Isabella," Rose whispered, wiping the woman's hair from her brow. "I'll put in a call to Dr. Bonaroti." Rose wiped her hands on the uniform's apron; angered the physician hadn't made it to the birth.

"No phone, Nurse Rose," Ian said, "'member last time yunz guys come down the house for—"

Ian began hyperventilating, his body shuddering rhythmically, bouncing him out of the chair. His desperation jolted Rose's own grief. She dashed toward the boy grasping his arms.

"That'll be enough, Ian. I need your help."

He looked up, snot flying from his nose, saliva at the corners of his mouth like a rabid animal, and she grabbed him from the chair, hugged him so tight he choked. She held him there, baby between them. Rose eased his pain with the warmth of her skin, hoping that she could stave off the sadness he'd feel as he grew up without his aunt.

"Now Ian. You need to go next door and phone Dr. Bonaroti." *Where was that damn doctor?* This was exactly why Donora needed to fund Rose for the next year. If her nearly one year serving as a community nurse had shown her anything, it was that they actually needed three nurses. Just two more months of funding and the program was shot if their data wasn't convincing.

Rose took the baby and guided Ian from the room. "Tell Alice to tell the doc it's an emergency."

She rubbed his back and wanted to say everything would be all right, but she knew nothing would be fine for young Ian. His uncle had a lust for booze and when he wasn't breaking his neck in the zinc mill, was inattentive even at his most benign.

Though she would have given anything to be one of those people who could lie to make someone feel better, she had discovered through the losses she'd experienced in life, she was not that kind of woman at all.

* * *

With candles finally lit and a mixing bowl of water by the bed, Rose wiped Isabella's crusting blood with a moist pledget. The blood had hardened into shapes, a map of where a life had drained from a body; the heaviest, black splashes were caked near the opening that should have delivered the world vibrant life instead of death.

Rose swallowed tears and cleared her throat. More could have been done for Isabella. If only there was more than one community nurse in town. No time for tears. She prayed for Isabella, repeating Hail Marys and Our Fathers hoping somehow the act would help usher the lost souls into the afterlife.

A door slammed somewhere in the home and Rose stopped her work. Her lips kept perfect prayerful time. Dr. Bonaroti barreled into the bedroom, stopped short behind Rose, kicking dirt up from the primitive floor. His unusual silence conveyed sorrow that a patient had met her end in the way she had.

"Doctor," Rose said without looking up from Isabella's leg.

"Rose." His voice was low.

She washed Isabella's legs. Her touch was firm, but gentle, scrubbing as though Isabella's spirit might feel the cleansing of her flesh. With her free hand, Rose fished around the bowl beside her for another pledget and held it up to Bonaroti. He shuffled around Isabella's body, taking his place across from Rose.

The doctor and his nurse bathed Isabella in silent, tandem rhythm that reflected their sadness and expertise in caring for patients for decades.

When they finished, Rose got the white sheet she brought with her and snapped it into the air, releasing its fresh scent. It billowed up and out before dropping and draping Isabella's still bloated shape. Bonaroti examined the baby and scribbled on his documents, lifting his gaze to Rose periodically. She met his eyes with a nod, noting that this death was particularly hard for him. In most situations, he was not afraid to infuse the moment with his dry sense of humor.

Rose wrapped the infant in a small blanket and marveled at her blemish-free face. Somehow they must be wrong; this infant, with no outward signs of death was really alive. Rose unwrapped the baby, listened for breath again, felt for the rush of blood where thin veins and arteries ran inside her tiny wrist. Certain the baby was dead, Rose tucked the precious bundle inside Isabella's arm as though they were asleep after a late night feeding.

"You're not going to try and baptize this one? Not going to call the priest?" Dr. Bonaroti said.

"I wanted to. But she was dead on arrival." Rose cleared her throat worried the tiny soul would live in limbo, caught between heaven and hell. She sped through another Hail Mary and asked God to let this one pass through the gates without baptism. That couldn't be right, sentenced to an eternity in limbo for lack of one breath and a splash of water over your brow? Rose didn't think it was true, but still her heart clenched in dread.

Rose took one final look at mother and child and smoothed Isabella's hair from her face, her fingers lingering, offering final comfort to a body no longer in need of human touch.

* * *

Outside the Greshecky's, Rose sent Ian next door to the Draganac's who agreed to take him in until his uncle finished working. Rose shifted her weight, hands on hip. In the early morning, the cool air mixed with her perspiration and chilled her. She waited for Doc Bonaroti to emerge from the house to discuss the coming day's plans. Though standing by herself on the hill above town, she was hardly alone. The familiar machinations of sleepless Donora kept her company.

Down below, carving the land nearly into an island, the horseshoe-shaped Monongahela River pushed northward. The "Mon," as locals referred to the river, fed Donora's steel, wire, and zinc mills—three full miles of industry. The town was located twenty miles south of its big steel sister, Pittsburgh, but was no less important. Incorporated in 1901, United States Steel had gifted Donora with its prized zinc mill in 1915 for the loyalty of the steel workers. Donora understood the power of steel and the way it fueled their existence.

Rose yawned and stretched as the last of the lights snapped off in the Draganac home, hoping Ian might sleep even for a short time. A burst of fire drew Rose's attention back down the hill. Like triplets, the three mills shared patronage, but each bore its own personality, voice and strength. The three industry siblings were the heart of the town—the reason Donora existed.

They shared veins and arteries in the form of rail systems, and each worked non-stop swallowing raw materials and spewing waste while producing steel to be flat-rolled and sheared, galvanized with zinc and finally driven into the world to gird the infrastructure that built and armed the greatest nation known to man.

The open hearth and blast furnaces were the family show-offs. Their fiery displays mesmerized onlookers with rushing flames, bringing people to a halt as though the hot work was a circus act. Even disposing of the furnace waste—the slag—inspired awe. Poured from rail cars the molten, lava-like debris lit up the sky as it spilled down hillsides in Palmer Park or into the Mon where it cooled and hardened, creating a sturdy riverbank.

Rose tapped her toe, keeping time with the firing of metal through molds in the wire-works—the loudmouth, most practical of the three mills. Its sensible nails provided never-ending uses as Americans clamored to build homes after the war. The rhythmic, measured beat of nails being shaped to industrial perfection accompanied life in Donora. It was a normal occurrence and expected, like breathing.

Rose checked her watch. Bonaroti and one of the funeral directors, Mr. Matthews, should be finishing up inside. Rose thought of Mr. Greshecky working in the zinc mill. That mill was the moody sibling. Everyone knew its value and so its punishing, scorching ways were overlooked. It produced a substance that protected steel from corrosion, keeping the products of the other two mills, rust-free, forever functional. The mill was so hot many workers toiled in four-hour shifts, rather than the typical eight.

Rose rubbed a knot in the back of her neck. Out of the corner of her eye, she saw a light go on in the Hamilton home and a flash of the missus as she passed by a window. Like the mills that never stopped, Donora's residents rarely did either. Sixty-five hundred of the fourteen thousand residents labored in the mills. Most of the men who weren't employed there worked in businesses that supported them in one way or another.

And the women and children—their lives were wrought by the mills every bit as much as the steel produced inside them. Up early to feed husbands off to the day shift, and staying awake late into the night hours to cook for sons on the night shift, the women worked nonstop; children ate dinner at odd hours and opened presents as close to Christmas morning as their fathers' shifts allowed. No one, nothing, in Donora was exempt from the body cracking, character-building work required of their lives.

And standing there in what would amount to the most quiet moments of Rose's day she wondered what it would be like to experience true silence, with no machinery underwriting every second of her life. She heard the slam of a door and looked over her shoulder to see Doc Bonaroti emerge from the Greshecky home, his dour expression making the ache in her neck worse.

Bonaroti shrugged then kicked at the curb. Rose knew he was discouraged if he was risking a scuff on the toe of his perfectly shined shoes.

Rose sighed. "So. What are our options for funding as we head into the last two months?"

He pushed his glasses further back on his nose. "Present our case to the Easter Seals society, Women's Club, Red Cross—"

Rose's teeth chattered, and she pulled her coat tighter. "Fanny has plans for the Red Cross donations."

Dr. Bonaroti nodded and held up his hand. "The new superintendent's wife is the head of the Women's Club now. She's willing to look at your data, to go with you to the Lipinski's and to another home of your choosing—"

"To *what?* To watch me work? No. Think of the patients. They aren't zoo animals."

Bonaroti set his bag at his feet and pushed up the arms of his suit-coat, revealing a trail of cheap watches people had used to pay him for his services. This was his way of reminding Rose that if citizens of a small town, even one with three thriving mills had to regularly pay a doctor with watches and the occasional hen, then she needed to make a damn good case for paying a community nurse.

Rose shrugged. "You're right. I made twenty-five hundred calls in the last ten months. We need three nurses if we need one. So, whatever it takes, I'll do it. We can't have more Isabellas."

Bonaroti pressed his lips together and pushed down his sleeves. He grinned, lifting his bag. "And a dentist, Rose. The Community Welfare Committee over in Moon Run springs for a dentist for the miners' families. Surely we can rustle up some cash for a dentist to take a look at all these mouths full of mottled teeth."

He started down the steps that served as sidewalks, a necessity in Donora due to the sharp angle of the hills. The fog was thick and hid him from Rose though she could hear his footsteps.

"Let's get my services paid for another year," Rose said, lifting her voice. "Before we add a dentist to the mix, don't you say?"

"Yes, let's." His disembodied voice carried over the groaning tugboats and screeching trains below.

Rose straightened and took a deep breath, wondering how she'd make it through the day with all that had to be done.

* * *

The time between a difficult call and arriving home gave Rose a chance to reflect, to feel gratitude, to pray. She plodded through the misty night, negotiating uneven cement walks, moving slower than she liked, the fog adding heaviness to the darkness of the early morning hour.

Around her, four hundred-fifty feet of mountainside lurched into the air, and slumped over the valley. Near the mills the narrow, soot-encrusted homes of its workers marched along the flatlands. Heading up the hillsides, houses were stacked; clinging to dirt and rock like children nestled to their mother's chest.

Rose enjoyed knowing the social makeup of the different sections of town and what that meant for her service to the people. Like a parent checking on children, opening bedroom doors and peeking inside to be sure they were sleeping peacefully, Rose did the same as she trekked home. She paused at certain addresses mentally ticking off whether all seemed well. She made lists of who she needed to check on the next day, which people might still be suffering after an earlier visit and who was covering up an illness that needed to be addressed in the first place.

One section of Donora called Cement City boasted cement walled homes, built to last centuries and keep mill smoke out of the house. They were designated for mill management and lower-rung hotshots. Overlook Terrace, at the other end of town, was for the superintendents of each mill. But streets like Murray Avenue, where Rose lived, were home to American born newspaper editors and immigrant laborers. Some folks had money tucked away in Mellon Bank, growing as fast as their post-war families and others had barely managed to save a few dimes.

Donora was full of people with all manner of education, breeding, and heritage. There were twenty-two churches and a synagogue in the compact town, yet somehow they managed to live happily. Rose knew much of the contentment stemmed from steady work in the mills. The promise of a secure source of income helped people keep soft hearts and open minds toward neighbors.

Rose reached her hodgepodge home, drew a deep breath and sighed. She would not have enough time to sleep so she surrendered to the work ahead, hopeful that her large family would do their part to help.

She grasped the oversized doorknob, and heard familiar huffing and puffing. Before she could turn, the mutt gently clamped her ankle with his mouth and licked her. Its stinking slobber wafted through the thick air.

"Stupid dog!" Rose shook her foot to loosen its grip and grazed the dog's muzzle. It collapsed into a ball, tail tucked in. Rose covered her mouth and squeezed her eyes shut. Go away, she thought, I don't like animals. Rose had learned lack of cleanliness was host to many deadly or debilitating diseases. So, she'd decided long before that when she met an animal that didn't carry disease or filth with it, she'd let it in the house.

Rose exhaled and stood over the pooch, disapproving of its shaggy fur, the ropey knots resembling the rags she used to clean house.

"I'm sorry I caught your nose with my foot, but you shouldn't be here."

It lifted its gaze and let out a raspy cry. Rose stared back, clutching her nurse's bag to her belly. "Now go on, you raggedy rags!" He bolted, leaving a fresh burst of sour odor of scabby filth in its wake.

Rose twisted the doorknob, threw her body against the side-door and heard the usual screech across the linoleum. Inside, she fell back, shoving the door closed. She tried to wipe the sound of Ian's sobs from her mind.

A rush of hot air from the radiator beside her flushed her face, and raised a rancid, bloody odor from her clothing. She looked at her watch. Five A.M. She felt every minute of the sleepless night. But *The Techniques and Expectations of Community Nursing Manual* demanded Rose immediately cleanse all used instruments and containers after a call. She swallowed a yawn and said another prayer for strength. Nursing meant everything to her; she was proud of her skill. To Rose, being a good mother was a given. She had no choice but to give her children a solid upbringing, but nursing gave her a sense of self-worth she'd never quite found any other way.

All she needed was a sip of water before she set to clean her instruments and start breakfast. Rose shook off her tweed coat. She sighed as she hung it on its own hook as per manual instructions, away from the other coats that draped the rickety coat-rack in the corner, behind the door.

Rose entered the kitchen and stopped short at the sight of her seventeen-year-old son hunched over the percolator, measuring coffee grains into the metal basket. Her jaw dropped at the sight of what he was using as a measuring tool. Urine sample cups. It didn't matter that Rose scrubbed them after use with the prescribed green soap until they gleamed; they were still vessels for bodily fluids.

"Johnny? What the hell are you doing?"

He emptied one into the basket. "Making coffee?"

Rose wanted to rip the cup from his hands and beat him on the skull with it, but didn't have the energy for it. "They're urine cups. You're damn lucky those college football scouts don't make surprise visits to be sure you fellas are as smart as you look on paper."

"Gee thanks, Mum." Johnny laughed, dumping the coffee into the garbage can. "I was wondering why we had six coffee measures." Rose got a whiff of alcohol as he turned toward her. He wouldn't drink on a school night? Not him. Not her baby.

"Geez-o-man, Mum, that blood." He covered his mouth and collapsed over the sink, retching.

Rose shook her head at his weak stomach, patted his back and leaned her hip against the sink. She sniffed near his mouth; the odor of booze was gone as suddenly as it had been there. Exhaustion must have been taking over her sanity.

She yanked open a drawer and flipped a worn dishcloth to Johnny. He wiped his mouth and straightened, leaning against the sink, mirroring Rose's stance.

Rose fluffed his hair, its Vaseline sheen lost during the night. "Go back to bed for an hour."

"Can't sleep."

13

Rose put her hand over Johnny's. "You have a big week ahead of you."

He stiffened. A grimace flashed across his normally affable expression. Rose was hard on him regarding his future, but she knew when to push and when to let go. An argument about the importance of college and a scholarship wouldn't help anyone at this hour.

"I was wondering," Johnny said. He squeezed Rose's hand and seemed to search her face for permission to continue. "Maybe we could talk about college. This week, before the game."

Rose closed her eyes and bit the inside of her cheek. She could not have this conversation again. "Sure, college. We'll talk about how you're getting a football scholarship and heading off to live it up in a fraternity house, smoking cigars after colossal wins and big tests. You just rest up for your game."

Johnny laughed. "I know. Good rest, good food, good game on Saturday."

Rose caught the mockery as he repeated the words she said to him many times. Johnny was a good kid and must have been tired, and Rose let his sarcasm pass. She could trust him, but couldn't trust that she would have money to fund the community nursing project another year.

So, she put her focus there—on her nursing skill and experience that would persuade the new mill superintendent's wife to direct any charitable funds she could toward the project. It wasn't in Rose's nature to ass-kiss and it would take all her attention and energy to do it well. Conflict upon conflict would not help anyone.

"You're a good boy, Johnny. Keep your wits about you and say your prayers and everything will be fine. You follow our plan and someday you'll be falling all over yourself to thank me."

He nodded and headed toward the hall, jumping to slap the doorjamb as if he were dunking a basketball. He turned back to Rose. "Oh, yeah," he said, "Something's going on with Magdalena. Said she's not roller-skating with the girls after school, even *if* all the smart boys are going to be there. She had *that* look, that scrunchy one where you know she's going to lay you out if you press her one more second."

Rose turned on the faucet and washed her hands. Magdalena was as moody as Johnny was jovial. They may have been twins, but in recent years they seemed to take different emotional paths through life.

"I'm familiar, yes," Rose said, pulling a coffee mug from the cabinet and setting it beside the percolator.

"Mum, this thing with Mag. I mean, I know you're busy, but this time you really should stop and just really listen. She needs you. That's all."

Rose nodded, but was already rehearsing what she'd say to Mrs. Sebastian to demonstrate her value, to persuade her that even the most destitute citizens deserved health care.

Johnny shrugged then spun into the air, whacked the doorjamb and disappeared into the hall.

"Next time, take a rag and wipe up there if you're going to be jumping that high, anyhow." Rose felt a smile squeeze her cheeks before sadness made her bite her lip. He was a smart kid. She could trust him, couldn't she?

"My sweet, sweet boy." Rose said to no one. "You just keep your shit straight and all will be well."

Chapter 2

Rose headed into the cellar to clean her instruments. She felt along the wall for the light. The paint lifted from the plaster like a leper's skin. The cellar was built to hold coal, a toilet and a cinder block shower that cleansed the bodies of smoke-caked steelworkers. The shower kept a marginal amount of soot out of the house. At least it made the housewives in Donora feel as though it did.

In a room dimly lit by one bulb, Rose waited for scalding water to fill the utility tub. The scent of bleach and green soap overwhelmed the space. Rose placed her instruments into the water to soak, and changed out of her uniform. She plucked the buttons and specks of Isabella's dried blood flicked off the fabric.

She shook her uniform down and stepped out of it. Only the hem of her slip was blackened from the mill smoke outside. She rolled down her stockings and analyzed them for future wear. For night calls perhaps, bleached to nearly nothing, they might pass.

Rose dunked her uniform into the water and rubbed at the material, scouring away thoughts of sadness and loss. In a second tub, hands plunged into the water; she scrubbed her instruments, intent on scraping deathly images from her mind with the cadenced movement of her work.

The sound of someone stumbling startled Rose. On the steps, arms extended above his head, stood Unk grasping the bare wood boards crisscrossing the low-slung ceiling.

"Sweet *Jesus*, you scared the living hell right out of me." His blaze-white legs caught her attention and her gaze trailed past his arthritic, cauliflowered knees to his veiny

16

thighs, and finally to his shriveled penis and dangling sacks.

"Ahh, Unk. Your *pants*." Rose snatched a scrap of rag, dried her hands and hurried toward him. "Where are your night-pants, old man?"

Unk's face whitened with the fight he constantly had with his bad lungs. "Rosie? The mills? Any word?" His words came out in a squeak.

He stepped further down and braced himself on the banisters. Rose grasped his torso to support him and shook her head. "You'll break your damn neck and be half-naked doing it. How'll that look when Doc comes to set your hip or your arm or whatever?"

Unk's slack jaw and narrowed eyes conveyed confusion. His chest expanded, thick with phlegm, and he coughed into his hand.

Rose sliced the air with her hand. "Stay in bed, Unk. Doc said not to wander the house at night. You'll snap your neck."

He begged Rose for some vodka. "Just comin' to get the money," he said. "Damn kid lost it again. And, a nip while you finish the instruments. I'll be good. Just sit here loungin' a bit. Don't want to be alone."

Rose ignored her sadness at Unk's beginning signs of dementia and settled him onto the stair. His breathing settled down. She certainly understood Unk's desire not to be alone—she'd grown up in an orphanage and the brittle pain from that experience still came to mind when she least expected it.

Rose reached above Unk's head into a small opening between the studs in the exposed wall, dislodging a bottle of vodka. She opened the lid and took a swig before putting it to his lips, cradling his chin as he swallowed. Rose closed her eyes and let the vodka warm her insides and dissolve the sudden helplessness she felt.

If Unk was wearing pants, his company would have been welcomed. She could not allow him to sit naked in a filthy cellar. She screwed the lid back on the vodka and tucked it back into its nest.

She took his elbow and guided him up the front stairs. "This has to stop." Rose said.

"Shut up, Rosie. You're just not that nice."

"Ah, you shut up, old man."

"I just wanted to get the money. He lost it again." Unk turned to Rose. He opened his mouth to say something else, but he never formed words.

"*Who* lost it again? Not Henry." Rose searched Unk's face for the answer. "Buzzy? *Again?*" The thought of her brother-in-law gambling away his pay was too much for Rose to handle that day, any day, really. For two decades, she and Henry had cleaned up his messes and she'd had enough. Henry assured Rose that Buzzy would not gamble again. And if there was anything in her life that was not a crock of bull it was the word of her husband, Henry.

Unk opened his mouth again, but nothing came out. The whites of his eyes were yellowed, his jaw slack, saliva at the corner of his mouth curving down his chin.

With her thumb she wiped away the moisture, and cupped his face, his prickly whiskers pinching her palm. She put her free hand on the small of his back and nudged him forward. He buckled and Rose positioned herself behind him, her shoulder in the middle of his back.

"Go on, Unk, I have you."

They stepped upward.

"Could solve all these problems," Unk said, "if yunz guys would just save some money for once."

Rose pushed against his body, to keep them both steady and heading upward.

"I see what you're saying." Rose rolled her eyes, knowing he understood the many ways Rose and Henry had shared and lost their money to family members, not their own careless spending. The dementia ripped his memory and when he tried to form coherent thoughts, he stitched facts and words together like a crazy quilt. Colorful, but not at all representative of their initial form.

"I can't shave you today," she said. "I'm due to show one hoity-toity lady the benefit of community nursing. Need to get her to loosen up her purse strings so our citizenry can keep in good health."

Unk grunted in response. His foot caught on a step, reminding Rose of when her children first learned to walk up stairs. She wished she had time to take extra special care of Unk.

But, if she couldn't get Mrs. Sebastian to fund the clinic, it would close until they found another revenue source. They'd been funded for one year—the project's first year—to see if Donora could even use one nurse the way Pittsburgh used dozens. Rose's thousands of home visits reassured her; the answer would be yes. They didn't need the entire operation funded, but enough for the over fifty percent of patients she saw who didn't have insurance or couldn't partially pay.

"I'll send Magdalena to shave you before she heads out to school," Rose said.

"She's cranky that one. A beauty, but touchy," he said. "And what about that money? Lost it again. Call Doc Bonaroti. He'll be in the know."

Rose and Unk stopped on the landing that led to the third floor. She bent over; resting her hands on her knees while Unk leaned on her back, digging his fatless elbows into her spine.

"It's not right to fib, Rosie," Unk said.

She craned over her hunched shoulder to see from his expression if Unk was purposely forming these thoughts. "What?" Rose said.

"Everyone's a liar, Rosie. Everyone. 'Cept Auntie Anna, 'course, not her."

Rose laughed. That didn't help narrow the fibbers' pool. A rectangular shot of daylight came through a window and lit the worn braided rug. The chute of brightness bulleted through the air, illuminating all the dust particles people never noticed until they blanketed the entire house.

"Oh come on, old man." Rose said and stood. She couldn't shake off the feeling that Unk was confused as expected, but maybe not completely off in what he was getting at. And, as her twenty minutes tending to Unk turned into forty, she decided transforming the living room into a convalescence room might not be such a bad idea after-all.

* * *

Sara Clara from The South. That's what they called her. It shouldn't have bothered her. But the way they said it, spit from clumsy Western Pennsylvanian tongues, it stabbed and mocked her, endlessly reminding her and everyone else she was an outsider. There in her shoebox-shaped bedroom she would burrow under her covers, taking shelter from the list of things to do that blitzed her at every turn once she left it.

Sara Clara ran her fingers down her throat and forced a cough to be sure she was still alive. Suffocating. The town, the family, the mills, the house—all of it recalled the dirty wool socks her brothers used to stuff in her face when they crammed her into the clothes hamper for the fun of it.

The difference was her former clothes hamper was gilded and she knew deep down, her brothers loved her. Nothing in Donora was gilded. And though everyone acted as if the glittering steel that belched from one end of town to the other was gold, Sara Clara knew the truth.

She lay in her husband's childhood bed naked except for a pair of yellowed underpants, and pulled the thin sheet to her chin and flung one arm above her head, the other draped out to the side, clawing at the mattress. Sara Clara wished Buzzy was beside her instead of slaving away all night then sleeping all day while she tried to make Rose and Henry like her, make friends with anyone, and raise a son in a town where no one had the time for her.

Years back, when Sara Clara had met Buzzy at a North Carolina bar full of airmen, Buzzy had gushed about his home. Oh, how all of the Pavlesics would love her, Buzzy had said. Everyone would. His face flushed with the tales of the way money was forged from the earth, ripped right from the ground the town was built upon. Like money grew on trees—it was the same thing, he told her.

But, it wasn't just the idea that Buzzy might make a fortune once they went up north that attracted her. It was the way he looked at her, as though she were a prize, as though he'd never seen a more beautiful, perfect woman in the world. That was what kept her up at night as she replayed every moment of their time together before they were married.

The love for her that she saw in his face and felt in his touch was like nothing she'd experienced. That and the possibility of money, to have the type of life she was used to, but in a new place, was enough to make her leap at the chance to follow love, to make a change.

She closed her eyes and tried, yes, there it was—the memory of that tender, glowing sensation that accompanied the smile when she agreed to marry Buzzy. Alone in his bed, lost in memories, she could feel Buzzy pull her into a kiss, his hands working their way down her body, bringing their marital promises to life. She was filled with longing, love and hope.

Then they arrived in Donora. All that thick desire was squelched like a coke oven dowsed by cooling water. She might as well have been from Siberia for all western Pennsylvania had in common with North Carolina. Sara Clara's finishing school education and refined Southern manners were simply not appreciated in a place where people (young, old, rich, poor, immigrant, native) allowed filthy mill shifts to shape their calendar.

It's not that she wasn't familiar with mill-life—her family owned three in Wilmington. But Donora's steel mills didn't just churn out the materials that built the country; the mills took lives in exchange—sometimes totally, sometimes just slices of your soul. She couldn't figure out how to live like that, to be content. Half dead, nothing could make you happy.

She shoved her hand inside her underwear. Usually, that simple act comforted her and allowed her to drift back asleep. But that morning was different.

Her mind wouldn't stop, fueled at first by anxiety. She thought of her plans to move Buzzy and their son, Leo, back to Wilmington. There was a time when she wouldn't have considered it after the way her own family had treated her. Disowning her, throwing her out simply because she married a Catholic Yankee. As if it were 1863. As if Buzzy were colored or something.

The radiator kicked on and blanketed Sara Clara with scratchy heat. She threw the sheet to the side and dangled one leg over the edge of the bed. Her fingers in her panties shifted, moving under the cotton to bring on that feeling she liked so much. If only Buzzy had a professional job. *His* hand would be down her pants.

She wove memories of loving Buzzy into sweet fantasies. She felt his lips on her belly, the erotic sensation of his hairy legs tickling when he spread her thighs apart with his. She moaned as if he were right here.

The sound of feet coming down the hallway broke Sara Clara's reverie. Before she could cover up, the bedroom door flew open. She shot up to sitting, mouth gaping at the sight of her sister-in-law standing in the threshold.

Rose held up her hand. "I'm sorry. I thought you were…"

Sara Clara pawed at the sheet, not managing to pull it up until the third grope.

"Holy mother of Pete," Rose said. She looked back toward the hall then started to leave.

Sara Clara felt herself blush. "Don't shout at me as though *I* burst into *your* bedroom when you were dealing with a nasty bout of insomnia!"

Rose turned back and narrowed her eyes.

Sara Clara was not about to let Rose get the best of her this time. Rose was always screaming at her about this and that. Not this time. "I wasn't expecting anyone to be awake let alone to fly into my bedroom," she said, leaping out of bed and snatching her robe from the bedpost. She shoved her arms through the armholes hard and heard a seam rip.

"That's it." Sara Clara said, twisting her hair into a bun. She glared at Rose. "What does a girl have to do for some privacy? I've tried for the sake of Buzzy and Leo. I've had it with this grey town and its black-hearted people!"

Rose wiped off a speck of Sara Clara's spittle that landed on her lip. She shook her head, unusually speechless.

Sara Clara smiled. She couldn't hold it in any longer, her hands flailed through the air. "I never see the sun. Everything's filthy. A cesspool! All I get is yelled at all day by you and—"

Rose crossed her arms. "If this cesspool's too much for you, you could start by simply picking up this room." She tossed a lump of Buzzy's dirty work clothes to the side with her foot. Under the pile were Unk's clothes, Leo's, and Henry's, too. Sara Clara swallowed hard. Her secret was out.

"You told me you finished the laundry yesterday," Rose said. "I should have known. Today's ironing day. How are you going to iron when there's nothing to iron?" Rose rubbed her forehead. "Everyone has to do their part." She shook her head, fist clenched at her side. "Just go back to bed. Or redd-up this mess. Just cut the bullshit. All that moaning. I thought you were crying again, that's why I came in. I was being sweet."

Like weather that snapped from stormy to cloudy with no warning, Sara Clara felt her anger evaporate into worthlessness. She had tried so hard to make Rose like her. Sara Clara dragged toward the bed, her shoulders hunched and feet shuffling, as though she were suffering from flu. This was Rose's idea of sweet?

Rose stepped over the clothing, bent and snatched something from the floor and stretched it in front of Sara Clara's face. "A guest towel? There's goddamn lipstick on this thing. Unk bought these...I asked you not to do that...I told you where we store your linens." Rose's jaw clenched and Sara Clara thought she saw tears welling in her sister-in-law's eyes.

Rose met Sara Clara's gaze. "You're not wiping your ass with these, are you?"

Sara Clara flopped back on the bed.

"Stop blubbering," Rose said.

Sara Clara sat cross-legged, tossing her hands upward, letting them fall and lifting them again. "I'm turning into a vampire bat, a rodent! In the mirror yesterday I swore my teeth were bucking out like a rat! This mill shift business is a little hard. Yes! I'm a little bazooka right now." She dabbed her tear-drenched cheeks with the bedspread and sniffled.

"I'm lonely, Rose. You get to run all over town being a nurse and I'm stuck here. Don't you see? I'm sorry it's so hard for you to understand what it feels like to live with people who don't even like you, don't want you there. To have no one who cares you're alive?"

Rose looked away and kicked a dirty sock to the side. Sara Clara thought she might have actually hit a soft spot, a point of entry into the heart of Rose Pavlesic—if she had one at all. Maybe Rose could understand? Sara Clara leaned toward Rose, waiting for an apology; just a whisper of commiseration would have meant a lot.

Rose finally met Sara Clara's gaze. "Pull it together. You'll waken little Leo. You're not a child."

Sara Clara leaned forward on the bed, wishing Rose would mother her. "I'm scared," she whispered.

Rose drew back. "Scared of what? Sleep? Cleanliness?"

"Every time Buzz goes into the mills, I think he's not coming out."

Rose ran the guest towel through one palm and then the other. "He's fine. He's got nine lives. At least. No, he's roach-like. He could live through Hiroshima."

Sara Clara's shoulders drooped.

Rose stepped closer. Sara Clara leaned in, expecting an embrace.

Rose squeezed Sara Clara's shoulder then patted it. "Everything's fine with Buzzy. He's fine." She stepped backward toward the door, stumbling over clothes.

Sara Clara felt as if Rose was taking the oxygen in the room with her.

"Look," Rose said, stopping. "You have to block out the fear. Just do what you need to do and don't think about what might happen if the worst comes along."

Sara Clara should have felt comforted by Rose's words, but instead she grew more angry. "If the mills are so safe then why are you forcing your son to live a life he doesn't want just so he doesn't ever have to set foot in one of them?"

Rose threw the guest towel to the ground. "That is none of your business. And *that's* the end of my sweet-act. You've pushed me over the line."

Sara Clara jerked her shoulders in defiance.

They stared at each other.

"Can't you just help me Rose? Please. Like I'm one of your patients, please. I feel so alone."

"This *is* me helping you," Rose said.

"You're mean."

Rose stood motionless. The corner of her mouth pulled tight, as if she were trying to hold back words. She headed for the door and then turned back.

"You have a job to do in this house. The rest of us depend on you to do your end of things. If you did that then you'd have less time to bellyache."

Sara Clara sat back up. "We are moving back to civilization!" she said. "Right after Christmas. We're headed back to North Carolina!" Sara Clara whipped the pillow, and it hit Rose in the chest and dropped to the ground in front of her.

Sara Clara thought she saw Rose smile under her scowl. Sara Clara drew her knees to her chest.

"You're not going *anywhere* until you pay us back, Sara Clara. So toughen the hell up and do the chores you're supposed to. I can't do one more task at home and still do the work I'm paid to do. So shut the hell up and do your part." Rose looked as though she had something more to say, but was silent. She closed the door and Sara Clara fell back on the mattress, hands over her face.

She had never felt so frustrated and helpless. She wondered if there was a way to make her life better, but no ideas came. She had made a vow to Buzzy. She was forever lodged inside a stifling life, in a town that sucked out all that was good, and she wondered if she'd live to see another sunrise. She decided that in Donora, home of the endless cloudy day, it was plausible the sun might not rise. And, she wondered, would she care if it didn't?

Chapter 3

On the edge of town a sign reads: *Donora: Next to Yours, the Best Town in the USA*. Donorans mean it, proud of the life they've built here, but they wouldn't begrudge someone else their dignity either. That said, they don't have time for lazy, arrogant fellas hiring on a mill crew. Those jobs required strength and skill and humility even though those attributes were not part of the job description.

Donora's heart beat inside the chest of sturdy immigrant bodies, forged from stock so nimble and willing that not even loss of limb or consciousness would keep a person floating in his own melancholy long. When things were really rough, before the war and unions, when the men worked the mills in twelve hour shifts then were stiffed for pay, Donora's steel workers refused to strike.

And it was this coarse, stubborn existence that seeded the life that Henry and Buzzy Pavlesic lived. The habits of their existence and the expectations of the town trapped them. They were lured into ruts, forced down the same path they'd already traveled and known to be wrong, as though they lacked the ability to simply lift one foot out of the muddy furrow and then the other.

When the two men reached their home, Henry sighed. He needed one hour to think of something other than their trouble.

Buzzy yanked at Henry's arm. "Christ almighty, Hen."

Henry had been hoping to avoid this conversation. Henry turned to see Buzzy shuffle his feet nervously.

Buzzy flexed his bicep trying to be jovial.

"I ought to use your head for a ram-rod and shove you through that door," Buzzy said. "What's with the fast-as-a rabbit routine this morning? You're not trying to dodge your little brother, now are you?"

Henry lit a cigarette and shoved his pack toward Buzzy. Buzzy drew a cigarette, put it to his cracked lips and Henry lit it.

"'Course not." Henry dragged on his cigarette, standing next to the side door that led into Unk's home—the house they all shared. Henry winced as he brushed his boot over the welcome mat.

The back of his heel smarted, scorched from the slag that had splashed onto his leg that morning. It would heal quickly, and he hoped to get enough soot off the soles of his boots. He didn't want Rose to bawl him out before he had his first cup of coffee. Still, that was the least of his worries this morning.

Buzzy thrust a forearm into Henry's chest, jostling him like they were still kids fighting over their only baseball mitt.

Henry shrugged Buzzy off. They weren't little boys anymore.

"You're gonna make me beg?" Buzzy said. "Please. I will, I'll do anything."

Henry could feel Buzzy's hot breath hit his chin. He couldn't bear to hear his brother's voice crack, see the panic well in his eyes.

"I *can't* ask Rose for money," Henry said. "The last time ran us about three hundred we didn't have. Not this time, not after everything else."

Buzzy clenched his jaw in response, stepped back, and slipped on a crumbling cement step. He caught himself, his playful mood changing to angry. He leaned back into Henry.

"I know what this is about. Rose hates me. She won't give me a chance. Never has." He picked up a pebble and whipped it down the hillside. "Thinks she's so much smarter than the rest of us, your kids are fucking geniuses. She runs this house like she's Henry Clay Frick and we're non-union steel workers in 18 fucking 92."

He grasped Buzzy's coat collar, the fabric, scratchy in his palm. "Don't *ever* talk about Rose like that. She's a little rough around the edge. Maybe a little nuts, but she loves this family as if it were her own."

Buzzy swallowed hard, but wouldn't meet Henry's gaze.

Henry thrust the coat back into Buzzy's chest. "I'll think of a way to get the money. It's not like these fellas are gunning for you, right? Give me time. And understand this. Rose has given us everything, never done anything but be herself. She's honest. That's more than I can say—"

"It's not like you're perfect either," Buzzy said. "If you recall a certain dame—"

"Shut the fuck up. I'll do what I can. For the brother you were before you turned into this heap of…I'll figure something out. I owe it to Dad. I promised him I'd watch over you."

A voice blasted from the sloped yard in the alley. Buzzy hearing his name called, pushed past Henry and bolted up the small hill toward Murray Avenue, the sound of his feet grinding over the barren dirt they called a yard. Henry craned his neck to see who was yelling but although it was morning, the fog was still grainy, heavy like pillow-fill.

Henry sighed. It was probably one of Buzzy's card-playing pals. What could Henry do? Fix the damn problem. He knew that was the answer, Henry rubbed his temples, acid gathering in his belly. The real question was which problem to solve first.

* * *

Henry lifted the door on its hinges and pushed, alleviating that horrific whine he meant to get around to oiling away but never did. With the door shut, dread cloaked him. He hadn't kept many secrets from Rose. Maybe he'd been afraid to. Or was he really the good guy he wanted to be all along?

Now, his fear of the truth—what Rose would make of the facts—had turned everything backward. He told himself he could get away with it, that he had time to sort things out. Denial and hope were two wonderful states of mind for Henry.

He stood in the shadows of the hallway, collecting his thoughts, watching his wife comfortable in the kitchen. He'd hoped long ago to have put her in her own home, make it "her" kitchen, but every time they were close, something snatched the money out from under them.

Sometimes Rose heard him come into the house, but this morning she must have been deep in thought. She didn't bark an order or wrap him in a hug or plant a kiss on his cheek. Henry watched her cooking and wondered what she'd do if she found out.

With one hand Rose cracked eggs into her favorite green Corning bowl. With the other she flipped hot cakes. Her lean forearms belied her power, both physical and mental. Her backside was round, but small, and the blue robe fell over her form like a fine dress, exquisitely highlighting her shape.

She slid across the floor, humming a slow, sad tune. It reminded him of what he'd heard earlier that day about the Greshecky woman. Clearly that wasn't a case Rose would let go of easily. Still she carried on with her chores. Most women weren't like Rose.

She was unsentimental, a machine, like the mills. She did what had to be done no matter how she felt. Nothing interfered with the way she operated. She just moved ahead like a rolling mill.

Rose wiped her hands on her apron then sniffed under her arms. Henry smiled. His Rose never did like a stench.

31

Her head jerked toward the small utility room off the far side of the kitchen. Her shoulders slumped and she scurried to the room, huffing and irritated.

He heard the storm door open—the one that led to the landing that they built from trash-heap wood and nails "borrowed" from the mill. The landing allowed Rose to store their garbage on the far side of the house, away from where the family would have to walk past it. What could have called her attention there? No one would ever climb that staircase except someone returning from dumping the garbage.

"You mangy mutt, Rags!" Her voice hit Henry's ears and his shoulders hunched bracing on behalf of the dog. He hated to see Rose yell at the sorry pooch. "I don't have time for this bullshit." Henry heard the door slam and watched Rose stomp into the kitchen still too distracted to notice him peeking in the doorway.

Henry was about to tell Rose not to be harsh with the dog. It couldn't help being a lost soul. But, he stopped when Rose tugged the icebox open and pulled out a package of bologna. She crumpled the wrappings against her leg before tossing them on the counter and disappearing into the utility room again. Henry heard the door open and hit the wall behind it. He slipped across the kitchen floor and poked his head into the utility room.

Rose stood at the open door; the dog was rolled into a ball, his snout barely peeking out.

"Now, you go away. You're not wanted here." Rose laid the meat in front of the dog's nose, patted the top of its head and backed away.

She left the utility room and ran smack into Henry.

"Hen?"

"Hey."

"What? The garbage doesn't put itself out."

Henry nodded and jammed his hands in his pockets. A smile pulled on the corner of his mouth. He wanted to tell her he knew she liked the dog.

Rose pulled his face to her, pecked his lips then the creases at the corners of his eyes. She held Henry's gaze like she was determining whether he'd seen her interaction with the dog.

Henry wrapped Rose in his arms, pulling her pelvis into his, kissing her neck. The salty taste on her skin after a long night of nursing excited him. She squirmed, sliding out of his grip, and his hand groped for hers before she completely got away. He pulled her back and smoothed loose hairs off her face.

Rose quickly covered her left ear with the hair he'd brushed back. After all these years, she was still conscious of him seeing her double earlobe—a congenital defect. In utero her ear had folded over on itself giving the effect of having two lobes.

"Later, Hen."

He wrapped around her, pulled her back against his belly, his chin on the top of her head, her hair smelling more like her than the shampoo she used. He could hold her forever, he thought. He was lucky to have any sex at all, let alone regularly. His friends often joked about the fact his wife was a nurse, and worked like a man, but he didn't care. The times she wasn't there with a tray of sandwiches, she was there with the sex. He loved that she was independent. That it was *almost* as though she didn't need him at all.

He kissed the top of her head. "I heard about Greshecky's wife—Isabella." She stiffened and he let her go. Suddenly he wanted to tell her what had happened at work. She would understand. He reached for her again.

Rose turned, tears welling. She shrugged. "Said a rosary for Isabella. She'll be in heaven with her baby...or maybe not, you know, no baptism..." Rose waved her hand in front of her face and pushed past Henry. She straightened the blue and white serving dish in the center of the table and sighed, as though her contentment had dissolved in an instant.

Henry knew, with Rose, she'd feel better soon. By evening she would have wrangled the good out of the bad and she'd be back to her normal self.

* * *

Buzzy rushed into the kitchen, heading for a glass of water. "How's my favorite sister-in-law?" He glanced at Henry then kissed Rose's cheek. She brushed it off with the back of her hand and looked to Henry for an explanation.

Henry's breath caught a moment and he coughed into his hand, forcing his body to relax. He knew Buzzy's routine. He was desperate, but he was only in phase-one desperation. He would try to charm Rose; he wouldn't attempt to bully her, not yet. If only Buzzy had listened to Henry and Rose.

Buzzy spread his hands, looking over the table, set with the dishes they bought every time they deposited money into Mellon Bank. "Where's the grub? I'm showered, I'm ready for food."

Henry limped to the table, brushing past Buzz.

Rose took a deep breath and released it as she went to the stove. "Food'll be a minute, Hen. Unk had a bit of, well, you know how things go with Unk." She pushed melting butter around one of three skillets.

"No matter," Henry said. He slumped into his chair and wrenched his WH Auden Chapbook—The Age of Anxiety—from his pocket and paged to where he'd left off during his lunch break.

Rose's eyes narrowed, straining to see Henry's foot as she carried blistering hot coffee to the table. "Are you limping from the old injury or did you get hurt today?"

Henry didn't care about discussing his injury. It was what would follow—the conversation regarding why he showered at the mill and *who* treated the burn that he didn't want to have.

Rose poured Henry's coffee and set it in front of him. He wrapped his fingers around the thick mug, brushing Rose's as he did. Henry knew the line of questioning that would follow. He couldn't help but get caught in Buzzy's heavy gaze.

"What?" Rose said. "I saw that look the two of you just passed like a bad dollar bill. What's in the vault? This isn't Mellon Bank, you know. Nothing goes in the vault without my say."

Henry pushed the conversation in a safer direction. "Little slag on my Achilles is all," he said. "Nothing new is in the vault." He grimaced looking down at his foot.

"That goddamn pol-ak," Buzzy said, "Vinski's going to get us all killed. Goddamn jackass is never where he should be." Henry was glad Buzzy's con-artist ways worked to his benefit from time to time.

"Let me have a look, Hen." Rose got down on her hands and knees and cocked her head, spreading open Henry's seared workpants. She drew in a breath as though it were she with burned skin. Henry looked at her rounded back, her muscles moving beneath her robe. His gaze slid back toward her behind. He patted it.

She sat back on her heels, face flushed. "It appears as though Nurse Dottie fixed a decent bandage," Rose shrugged. "For now it's decent. Her work doesn't always stand up over time."

Henry knew Rose's deep dislike for Dottie Shaginaw and treaded carefully when it came to praising Rose's rival.

Rose went back to the eggs, Henry, to his poetry.

Buzzy snapped the newspaper open and began reciting the headlines. He shoved Henry's foot with his.

Henry lifted his gaze from his chapbook and shook his head. He was not ready to beg Rose for money to cover Buzzy's irresponsibility, again.

"I saw that," Rose said.

Buzzy pulled out the wooden chair beside Henry and rotated it. He straddled the seat and rested his forearms along the back. "Saw what?"

"That foot nudge," Rose said over her skillets. "What are you two up to? You owe money, again, Buzzy? Unk was mumbling about money lost again..."

"No! Rose you know I've changed."

Rose stared at Buzzy then Henry. Henry felt sweat on the top of his head. He opened his mouth to tell the truth, but Buzzy was already filling the air with what he considered quality thoughts.

"That polak Vinski's gonna get someone's hand sheared off," Buzzy said. "If he isn't made to tow the line. I don't know what the USW'll have to say about that jackass. We fought long and hard to form that union, to be protected from the white hats, but who'll protect us from our own? Son of a bitch'll cost you, um, me, I mean, some fella at least a week's pay if that jug head Nelson finds out."

Henry leaned forward on the table glaring at his brother. Damn Buzzy, Henry thought, subtle as a jackhammer.

"Just read the paper, Buzz. How about the Steelers this week? Who they playing?" Henry gritted his teeth.

"*Who* lost a week's pay? I'm not stupid you know." Rose poured the eggs into the pan and scraped them into tiny, buttery bits of heaven.

"No one, Rosie," Buzzy said with that smile he'd used to get what he wanted all his life. "All's well on the Murray Avenue front. Everywhere else, though, well, everyone's an asshole these days, Rosie. Except Hen, here that is."

Rose slapped a lid on each of the skillets on the stove, turned off the burners and sauntered over to Buzzy and Henry wielding a spatula as though headed into battle. She poked it into the air at the two of them.

"What's all the code-speak, bullshit Buzzy? If you think I'm not aware that you're rambling an awful lot of nothing to cover up something then you're crazy."

Buzzy held his hands up in surrender.

Rose narrowed her eyes at him.

Henry forced his attention back to Auden hoping to convey nonchalance.

"Just yammering after a hard night's work." Buzzy nearly dropped his coffee mug.

Henry glanced at Buzzy, noting his clenched teeth. It made Henry think his brother was more nervous than he originally supposed. Maybe the fellas shouting his name earlier weren't simply his buddies. Maybe Buzzy wasn't playing a friendly card game anymore.

Apparently, though, Rose was appeased. She tossed the spatula on the counter, and stalked into the utility room.

Henry leaned forward, hissing his whisper at Buzzy.

"What the hell was that?"

"Just trying to soften things up before you let the boom down. That's all, just trying to help."

"Well, no thanks, Buzz, old boy. Keep your trap shut."

Rose came back in the kitchen, eyeing the two of them suspiciously.

Henry's nerves were on edge. He tapped his book of poetry. "This Auden gets me thinking." He lifted the book in Rose's direction. "I think he's suggesting technology is looming too large. That it's scraping away at our common sense, our connection to each other…"

"That's what that book's about?" Rose said.

Henry shrugged. "I'm getting a little of that from it—a little cynical, a little hopeful. Like when I think of those mills, all the incremental elements that have to fit perfectly together in order to produce a single steel thread. When I think of that wire! Sometimes it all seems parochial, sometimes it seems like the most worldly work a man can do."

"Don't romanticize that mill," Rose said. "The seventeen-year locusts have more of a social life than you fellas. Every seventeen years those little bastards come out of the ground, mate, and eat each other or some shit like that. That's no existence for anyone, man or insect."

"Easy nurse, Pavlesic," Buzzy said, "I think the guy's had enough injury without your insult lumped on top."

"Stuff it, Buzzy."

She patted Henry's shoulder. He grabbed her hand and pulled her closer.

"We have to talk, okay?"

Henry tried to interpret Rose's body language, determine whether her stiff posture was due to Buzzy being there or if she knew something was going on with him.

Buzzy slid the Donora Herald American from the table and snapped it open again in front of his face. "Oh looky here, Truman's about to lose the election to Dewey. Nice. Another jackass running the world. Just what we need."

"We'll talk all right," Rose said, "but I'm busy this morning. Doc Bonaroti set me on that Sebastian woman thinking I can get her to pop open her Chanel handbag for the sad sacks of Donora. He's convinced I can persuade her to fund the clinic."

"He's right," Henry said.

Buzzy dropped his paper and put his hand to his ear. "I think I hear Magdalena calling."

"Ass," Rose said and ambled toward the hallway. Henry watched her disappear from sight, and from figuring out she was right to suspect Buzzy was in trouble again, and Henry was privy to it.

Henry hadn't realized he'd been holding his breath until Rose left the room and he was assured Buzzy couldn't reveal anything. Henry took the moment of peace and turned back to his poetry. He slipped into Auden's world of poetic, human interaction, thankful Rose was too distracted by her lack of clinic funding to push either of the two men on any matter at all. They'd been given a reprieve. For how long, Henry didn't know.

* * *

The looks that passed between Henry and Buzzy troubled Rose, but not nearly as much as the recurrent images of Isabella and what it would mean for the Greshecky family. She covered her mouth, feeling like she needed to shield herself from an unseen, malignant force. The sound of furniture being pushed across the floor above her called to mind Sara Clara—the obvious, futile presence in the house.

Perhaps the noise above was evidence that Sara Clara was finally going to contribute to the household without any more fuss. But, even thoughts of Sara Clara laying around in bed all day instead of contributing to the family, would have to wait.

Rose rapped on Magdalena's door. No reply. Must be in the bathroom. Rose crossed her arms and tapped her foot, waiting. Magdalena's door opened and she slunk into the hallway using the wall for support.

"You sick?" Rose said, remembering Johnny reporting that Magdalena wasn't going skating this afternoon, the norm for months.

Magdalena shook her head. She wrapped herself in her arms and sat on the stairs. Her bony knees peeked up from under her skirt. She tossed her head and her silky locks swung and draped her back, ready for Rose to go to work.

She settled on the crooked step behind her daughter, the fresh odor of Camay and Breck shampoo wafting up as Rose lifted Magdalena's chestnut hair.

Magdalena sighed and scowled over her shoulder, silently warning Rose to speed it up. But, Rose loved these moments, the opportunities she had to touch her daughter—do her hair, help her dress, button a blouse. Once Magdalena barreled into her teens, she had careened right past Rose, with barely a look back.

Rose had tried to forge a close relationship, create that happy friendship she saw some mothers and daughters share. Rose had to settle for the reassurance she was raising her daughter right and giving her opportunities to have a life, a career without money-worries. Rose had nothing in the way of a stable beginning to life. Luckily she'd had nursing to fill the gap left by her childhood, the craggy hole that remained after Rose trusted people she shouldn't have.

Rose shuddered. Growing up in an orphanage left her with painful memories so deep they'd shock her, and surface with a sight or smell or a feeling and invoke something she'd forgotten. But in being a good mother to Magdalena and Johnny, she had thought she could heal her past pain, her past sins.

At the very least she could be vigilant about how her children looked and dressed. Rose knew what it was like to be clad in tattered clothes with shoes worn through to the pads of her feet. She knew what that did to a person's soul. She understood the value of dressing well, and it wasn't about shallow expressions of wealth. A girl's appearance was the quickest way to send the message about herself, who she wanted to be or thought she was already.

Only on the days when the orphanage was expecting nervous, fashionable couples, looking for a child to adopt, did someone touch Rose in anyway remotely nurturing. Those days the women at the orphanage would do Rose's hair. But it wasn't a loving gesture, more of a yanking, the sound of a comb thwacking through knots as Rose's head snapped back and forth with the grooming. The memory of it made Rose shudder.

Rose treated Magdalena's grooming as an act of love. She'd never tugged Magdalena's hair. She cherished every quiet moment with the comb she had.

Rose's eyes began to burn at the thought of Isabella and her infant daughter. They would never have these moments. Rose would never say it out loud, but if not for Ian being without Isabella now; Rose thought it was better both mother and daughter died at the same time. To live without your baby. Rose's eyes filled. She knew what that meant. She couldn't start thinking about that. She didn't have the time to feel something so raw.

"Mum? How old were you when you got married?"

"Twenty."

Rose put the brush in her mouth and ran her fingers through Magdalena's locks, remembering the picture of her and Henry on the baseball field, getting married at Forbes Field on the pitcher's mound, that photo in Life Magazine, showing her as happy as she'd ever been.

Rose ran the brush back through Magdalena's hair. "That day was spectacular. Wow, that sun. We don't get sun like that often. Fat and yellow as can be." Rose wrapped the gum band around the hair and gently pulled Magdalena to standing with a sigh.

"Why?" Rose said.

"No reason."

Rose wondered if everyone was bizarre today on purpose or if they just couldn't help it.

Magdalena looked over her shoulder at Rose. "Daddy's perfect. I want a man just like him."

Rose raised her chin at her seventeen-year-old daughter trying to see inside her soul. What did she really want to know with this line of questioning?

Rose put the brush into her robe pocket.

"You're not worried about that bullshit are you? Boys? Pal around with the gang all you want, go roller skating with Susan and the Delany boys and so forth, but there's no time for complicated love bullshit, right now."

Magdalena stiffened and drew away.

Rose recalled her conversation with Johnny. "Wait, but you're not going skating today? Johnny told me. You sick?"

Magdalena shrugged and put her hands on hip, chin in the air, and for a second Rose saw every bit of who she was in her daughter.

Magdalena blew out her air as though she'd just been told to clean up Unk's waste. "Can't a person be under the weather in her own house without the community nurse taking her temperature every five seconds? It's this test I have. I really want that scholarship. Okay?"

Rose was relieved by Magdalena's words and she gathered her into a suffocating hug. Rose believed she would be able to feel any real trouble coursing through Magdalena's veins if she just held her tight enough.

Magdalena went stiff and tried to pull away. Rose gripped harder, until the girl had no choice but to embrace Rose back. Rose felt her daughter's arms slide around her back and she laid her head on Rose's shoulder.

"I'm proud of you, Magdalena."

Magdalena nodded into Rose's shoulder.

Satisfied, she gripped Magdalena's shoulders "Okay, move it," Rose said, "Lots to do, right? Just remember you can do anything you set your mind to, Magdalena. There are no limits on your future. None."

Rose patted Magdalena's back, spun her toward the kitchen and smacked her on the behind as though sending a horse out to pasture.

Magdalena looked over her shoulder, face twisted up with confusion before she disappeared into the kitchen.

Rose never had to worry about Magdalena being a wayward sort—a poor decision maker. No, Magdalena had everything Rose never did. No black holes marring her soul.

She'd given Magdalena and Johnny all the love and security they needed to grow up and make the right decisions. She didn't have to waste her time wondering if they were okay. And that was as comforting as anything to Rose.

* * *

Rose stood just outside the kitchen doorway. She leaned against the wall, gripped by exhaustion, remembering she had only slept a few hours before she'd been called out to the Greshecky's to deliver Isabella's baby. She could hear her family, the lot of them, gathered in the kitchen. At that moment, she wished they would all disappear and she could go about her business without interference.

Rose grimaced. She wanted to obliterate that awful thought, but it was there to stay. She prayed for peace and the ability to be content with what she had, this family. But, she and Henry had worked hard to put money away for a nice family of four to purchase a home. It seemed so simple. Save more than you spend. Reasonable. Especially when both parents did work.

Yet, there was still no house for the Pavlesics. Not when family members needed to borrow from their savings, or stole it. Or gambled it away. Because family staying together in the hopes of making a better life took precedence over everything.

The Pavlesics lived enmeshed like prickly strands of hemp, twined together, abrasive, but strong from one end of the rope to the other. The rope may have been strained from the hemorrhaging of their joint bank accounts, or by

43

petty arguments and useless jealousy, but it was as stable as it needed to be. The damage wasn't even noticeable from certain angles, or over time.

Rose told herself to toughen up. She should go to her family, to Henry for comfort. But she had never been able to verbalize her feelings as she wished she could. She was grateful for Henry and the family he'd given her by marriage, but still, even with them seven feet away she felt alone in every way.

The steady hum of conversation, punctuated by Buzzy's guffaws and expressions of "you don't say!" kept Rose from moving. She couldn't shake the heaviness in her chest. She took a deep breath and exhaled as she peered around the wall.

The family sat sausaged at a table intended for six, shoulder jostling shoulder, squeezed so tight that Rose often let the coal go low during the course of a meal for all the warmth generated by sheer body heat and a hot argument. Buzzy's and Sara Clara's child, Leo, and Johnny and Magdalena sat along one side of the beat-up Formica table.

Auntie Anna, an elephantine white-haired woman sat at the far end of the table, grinning at Leo. She fingered the leather strings around her neck that held her bulging suede sack of cash between her shapeless breasts. Unk was at the end closest to the stove, rubbing his temples, lost in his thoughts or simply confused by the banter.

Sara Clara's wide smile and cheerful expression was in full force. She was clearly over her earlier mood or faking it so no one besides Rose would know of her melancholy. Her neat figure was made more alluring by jeans, showcasing her long, trim legs, and a form-fitting, coral cardigan pushed her breasts out over the table as though Isaly's had purchased advertising there and demanded Sara Clara make a sale that very breakfast.

The picture-perfect twenty-three year-old sat cinched between Henry and Buzzy. Sara Clara's wavy hair, silky as exquisite Japanese threads, was gathered in a ponytail and made her appear sophisticated; the same hairstyle made Magdalena look innocent.

Rose shifted her weight and fussed with her hair, pushing strays back in place, squeezing her bun, a jumbled mess after a long night. She'd been too busy to shower and observing Sara Clara prompted a surge of envy. Sara Clara did nothing to help out at home, but always looked stunning for her job of Queen Do Nothing All Day.

Sara Clara's purring at Henry made Rose cringe. The woman-child bestowed all her attention on Henry, every blessed day, probing him for stories about his days as a Pittsburgh Pirate.

Rose sighed at Sara Clara forcing Henry to relive the best and worst stretch of his life as though it were her story, too. It called up too much emotion for Henry and it unnerved Rose. The exercise excited Sara Clara, satisfied with the stories of another life rather than having her own.

"No, why of course, I understand the decision to go to the Pirates instead of accepting that chemistry scholarship," Sara Clara said, and swept her petite, manicured hand over Henry's forearm, resting above his wrist. "But Henry, *reallllly* a Pittsburgh Pirate. What tales you have to tell!"

Rose was pleased to see Henry worm his arm away and run his hand through his hair. She hadn't realized she groaned in response to Sara Clara's inquisition until the whole family turned toward her. She moved quickly to kiss Auntie Anna good morning, and saw the family's plates were empty. No one had served the food. Like always, they waited for her.

"I ain't *hungry*," Auntie Anna growled at Rose. "Gonna count the money n'at. Think we're 'bout flush for that house you been talking about building." Auntie Anna pulled her money pouch—the one she never removed unless Rose was forcing her to bathe, or was checking her for repeated bouts of pneumonia, or adding more money.

Rose spoke to Auntie as though soothing a wild animal, tucking the sour smelling sack back into Auntie's shirt, telling her that they would certainly count the money on pay day—Friday. Rose had been depositing funds into the bank on behalf of her family, but still gave a portion to Auntie Anna, as was the tradition for all of them. Rose would have liked to put all their pay in the bank to make sure it grew at the rate it ought to, but it wasn't Rose's home and despite Auntie Anna's diminished abilities, no one was ready to take the last scrap of her dignity. Besides, from the lessons learned in 1929, Auntie Anna was as safe a bank as Mellon at the bottom of the hill.

Buzzy lit a cigarette and waved the smoke away from the table.

Each payday, Buzzy, Henry and Rose forked over their pay, into the family pot so that as soon as possible, each person could purchase their own home. Unfortunately, illnesses, Buzzy's irresponsible ways, and a house-fire had filched the family funds from Rose's open hand so many times she wondered if she'd ever have the opportunity to live the way she'd imagined.

She dreamed it so much and so long, she couldn't admit it might never come to be. She thought of the orphanage, lying there as a child on rickety cots, slotted between thirty-one other girls, frigid breezes lifting thin sheets and keeping her from drifting into the safety of sleep. During those sleepless nights she formulated the life she'd wanted to live. And really, all that she desired was a small, warm, clean home, a safe home, filled with love.

Rose washed up and served the food, distracted by a spike of hope that Auntie Anna might be right. Maybe they did save enough money for Rose and Henry to buy their home. Rose plunked eggs onto the plates as the conversation drew her from her own mind.

"Having their ninth child?" Sara Clara squealed. "Why, aren't they aware of *methods?*"

Henry dropped his head into his hands, elbows on the table, he rubbed his temples.

"What's a method?" Johnny said.

Sara Clara leaned across the table, "Family planning. Margaret Sanger? Surely having a nurse in the family means y'all are enlightened on these matters."

Johnny drew back, face crunched up.

"Marital Relations?" Unk's gravelly voice cut in.

Henry shot his hands into the air like someone scored a touchdown. "Holy Christ! Do we have to talk about this?"

Rose cleared her throat, working around the table, getting to the bottom of the first pan of eggs.

"Humph. They could adopt the baby out, you know," Sara Clara said. "Why Buzzy, didn't you say that mill nurse Dottie Shaginaw wanted to adopt a baby?"

Buzzy looked at Sara Clara as though she suggested he lop off a limb. "Adopt out? Are you nuts? If you have a baby, you keep it; it's not some extra dog for Pete's sake. You raise the kids you make. That's that."

Rose's careful plunking of buttery eggs onto plates faded to scraping burnt grease so hard that the screeching of metal on metal silenced the discussion. Rose shrugged and went to the sink. She tossed the pan into it and ran the water trying to blot out the conversation at the table for a moment, but then couldn't stop herself from listening as the conversation resumed.

Buzzy stabbed at his eggs. "You know an adopted child is never treated the same as the real kids in the family. Better off dead. Besides, Dottie's a little off center if you know what I mean?"

"Off center?" Johnny said.

"She likes...well, other nurses, if I could put it delicately, Johnny boy."

Nonsense. Rose fumbled a second skillet of eggs, making it crash back onto the burner. The breakfast table was not the place for this type of talk—about adoption or Dottie. Diamond Dottie with a child? She was still a child herself, cocooned in her girlhood home, spoiled by wealthy parents, only working as a nurse out of boredom. If she really cared about people in need she'd be a community nurse.

But off-center? Rose didn't believe that. Dottie was much too interested in flirting with Henry every chance she had to be even a little interested in women. And, she certainly couldn't handle a baby. Rose picked up the frying pan without a potholder and dropped it immediately, bouncing some eggs out of the pan. She scooped up the eggs and glanced over her shoulder to everyone staring at her again.

"Excuse me. Sorry. I didn't say anything." Rose pursed her lips, irritated by all of them. She pushed the plug into the drain and filled it with hot water and soap. She shuddered as she replayed Buzzy's words in her mind. He could be so cruel. He knew Rose had grown up in an orphanage, and had desperately wanted to be adopted. It's not as though Rose were still in that situation, but to hear such heartless statements regarding unwanted children...well, Rose thought, unwanted said it all.

Rose shivered even in the heat of the kitchen. Was it the change of life already? She was only thirty-eight. She told herself Buzzy didn't know what he was talking about. Trouble was, his ideas weren't any different from most folks.

Rose was half-listening to her family when she heard Magdalena's voice come over the din of the others. "Well, I suppose this is as good a time as any to say this."

Rose turned to her daughter, rubbing her arms to stave off the goose bumps crawling up them. She wondered if Magdalena was going to request they all say a prayer for her and the test she needed to take.

Magdalena straightened in her chair. "I'm quitting school to start an apprenticeship with Ms. Hakim. She said I've got a stunning ability to sew a straight, tight line, that I could babysit for her in between learning to perfect my dressmaking skills."

The silence in the room was as startling as Magdalena's announcement. Everyone gaped at Rose, clearly waiting for her response.

She could not think. Her hearing must be going. She grabbed the skillet with bacon and stomped to the table and shoveled some bacon onto Sara Clara's plate. She must not have heard right.

Henry cleared his throat. "If Magdalena really wants to be a seamstress, well, I think it's something to consider. Maybe she has too many responsibilities compared to other girls, too many expectations that suit boys better."

"She's a big girl," Rose said as she scraped bacon from the bottom of the pan for Buzzy's share. "School is the first responsibility on the list of shit she has to do as far as I'm concerned."

"She's still a baby," Henry said.

"I thought I might—" Magdalena said.

"She can decide," Henry said, "if her future means four years of college with men who may not be ready for a woman as smart as they are. I understand—"

Rose grunted and slammed her spatula into the pan. "My daughter will not quit school to sew of all G.D. things. No!" Rose slapped the pan with the spatula several times, anger overtaking her senses.

"Hello? I'm right here!" Magdalena pounded her fists onto the table once, rattling the place settings.

Rose pointed at Magdalena with her spatula. "She's still a *baby*! She can't make her own decisions! That's what the hell we're for!" Rose wiped her brow with the back of her hand. This was not what she needed on a morning like she'd already had. She needed a swig of vodka, needed to calm down.

Sara Clara patted Henry's hand. "It's okay, Hen, everything'll end up fine."

Rose stared at Sara Clara's manicured fingers patting Henry. Rose wanted to smack Sara Clara's hand away.

"Oh, *now* you know everything will be all right, Sara Clara? Now *you* know, huh? A damn miracle, right here in Donora," Rose said.

"Mum," Magdalena said. "Just because I want to sew doesn't mean I'm not as smart as you thought I was. It doesn't—"

Rose smashed the spatula into the pan again. "It means you have nothing to your name if that's the path you take. You have no idea what it's like for women who are at the mercy of their husbands. You have never seen—"

Sara Clara tapped her knife against her coffee mug. "Now Rose, there are some things a woman simply can't worry about. Isn't that the advice I recently heard you offer?"

Rose glared at Sara Clara. What the hell was happening? She did not have the time to engage Sara Clara or any of them in a reasoned argument. She would deal with them later and they would do what she wanted because she loved this family and Magdalena would forget about this sewing. Suddenly, all Rose wanted to do was head off to the world of nursing, where nothing ever went as expected, but where Rose always had the answers.

"The Texaco Star Theatre's on tonight, right?" Johnny said. It was just like him to inject some levity. "Eight pm. Maybe that blond sweetie pie will be back to sing another show-tune or two."

Rose usually appreciated breaks in the tension like that. That was normally all she needed but her arms felt as though they were wrapped in steel, as though her body finally recognized the decades of tireless work she'd used it for and gave up.

Rose stalked to the stove and tossed the pan back onto it. "Serve yourselves," Rose said bolting from the kitchen. All she could do was flee. She did not have the luxury of sitting around messing up people's lives.

Chapter 4

Rose tried to calm herself by taking deep breaths. She stared at her bedside table, knowing the vodka was inside it, wanting it like a man wanted a shot and a beer after his shift. Like every Pennsylvania mill town, Donora had bars tucked between shoe stores and five and dimes, hardware stores and churches. No matter what was standing there, a watering hole of some sort was wedged next to it.

The men worked hard enough during a sweltering, backbreaking shift to justify stopping for a drink on the way home even if work ended at seven in the morning. Still, many a housewife met her husband at the gate on payday to collect the wages, to make sure the money wasn't sucked back with whiskey and Iron City beer.

Rose couldn't stand it any longer and yanked open the stubborn drawer. She was tired and the booze might slow her down even more. But she argued to herself, a nip of vodka might numb her anger enough to refocus on what lay ahead that day. She stared at the flask. She deserved a sip. She thought of the men who left their shifts. They loved a good boilermaker—a stiff drink that consisted of a shot of whiskey—glass and all—plunged into a herculean-sized tumbler of beer that they guzzled down as though they were stranded in the desert.

That was what Rose felt like, traipsing through the hills, caring for dozens of families in just one day. Her throat would be choked with soot after her shifts, and just like the boys at the mill, she needed a shot, but took it at home, at some point during her day. She would throw back the booze like prohibition was minutes from reinstatement. A nice shot provided cover from time to time. Or a tall cool one allowed her to blow off steam. Either way, the booze was anesthetizing, a gateway to getting by or getting through.

She reached in the drawer and ran her finger over the embossed flask. In and out. Rose drew deep breaths, unable to block out Sara Clara's, Magdalena's and Henry's words from her mind. Why would Magdalena give up all that she's worked for her entire life? She had a scientist's mind. She was Rose plus she had the advantages of a loving family, and stable home, a sturdy path to academic and then career success. Not a young girl's typical journey, but her daughter wasn't ordinary.

Rose scolded herself, told herself not to worry about nonsense, that Magdalena was only momentarily frustrated and worried about her pending scholarship. Rose knew Magdalena was a smart girl, but she knew a lot of the world's big problems stemmed from lack of education, more than a dearth of smarts.

The question most burning Rose was why Henry would pretend it was reasonable for Magdalena to quit school. He knew a woman needed her independence. The only way to guarantee that was through financial security. And seeing as Magdalena was not heir to a fortune, her mind would have to provide for her. Rose had taught her daughter since the first time she whispered sweet words in her ear: You are magnificent Magdalena, you keep your wits about you, you work hard, be great.

She didn't have time for this. She had to meet Mrs. Sebastian, the wife of the new mill superintendent, at ten A.M. at the Lipinski home.

Rose opened and closed her hand around the flask of vodka. She shook her head, paralyzed by fear she'd take a drink; motivated by the desire for one. She closed her eyes, the events of the morning causing her as much anxiety as her ambivalence about taking a drink.

She exhaled her frustration, unscrewed the lid and tossed a mouthful of vodka into her mouth. It stung like an angry wasp and hit her stomach like needles. Her shoulders hunched forward and she resisted her gag reflex. With the edge of the bedspread, she wiped her mouth. Her heartbeat slowed and she rubbed her chest below her collarbone.

Rose replaced the lid on the flask and shoved it to the back of the drawer. She leaned over the side-table, gripping the edges. She wanted more. But, no. One shot was enough.

Walk away and get dressed, she thought. She squeezed her eyes shut.

No.

Just one more.

She rifled through the drawer for the flask. In hand, she unscrewed the lid and took her shot. The alcohol spread through her body. Magdalena's announcement, Henry and Buzzy's breakfast shenanigans, all of it made her think she was losing everything. She needed to employ logic and rid herself of blind uncertainty that only led to self-fulfilling prophecy. And, not the good kind.

She threw open her closet door and pushed aside her freshly ironed uniform and good church dress. She knelt on the floor and rammed three hatboxes to the side. Her breath short, she crawled deeper into the closet, groping along the wall where the side met the back and popped open a hidden door. Her chest heaved as she focused on the orderly rows and stacks of non-perishable goods. Everything was there in the exact order that she left it.

This stash of foodstuffs was as important as saving money, she thought. And hidden here, no one would find it. She ran her fingers over the cans of beans, soup, spam—anything that would keep. She would have everything they needed to survive if needed and she wouldn't share a bit of it with lazy Sara Clara.

That woman could starve and wither like an autumn leaf. She crossed herself at the thought. Please God help me, she thought. She felt her focus scatter. Everything and everyone should have been in its place, yet it wasn't.

She crossed herself. Please God; help me get through this day. She had always tried to be a good Catholic. Well, ever since Sister John Ann showed her how much she needed to be. She tried. She did everything she could to follow the rules.

Rose squeezed her eyes shut, still running her fingers around the tops of the cans. She wanted her doubts to vanish. But, despite the constant confession of her sins, the penance of Hail Marys and novenas, she was still angry with God. But, too afraid to discount his power. She knew she was wrong to be angry with Him, so she proceeded in life as though she were not.

* * *

Johnny stood near his mother's clothes closet, bent over, hands on his knees, trying to see what exactly she was doing. Her feet, the splotchy, blackened bottoms of her slippers swerved and jerked as she messed with something in the back where he couldn't see. He'd caught her in the same position a couple of times. Once, he snuck in while she worked and fished around, sure she stashed Christmas gifts there but found nothing. Johnny felt his mother kept a part of her hidden from the family; no one knew her as well as she knew them and this closet was part of what made him think that.

The sound of metal clanging and paper crumpling drew him closer. "Mum?"

Rose gasped; feet suddenly still, one foot slightly raised in the air, the other toe, jammed into the matted carpet. And then she was moving again. She backed out, shoving things around as she did.

Rose stood and pulled her robe tight around her.

Johnny's eyes darted from Rose to the closet and back again. He was nervous, but tried to exude confidence. He knew his mother responded positively to mutual strength more than she did to weakness.

"I need to talk to you." Johnny saw a crescent of greasy soot on her shoulder. He flicked it with his finger, smearing it.

Rose pushed Johnny's hand away and brushed at the soot, smudging it more. Johnny knew that would infuriate her, but she seemed more jumpy than angry, shuffling him away from the closet, kicking it shut with her foot.

"G-go, on." Her words came out in a stutter for the first time in Johnny's life.

Again, he glanced over Rose's shoulder at the closet. He made a mental note to poke around in there later.

"Get on to school," she said. "You've got plenty of school work to do and you need to have the grades like the fellas from the class of—"

"Mum, *please*. I'm not like those fellas from forty-four and forty-five. I love playing football with the fellas for sure, but I am not looking to break my neck in college."

He couldn't get the right words out. He searched for a sign in his mother's expression that she would be open to what he had to say. He reminded himself to be confident, to simply push the words into the world.

He took Rose's hand and squeezed it to get her full attention. "I want to play music."

Rose clenched her jaw and pulled her hand away. "What the hell's in the water today? Is this some sort of 'jag Rose day' I'm not aware of? Music is a direct route to the mill. It'll be as if you signed on a shift the day you graduate from high school. Hell, why even finish high school if that's your plan?"

"But—"

Rose shook her head. "And now look it here, all your yammering has influenced your sister. Do you know how smart that girl is? And she's plotting a life *sewing* of all things."

"I'm trying to tell you I have other opportunities."

Johnny felt his legs go rubbery and he sat on the bed. Why did he think they could talk about this, that he could change her mind? She had taught him to be strong. This was his chance to show her he learned that lesson. He swallowed and stood back up, looking at his mother right in the eye.

"I just want you to know I, uh, might take those opportunities."

Rose sighed. Now she took his hand, stepping forward, forcing him to sit back on the bed. She re-combed his immaculate hair. He waited for her to rant, but she didn't. Maybe the Magdalena thing took more out of her than he realized.

"My parents died of the flu when I was two; I lived in that wretched orphanage. Every time we save money, someone in this family loses it or steals it or borrows it. Not to mention the depression years. It took almost nothing to go from having everything we needed to buy a house to nil. If a person's wealth is in his mind, an education, *that* can't ever be taken away. That's the safest investment a person can make."

"I would say the same is true for a musician. A good one."

His mother was petrified of losing him in a mill accident or to booze, or to a lazy girl who couldn't keep house. But Johnny had no intention of working in a blistering mill. His mother simply didn't know how good he was at music.

"It's my *job* to tell you what to do," Rose said. "It wouldn't be responsible if I didn't open up the world to you, so *then* you can make the choices you want. That's what's wonderful about America. The parents just have to be smart enough to know their kids can do better than them and care enough to make it happen. So, when you talk to the football scouts this weekend. Don't say 'yunz.' They'll look at you different if you speak properly than if you speak like a buffoon. You'll go to college. You don't have a choice. End of discussion."

"Julliard is a college—"

They locked stares.

"I will work so hard, Mum. In New York City. I've talked to a fella there. No way I'll fail. You're my mother. I hail from Donora where the only failure is not trying. I'm not Buzzy."

Rose's eyes conveyed a kindness she didn't always reveal. She put her hand on his shoulder. "You'd be better off if you were dumber. Not that you're a genius, but you're not dumb enough. I don't think music school is the answer. I don't think—"

"Hey, how 'bout a swing around the living room before I leave for school?" He cocked his head and his lips slid into a half smile that never failed to soften his mother. Rose shook her head.

Johnny couldn't live the life his mother had plotted for him, but he loved her so much it hurt. He was sure he could get her to go along with his plan if he tried hard enough. He had a few more days to convince her, to get her ready to meet the man who would change his life.

Johnny stood and leaned on his toes and broke into a full smile. She tilted her head and shrugged. She was clearly finding his idea reasonable. By the end of the week he might even convince her to forget about having the Notre Dame scout over for grub. By then, he might actually have everything he wanted.

He took Rose's hand, pulled her into the hall where he'd set the Victrola spinning. He dropped the arm and the sax introduction for "In the Mood" began. Rose's favorite song.

He spun her down the hall. His father stood there, hands in his pockets.

Johnny heard pounding on the door. "The gang's here. Gotta get to school on time." He broke away from Rose, glancing back to see that she was smiling at him, making him feel as though there was room for him to make his world right.

* * *

As soon as Johnny dashed out the front door Rose was struck by his absence. Henry took her hand, his familiar calluses hit her palm in the spot they always did. Resentment sputtered through her body—irritated that he'd taken up for Magdalena before they had a chance to discuss the fact she was throwing her life into the toilet for no good reason. She refused to look at him and started back down the hall.

Henry came up behind her and grabbed her by the waist. He turned her around, forcing her to face him. Henry wore his half smile, lips not parting even as his eyes squinted. He kissed her forehead and cheeks gently and she stepped against him, his smooth steps leading her to a slower rhythm than the music suggested.

"I'm goddamn angry you kept that from me. It's bullshit, Hen," Rose said into his ear. "You conspiring is..." Just saying the words was like a million knives in her pride, eviscerating her position in the house. Magdalena had trusted Henry over her. She had gone to him her whole life with little tiny things, but *this* was important. This wasn't about a dance on a school night or buying an extra sweater. Henry knew Rose believed in getting an education above anything else; he'd always agreed, yet there he was, approving of Magdalena's irresponsible plans.

Henry pulled Rose closer, her chest against him, his lips brushing her ear as he unknotted her chignon in a single swoop. His fingers combed through her hair. His other hand sat gently in the small of her back making her body meld into his.

They danced their way back toward the bedroom, the passion that marked their relationship for nearly two decades was reborn as Henry lay Rose on the bed and slowly, artfully, and as though there was nothing else in the world that mattered other than her being, pulled her robe open and ran a hand up her slip.

And, the two knew what they meant to each other in a way that they never seemed to find the words to convey. She closed her eyes and let his hands wander over her body. She rubbed and squeezed him; her legs wrapped tight around his waist, and smelled his skin, the familiar scent of sweat from the night still there in spots his shower did not reach.

His lips on hers, his body inside, he unbolted her heart and filled the emptiness. Rose had never felt love the way she did when having sex. It was the most potent form of it, the only way she felt she belonged with Henry completely. And so, there was never a time, never once, that she said no.

* * *

Rose sighed as Henry rolled off of her and onto his back. She looked at his tranquil face, the way he appeared completely at peace when his eyes were shut. Nice for him. Other than the few minutes during sex Rose couldn't seem to find peace in any aspect of her day, eyes closed or open.

She sat up and swung her feet to the floor, stretching her arms above her head. She went to the dresser and took the fresh washrag from a drawer. Its fluffy, terrycloth loops were long flattened into near-useless cotton.

She looked over her shoulder at Henry. How could he have agreed that Magdalena should quit school? Rose dipped the cloth into the water basin, rung it out and rubbed it with her beauty bar to add a scent that would freshen and cleanse.

He had never lied to her before. With the cloth she rubbed her neck, her underarms, scraping away the dead skin. She imagined Magdalena confiding in Henry, discussing how they would keep it from Rose until just the right time.

She whisked away the sweat and filth between her legs, rinsing the cloth then running it down her ankles to her feet, between her toes. She tried to cover up the sadness those realizations brought by focusing on what lay ahead—the data she needed to present to get the funding from Mrs. Sebastian.

Henry coughed making Rose turn back to him. He tamped out his cigarette in the chunky, glass ashtray beside him and scratched away on the yellow legal pad he'd kept in his bedside drawer.

"Get some sleep," Rose said.

"Yeah," Henry said as he continued to write.

Rose shook her head and toweled off her legs. She was always caught off guard by the way Henry attracted her, zapping away unease or anger or worry for the moments that their sex lasted. Then, like a window snapping shut, the closeness was gone and the hurt that she had closed off was instantly back.

"You need a day off," Henry said.

Rose pulled her stockings and undergarments from a drawer and slammed it shut.

"You'll see. With some rest, everything will be fine," Henry said. He normally pushed Rose to confide in him when she was angry—as much as she ever could—but this time he seemed as unwilling to cross the divide as her. That made her even angrier.

Rose laid her slip on the bed, pulled on her underpants and garter-belt and sat down, forcing Henry to move in toward the middle. She glimpsed the yellow pad of paper as he shifted. Doodling. He had something to say to Rose, but she didn't have time to lure it out of him.

She fixed her bra straps over her shoulders and hooked it in the back.

"Just one day," Henry said as he ran his finger under her bra strap and then caressed the back of her neck.

"One day?" Rose wound the Big Ben clock listening as the gears tightened. "I've got a home visit to show the new superintendent's wife that her money would be well spent in our community health clinic. I should check in on Meanie and Slats before seeing if Big Martha will deliver today."

The clock's heavy ticking set her pace. She lifted her leg and rolled a flawless white stocking over one foot and up her leg. She snapped it to the garter and smoothed the whole stocking from toe to thigh. Henry toyed with the garter and she eased his hand away.

She rolled on the second stocking. "You fix this with Magdalena and then I'll feel better." The sound of paper crinkling drew her attention to Henry who was folding up a yellow, legal pad piece of paper.

"We don't need a conversation about how crazy her little announcement was this morning. Neither of us has the time."

She stepped into her slip.

Henry lit another cigarette. "What would you do if you knew something you shouldn't, but because you knew it, you should do something that may not be the right thing?"

Rose grimaced. Henry was always spouting philosophic "what ifs" that at one time Rose used to entertain. They'd become background noise to her, well, she wasn't sure when, but they floated through the air, entering her ears, but not sparking any intellectual interest.

"You just tell the truth, Henry. That seems to be the best way to avoid stepping into dog-shit, don't you think?"

He shrugged, tapping his pencil on the yellow pad. "Like when there's information you're supposed to know and facts you're not…"

Rose laughed and went to the closet. "Like when our daughter confided in you that she plans to toss away her future like dirty toilet paper?" She removed her uniform from her closet.

"Don't ever do that again. Keep a secret," Rose said, wishing she could wrench the words back into her mouth, knowing that she'd kept secrets from Henry she would never want to have to make up for. But still, this was different.

"Rose." Henry appeared to feel all the guilt Rose thought he ought to, having kept such a secret. "I didn't—"

A knock on the door stopped Henry from finishing his thought.

Sara Clara's voice was muffled behind the wood door. "Doc Bonaroti said, Mrs. Sebastian confirmed, Rose. Don't be late."

Rose groaned. As if she'd ever been late for anything.

"The Doc said that, not me. Don't be mad at me," Sara Clara said.

"Oh I'm mad, Sara Clara," Rose said.

Rose pulled her blue uniform over her fresh, white slip, its delicate lace, immaculate from Rose's laundry skill as she did not let Sara Clara near her clothes. "So, spill it, what were you going to say?"

She glanced at Henry who was back to scribbling.

"Later," he said, his voice conveyed that he was pouting. "Sounds like you have to run."

She straightened the white, crisp collar and slipped into her best black, pumps—she had to show Mrs. Sebastian that in the work of a community nurse, the uniform was as important as what she did.

Rose turned back to Henry and saw the yellow paper sticking out from his pocket. She tugged on it. "Is this part of the poetic question of the day?"

"Hey," he took the paper from her and set it on the side-table. "A moment of weakness is all. Nothing you ever…"

Rose put her hands on her hips and raised her eyebrows. She motioned to the yellow paper.

"It's nothing Rose. Just a little crisis of conscious is all. Nothing you've ever struggled with, I know."

Rose bit the inside of her mouth. She was choosing to let this pass. She had plenty of clock-time to get to the Lipinski home, but she needed to gather her thoughts and Henry's nonsense wasn't helping her do that.

"Don't be sarcastic, Henry. Do what you know is right. Neither of us has the time for horseshit. I'll take this little conversation as your apology for not telling me our daughter was dabbling in a vat of stupidity in her off-hours." Rose took his face in her hands and gave him a quick smack on the lips. "She's a scientist not a seamstress. Talk to her. Magdalena likes you better, after all. And, I'm operating on the notion that this is the end of your clandestine affairs, right?"

Henry nodded and tamped his cigarette into the ashtray. He stretched out in the middle of the bed, pulled the covers up to his chin and fell, it seemed to Rose, instantly asleep. She stared at the yellow paper he'd put on his side-table, the top half of the fold bouncing up as the radiator pushed heat into the air. Rose picked it up, but the clock caught her eye. She shoved the paper back onto the table and kissed Henry's cheek before closing the door on the tiny, stale room.

* * *

Many believed a community nurse was essential to small town healthcare. She was the bridge between families and the ever-changing world of health and hygiene. Rose and Dr. Bonaroti had discussed the matter for years, but because the town of about fourteen-thousand citizens had eight doctors and several nurses at the mill hospital, it took extensive time and energy to raise the initial funding for Rose and their clinic—the place that offered care for women, children and non-mill employees. She and Bonaroti had only managed to implement their plan in the past year. And, their work had yielded results.

Across the country strategies mounted in how to win the war on communicable diseases. Rose was a voracious researcher, both borrowing and writing her own plans to best deliver pre-natal and postnatal care for mothers and their babies. She encouraged the thrust to assimilate immigrants into the American way of post-war life as the practice grew sharper and more prominent in large cities and small towns.

Nurses were charged with everything from showing a family how to manage their money, clean their home and sew clothing, to making regular visits to polio patients and treating acute viruses and infections like tuberculosis. This work inspired Rose more than her hospital job in a neighboring town had ever done. Even before she was a community nurse she'd always been available to help this person or that back to health, but that wasn't the same as having a structured clinic and services available to an entire town.

She didn't dislike nursing at the hospital, but it was inside this community network of delivering services to people whose needs were subterranean and wide-ranging that Rose found her true love and security. In the face of other people's weaknesses, Rose brought strength. She could help anyone with anything, whether they wanted the help or not. She showed them what they didn't know and why and how they needed her.

Rose headed down the hall from her bedroom and turned off the still-spinning Victrola. She found Leo seated on the chair by the front door, the top of his head just under her hanging nurse's bag. His eyes were closed as though he'd dozed off.

"What are you doing?" Rose said.

Leo's eyes snapped open. "Why hello there Sweetie! Mum and Dad said to go with you for today."

Rose couldn't help but be charmed by Leo's pet name for her. Still, she didn't want to schlep him around town. She was not a babysitter.

"Mummy went shopping. And Daddy's sleeping."

Rose sighed and dragged Leo into the kitchen where she sat him in a chair. She brushed the crumbs from the tabletop into her hand. "Dammit. Can't anyone else in this house clean anything?"

Rose averted her gaze from the grease stained stove that Sara Clara must have overlooked as she attempted to redd-up the mess. The breakfast dishes teetered in the sink; dirty as when Rose had charged out of the kitchen. Rose would have to simply walk out the door and forget that no one cared enough to clean up after themselves.

"Last time you came with me," Rose patted Leo on the shoulder. "I could have strung you by the toes by the end of the day. I'd have let you swing in the wind for decades if I wasn't so, well you said, it, Sweet." Rose grabbed the washcloth that was drying over the faucet and smelled it. Fairly clean. She turned the water on to hot and waited for it to heat.

"Remember, don't make a peep while we're at these homes. If need be, I'll put you to work and you'll pretend that you help me locate people who need our services. Like that girl in McKeesport who's famous for bringing indigent and lazy people to their clinic that we read about...well, you're no dummy. Just follow my cue and first and foremost, be quiet."

Rose wet the towel, grabbed Leo's cheeks with one hand and scraped at the crusted eggs and toast at the corners of his mouth. Naturally, he didn't brush his teeth that morning. She yanked his mouth open and scrubbed his teeth with the cloth. He giggled even as he cringed, making Rose fall even more in love with him than she already was.

"You'll sit on the porch while I do my exams and I might even have to send you walking ahead of me if someone is infectious, but I don't see the infectious crowd until the end of the day, so to not spread disease." She grabbed his arms and squeezed them. "You do what I say or I'll smack your ass."

He looked up at Rose, eyes wide. His lips parted as though Rose's words had stolen his breath, and pulled her into a hug, nodding agreement.

"Well, okay then." Rose wormed out of Leo's grip. "Let's go. Being late is unforgivable, you know. I have told you that before, hmm?"

She flicked her hand toward the hallway, sending Leo in that direction. Rose passed the family pictures in the hallway as she headed toward the door. Johnny's photos revealed different expressions—an open-mouthed guffaw, an angry scowl, a pensive wonder whether taken seconds apart or years revealed yet another part of who Johnny was.

Magdalena wore the same dark, knowing expression in each of hers. She wasn't joyless in the photos, but she wasn't grinning either. Rose couldn't really say what Magdalena might have been feeling in any of them and that made Rose wonder if she knew Magdalena at all. Rose touched one photo, traced Magdalena's perfect jaw line grateful that Henry would set their daughter back on the proper path to college.

The last picture she passed was of Rose at fifteen, sitting in a room full to bursting with people. The blurry background blotted the fact she was in an orphanage but somehow it gave off a glow as though it was a mansion peopled with folks who loved her rather than exploited her.

Henry loved her in the photo, her appearance—her utter contentment; he insisted it stay there. Rose felt a chill as she pushed away the memory of the day the photo was taken, as the soul shadow that had haunted her for decades showed itself in that hallway.

She shuddered and crossed herself, asking God to forgive her, and she reminded herself to get to confession by late afternoon. Leo craned around the doorjamb. His hat perched on his head. He held Rose's nurse's cap out to her. "Here, Sweetie."

Rose drew back, surprised at the sight of Leo's dirty fingers, his oval fingerprints dotting her pristine, white and navy nurse's cap. She would have scolded anyone else. She took the cap and fitted it to her head then squatted down to Leo's eye-level.

"Jesus, Leo. That's really thoughtful. I don't think there's another person in this house who would bring me my hat. You're a definite doll, you are." I wish you were mine, she almost said.

"Now, don't touch my cap again. Look at what you've done. Your teeny fingers smudged up my whites."

He stuck out his bottom lip.

"Not to worry, it'll be every hue of grey by the time we get around the corner." She tussled his hair and ordered him to wait by the door while she scrubbed her hands then loaded her bag with fresh pledgets, sterilized brushes, urine cups, green soap, the sanitary pads she'd made from old flannel, in all—more than seven pounds of weight across

Rose's arm for her trek around town attempting to create a healthy living environment for all who lived in Donora.

* * *

Rose stood on the porch, chest rising with calming breaths, running the data through her mind. Twenty-five hundred bedside visits, one and a half hours per work day in Bonaroti's clinic, one hour per week for new mother conferences. And that only began to cover the town's needs. Rose took another deep breath. The woman will fund the clinic; Rose said to herself and pulled out her map of Donora.

A flash of red drew her gaze to the gauzy fog. A cardinal hopped over and flew from one porch roof to another. A good omen, Rose thought, and spread her map out on the porch. She ordered Leo onto the floor to go over the path she was about to take.

She had five minutes to spare before heading toward the Lipinski's. She'd been showing Leo the maps each time he went with her. If he was going to traipse all over town, he needed to know where he was and where he wasn't in case he needed to head home alone.

Rose pointed to a spot on the map, the Lipinski's, and several others she was due to see that day. She had Leo recite the path they'd take, street names and all.

Leo scratched his nose. "Where're the hills?"

Rose squatted down with Leo and pulled his hand from his face. Impetigo spreads like news of a new floozy in town when kids start scratching and picking and rubbing around the nasal passages.

"There ain't no hills on that map," Leo said.

"*Aren't any hills*, Leo. Not ain't. Never ain't." Rose ran her finger from the Lipinski to the Nemoroski home—a place she'd never been to—on the very edge of the north end of town. Leo traced the same path with his tiny finger on top of Rose's. Leo was right. The map, a one-dimensional version of town, was misleading to say the least.

On paper, Donora mostly appeared to be broken into neat squares and rectangles, with roads forming odd polygon shapes in the middle of town. But, overall the map's layout gave the impression that the land hugging the horseshoe-shaped river was flat and easy to navigate. In reality, it was as though God had seized a section of the perfectly plotted land and lifted it up, shifting everything so roads that appeared parallel weren't. The natural landscape forced homes to curve into hillsides, butt against stone walls, and dangle from plateaus, creating tiers of town, as if tightly knitted homes were fixed into the mountainside with glue and a prayer.

Steep sets of stairs acted as sidewalks up arrow-straight avenues, paved in cobblestone, cement, dirt, gravel or coal depending what was available at a given time. The steep landscape made Donora the perfect place for fog to inhabit on a daily basis, and added to the darkness the mills contributed on a round the clock basis.

"Don't smudge up the bag," Rose said. "Did you make bubbles? You can't traipse around other people's home, using their bathrooms."

"I can use a tree," Leo said.

"Not on the *last* day of your life, young man. This isn't bumpkinville like where your...oh forget it. Let's get going. You're young. Your bladder's good."

* * *

Rose and Leo headed off the porch and a voice cut through the dense fog. Mrs. Saltz crossed the street and started up the steps. If Rose hadn't known the voice, she'd recognize the shape of the woman—the cat always sitting on her shoulder made her look deformed.

The stout German neighbor woman spoke broken English and refused to leave her hot-tempered husband despite his actions putting their family in repeated, but varied types of peril. Rose blew out frustrated air. She could not be late for Mrs. Sebastian.

"I have Joey on my list for therapy tomorrow," Rose said to Mrs. Saltz as she started down the stairs. Rose noted Mrs. Saltz's red, swollen cheeks. The cat was licking her face. Rose cringed. Could there be a filthier animal? Worse than dogs.

Mrs. Saltz's eyes were bruised and a small cut had crusted to black blood at the corner of her mouth. Rose hardened against the pity she felt for the woman. She had tried to help her, dozens of times—at least forty documented nursing visits for all manner of things, but the success of a community nurse required the family to be committed to change.

Mrs. Saltz wept into her hands, then balled them up and covered her eyes. Rose wondered if that was the stance she must have taken each time Mr. Saltz hit her.

"There's a family in Lancaster that would happily take you in. I can't help you if you don't let me. You said you had family in Ohio..."

Mrs. Saltz stood, crying, curling up like a dying flower, not saying anything. Rose sighed impatiently and the cat leaped onto her shoulder and clung to her back. Rose whapped at the cat over her shoulder and spun and spun around.

Mrs. Saltz reached up toward Rose and with a sudden burst of energy ripped the cat from Rose's shoulder and put it back on her own. The cat meowed, showing its teeth then hissed at Rose while Mrs. Saltz continued wailing.

Rose's heart thumped and crushed her chest. "Keep that damn thing away from me." Rose was about to say or she wouldn't come see Joey. But Rose could never hold a crazy mother against a sick boy. Part of her job was to turn the family around, not judge them. But still. That cat was like a deadly weapon as far as Rose was concerned. "Damn cat," Rose said quietly.

Mrs. Saltz slid her fists under her loose jowls, eyes narrowing, her rectangular face quivering. "My husband, your husband. They the same. Buzzy. They the same. Men all the same. Gambling, women…" her voice cut out like radio static.

Leo reached up and patted Mrs. Saltz on the elbow. The woman stopped wailing, stared down at Leo then made a break across the street. Gone, as though Leo's touch had wakened her senses.

Leo scrunched his face and shrugged. "Sweetie?"

Rose felt the same confusion that she saw grip Leo's expression.

He pointed in the direction of the fleeing Mrs. Saltz. "Of course all men are the same. We all have penises, right?" Leo lifted his coat, thrust out his crotch area and looked downward as though checking to be sure he still had one.

Rose sighed at Leo's innocence. She knew what Mrs. Saltz meant except for her reference to Henry. He was not a gambler. And he certainly did not have women. Not since he married Rose 18 years before.

"Leo my boy. All men are *not* the same. Penis, yes. The same, no. At least I pray that's the case." Rose had never distrusted Henry. Well, once or twice, but she'd always investigated and discerned her suspicions of adultery to be unfounded. No, Henry might not be perfect, he may have hid some information regarding Magdalena, but Henry Pavlesic was *not* a cheater.

"Come on, Leo. Take a good lesson from Mrs. Saltz. You sure as shit better be able to take care of yourself because a person with no course of action planned, no education, and no money in his pocket is helpless and that's no way to be."

Rose thought of Magdalena loosening the ties on her secure future by saying she might quit school. Perhaps she needed to give Magdalena a refresher in how many ways life can go bad.

"Mrs. Saltz's housekeeping habits allowed Polio to have a field day with her son," Rose said. "Everything has its use, every person, too. So you better have some toughness about you or you'll end up crying all day with a damn cat perched on your shoulder like a crazy."

They headed north to where the Lipinski home was located high above the zinc mill. Leo nodded and grasped Rose's hand. Despite the fact his hand was joined with hers it was clear to Rose that he could feel none of her concern about what had transpired since the moments she was called to the Greshecky home early that morning.

He sensed none of her anxiety, that she was having trouble focusing on what lay ahead, even though she had never been able to leave the pain of what lay scattered behind. And for that, she smiled at Leo, wishing she was more like him.

Chapter 5

Life was slowly returning to prosperity by 1948. Rationing had ended in 1946, nylon stockings were available again and you could sell your fifteen year-old car for the same price you bought it for new. But, it only took one bad loss—a huge hospital bill, a broken appliance, or a job loss—and your account would be wiped out.

Like many Donora families, the Pavlesics had money for food and clothing and some savings. And, while a budget still ruled the day, if they were careful they could soon build their own home. If they paid off the final chunk of Buzzy's debt and he paid them back, that is.

Things in the world were looking up, what the war took away from the newly unionized steel workers—pay-raises during the war—it tried to give back in benefit packages that helped people feel as though they were getting ahead. Donora was a boomtown—it had fueled the war and now every ounce of steel it turned out was wired into a bridge, nailed into a house or bolted onto a car driving down an elm-lined street somewhere in America.

The endless stream of smoke was a good thing—a sign that everyone was working in the mills or in a job that supported the mills. Rose and Dr. Bonaroti were determined to make health care a part of that prosperity, and get their funding from all that profit.

They thought they could persuade the Women's Club and Easter Seals to fund and stock the clinic and thereby push city council to at least partly fund Rose's position with community chest monies. With new mill benefits packages, Rose and Bonaroti figured approximately fifty-four percent of her visits could be funded by insurance.

Some families could partially pay out of pocket and the rest would need assistance. Then there was the need to pay for instruments and materials. Rose couldn't hand-make sanitary pads forever.

Rose and Leo reached the Lipinski's address. From where they stood, three tiers of steps led straight upward to the house. From the sidewalk, Rose saw the rickety porch boards and a glimpse of the second floor dormers. She pulled Leo's hand, yanking him up the first few in a set of twelve. She let him go up another two steps and then turned him toward her. He was high enough to be eye-level.

"Now listen," she said. "Set up camp on the Lipinski's porch and, here, take this set of marbles and occupy yourself. Not a peep and there's a pop and some Klondikes in it for you."

Leo grinned and raced up the remaining steps, stirring up the soot that had gathered on the wood. Lipinski's clearly did not keep up with their sweeping. Near the top he disappeared from Rose's view. She was suddenly aware of the fog, the way it hid her nephew as he moved further away. It would certainly have lifted by the time she was done with this call.

Rose stepped back down to the wooden plank sidewalk. She crossed herself and began ticking off important points one at a time. Parts of Herman Biggs' famous quote came to Rose, "Investment in public health can regulate illness and death. Investment and education are primary." Her nerves had suddenly done away with the exact words, but the gist of his sentiments looped over and over in her mind.

The sound of someone's voice from behind startled Rose. She spun around to see a slender blond woman in a fitted aquamarine suit. The woman wore a delicate hat which Rose knew at a glance was silk velvet, with a taffeta ribbon and the finest netting covering her eyes.

The woman moved closer and Rose realized they were about the same age—late thirties or early forties. Rose's gaze darted to the woman's perfect shoes, the exact shade of blue as the suit, with crystal and lace flower appliqués that Rose had only seen on brides and in Hanson's Finest Women's Wear storefront.

Rose offered her hand. "I'm Rose Pavlesic, Mrs. Sebastian."

"What makes you so sure?"

Rose pulled her hand back and hugged her bag into her body. "Oh. I'm sorry." Rose shook her head and stepped out of the way.

Mrs. Sebastian nodded and smiled with her mouth closed, "It is me."

Rose's mouth screwed up at one corner. This interaction threw her off balance.

"My daughter's on her way, a block behind me or so. She's a little fragile that one, but she won't let me help her a bit. Stubborn as the dickens. I don't take her with me much, because she gets winded, but I insisted she come today. I thought it might help for her to see that there's no artificial measure big enough to plug the gaping hole that is poverty. Not even with well-meaning people at the helm. Here she is."

Rose didn't like what the woman said or the way she said it. She was not accustomed to being in this position— one where she had the information, but not the power. This would require the same precision as neurosurgery in Rose's estimation. Same result if she screwed up.

Behind Mrs. Sebastian, traipsed a twentyish woman with shoulder-length auburn hair and almond shaped, dark eyes. She wore a cocoa-colored woolen suit, and brushed it nervously with a slim gloved hand. Her chest heaved for breath. Rose reached for her, to support her as she caught her breath.

"You all right?" Rose said, close enough to smell the girl's fruity perfume. Rose felt her forehead with her palm and then the back of her hand.

"This is Theresa," Mrs. Sebastian said.

Theresa smiled through gasping breaths and gently pushed Rose's hand away.

Rose glanced at Mrs. Sebastian who nodded. Rose backed off, turning her attention to Mrs. Sebastian.

"I'll be frank, Mrs. Pavlesic. I'm accustomed to offering my time, talents and money to the arts," she said. She cocked her head giving Rose the sense the woman was speaking to a child rather than a skilled nurse with years of experience. "I was a ferocious supporter of the symphony in Pittsburgh. In Gary I was the head of the Women's League of Arts and Music. But, my husband thought it was important to at least entertain the thought of carrying on the work of the superintendents' wives who preceded me. Well, I just wanted to let you know what you're up against. I believe the community chest is better choice for funding a clinic."

"That won't cover the whole project." Jackass. Rose's jaw tightened. She fought her rising worry. This was going to be harder than she thought. She'd been so distracted by her family problems that she'd miscalculated. She should have known. "Maybe we should begin in the clinic with some hard statistics," Rose said pointing over Mrs. Sebastian's shoulder. "Maybe you'd be more comfortable with a set of numbers."

"We're here now," Mrs. Sebastian said. Her eyes hard on Rose's, her words, icy. Rose hit a nerve. That wasn't what she had intended. Rose shifted her weight and patted her bag.

You can do this, Rose told herself and turned toward the stairs swinging her hand upward, offering the woman the first step up. It was then, when Mrs. Sebastian turned that Rose realized the woman was pregnant. A slim hipped woman from the front, in profile, her round belly was displayed.

"Oh, well, are you sure, this is quite steep, three flights of steps." Rose didn't want to condescend; she wanted to be respectful of the woman's condition. She was quickly losing confidence that she'd chosen the right set of families to demonstrate the town's needs, but dismissed her nerves.

Mrs. Sebastian popped open her shantung clutch and dug through it. She produced a thin cigarette and a chunky Zippo lighter. She held her handbag under her arm and lit the cigarette. "Let's just hope this journey into the clouds via a less than sturdy staircase is worth the risk." She chucked the hefty lighter back into the purse.

"Perhaps you could hold my bag?" She handed the dainty purse to Rose who rubbed the buttery fabric between her thumb and finger. Rose hoisted her nurse's bag over her shoulder and offered her empty arm to Mrs. Sebastian to help her up the crumbly steps.

Mrs. Sebastian bent over Rose's outstretched arm and ran her finger over the shabby spot in the tweed where the bag straps had laid over Rose's arm each day.

Rose looked away, her cheeks burning. She prided herself in the care she took in preserving all her clothing, her presentation. But as any community nurse knew, hauling a seven-pound bag each and every day of the year wore at one's coat.

"Evidence of hard work and the need for a nurse in town. Right there on that arm." Rose nodded.

"Hmm." Mrs. Sebastian lifted her chin and turned her attention toward the rising stairs.

By the time they reached the top, Rose had diagnosed Theresa as having asthma and had, in her mind, cobbled together several different protocols that might help alleviate the girl's spasming bronchial tubes. And, maybe that—helping Theresa—would sell her mother on Rose's skill and the benefit of community nursing care.

* * *

Rose cringed when they reached the Lipinski's porch. Leo wasn't there. His footprints, where his small shoes lifted the soot away, left white tracks instead of black: he'd gone around back. He probably saw the Huston boy and that would occupy him more than a bunch of marbles. Mrs. Sebastian took a drag from the cigarette as though it would allow her to catch her breath.

Rose wanted to tell her about some very important doctors who had done some preliminary research and found cigarettes caused babies to be born small and more helpless than usual. She would wait to offer that bit of information until she was sure she was getting the money. Or not.

Rose explained to Mrs. Sebastian and Theresa that she'd selected two households to demonstrate the role of community nurse and its clinic—one, a home full of people who'd learned from Rose how to create a healthy living environment even though poor, and two—the Lipinski's—who'd just allowed Rose one visit so far. Rose hoped the contrast of the two households with similar histories, would demonstrate the significant impact a community nurse had on the public.

Rose filled Mrs. Sebastian and Theresa in on the Lipinski situation: a widow who has not recovered from her husband's sudden death when he slipped and fell into a vat of molten steel incinerating him. With no pension and the amount of his last check in dispute, she had not found the energy to care for her six children. The oldest, a twelve year-old, had stopped attending school, the others never started. Even before Mr. Lipinski's death, the family did not adhere to strict hygiene practices and the children suffered from lice, scabies, rotten teeth and malnutrition.

"Aren't some families lost causes?" Mrs. Sebastian said. "Giving money to the theater means it is used constructively right away." Mrs. Sebastian flicked her cigarette into the hillside off the porch with her thin fingers.

Rose silently admitted she'd often thought the same thing upon entering a rancid home. But her stomach churned hearing Mrs. Sebastian be cavalier about a family whose head died in the very mill that lined her husband's silk pockets. Rose pushed her shoulders back. She had to be careful not to offend Mrs. Sebastian.

Rose nodded and pushed a smile to her lips. "Pathetic, yes, but lost causes? No. That's why I'm proud to carry the black bag of public health. There's always something to teach and someone to learn." Rose drew back, the corny wording felt phony, as if she were advertising during the Original Amateur Hour.

Mrs. Sebastian took her purse from Rose, stepped up to the pitted wood door and rapped on it. Rose worried the Sebastian women were not ready for this, but it was too late to change her course of action. Rose knocked again, and after no response, pounded on the door.

Rose waited, her ear turned to the door. With no sounds coming from inside she pushed open the door and poked her head inside. A stench of spoiled, cooked onions and greasy meat made Rose's stomach heave.

Rose heard rustling in the space in front of her. "Mrs. Lipinski?" The rooms were so dark that even coming in from the fog, Rose's eyes couldn't make out what was in front of her.

She reached back and waved Mrs. Sebastian in, and heard her sharp intake of air. Rose hoped the woman would maintain an expression of neutrality and not embarrass the family.

"Mrs. Lipinski?" Rose stepped further into the house, turning her ankle on a shoe. Dammit. This may be too good of a "bad" example. She kicked the shoe to the side then felt along the wall to the point where she hit the light switches—one button to push on, the other for off. She pushed one then the other. Neither lit the room.

A gravelly female voice came from inside the room. "Can't spare no extra to burn lights in daytime. Fog'll clear soon 'nough."

Mrs. Sebastian let out a startled squeal.

Rose shuffled along the wall, remembering a lamp near the unlit fireplace. If she didn't bring on some light quick, Mrs. Sebastian would leave without the opportunity to see what Rose's work entailed.

Rose heard the grainy snap of a Zippo. Mrs. Sebastian's lighter provided just enough light for Rose to reach the fireplace. She twisted the tiny knob on the side of the lamp and weak yellow light lit the room. The light, like a magic wand, revealed five people sitting around their mother, shielding their eyes from the sudden glow. Mrs. Sebastian was backing out toward the door, bumping into a wide-eyed Theresa.

Rose grasped Mrs. Sebastian's hand and patted it as though she were a child. She wondered if the woman had ever been in a home like this, whether she'd always been wealthy enough that not even the depression had lifted the shade on the ugliness of poverty. Rose coaxed a reluctant Mrs. Sebastian into the room, introducing her to Mrs. Lipinski, and five of her children.

"Marie's up in 'er room, n'at," Mrs. Lipinski said, never lifting her gaze from the floor. "Go on up and check 'er out. She ain't been dahn in two days. Not even fer her favorite. Bacon."

Rose nodded then knelt in front of one of the children and whispered. The child, who Rose quickly realized was a boy dressed in girl's clothing, nodded and gave Rose his ladder-back chair then nudged his sister and sat with her in the next chair.

Rose pulled the chair one foot away from the wall and laid her coat over the ladder-back. The weight of the coat, snapped off its back.

"I am so sorry," Rose said to Mrs. Lipinski. "I'll have my Henry come fix that this very afternoon." Rose glanced at Mrs. Sebastian. Her eyes were closed and her mouth was moving, in prayer Rose guessed. That could be good or bad.

Mrs. Lipinski stared at the wall of windows so blackened from soot they might let in barely more light than a wall. Rose asked another child to sit with his mother and offered that seat to Mrs. Sebastian.

Rose dragged another broken chair toward Mrs. Lipinski for Theresa to sit on, but the young woman was backed up completely against the door. Rose walked her to the chair beside her mother. She squeezed her hand. "It'll be okay. You'll see." Theresa shuffled across the floor and nodded. Mrs. Sebastian sat beside Mrs. Lipinski, as close to the edge of the chair as she could, appearing to breathe through her mouth rather than her nose, to block the odor of the home, Rose guessed.

Mrs. Lipinski shifted her gaze from the windows to Mrs. Sebastian's profile. "Like yer suit. Ain't one of them convertible suits, that there's a real one. Had me one of those once 'pon time."

Mrs. Sebastian fingered the collar on her suit jacket. One of the children was creeping across the floor on all fours, lured by the crystal shoe appliqués that reflected every last bit of light in the room. Mrs. Sebastian watched the child inch closer. The woman's face froze in a grimace. She pulled her body taller, tighter into herself.

Rose worked as efficiently as possible. She might have made more inquiries about the general state of things had this been a typical visit, but she needed to get at the crux of the problem and move onto the other family—the one who'd become a prime example for the benefits of community nursing.

She removed newspapers from her bag, put some of them under her arm, spread a set on the now backless chair seat and lay her bag on it. She folded the remaining newspapers and turned them into bags to carry soiled linens. Another would be used for after-use instruments, and the third for waste to be thrown out.

In the kitchen Rose scrubbed her hands with the green soap she'd left at the Lipinski's house three days before. She just managed to avoid touching the pile of dirty dishes in the sink while she washed up.

In the front room, Rose opened her bag and removed the sanitary pads she'd sewn. "These are for your monthly cycles, Mrs. Lipinski. The flannel's good, but like I said last time, you'll need to soak them and wash them in the hottest water to maintain their usefulness."

Mrs. Lipinski began to rock in her chair as though she were into another world.

Rose handed the pads to a trembling Mrs. Sebastian to hold. She looked at Rose and held her gaze as if to say, don't you dare leave me alone with these people. Rose gave her an encouraging nod and she wondered if she should have instructed her on how to interact with a different class of people.

Mrs. Sebastian nodded back, though appeared to be in shock. She ran her hand over the flannel. "Why these," she cleared her throat, "are fine pads, the stitches..." Her voice shook as she faked a casual tone.

Rose pulled more fabric from the bag, and turned her attention to Mrs. Lipinski. "And I bleached these flour sacks and made underwear for you and the children. Nothing ever lasts as long as good flour-sack underwear. I was raised on them, myself." Rose hesitated, knowing she needed to follow protocol and ask Mrs. Lipinski to assist her in caring for Marie.

As soon as the question was out of Rose's mouth, Mrs. Lipinski turned away, unwilling or able to get out of the chair. Rose was not about to wrestle the woman up the stairs and decided she would explain to the Sebastians that working with the Lipinski's would require a multi-layered approach. It would take time to make the simplest changes with them.

Rose smiled. "Now, I'll leave you ladies to get acquainted while I tend to Marie."

Rose felt her way up the staircase into the bedroom at the top of the landing. She didn't think it was possible for a set of steps to be skinnier and more treacherous than her own, but in homes like this—where additions were cobbled together with nails the homeowner stole from the mill and wood that was rummaged out of garbage heaps she was reminded self-pity wasn't allowed.

Rose crossed the threshold into Marie's room, passing through cobwebs. She batted them away from her face and cleared her throat. In the shoebox-shaped room a narrow bed and a coal stove stood by a closed window; an arthritic table perched at the end of the bed.

Marie lay still as a corpse. Rose bent over her and waited for warm breath to hit her cheek before she began her work. She moved toward the magazine-sized table and checked over the things she'd prepared for the family to care for Marie—everything was exactly as she'd left it. They had ignored her instructions.

Rose readjusted the items: green soap, brush, tea, and spittoon that would ensure Marie had a place to spit her mucus, but not to be promiscuous about it, to keep the spread of disease to a minimum. Rose placed the thermometer and stethoscope on the table.

The girl was too still, prompting Rose to hurry. "Little Marie?" Rose, sandwiched between the mattress and the coal stove, inched toward the two-year-old. She pressed the skirt of her uniform against the back of her legs so it wouldn't catch fire.

Marie stirred. Rose's shoulders dropped, releasing tension she didn't realize she was holding. She lifted Marie's hand and turned it wrist up. She ran her finger over the pale, soft skin, the one section of the girl that seemed clean. She settled her fingers into the center of the clammy wrist and counted the beats for ten seconds. Eighty beats per minute. Rose liked to see a child's resting pulse around sixty, but eighty was greatly reduced from the one hundred-five it was the day before.

Rose put the back of her hand on the girl's cheeks then forehead. Her fever broke as Rose predicted it would. But her face was sticky. Rose touched her again with her fingertips. Sticky. She ran her hands over the scratchy blanket. Sticky. What the hell is this shit?

Rose knelt beside the girl and sniffed. Sweet. Not sugar. "Marie? What *is* this?"

"Juicy Juice." Rose wondered if the girl's slurred speech was the mark of the emerging language of a two-year-old, but the lolling of her head made her appear more like a drunk than a two year-old on the mend.

What the hell was juicy juice?

Rose sniffed the girl's face and blanket again. The wet wool odor masked the scent of the sticky stuff. Rose didn't want to do it, but decided to since a little girl's health was at stake. She licked her fingers then looked at them, turned toward the fire and peered closer at her fingers. Purple. What? Rose shook her head. How could a sick girl be sugared in wine?

A drop of liquid hit Rose's scalp. She looked up at the dark ceiling and squinted. Something was definitely leaking. Rose bent over the bed just above Marie's face and turned her face upward, waiting for a drip.

Plop.

Wine. Definitely. Rose growled. Marie was drunk from a steady drip of homemade wine. Elderberry, of course, was du rigor in Donora in October. Rose struggled to stand and her skirt licked the stove just enough to catch a flame.

She yelped and Marie giggled at the sight of Rose's uniform blazing. Rose ripped the wool blanket from the bed and smacked at the flames, putting them out. But, not before the flames had seared the hem of her uniform.

Oh, this was not good, Rose thought. "Okay, little Marie. Out of bed, now." Marie reached up but didn't, or couldn't, move. Rose scooped her up and flung her over her shoulder, taking her downstairs. In the front room Rose settled Marie onto Mrs. Lipinski's lap and spoke to her about the wine and the neglect, telling her the girl could not go back into that bed.

"That there wine? Holy shit on a brick! I fergot the wine." Mrs. Lipinski began to rock Marie, finally conscious. "That was Boguslaw's wine. Fermentin' he said. Just a bit of time, he said. But, he got swallowed by that there slag and I fergit, I fergit everthing."

Rose sighed, torn between knowing what her job required and what she wanted to do.

"Must've blew out of the barrel n'at?"

Rose nodded. She would send Henry and Buzzy before their shift to do some repairs. They had an extra lamp; some rags. She didn't have enough resources to furnish and clean up everyone's home, but she couldn't let this go. Her job was to help people help themselves.

She should contact Fanny at the Red Cross and file a complaint regarding the dangerous state of this home. Still, Rose believed she could change this woman's life and not have to move her out of her home to do it. Stupid, Rose thought. That wasn't the best plan. It might be the worst, in fact.

"I'll give this outfit three weeks, Mrs. Lipinski. You *have* to have your household up and running, the children who are school age, back in school, the home lit, the rotten food gone, or I have to take the next step. Why don't I send Father Slavin to see you? He's a whiz at getting people back on their feet."

"Can't afford to be religious."

"It won't run you a dime," Rose said.

Mrs. Lipinski pursed her lips, but nodded and squeezed Marie, smiling through tears.

Rose hauled the pot out of its cupboard and filled it with water. She lit the stove and shoved the soiled linens from Marie's room into the boiling pot while barking a list of orders to Mrs. Lipinski. The woman seemed remarkably lighter in mood when Rose and the Sebastian women headed for the door, but Rose was unsure of the decisions she just made.

Was she showing off for Mrs. Sebastian, suffering from hubris? Thinking she could change things that might be impossible to alter? It wasn't as though Mrs. Lipinski's problems were all caused by her husband's death. But, Rose had work to do and wouldn't have time to reconsider her decision until later. And lucky for Rose, she was good at simply moving on.

* * *

When the door closed behind them, Rose exhaled. So did Mrs. Sebastian and Theresa, as though they'd all been holding the same breath since the moment they set their heels inside the Lipinski home. Rose would let Mrs. Sebastian have a moment before filling her in on the next visit. Or, perhaps Rose should report the numbers related to poverty and health care and how it affected costs, education, quality of life, longevity, everything.

Mrs. Sebastian unclasped her bag and rifled through it. She pulled a cigarette and Zippo out and held one to Rose. She shook her head. Unless there was a flask of vodka or her checkbook in that purse, the woman had nothing that could help Rose right then. Rose smoothed her coat, making sure it hid the length of the burn from the stove in little Marie's room.

Theresa let out a groan then burst into tears, startling Rose. The young lady huddled up to her mother, latching onto her arm. Her face crinkled up in pain. Seeing how affected Theresa was moved Rose. She wasn't accustomed to being taken by such emotion.

Mrs. Sebastian shooed her daughter away. "You'll be fine, Theresa. Remember, you don't actually live in that home. You don't need to get all blue and...I just wanted you to see...oh, please start down the steps, so you don't get winded."

The girl followed her mother's orders and disappeared down the way, still crying.

Rose was concerned about Theresa but knew that wasn't her responsibility. She looked over the hills. The fog had burned off and left the sun a silvery moon rather than an egg-yolk sphere.

Say something. Rose wanted Mrs. Sebastian to signal that she was ready to fund the clinic.

As if she sensed Rose's thoughts, Mrs. Sebastian held up her hand. "I need to further absorb what I saw." She swung her hand back into her chest as though wanting to dislodge a chunk of meat from her windpipe, and bent forward, shaking her head. "It's indescribable."

Rose nodded, keeping her face relaxed, her outward professionalism intact despite her insides contracting with nerves. This was good, Rose thought. Like the cleanest windows revealing the worst circumstances of a person's life, Mrs. Sebastian saw the need and was clearly impacted.

Rose was sure the woman would not walk away without emptying her wallet.

Rose would give Mrs. Sebastian time to collect her emotions. She turned toward the view down the hillside—bright compared to before—a colorless backdrop for the blast furnace fires and busy citizens scurrying here and there. It reminded Rose of pencil drawings she'd seen by Raphael Soyer, beautiful even without dazzling hues.

Bright as the late morning seemed in comparison to when they went into the Lipinski home, the smoky waste from the mills obscured her view of the town across the river. Rose watched Mrs. Sebastian out of the corner of her eye, waiting for the right time to continue her sales pitch.

The sound of feet thumping over the wooden porch made Rose turn. She'd forgotten about Leo. He flung himself into Rose, and she patted his back.

"Why Leo. Meet Mrs. Sebastian. She is the wife of one of our leading citizens in town. *She* is very important."

He cowered behind Rose. She pulled him out from behind her. "Shake her hand."

Leo stretched his hand to Mrs. Sebastian but didn't look at her.

"Make eye-contact Leo," said Rose. "You know the proper way to greet a grown-up."

Mrs. Sebastian shook Leo's hand and looked at Rose.

"My nephew. You know how those things go sometimes…maybe not. But he's a good boy this one. Smart." Rose patted his back as he grinned at her.

Mrs. Sebastian exhaled deeply, clutching at her chest again. "Well, thank goodness. That would have stopped this outing cold—a nurse with a young son, traipsing around town, in questionable situations with questionable people. A woman should be in the home. If it's a proper one."

Rose's earlier exhaustion set back in and Rose swallowed a yawn and forced a smile.

"Mrs. Sebastian and I have one more home to see and we're short on time. So, why don't you see your way home, Leo?"

Leo clutched at Rose's torso, not willing to leave.

Rose pried off his hands and she squatted down to his level, lowering her voice. "Go on home, Leo. Stay on the walks and be polite. Don't chitchat and keep people from their daily round, sit your ass on the steps until your father or uncle Hen wakes up. Don't light the stove, don't waste electricity, don't...just *sit* there. Read the funnies. And I'll be home just as soon as I can."

Rose patted him on the behind, sending him on his way.

Mrs. Sebastian held her hand palm-up. "Feels like rain."

Rose was relieved the conversation changed course.

"No," Rose shook her head and pointed northeast toward the zinc mill, toward Mrs. Sebastian's home. "See the smoke there, running across the Mon?"

"The black smoke?"

"No, the whiter, yellowish smoke comes from the zinc mill—across from your house."

Mrs. Sebastian adjusted her gaze and nodded.

"The plume runs directly over the water, to Webster."

"Like a river," Mrs. Sebastian said.

"Well, when that plume runs over your house instead of over the river, that's when you know rain is coming." Rose raised her hands into the air. "Not a bit of wind."

"A plume? Huh." Mrs. Sebastian said. "We get plenty of smoke without a funnel of soot rushing overhead. Theresa suffers from all manner of issues and, well the list is long in regard to how she suffers. There are times I think the smoke causes her more distress. But others say, many doctors have said, no. She's just weak, and sometimes, well, I'll deny it if you repeat that—what I said about the smoke making her sicker."

Mrs. Sebastian turned her back to Rose, sucking on her cigarette.

Rose didn't think Mrs. Sebastian's words were an invitation to confide so she changed the subject. "The second home I have on the list is quite different from the Lipinski's." Rose explained to Mrs. Sebastian's back. "The Hornack home is two doors down. The mother died giving birth to premature twins." When Rose delivered them, she thought the babies would die, too, but they didn't.

She outlined the care plans she had enacted to Mrs. Sebastian. She had contacted Mr. Hornack's sister and she came to live there and while the Mister continued his shifts, Rose mentored the sister to care for the fragile babies. Rose organized the home (the pregnancy had left the mother unable to keep house and the husband unwilling to do it for her) and arranged a breast-milk bank with thirteen women willing to donate their extra breast-milk to the cause.

Rose constructed warming tubes from bicycle tubing to keep the babies' temps up, and trained the father to do the housekeeping he never would do before his wife had died. He and his sister lived up to all the standards of hygiene to discourage diseases like polio, TB, flu, and skin infections as directed.

Mrs. Sebastian flicked her cigarette onto the dirt hill beside the porch, but didn't face Rose.

"A breast-milk *bank*?" Mrs. Sebastian lit another cigarette then rested her hand over her belly, nearly singeing the fine blue material of her suit. Rose waited for her to spout something off about women should keep their milk to themselves.

"Now that's a bank a girl could get behind," Mrs. Sebastian said. "I wonder if I could…when this baby comes, make use of that bank." She rubbed her belly, looking down at it.

Rose hid her initial inclination to frown at the woman. This was an opening, a bit of leverage. Perhaps she could lure Mrs. Sebastian toward funding the community nurse if she saw a need for it herself. She would tempt the woman; make her want the service, something that perhaps she could not have.

"I'm sure with this not being your first pregnancy, you'll be an old pro at nursing your baby. Even though you're more mature than a lot of mothers—uh, that sounded atrocious. I didn't mean to note your age." Rose meant to note it. She didn't feel very warm toward the woman.

Mrs. Sebastian swung around to face Rose. Rose stiffened, waiting to be scolded. She should learn to keep her mouth shut.

"I like you, Rose Pavlesic, nurse Pavlesic."

Rose's eyes widened. She hoped the woman wouldn't pick up on Rose's worries.

"Dr. Bonaroti said you were forthright. Therefore, I feel I can be honest and say that our Theresa—she's twenty now—was adopted. That wasn't easy. We didn't quite adjust as I had hoped. At the time I thought not breastfeeding might be part of our difficulties. But now I don't want any part of the baby suckling, even this one who will *really* be mine. Isn't it strange the way the world works?"

Rose held her hand up. "Adopted?" Rose had assumed Theresa must resemble Mr. Sebastian more than the Missus.

"Yes, and you can understand that I'm the age that many women have their sixth or eighth child, but this one will be my first. And if some other woman, more comfortable with being milked like a cow than I am, is willing to bank her milk then I'm willing to buy it. At my age, having a baby, dealing with, well all of it...I can't say I'm ready for this."

Rose's face seized, possibly revealing her confusion and disgust, neither of which she wanted to. She forcibly relaxed her expression. She felt her lips quiver under the strain of a phony smile.

Adoption.

The word thrust Rose back to that day. That day, that one.

Rose saw something out of the corner of her eye and jerked toward it. Nothing. Just the soul shadow. She rubbed her arms, staving off the familiar chill brought on by memories she would rather bury.

"Well," Rose said. "I'm sure we can make arrangements, especially since you're willing to pay."

Tingly heat rushed through Rose, as she tried to shake off her past. She grasped the railing at the top of the steps. "Shall we go?"

The rusty metal shuddered under Rose's weight as she waited for Mrs. Sebastian to move along. She wondered if the feeling of shame would ever go away. Rose caught herself doing the sign of the cross.

Mrs. Sebastian joined Rose. "I've embarrassed you."

"No, no. I'm a nurse. I've heard it all." Rose cleared her throat and re-established the tight smile on her face. "It's my schedule. I'd really like to show you—"

"I saw plenty." Mrs. Sebastian pulled on her gloves, the soft leather teasing Rose with finery she may never enjoy herself. "I'll speak to Mr. Sebastian this evening and then well...I'd like you to examine our Theresa, thoroughly. She had an appointment with Dr. Bonaroti and he suggested you were the best for follow-up."

"Theresa, yes. Absolutely." Rose met Mrs. Sebastian's gaze knowing she needed to force the woman to say yes to the funding very soon. "Tomorrow?"

"I'll arrange my schedule."

Rose gripped the handles of her bag and pushed back her shoulders. "What about—"

"There's time for that later," Mrs. Sebastian said.

Rose wanted her to clarify what Mrs. Sebastian meant, but reconsidered, thinking she shouldn't push. Rose knew her strengths and if she could offer Theresa relief from asthma, it would go far to hook the Sebastians' interest in the clinic.

Rose cleared her throat to stave off her building desperation. "Tomorrow, then." She didn't like to be patient, but she knew with this woman, it was her only choice.

They headed down the steps to where Theresa waited. Rose offered to walk Mrs. Sebastian to the trolley or wake Henry to borrow a neighbor's car. But Mrs. Sebastian declined saying she'd prefer to walk with Theresa, to think.

Rose looked down at Mrs. Sebastian's shoes. One of the exquisite appliqués was missing. Rose shut her eyes, wondering what other damage had been done to Mrs. Sebastian's clothing in the Lipinski home.

"Your shoe."

Mrs. Sebastian turned her slim foot back and forth as though the action would make the appliqué reappear. "Yes, I know. No sense in going back into that nightmare to root through the debris for a piece of glittery shoe décor. Besides, everyone can use a little piece of shiny glass something in her home. Don't you agree?"

Rose watched Mrs. Sebastian and Theresa weave in and out of the crowd of grey suits and everyday calico dresses of housewives headed out on errands, and felt a tinge of hope. Rose said a quick prayer that Mrs. Sebastian saw the experience as Rose had—as proof that her role in the community was vital. But, she wasn't so sure she had shown that. She wasn't sure at all.

* * *

Someone was shaking Henry like a martini. He opened his eyes, blurry and dry, and rubbed them. Who was bothering him? He swung his legs over the side of the bed to see Sara Clara. She dug her cotton candy colored nails into his shoulder, whispering, like a snake hissing.

"I need your help." Her heavy, lavender perfume turned his stomach, but her face, its perfect porcelain, heart-shape made him want to pull her into him and hold her as though she were his wife. He pushed her away.

"What the hell's half acre are you doing?"

"Rose is gonna string me up."

Henry saw Sara Clara's face strained with fear. He'd always thought Sara Clara put on an act, being afraid of Rose, a performance of insufficient housekeeping skill so Rose wouldn't actually ask her to do anything around the house. But this time, it was clear, Sara Clara was scared to death.

"Get the hell out. Get Buzzy up," Henry said.

"No, Henry, it's not another burnt roast. It's that *woman*, superin-whatever y'all call it; she's here for her own little home visit she said. Rose. Is. Going. To. Fry. My. Kiester. This woman makes Rose seem sweet. A girl is with her. Beautifully dressed. Rose is gonna have my hide."

Henry's mind was half-asleep as he ripped away the blankets and pulled on his jeans. Sara Clara must be mistaken. He grabbed a white undershirt and then threw it back and took a more tailored shirt, two toned with buttons down the front.

He went to Rose's wash table, threw water over his face and wet his hair back with a comb. He scurried to the room at the front of the house, but no one was there. Henry jogged down the hall to the kitchen, paused and saw two very well dressed women, the younger one, not much older than Magdalena. This was going to require his best gentleman act.

Henry sauntered across the floor and extended his hand to the elder of the two as though they were meeting at a charity ball instead of in his kitchen, with him barefooted and barely awake.

"Mrs. Sebastian."

Her handshake felt like a dead fish. Henry pulled away noting his black nails, wishing he was cleaner.

"We were just leaving."

"I know Rose would want you to have some tea. Rose...was she expecting you?" Henry looked around the kitchen and scratched the back of his neck.

"Why, no."

Henry suddenly saw the kitchen through the eyes of a stranger, the mayonnaise on the countertop, chicken scraps littered on the stovetop. Mrs. Sebastian lifted and replaced her blue-shoed foot on and off the floor like a ticking clock, seemingly mesmerized by the sticking sound that emanated each time she did.

Henry bit the inside of his cheek when he realized the smartest thing was to let the woman leave before she looked any closer at the mess. "I'll let Rose know you came by."

Mrs. Sebastian nodded and surveyed every inch of the kitchen as she headed toward the doorway. The younger girl had wandered into the hall and when Henry got there she was moving down the hall, one step at a time, smiling at all the pictures on the wall. She stopped at one of Rose, Henry, Magdalena, and Johnny. With a spindly forefinger she touched Rose's image, tracing her hair as though she could feel the real thing, as though she were being absorbed into the photo.

Henry opened the door and Mrs. Sebastian ushered her daughter away from the pictures. Theresa shuffled along, looking over her shoulder. Henry caught a final condescending scowl from Mrs. Sebastian and couldn't stop himself from tapping her on the shoulder. She turned to face him.

"My wife," Henry stuttered. "Nurse Pavlesic. She's the best at what she does. There's not another nurse like her in the world. I promise you that."

"I'm not sure that's my question." Mrs. Sebastian disappeared out the door.

Henry realized how bad all of this was for Rose. For the clinic.

Back in the kitchen, he tried to help clean up the mess. Sara Clara was not an apt homemaker. Henry felt the frustration that Rose must have experienced nearly every day. His sister-in-law came from a long, privileged line of southern belles and if it weren't for getting pregnant by Buzzy and disowned by her family, Sara Clara never would have set foot past the North Carolina border let alone set up house in a steel town like Donora.

Henry realized for the first time something that Rose had known all her life. It didn't matter whether a woman's home was constructed with thick burgundy bricks, grey-blue cement, pitted, wood planking or corrugated metal sheets. What mattered was that she damn sure treated it as though it rose up from fields of gold and had been carefully shingled in spare diamond brooches. If there was a surface in a home—it ought to sparkle.

Dirt and disorganization was the bane of every woman's life and the presence of it distorted truth and reality and well, there was simply no place for it, Henry saw right then.

He knew Mrs. Sebastian would not hold the mess she witnessed against Henry or Sara Clara. It would be pinned on Rose like a badge of shame, marring the chance Mrs. Sebastian would support the clinic.

Henry scrubbed at burnt chicken grease on the stove with his nail, rubbing so hard he thought his finger might bleed. He could not imagine life without Rose being a nurse. He'd had a glimpse into that world seventeen years before and it wasn't a scene of grace. It was the worst few months of both their lives. It was then that Henry did what he did. And though he couldn't take it back, he had done his best to never repeat it. He hoped that counted for something when the whole thing crumbled. He hoped it counted for something.

* * *

Rose saw ten more families that Tuesday. After she checked, taught, treated her patients, and delivered acts of kindness and compassion, she arrived back at 2 Murray Avenue with a pinching dread in her chest. What if she could not secure the funding? What would her patients do?

Inside the house, sweltering dry heat blew past her as she went through the kitchen to the utility room. Rose assumed Sara Clara would be washing the clothes that she'd seen in her room that morning. Rose would clean her instruments upstairs instead. No point in fighting over the tubs after such an exhausting two days.

She glanced back at the kitchen. The tower of dishes that had been in the sink early that morning was gone. The countertops were cluttered with rags and a row of coffee mugs. Still, at least something had been done while she was out working.

She shed her coat, dropped it over a hook, sniffed under her arms and grimaced. A shower would come the minute she finished with her implements.

Rose scrubbed her bottles and brushes with green soap until her forearms cramped. She replaced the depleted supplies she had on hand, wrote order slips for needed provisions and penned the narratives that depicted every aspect of her visits and the plans for future ones.

These responsibilities were satisfying to Rose—a beginning and an end to them with a simple yes or no to whether she'd been successful at that part of her job. Though a niggling worry poked at Rose, she felt it would be impossible for Mrs. Sebastian to ignore the value of her work. She closed her notes and smoothed her hand over the leather cover. She needed to sleep and pray and get to confession. With those things in place she would be able to do her work to the standard she expected.

She went back through the kitchen even more confident she had made Mrs. Sebastian's purse rain like April. Henry and Buzzy sat drinking coffee. She poured herself a cup.

"Say, boys. How about I make you a sandwich with your coffee and then you head over to the Lipinski's." She arranged thick ham and cheese onto white bread.

"Fix the broken chair, get rid of the wine barrels, and make sure the McClatchy's, down two houses from the Lipinski's, have coal for their stove."

Henry scratched his stubbly chin and agreed to the work while Buzzy slurped on scorching hot coffee, scowling between sips.

Rose snapped her fingers in front of his face. "If I'm going to watch your son all damn day, you're gonna give me something in return, Buzzy Pavlesic."

Buzzy snapped back. "Leo's here. Kid woke me two hours ago."

"He was with me most of the day. Just about ruined my quest for money from the superintendent's wife. Not to mention your wife has yet to do her chores on time." Rose hated to be critical of little Leo, but the words flowed. She rubbed her tired eyes and yawned.

"You can bully your patients, Rosie," Buzzy said, "but you're not *my* boss. You're not my nurse. Jesus Christ almighty, stop nagging. And, just so you know, I'm not the only one sick of your neb-nosing like you're boss of everyone. Superintendent of Health, or some shit."

Rose ripped Buzzy's coffee cup from his grip, swishing hot coffee onto her hands. "Dammit! Why don't you just skidoo, Buzzy. And shut your trap while you're at it."

Buzzy shrugged and slapped his palms onto the table. He pushed to standing. "Fine. This house is a shithole anyhow. No sense in hanging around when my family's privacy is violated every minute of the day."

"Ummhmm." Rose wiped her wet hands on her uniform.

Henry stepped in front of Rose, blocking her view of Buzzy as he faded out of the room. Henry kissed Rose's forehead. She pulled back, glaring.

"Ignore the bastard. I do."

Rose nodded.

He gripped Rose's arms and squeezed. "I need to tell you something."

"What now?"

"Mrs. Sebastian." Henry drew and released a deep breath. "She stopped by earlier."

Rose wiggled out of Henry's grip. Her heart contracted in fear. "She. Did. *What?*" The house was not ready for company when Sara Clara had the only hand in housekeeping.

Rose covered her mouth. "Without calling first? This house? She was in *this* house?" Rose's gaze shot around the kitchen, taking note of everything that was out of its place.

Henry took Rose's hand from her mouth and held it against his chest. "She was here to make sure you weren't leaving young children at home to take care of other people's problems, not to inspect the state of our housekeeping."

Rose took her hand from Henry's and balled her fists at her sides. That was exactly what the woman was doing there.

"It's all right, Kiddo," Henry said. "She told Sara Clara she grew up in similar circumstances. Sara Clara explained the mess." Henry dug his hands into his pockets and shrugged.

Rose stepped back, looking around. "This isn't pristine, what I'm looking at here, but it's not a mess. Not like when I left this morning. Exactly *when* did Mrs. Sebastian show up here?"

"Well, Sara Clara had prepared lunch for a lady friend she'd met shopping as well as Johnny's gang, and well, you can picture..."

Rose closed her eyes and dropped her head back, surrendering to the images that shot though her mind.

"I'll kill her. My God, I'm gonna kill her. It'll be quick and clinical, minimal blood, but if I have to set eyes on her again, if she causes me to lose this money I don't know what I'll do. How many things will your brother and his wife ruin?"

Rose looked at her shaking hands. She felt disconnected from what was normally her strength—managing the way the world saw her and her family. What was happening? She realized she'd skipped confession, and her rosary, even her prayers had been lackluster.

Henry's voice was washing over her, but she couldn't hear the individual words. She needed to get a hold on her life again. And, that always started with her rosary. Her kitchen rosary. She needed to feel the weight of the wooden beads between her fingers. She ripped through a drawer in the hutch.

"Rose. It's fine. I think she understood."

Rose shook her head as she laced the beads over her wrist so she could finger the crucifix. It was the only thing that could help her now. She'd been told once that her lazy attention to Catholicism was the root of her deep pain and stupid decisions. She believed Sister John Ann when she had said it.

Her fingers slipped over the beads, but her thoughts didn't go to her prayers. She knew what Mrs. Sebastian would be thinking. That Rose belonged in her home, cleaning, keeping it the way she was telling all the women around town to keep their homes.

Henry guided Rose to the table, put her in a chair and sat across from her.

Rose ran her fingers over the beads. "Did you explain that Sara Clara couldn't keep a house if God himself swept up the shit ahead of time? That household debris literally falls from Sara Clara's body? Did you tell her your brother and his wife are like human colons, expelling shit at regular intervals throughout the day?"

Henry leaned toward Rose, his forearms resting on his thighs. "I'm sure Mrs. Sebastian understood."

"I'm sure she didn't."

Henry sat back in his chair. "People understand these things. Family."

"Not everyone."

Henry shrugged. "Give her a chance. She seemed nice enough. Her daughter was here, too. She said you were heading there tomorrow. To check out the daughter's lungs or something."

If Mrs. Sebastian didn't cancel Rose's appointment with her daughter the next day, that was a good sign. Rose told herself everything would be okay. "She said that? At what point in the visit did she say I had a call at her home?"

"When she was leaving."

"Leaving. Yes. All right." Rose nodded. She put her hand to her chest and felt her heartbeat slow.

"Listen Rose, tonight or tomorrow, we need to talk."

Rose forced a laugh. What else could there be? "Why not now? Might as well drop all the bombs the same day, right?"

"Yeah, might as well."

Buzzy popped back into the kitchen. "Let's beat it, brother Hen. We've got extra money to make." Buzzy rubbed the palms of his hands together. "Rose, Mr.

Masucci was looking for a couple fellas to take his painting overflow—houses on the north end of town are peeling like bananas in a monkey cage. Said he'd make it worth our while." Buzzy rubbed his thumb over his fingers to show he was expecting money.

Rose lifted her chin to Henry signaling that he might as well head out. The sooner Buzzy could repay them the better.

"But, don't forget the Lipinski family," Rose said. Henry kissed both cheeks then her lips before leaving. She touched her lips where his had just been. She couldn't stand Buzzy always whiny and worrisome. If not for Leo, she might cut her losses and tell Buzzy and Sara Clara to hightail it the hell out of town.

As the two men left the house Rose could still hear Buzzy's voice cut through her. Saying he was too exhausted, he didn't have the time to help others, on and on. Buzzy never failed to make her wish he could *feel* how lucky he was, to just once really lose something that couldn't be replaced, just one thing, just once.

* * *

No point in waiting around wishing. Rose kissed her rosary and put it back in her drawer. She cleansed her hands and arms and began to prepare roast beef, green beans and mashed potatoes for dinner. Once the roast was bedded down in the oven, she baked a chocolate cake, put on another pot of coffee, and did two shots of vodka.

Rose then gathered the laundry that Sara Clara hadn't done and traipsed down into the cellar. Where was Sara Clara? Rose fumed at the sight of wet clothing, hanging over the washtubs, dripping as though recently abandoned.

Rose's stomach clutched when she saw a scribbled note, in Sara Clara's handwriting clipped to the clothesline that draped from one rotting beam to the other. Rose snatched the paper and slogged to the far corner of the cellar, yanked the string where a second bare bulb lit up.

> *Dear Rosie,*
>
> *I started a load of laundry during my lunch break. (I fed John and the fellas from the school and they were shootin' mad you weren't there to prepare their meal) and as you can see, something was in the load that turned everything in it grey. I decided rather than ruin it more, to leave it for you, so you could cool down before I get home for dinner and you string me up by my toes. I am sorry, Rosie. You may take the funds to cover the towels from my strike-can. I've hidden it under the sink, behind the rat poison as all the women in Donora do. I have become one of you."*
>
> *Truthfully frightened at the thought of your pending response to this news,*
> *Sara Clara*

I'll show her shootin' mad, Rose thought.

"Sara Clara!" Rose bellowed.

No answer. Rose knew her voice would carry through the heat registers, that Sara Clara could hear her. Rose waited for the sound of Sara Clara's feet rushing down the steps, to really apologize for this. She'd had enough.

Rose tried to remind herself that she was lucky to have a family. *Not this family* kept flashing through her mind. Henry, yes. The kids, yes. The rest of them? *They* were quickly ushering her to a shallow grave.

She screamed for Sara Clara again. No response.

Rose's shoulders slumped. Frustration exploded inside her. She gritted her teeth, crumpled the note, threw it so hard her shoulder felt as though it separated, and she stomped back to the washtub.

She lifted items from the water—Buzzy's blackened work-shirt, Rose's embroidered wedding hand-towel which now boasted blotchy Rorschach-like shadows over the delicate flower garden Auntie Anna had handmade eighteen years before.

Rose stared at it, pulled it taut then chucked the towel back into the rancid water. She couldn't fix that mess. Not right then. Rose hadn't felt lethargy, the kind of fatigue that swelled her bones, in decades. Rose suddenly couldn't stop the helplessness from washing over her, making her want to hide.

Rose trudged up the creaky stairs made of mismatched wood planks and told herself to forget the laundry, and just do her reports and go to sleep. If no one else in the house was going to do their share, why should Rose do more?

* * *

Rose gathered her papers, notebook and pencils then closed the bedroom door. She had dinner warming in the oven, the cake in the icebox, and coffee ready to go for the family's supper. She was too tired to be hungry herself. She'd just do her work then have a quiet meal alone, sneak a peek at Texaco Star Theatre at 8:00 pm and nod off for the night. In bed, writing her plans for the next day, she was too tired to stay awake and her mind was too fuzzy. Finally she simply fell asleep.

Rose felt a hand on her shoulder then Henry's whiskers against her cheek.

She rolled onto her back, pencils and papers falling off her body. "What time is it?"

"Ten." Henry showed Rose her clock and replaced it on the bedside table. "I'm leaving for my shift. I didn't mean to waken you."

She shifted again and the papers and pencils fluttered to the floor. Henry bent to pick them up. He piled them neatly at the foot of her bed. Her sleepy vision blurred and she wondered if she would remember this in the morning.

He looked as beaten as Rose felt. Finally more awake than asleep, Rose felt a jolt of fear that something was happening with Henry. Something she should know about. "Hen. What's wrong?"

"Something at work that's been bothering me. And I just want to let you know that I love you, no matter what."

Rose sat up on her elbows. She squinted. He was probably feeling all the guilt he should have for keeping Magdalena's secret from her.

"I said I forgave you for the Magdalena thing. You said you'd fix it, I said don't let it happen again. You're covered, Hen."

"No. It's not that. This morning when we were talking and I said sometimes there's a right and a wrong thing. I've been thinking all day, I'm making too big a deal out of it, I just need to—"

"You're rambling."

Henry leaned into Rose and kissed her hard on the lips. She gave into the kiss feeling familiar affection at being the object of Henry's attention.

He held her face, caressing her cheekbones with his thumbs. "I just wanted to get your thoughts on something. That's all. But you're tired. You always do the right thing and I know. Now I know."

Henry stood and went to the door.

"Hen!" Rose glanced at the clock. He was going to have to sprint down to the gate to make the shift change. He didn't have time to quell her confusion, but she couldn't let him leave the room.

He raised his eyebrows at her from the doorway.

"Just be careful." What a stupid thing to say. What she wanted to do was order him to stand there and reveal what was behind his wandering queries. But she didn't want his pay docked or for him to be fired for tardiness.

The thought that Rose might never see Henry again brought to life a dull fear she hadn't felt in ages. Rose collapsed onto the bed, her heart thrashing in her chest. She felt like she couldn't breathe. She lay still, willing her body to listen to her mind, to understand, Henry would be home, that worrying about injury or death when he went to work was not worth her time. There was no way to keep him safe. He was good at what he did, that though other men were maimed and killed in the mill, they were not as strong or smart as Henry.

What was happening to her? Maybe Sara Clara was getting to her in more than one way. Maybe it unnerved her, having the young woman there, a set of eyes that hadn't seen how bad work in the mills was before there were eight-hour shifts, or unions, a sense of control over their lives. Maybe it was reflecting back a truth Rose knew existed—she didn't want her son anywhere near the mill. She would mourn Henry forever if he died, but she would live. The death of her children? Well, they could put her in the grave with them for all she'd be able to handle after that.

With the last burst of energy Rose slid out from under the bedcovers, slipped out of her clothes, into a nightgown, and back into bed still not bathed. Her head felt heavy on the pillow and she hoped sleep would remove all that had stained her life that day. For that moment, she believed that was possible.

Chapter 6

The benefits of uninterrupted sleep were never to be underestimated. At five in the morning Rose woke, her mind sharp. She rolled into Henry's side of the bed, the sheets cool from the absence of his body. She rubbed her eyes, crossed herself, and said a short prayer for his safety. Then she offered one for the others. Inside her words to God, she felt protected as if she and He stood within her clasped hands, sheltered by His grace. She pushed her folded hands to the ceiling three times and hopped out of bed.

Rose pushed back the curtain as she did when she woke each morning. She squinted. She had expected to see the lamplight at the neighbor's house illuminating both of their back yards but she could only make out a cottony glow that didn't beam past the lamp itself. Were the windows that dirty? She rubbed the glass then examined her fingertips. There was soot on her skin, but not enough that it would make the early morning sky appear charred as it did. She shrugged. She pulled the curtain back into place, sure the sun would burn back the fog by noon.

She headed toward the bathroom, tripped over a raised stretch of carpet in the middle of the hallway and stubbed her toe. Her knee ached and brought back the memory of Isabella, and Rose faltering as she headed down the dark hall to the woman's bedroom. Chills ran up her spine. She was struck with an image of the lifeless Isabella and her dead baby tucked in the crook of her arm.

She ran the faucet in the tub, and bent over the edge, her knees digging into the cracked tile floor. Rose scrubbed her scalp and hair under the soothing water, as she shook off the memories of Isabella. Early in life she'd learned allowing herself to feel pain—physical or emotional—caused her to lose the ability to make good decisions, to be a good person, to function at all.

Finished with her hair, Rose plugged the drain and slipped into the comfort of full submersion, thinking that a total cleansing to baptize the day was what she needed.

With her to-do list reeling through her mind, a freshly bathed Rose breezed through the dusting and sweeping on the main floor then tackled the laundry mess in the cellar. At the top of the stairs, she pulled the string to the bulb, and cast the stairs with feeble light. She brushed aside cobwebs at the bottom and looked up into the wooden crosshatched supports before ignoring their filth.

Rose passed the coal cellar and jumped as the metal door swung open. She heard the coal man's shovel scratching into inky mounds of coal outside, then a load hitting the floor in chunks; smaller shards splashing like black water.

"Hey there Nico," Rose said.

"Rosie." The coal man peeked through the hole in the wall. "Milk man nearly broke his neck on them steps up to yunz guys' utility room—up by yer kitchen."

"I told him to leave it out front. On *that* porch sixty-seven times, I told him."

"Tell 'em again," he said. "Fore he breaks his neck n'at."

"He breaks it, then screw 'em, I warned him," Rosie said.

"I'll pass that along," Nico said.

Rose nodded.

Past the cinderblock shower, past Unk's workbench where each tool had its hook, and on the underside of the shelves, baby food jars hung like glass bats. Unk had screwed the lids of baby food jars into the wood and each jar, turned into its lid, was suspended in the air, boasting its contents, as neat as Rose could ever imagine tiny construction items being stored.

At the back of the cellar Rose dunked her hands into yesterday's wash water, feeling around for the carcasses of her beautiful tea and hand towels.

She smiled down at the linen. A small segment of the embroidered flower garden remained in full bloom, somehow still vibrant blue, pink and red. Rose crossed herself, thinking she'd been witness to a miracle that morning as she cut the salvageable part—a four-inch segment—from the ruined towel and tucked it into her jeans pocket. She fingered the rest of the sopping, grey towel then threw it into the garbage.

She snatched it back out. So few things she owned were markers of the day she married Henry. Even ruined, she couldn't bare to throw out Auntie Anna's work, her gift to Rose at a time she had nothing. A surge of anger toward Sara Clara flooded Rose. She said a quick Hail Mary, but the resentment had taken root and stifled the prayer.

"I have news." Rose turned from the wash and met Henry's gaze.

"Mother of God, you scared the living daylights out of me."

He limped toward her.

"Oh Hen, your foot? How's the Achilles?" She craned around him to see the back of his leg, looking intact.

He touched Rose's cheek. "You crying?"

Rose winced. "Course not. What's news?"

Rose turned back to the utility tubs. "Well Hen, what?"

"Magdalena's skates. Did you see them under the stairs there?"

"That's what you want to talk about?" She clipped the scrap of ruined fabric to the clothesline above her head then drained the washtub. She still needed to rewash what Sara Clara had simply matted down with water. She could feel Henry watching her. He was a man of few spoken words, but normally, if he stood there looking like he had something to say he simply said it.

She heard him exhale.

"It's not good."

"What? Magdalena's quit roller-skating along with school? You're worried about that over the fact she wants to quit school? Come on, Henry."

Henry crossed his arms and looked away.

"What?" Rose said.

Henry met Rose's gaze. "I got fired."

She turned from him and buckled, catching herself on the edge of the tub. "What?" Buzzy's words from the day before came back to her.

Henry sighed.

She straightened but didn't face him. "Because of dumb-ass *Vinski?*"

Rose could hear Henry shift and sigh behind her.

"No, Emmanuel Knight."

Rose spun back to Henry. "Manny? The colored fella who coaches Johnny sometimes?"

"He deserved the promotion. Before any other guy in that entire mill. He knows more than—"

Rose leaned back against the tub for support. "So *you* had to get involved?"

Henry pulled a wet shirt from the laundry tub and started to feed it through the ringer. Rose snapped it back and tossed it into the tub, turning on the faucet to re-soak the damaged clothing. They had often discussed the way colored men were overlooked in the mills, but never in terms of giving up his job up for the cause.

Henry held up his hands in surrender. "Something snapped. I couldn't watch them give it to someone, someone pretty dumb, over him again."

Rose felt like the restful sleep she had gotten, never happened. Her arms and legs felt heavy, her stomach churned at the thought of Henry losing his job. How would they pay their bills?

"Look at me, Rose."

She stared past him.

"It was right to say something," Henry said. "Sometimes a fella needs to do the right thing."

Rose turned and fed the shirt through the roller, pushing the handle, pulling it so hard her wet hand slid off every other turn. "I know, I *know*. It's not fair. Nothing's fair. That's a first-grade lesson in social studies, Hen. You're smarter than that. We're almost done paying off Buzzy's debt. We're *so* close." Rose lost her grip on the handle then picked up the roller and tossed it into the tub. Henry had no idea what it's like to have nothing. She couldn't live like that again.

"You could have just written a poem about the injustice," Rose said. She instantly wanted to take back the words. She put a hand to her forehead, wiping away the sweat. She couldn't look at Henry, couldn't stand to see the hurt in his expression. She turned the water back on and let her hands dangle in the tub.

Henry stepped behind Rose and rubbed her back. "Well, you know how everyone kisses my ass because I played ball for the Pirates, and my purple heart, they crawl up over each other's backs just to buy me a beer. I thought they'd listen. I forgot they didn't really give a damn. Still, I did the right thing, Rose."

She knew it too, but it still pissed her off.

Henry ran his finger down the small of her back. Rose stiffened, agitated, mad that she found the word "stupid" so readily at her lips, just barely able to keep it locked inside her mouth. The phrase "You dumb hunky," kept popping into her head. She wanted to scream it and beat him with it.

"I'll get work," Henry said. "You know these fellas on McKean will hire me. The chance to put my mug in their windows. An ex-Pittsburgh Pirate? I may not be Stan Musial, but you know I'll get work. This town is doing well. I'll get other work."

Rose wished Henry was Stan Musial, the Donoran who'd gone on to make $50,000 a year playing a game instead of throwing out his shoulder after just six seasons.

Henry held a towel out to Rose, and she took it and rubbed her chafed skin with a heavy exhale. "Town's doing well," she said. "But, you can't piss people off. Every blessed business in town depends on the mills, Hen. Christ Almighty, even Deborah's Shoes and Gloves. No one's going to hire a loudmouth, even one who played for the Pirates."

Rose loved Henry because of how he saw the world, she just wasn't prepared to live with the consequences. She pushed the towel back at him. He hung it over the rope above them.

"You know I agree with you," she said, "but you shouldn't mess with mill hierarchy. Just do the right thing and come home to your family in one piece."

Henry nodded and lit a cigarette. "That's what I thought I did."

Rose bit the inside of her mouth.

Henry's silence said he was disappointed in her reaction.

"You'll take Leo while I look for work?" Henry said.

Rose lifted her shoulders and let them drop. Maybe Buzzy needed a diaper change, too. Maybe a rubdown and spoon-fed breakfast.

"Buzzy's got to sleep. Sara Clara's under the weather."

"Jeez-o-man! Lord knows we can't have those two care for their own kid."

Henry looked away. "I can watch Leo tomorrow once I get a job and catch up on shut-eye."

113

Rose didn't mind Leo traipsing around with her; she just minded that everyone else treated her as though she were a donkey. Why not load up the old girl?

Rose was losing control of her focus, her list of things to do that day. "I have to see to that young woman with respiration issues—the Sebastians' daughter, Theresa. I need that funding more than ever now. We can't all be out of work, can we?"

Those words burned Rose's lips and she knew they chiseled at Henry's ego. There was nothing worse than a shrew belittling her husband, let alone one that actually had more financial leverage and a reason to belittle him.

Rose wanted to let this go, to let Henry go sop up his pulverized pride, but she couldn't.

"Do we even want the same things anymore, Henry? The house like we always talked about? Getting out from under your brother? You keep making these decisions as though I don't exist. I mean, Magdalena is allowed to quit school of all things? She needs to be independent, able to care for herself no matter what—"

"You know we want the same things. I care about my family, our family. I know they're hard to handle, but they're ours. That means something."

She threw a shirt into the water and stomped away.

"Does it mean *something*, Henry? I guess you're saying I wouldn't know?" Rose didn't wait for his response; she slammed back through the cellar, back upstairs to get ready for work. She felt as if she was losing everything; she could not ever go back to the poorhouse at Mayview. Not for anything, for anyone.

Henry called to her but she pretended not to hear. She wanted to stop and talk and help soothe her husband, but she couldn't and as she closed the door on further conversation, she was hit with the urge for a smoke and a stiff fifth of vodka.

* * *

Rose dressed quickly, double-checking her uniform. She was heavy-handed with the starch when she ironed and never more grateful of the care she took with her clothing than when she slipped on the uniform to visit Mrs. Sebastian that day.

Every crease and plane lay as it should, giving Rose confidence. Her backup pair of shoes boasted a nice, clean shine. The soles were worn nearly through to her skin, but they would do for a while more. Finally, she brushed and twisted her thick hair into a bun that gave her a polished appearance.

Rose took a deep breath as she entered the kitchen. She was fuming at just about everyone in the room. Each seemed to occupy his or her own special level of uselessness, but Rose wouldn't point that out just then. Certainly, she was not perfect, she reminded herself.

She kissed Unk's head and gave Auntie Anna a tight squeeze. She patted Leo's back and told him to hurry, to go get dressed as he was assigned to her for the day. The normal family banter was non-existent; the mood was wrapped in terse silence. Sara Clara wasn't wearing lipstick and her face was as grey as the laundry she had ruined. Magdalena sat head in hand, lifeless as Sara Clara. There was a bug going around, Rose probably brought it home to them herself.

She plucked a piece of bacon from the serving platter. It was surprisingly crisp. She wondered who had cooked it, but refused to ask. The clink of forks and knives on china punctuated the hush. Her stomach should have been growling, but it turned over on itself instead.

Johnny grinned at Rose. He looked as though he had not spent the night drinking, thank goodness. Rose sighed, his ease relaxing her. She didn't want all this strain in the house. She would try a different tact with Sara Clara. Rose would not yell at Sara Clara for ruining her embroidered towels. Besides, she needed to have the sense of goodness around her before meeting with Mrs. Sebastian, and pointing out Sara Clara's shortcomings hadn't forced her to pay any more attention to detail.

"Sara Clara," Rose said as Leo came back into the kitchen with his coat in hand. "Don't forget to make the shopping list." She couldn't ruin that, Rose thought. "Friday's payday, after all. You know what should be on it after nearly a year here. Johnny and Magdalena can put together jumbo sandwiches for lunch if I'm not here to make something better."

Rose tapped her foot not sure she should order Sara Clara to do more.

Leo draped himself around Rose's midsection. Rose smoothed his hair off his forehead.

"Oh, and Sara Clara," Rose reached into her junk drawer and pulled out a glob of pink putty and kneaded it. "The walls in the front are black again. Remember how I showed you to use the putty?"

Sara Clara glanced at Buzzy then nodded making Rose think she didn't really remember.

"Just press it on the wall to lift the soot and when it's blackened, knead it until it's pink and start again."

Sara Clara nodded.

"And costumes," Rose tossed the putty to Sara Clara. "We need to finish Leo's Halloween costume. I fitted him, you sew. Big parade on Friday. You'll see why Donora's so special once you experience the Halloween parade. And don't forget to mail your bills. It's Wednesday."

Sara Clara forced a smile and nuzzled into Buzzy who put his arm protectively over her shoulder.

"I can do that, Rose," Sara Clara said.

Rose saw the question on Sara Clara's face, wondering if Rose was going to yell about the ruined laundry. Rose patted her uniform pocket where the scrap of intact flower garden embroidery was nestled. "But don't touch my wash. I'll handle that." And Rose was out the door, Leo flying behind her.

* * *

The crisp air nibbled at Rose's cheeks and nose as she and Leo stepped into the thick fog—bristly, Irish woolen-like fog—still murkier than normal. Was it earlier than she thought? She looked at her watch—eight-thirty. Rose thought perhaps the fog had settled thick to reflect her dark mood or maybe she'd stepped inside one of Henry's bleak poems.

Rose reminded herself that Mrs. Sebastian's funding was more pressing at that moment and feeling sorry for herself would only make her reek of vulnerability or resentment and cause Mrs. Sebastian to question her abilities.

It was paramount for Rose to present herself as immaculate, organized, and strong especially after Mrs. Sebastian stopped by her home for a surprise visit. Mrs. Sebastian was the sort of woman who could read folks, the kind who lived in a world peopled with slick operators who made decisions on intangible impressions as much as simple facts. *Those* people made their livings by feeling out other folks and either exploiting or joining forces with them.

Rose would be formidable. She yanked on one glove then pushed the leather down on her fingers. She would be a woman Mrs. Sebastian wanted to support, whose name she wanted linked with hers. Rose pulled on the other glove. She would carry on the work of treating the kind of people she had once been—the kind who needed assistance just to get out of bed in the morning.

Rose knew what that felt like—not wanting to live, but too weak to do something to bring about her own death.

KATHLEEN SHOOP

She recalled the last time, thirty years before, a family had considered adopting her. Standing in her foggy yard, fully grown, Rose covered her ear, flinching from the memory, the woman who had dragged her by her defective earlobe, shoving her in the closet, twisting her ear as though trying to remove it, screaming that Rose's haughty attitude had turned the family sour on her more than her ugly ear. Rose had only been trying to appear to be intelligent, not sassy.

As a teenager the desire for death revisited her. At sixteen she failed at selling herself to...well, she wouldn't dwell on that. Leo bumped into the back of Rose shoving her out of her thoughts. "We goin'?"

She looked down into his serene face. The result of her yearning for death had taught her that in order to live, she found people who needed her, even if they didn't want her.

Leo wormed his hand up Rose's coat sleeve and tickled her arm and she kissed the top of his head.

With newspapers under her arm, the Black Bag of Public Health strung over it, and Leo bounding along beside her, they walked down the center of the adjoining yard—the Tucharoni's. The window emitted a picture of light and shadow, the fog making it an impressionistic painting. Beside the door were seven jack-o-lanterns, neatly carved and awaiting candles on Halloween. Rose wondered if the family had known to make use of the pumpkin for pies and bread, and roast the seeds for a special treat. Mrs. Tucharoni stood at her window, rubbing the glass with her palm, peering through the clean spot. Rose hoped she and Leo were hidden in the fog, that Mrs. Tucharoni would not come out to talk. They were fine as neighbors, but Rose did not have time for friends.

Leo was bent over his shoes, attempting to tie them. Rose refused to help; she didn't want the kid to be lazy and dependent. Rose shifted her weight and checked her map.

When he was done, she tussled his hair. "Time to hustle, Leo."

They walked slowly down the pitted, dirt alley and emerged at Fifth Street, a plateau overlooking one hundred eighty-eight steps that ended at the bottom of Prospect Street. A man jostled them from behind, hat in hand, clearly late for work.

"Scootch over, Leo. So folks can get by." Rose and Leo descended the stairs, greeting people who moved past them faster.

"How yunz doin' today?" one person after another said. Rose was grateful no one stopped her that morning to discuss a medical problem. She needed to get to confession.

"Too foggy, today," Leo groaned. He grasped Rose's hand, startling her. She squeezed his, feeling a sliver of contentment in their grip.

Rose narrowed her eyes, peering across the way, trying to make out buildings that were usually easy to see. "Nah, same as always, Leo. See—there we go, the blast furnaces over there." Rose pointed to the right where blazing fire shot into the sky and carved space out of the thick fog. Rose smacked her tongue off her teeth. Sulfur. More than usual.

"That smoke and fire is money in the bank, Leo," Rose said, "Sun must be a little lazy today, is all."

At the bottom, they turned left and headed north down the sidewalk, past the Methodist church, weaving in and out of pedestrians. Tugboats moaning, nails firing, steel being sheared and shaped, trains howling, and church bells ringing—each sound melded with another, narrating each step Rose took.

She walked smack into the postman, Sparky, knocking him over. Rose and Leo helped him pick up his scattered mail.

"Guess we both better wise up and fly right when it's this foggy out," he said. "Smell that filth? As though I stuck my head right inside the furnace down home."

"Always is foggy in the morning, Spark," Rose said. Something was off about the fog, but it wasn't something that made sense to say aloud. "You know that better than anyone. Sorry for knocking you to heck."

Rose grabbed Leo's hand, moving as quickly as the fog would allow. They were silent, Leo's gait double-speed, but in synch with hers. Rose went over her list of sins for the past few days, preparing for confession as she nearly fell off the curb. She pulled Leo out of the street several times as the fog kept the light of the streetlamps from illuminating the area below.

Their normal five-minute walk to St. Dominic's took noticeably longer. When they reached the soaring house of worship Leo stopped to pluck a stone from the sidewalk. He pocketed it then met Rose's gaze, and pointed past her. "Hey a dog!"

He rushed to a mound of rags as it emerged from the fog.

Rose groaned. "Shoo dog, go on home!"

"Sweetie, a dog. Look at him." Leo shoved his face into the side of the dog. "He needs a home!"

Rose cringed and held her breath as though she had been the one with her face buried in the putrid fur. "Go on, shoo dog!" she said again. "Stop looking at me. Get on home."

A man emerged from the fog, rummaging through his briefcase and nearly tripping over Leo and the mutt. Leo sprung backward and the dog disappeared.

"Life-lesson number thirty-five, Leo, don't be so easily distracted. It only leads to mischief."

Leo burped, the scent of bacon wafting up to Rose. Rose ignored him and readied her mind and heart for confession.

Yellow bricks and stone steeples loomed as they headed up the steps into Church. Rose dragged open the hulking oak door and entered the foyer. Her nerves calmed at the sight of the ornate mahogany altar at the end of the center aisle. Painted saints all around the church made Rose feel as though she were in the company of friends.

Rose's heels hit the marble floor, the sound of her steps echoed as she walked into the sanctuary. She crossed herself with holy water and the scent of candles and flame floated from the vestibule to her left.

She tried to walk slow enough to quiet her clicking heels. Rose looked reverently at the altar, a bastion of tranquility, power, answers, everything. She wished she never had to leave the church.

She heard splashing and turned back. Leo was dousing himself in holy water. Rose sprinted toward him, heels clicking madly. "Damn Sam, Leo what the hell're you doing? That's holy water! With a capital H. I'll drown you in it if I see you messing with it again!"

Rose yanked the hat off his head, dragged him down the aisle and planted him in the pew across from the confessional. Someone was already inside so Rose stood at the door hoping her presence would somehow be noticed. She sighed and looked at her watch. The fifteen minutes she'd had to spare were almost gone.

Whoever was confessing inside was speaking at a volume more suitable for a bar than a confessional. The voice—the rhythm that shaped it—was familiar, but Rose could not place it as the words were muffled by thickly carved oak. She slid into the pew out of politeness and took the time to pray for Henry and her children.

The door flung open and Sara Clara from the South waltzed out, straightening her hat.

Rose stood, gripping the back of the pew. "Je-*sus*, you're not even Catholic."

"Mama!" Leo scrambled past Rose's knees and dove into his mother.

"I was simply trying to fit in. I told you, Rose; I would do my best to...oh forget it. Unk drove me down—" Sara Clara rubbed Leo's hair and knelt down in front of him.

Rose clenched the straps of her bag. "Unk! Whose car did he drive? Oh forget it, Sara Clara. I'm busy."

Sara Clara's efforts were good and noble, and the woman did have a lot to confess in Rose's estimation, but a person didn't just crash into confession as step *one* to becoming Catholic. Everyone knew that.

* * *

Rose entered the confessional where she dropped onto the kneeler. She fished her pearl rosary from her pocket, the only valuable jewels she owned, and held the beads to her forehead, eyes closed, waiting for Father Slavin to get things going.

He shifted behind the screen, but didn't say anything.

Rose didn't have time to wait for Father Slavin to begin and jumped right into her confession. "Forgive me Father for I have sinned. It has been two days since my last confession."

"Go on." An unfamiliar, deep voice filled the confessional.

Rose jerked and put her nose to the screen to see the large outline of a man, double the size of tiny Father Slavin. "Who the hell are you?"

The priest's shadow moved toward the screen, close enough for her to feel the warmth of his breath on her chin. "I guess we can tack on another rosary for cursing in church," he said and laughed. Rose saw his form slide back from the screen into a more relaxed position. "I'm Father Tom."

"We don't call priests by their first names around here."

"I'm a little different. But, I'm a priest all the same, with plenty on his plate today, so let's move it along."

Rose's jaw dropped.

"Well?" Father Tom shifted behind the screen.

"You've thrown me off."

"Why don't you just go on and start at the top."

Rose was offended that the priest she'd never met thought there must be a "top" to start at. It didn't matter that there was. "I'm sorry. This is a mistake. I have work to do."

"Well, you'll be pleased to know Father Slavin will return in few days or so. Until then, why don't you do yourself a favor and unburden with me. We're all the same, us priests."

That sounded wrong. Rose squeezed her eyes shut. Should she just wait for Father Slavin? That wouldn't help her soul to wait, she decided, and Rose rifled through her list of curses, unpleasant judgments and questionable deeds. She watched the priest's shadowy form shift back and forth as though more or less curious depending on the sin she was confessing at the time.

She took a deep breath as she wound down to the sin she always acknowledged in her mind but never aloud, never to a priest, never to anyone who hadn't been there to see her bad deeds in person. The discussions about adoption at the breakfast table the day before, then with Mrs. Sebastian, the tenuous funding—a confluence of sin and anxiety made Rose decide she was experiencing a sign.

She needed to finally say the words aloud. Perhaps this strange priest was exactly the one who should take her biggest sin once and for all. This Father Tom must have been accustomed to silence because he sat as still as any of the statues on the other side of the door.

Rose took a deep breath, on the verge of hyperventilating. She clutched her bag tighter to her stomach, her hands sweating around the leather straps. "I confess that I engaged," she said and took another shaky breath. She wanted to say it, and have a priest, anyone absolve her, but she couldn't say the words aloud. As usual, she said them instead to God, silently in the safety of her mind. *I had relations out of wedlock, had a baby and gave her away for adoption like she was a sack of extra sugar.*

Father Tom's shadow straightened and he leaned toward the screen. That small act made Rose's air leave her lungs. The priest must have read her thoughts. In over a decade of silent confession of that one sin, Father Slavin had never moved a muscle. Rose drew back exhaling.

"Years," her words caught in her throat. She cleared it. "Years ago...I can't say it."

"You still carry this guilt, as though it were yesterday? You haven't a bit of relief in, well, how many...?"

"Twenty. Years, that is."

Rose didn't know what to make of the question. She'd never been questioned in confession before. Father Slavin just allowed her to rattle on, then doled out her penance.

"If you've confessed, you've been forgiven. Would you say you have godly sorrow in your heart?"

Rose nodded and squeaked out an "umhmm."

"You have been forgiven, your sins are erased like chalk from a board—"

"You can't just *erase* something." The quiet of confession brought back the past day's events. She tried to explain, but couldn't say the words out loud. *The dead baby I delivered, and twice, twice, adoption was mentioned in casual conversation, it was like they knew what I had done. I just feel...suddenly...disjointed, exposed. I have this feeling I will never be forgiven. I gave that baby away like trash and I knew better. I'd seen what happened to some adopted kids.* "But, God does forgive and coming to confession should heal you."

"You don't know what I did and confession isn't about healing," Rose said. "It's about suffering so I will be granted eternal life. Or it gives me a chance to make up for my sins by the time I meet the big guy. I haven't done another horrid thing in my life since then. Sinful, yes. But not…not unforgivable."

Rose could see him shift, his shadow shrinking, as he must have reclined against the wall.

This broke Rose's train of thought. "Hey, look I have to go." Rose held up her black bag as though he might be able to see it through the screen. "Give me my penance."

"Well, if that's all you need."

Rose rubbed her forehead, holding in the rudeness she wanted to let out. Confession was about duty and preserving one's soul, not needing, just doing and being and carrying out a proper life.

Now, Father Tom's silence made Rose think she may have hurt his feelings. She didn't have time to care. It wasn't as though this priest was going to be a fixture at the church. He assigned her two rosaries and some extra Hail Mary's. But his issuing of the penance lacked the bluster she was accustomed to.

Rose nodded and stood. "And just so you know, that woman in here before me? Not a Catholic."

"So you're a rule follower. I wouldn't have guessed," the priest said as Rose was shutting the door.

"As I should be," she said to herself, and noted her heart did not feel lighter, as she expected. She looked over her shoulder at the priest's door. With that priest offering confession, Rose decided, feeling unfulfilled made sense. He had offered as much of a soul cleansing as a confession offered by Leo. Father Tom should be disappointed in his performance. Rose would have been if she were the priest. She started down the aisle, heading into the world where she would be sure not to leave *her* work half-done.

* * *

The nurse and her charge stepped onto the Sebastian's back porch. Only five homes stood on Overlook Terrace, an enclave carved into land below the Gilmore cemetery and above the spewing zinc mill. The home was a stunning red brick colonial revival, not as symmetrical as a four square but not as angled as a Victorian. Rose imagined it with the soot stripped clean from the brick pristine as the day it was built. Like anyone who performed a service at the home, Rose entered by way of the kitchen at the back of the mansion.

Leo pinched his nose shut. "Ewwww," he said.

The sulfur stench stunk up the whole town, but above the zinc mill the odor was nearly solid to the senses. The bulk of the smoke raced across the Monongahela, winding over Webster on the other side of the river, but enough of the debris coursed up the hill to the Sebastian's home that a foul smell was often present. The plume carried the stench as though it were a second river, drenching everything the liquid one didn't.

Rose characterized the Terrace section of town as "the desert." She'd seen photos of Arizona and there wasn't a difference between it and what she was looking at. Except that many hills in Donora had less vegetation—no cacti with their own beauty, nothing but the great mill spitting its insides into the air, letting its residents know all was right with the world; Donora was productive and financially healthy.

Rose sat Leo on the porch bench, told him not to move and gave him the missalette she'd taken from the church. He might as well be educated in Catholicism if his mother was going to pretend to be one.

"But I can't read," Leo said.

"Just stare at the blessed thing. The words will leap into your head like a frog. That's how it happened with your cousin Johnny." Everything came easy to Johnny, and while that was a comforting thought, Rose sometimes wondered if he'd be able to handle adversity as well as success. He never practiced that before.

Leo's lips quivered and his shoulders jumped with uneven breath. Rose knelt down in front of him. She squeezed his knees. "I'm joshing, Leo. Just sit and enjoy the peace. You'll be in first grade next year and then you'll learn to read. Think about the mill on the other side of this grand home and focus on how you'll never, ever work there. That's the idea you need to sear into your mind right here and now. You need to go to college and get the hell out of here."

"This place is great. I hear you say that."

"It's confusing, Leo, I know. You *should* appreciate this town. It'll make you tough. These mills produced more steel last month than any other in the world. Donora's steel...well, it's in everything, but that doesn't mean your future is in that mill."

Rose's eyes began to burn with zinc mill smoke so potent it peeled paint from siding. She coughed into her hand and looked around the dark porch. The fog should have been lighter by then.

She squeezed Leo's knees. "What you need to take from this town's greatness is simply its muscle and will and determination. Get an education so that the only position you'd be qualified to hold in the mill is goddamn superintendent of the whole shebang. You can be anything you set your mind to."

Leo nodded along.

Rose smiled and picked up speed. "There's Stan Musial, need I say more about him? And Lee O'Donnel's a knee surgeon for athletes. Julia Keefer's a doctor, a woman! There's a reason we're known as 'The Home of the Champions.' Judges, lawyers, athletes, professors and scientists have come from Donora. I could name fifty of them right off the bat if I had the time."

Rose readjusted her bag over her arm. The key to their achievement was that they left Donora, taking with them brawn and drive, but leaving behind all that made life harder to live than not. Rose wanted that success for all her children, including her nephew Leo.

Chapter 7

Rose balled up her fist and knocked on the back door. She had not figured out how to excuse the ramshackle appearance of her home Mrs. Sebastian had witnessed the day before. If Henry's explanation for the messy house did not suffice, then no meek apology on Rose's part would help.

The more Rose thought about it, the more offended she was; the woman stopped by unannounced. No other superintendent's wife had done such a thing. Rose told herself to put aside her embarrassment. It would take all that she could muster to appeal to Mrs. Sebastian's ego and make her believe the clinic was part of her very own grand-scheme.

It was Mrs. Sebastian who opened the door for Rose. Maybe this woman was different from most of the wealthy folks Rose had come across. Maybe Rose had misjudged her. The pregnant woman wore silk, coral colored slacks with a white blouse that wrapped around her compact, pregnant belly. She wore silk mules that matched her slacks.

A long cigarette dangled from Mrs. Sebastian's crimson lips. She smoothed the golden waves that careened down the side of her face. Rose searched the woman's face for evidence she thought Rose was incapable or inadequate.

Mrs. Sebastian rubbed her belly. "Excuse my casual attire. I'm feeling a little balloonish to be confined in a suit, today."

Instead of spitting laughter at the woman, Rose nodded as though she agreed, as though the pants cut from formal gown fabric were informal simply because they were pants.

Rose removed her gloves one finger at a time and shook Mrs. Sebastian's hand, stunned by its buttery softness. Mortified that her hand was sandpapery, Rose wanted to yank it free, but she only shook harder. Her hands were the cost of actually making a life rather than watching it go by and she wouldn't let vanity push that aside.

Mrs. Sebastian pulled her hand away and took a drag off the cigarette. An image of Mrs. Sebastian seeing Rose's home flew through her mind, making her feel naked. She leveled her gaze on Mrs. Sebastian. She wouldn't let her shame show. Every second Rose spent with this woman was an opportunity. Mrs. Sebastian leaned against the wall, her skin suddenly pallid.

"If you're not feeling well, I can examine you," Rose said. "We offer the best in modern care through the clinic. Post-natal instruction as well. I'm sure you've been cared for throughout your pregnancy but—"

"No, no. I'm fine. If those mill hunky women can give birth with nary a—"

Rose cringed but tilted her head in a casual way to attempt to convey the "mill-hunky" reference did not apply to her.

Mrs. Sebastian's face reddened and she poked at the cuticle on her thumb. "That was rude, I apologize."

Rose crossed her arms. Stay calm. Let her be in charge, Rose told herself. Rose was sure the way to the money was through a connection of some sort. Anything. There must be a way to create a sense of friendship where there would never be any. Rose's thoughts didn't work this way. She was viewed as an expert in town. There was no reason to hide that part of who she was.

"The river of ignorance flows both ways when it comes to social strata and economics," Rose said.

Mrs. Sebastian narrowed her eyes at Rose.

"All the current research has shown women, even well-to-do women," Rose said, "can be plagued by pregnancy complications. That's why my position, the clinic, is so important. But I'm sure you fully understand that."

Mrs. Sebastian held Rose's gaze while taking another drag off the cigarette. Rose waved the exhaled smoke away from her face and forced her jaw to relax.

"We meet the needs of families who are in crisis, or uneducated in proper hygiene or those who simply want to ensure the greatest health for very capable, paying families. Like yours."

Mrs. Sebastian began to walk through the kitchen. She waved Rose past the butcher-block island in the center, past the kitchen table and built-in closet with flower-bordered china and etched crystal stemware peeking through glass panes. Mrs. Sebastian's heels tapped the tile then were silenced when crossing over small throw rugs that directed their way. Rose would have been exhilarated by her own healthcare spiel if seeing the Sebastian home didn't make hers seem desperately deplorable. Focus, Rose thought.

"I won't mince words," Rose said and quickened her pace to keep up with Mrs. Sebastian. "I gleaned from our talk yesterday that you appreciate candor. Funding from you is imperative. It would ensure that there are no gaps in service, that I have my position, that I'm available to not only help people in crisis, but to maintain healthy standards and educate the populace on how to care for themselves so that some day community nurses won't be needed."

Mrs. Sebastian stopped and turned to face Rose who nearly ran her over. The woman's face twitched with a flash of anger. "So you're working your way out of your job? You'd prefer to spend a little more time at home?"

Rose drew back and felt her confidence shudder. She ignored the stream of sweat that coursed down her hairline, past her ear. Rose felt old embarrassment and fear return; As a child barely dressed, lined up in a cold room on a cement floor so frigid it numbed her bare toes, standing there, no family, no advantages, with nothing but raw smarts. There on Overlook Terrace, with Mrs. Sebastian, Rose felt that petrified child reappear.

"Wouldn't that be nice," Rose cocked her head, "if there were no need for a community nurse? Wouldn't you like to be part of the solution to poor hunky women and their appalling living conditions? I'm sure you'd like to be a credit to that movement. A woman like you."

Mrs. Sebastian rolled her eyes then seemed to search Rose's face for the answer to some unasked question. Rose felt a trickle of strength return.

"Go on." Mrs. Sebastian turned on her heel and continued into the front hall. Rose kept up beside her. "Continue, nurse. Fascinate me, because, no," Mrs. Sebastian lifted her forefinger into the air. "I'm *not* sure I want to be part of anything that probably will meet with failure."

Mrs. Sebastian licked her shiny lips and circled the oval table under a chandelier with endless crystal tentacles. She rooted around for something in a footed, blue and white bowl. Rose took the moment to note the bulky plaster molding that belted the fifteen foot ceiling, tinged yellow from cigarette and mill smoke; the hand-crafted moldings were just one mark of supreme wealth.

"Well? Dazzle me," Mrs. Sebastian said.

Rose stepped forward onto the Oriental rug, across the table from Mrs. Sebastian.

"If I could compel you to funnel the Women's Club monies to fund the clinic, its operations, for at least a year, I think I could convince council to find alternate funding sources. But, to simply not contribute after we have seen such promising results? It would be dire. In just one year I made two thousand five hundred thirteen visits. And I didn't even get to everyone." Rose thought of Isabella. "I doubt you want to be responsible for causing an entire town to lose their safety net."

Rose caught her reflection in the gleaming wood. From the bowl, Mrs. Sebastian produced more cigarettes and Zippo lighter.

"That's dramatic." Mrs. Sebastian said.

Rose refocused on Mrs. Sebastian and put her hand inside her coat pocket. She fingered her rosary.

"Truthfully," Rose said, "We—Dr. Bonaroti and I— could use a *second* nurse for visits and a third for the schools. Not to mention a dentist. Not that I'm requesting funds for such a thing, but I made over three hundred visits in August—the height of polio outbreaks. The work never ends even in a slow month. Someone's always snatching me into her home. Unlike most nurses who have to figure travel time into their day, I don't. What you're getting from me is pure substance. I rarely stop for lunch." Rose rambled, but she didn't know if this would be her last chance to fight.

"No lunch?" Mrs. Sebastian raised her eyebrows and ran her unlit cigarette through her fingers.

"I have a full report." Rose bounced the Rosary beads in her pocket. "If you'll come to the clinic on Friday I can walk you through everything. And, the report in conjunction with what you've seen with your own eyes at the Lipinski's, I'm sure you'll fund the initiative."

Please, she thought.

Mrs. Sebastian's expression appeared reflective as though Rose was having an impact. She tapped her nails on the table. "I haven't had the opportunity to consult Mr. Sebastian. I'm torn. Seeing you here, like this, like you were at the Lipin-whatever their name is, impresses me. Seeing your home as it was yesterday concerns me." She lit her cigarette and tossed the lighter back into the delicate bowl.

Rose marveled at the fact it didn't break, that the woman would be so careless.

"Even if I were to fund the clinic itself," Mrs. Sebastian said. "I'm not sure it would be morally responsible for me to fund *you*. A woman's place is in the home. With her family." Mrs. Sebastian headed up the sweeping staircase.

Rose unbuttoned her coat as they climbed, hotter than before. It wasn't as though she were working as a waitress. She was a nurse, for Pete's sake, Rose wanted to say. She could not let Mrs. Sebastian further consider this line of thinking.

"If you simply allow me the opportunity, you'll see the clinic is imperative and that my working there is central to its success."

"We'll see, yes." Mrs. Sebastian's voice was lighter almost as though a toddler had requested an extra cookie for dessert.

It wasn't as though any old nurse could be a community nurse. It took a different type of person to do that job. Rose held her breath. She wouldn't be able to face herself each morning if she failed.

Mrs. Sebastian drew her slender fingers through her hair as they rose up the staircase. "Oh, and Mr. Sebastian's in-house this morning. He needed to oversee the installation of the office furniture downstairs. I said, we live right across the street from the mill, do you really need a full office here...well, never mind that, I'm sure that's the last thing you want to hear. But, you'll meet him today."

"I look forward to it." Rose traced her finger up the molded mahogany banister as they went, slipping it into the carvings. At the top landing Rose lifted her fingertip. Perfectly clean.

"I have a girl," Mrs. Sebastian said.

Rose wiped her hand against her side.

"Irish. She dusts every surface of the home. Like clockwork. When we moved to Donora, I never thought it would mean all this soot. Not that Gary or Pittsburgh were sites of sun and clear views, but this. This is like nothing I've seen. I'd rather a home on Thompson Avenue if we have to live in Donora."

"Those homes are ordinary compared to yours."

"The smoke, though. Theresa's breathing has never been good, but since moving here, it's worse."

Rose felt a surge of energy. This was her chance. She slipped out of her coat, juggling her bag, relieved Mrs. Sebastian had moved the conversation to a topic that allowed her nursing acumen to do the persuasive heavy lifting. "You don't see signs of TB, a lump behind the ear, any infection at all?"

"You tell me."

Rose exhaled. Yes, she thought, yes, I will.

* * *

Mrs. Sebastian excused herself, telling Rose she had a phone call to make. Rose smoothed a section of her newspaper over the chair by Theresa's door. On top of the papers, went the bag. Another black and white uniformed maid popped out of a doorway stating that Rose would have to use her own green soap because the Sebastians had none.

Rose scrubbed up to her elbows under the maid's watch. A family with the means of the Sebastians should have everything on hand for a visiting nurse. Certainly Mrs. Sebastian wouldn't expect Rose to absorb the cost of basic toiletries. Rose dried off her hands and arms.

"Could you let Mrs. Sebastian know that we need the supplies for after the exam and that she should join us?"

The maid's face crinkled in confusion.

Rose smiled. "She knows I'm here."

Mrs. Sebastian poked her head out of a door ten yards down the hall. "I see you have everything. I have some business with the arts committee at hand." And, she disappeared back into the room as though never there.

Rose shook her head. Mrs. Sebastian wouldn't be attending her daughter's exam? Either she was more vacuous than Rose had thought or it was a sign she had already decided Rose's work was not useful.

Rose caught up to the maid and requested a set of fresh towels, a pot of boiling water for after the examination and a fresh set of sheets. Rose tapped her foot and seethed while she waited.

Any other mother who was capable of doing so, Rose would have ordered into the exam to assist. But she couldn't yet read Mrs. Sebastian and she controlled everything. Rose's impatience for the towels and sheets was tinged with disappointment. She was compromising the procedures she knew were in place for a reason. Yet, there she was, letting it happen. There was no excuse for this parent to not be present. This woman who had judged Rose's home situation as lackluster did not seem to care about the health of her daughter.

Rose paced the hall hoping to draw Mrs. Sebastian's attention. The idea of public health nursing was to educate families on caring for their family members. She could wait no longer. She bent down at Theresa's door and turned the doorknob with her elbows to keep her hands sanitary. *Dammit.*

She crossed the threshold then turned back, stuck her foot out to keep the door open and craned her neck out the door. Was Mrs. Sebastian really going to ignore home-visit protocol? If Rose even caught a glimpse of another maid she'd order her to witness the examination.

Someone in the home had to be sure the girl was receiving the proper care, especially since yesterday Theresa seemed relatively strong and was now so weak she couldn't get out of bed, for Pete's sake. The only sound Rose heard aside from the outside noises of the mill cranking and the tugboat groaning was the steady ticking of a grandfather clock beside Theresa's door.

Rose took some newspaper from under her arm and laid it across a small portion of a tall dresser. She turned and finally took in the room. Everything, the walls, the spread, the knickknacks were made of or embellished with pink.

Rose didn't realize it until that moment, but she'd envisioned a room before, dreamed of having a welcoming pink room where nothing soiled it. In reality, it was creepy. As sterile as Rose liked her life, that moment revealed that things could be too perfect, even for Rose.

The girl lay there, swathed in rose-colored covers, up to her chin, her hands crossed, one over the other, over her chest as though she might be resting in a coffin. She coughed.

Rose moved toward the bed. "Theresa?"

No response. Rose should have turned to the dresser, grabbed her stethoscope, thermometer, and notepad, but she couldn't move. The sight of Theresa, her thick, auburn hair fanning around her head, high cheekbones, bow-lips, kept Rose standing there. She told herself she was listening to her breathing, a legitimate clinical act. But really, Rose was just staring.

Rose jumped at the sound of Mrs. Sebastian's voice then put her hand out and walked toward the woman to welcome her into the exam.

"I was just looking Theresa over before I do a full exam. Please, join me. I need you to fill in the timeline between when we were together yesterday and right now."

"I have a full day's activities—a phone call into the president of the Ballet board."

Rose nodded, struck by Mrs. Sebastian's indifference toward her daughter's health.

Rose felt a burst of confidence and recklessness all mixed together. Maybe it was the stress of the day, but she couldn't hold her thoughts in even though she wanted to.

"Funny," Rose said. "What you saw at my house yesterday, I know how bad it looked. But you never gave me a chance to explain. And yet, here I am, judging you because you appear so uninterested in your daughter's care. But, appearances aren't everything, are they?"

Mrs. Sebastian looked toward Theresa on the bed as the maid stepped into the doorway beside her boss. "A call, Mrs. Sebastian. For you."

Mrs. Sebastian nodded and waved her away, watching her leave the room. She looked back at Rose. "You don't know what our life is like."

"Exactly." Rose said sweetly and gently as though she were agreeing with a friend on some inconsequential matter. Mrs. Sebastian left the room, glancing over her shoulder as she did. Rose knew she was close to the edge of decorum, but she had a job to do for the next two months and future funding or not, she would not let this woman be careless with her daughter's health.

Rose recalled Mrs. Sebastian's words regarding the adoption, the notion that she never connected with Theresa. Rose had thought she meant that they hadn't bonded at the beginning, but it didn't appear as though the two were especially close even after twenty years. Rose told herself to feel sorry for Mrs. Sebastian. She may have had all the money and things she could want, but strained or not, Rose's relationship with Magdalena was surely more intimate than what she saw here.

Rose thought if she saw Mrs. Sebastian as having a weakness, Rose would not be so intimidated by her. She went to the bed and lifted one of Theresa's manicured hands then the other placing them at the girl's side. Rose lowered the covers to give her body some air.

Theresa stirred, stretching then contracting, her head off to the side, a peaceful picture even in the context of what her mother described as a lifelong illness. Rose instinctively smoothed Theresa's hair back from her forehead.

A shadow fell over Theresa and Rose looked up from her patient. A man, Mr. Sebastian, Rose guessed, stood over the bed.

He ran the back of his hand over a section of Theresa's hair. "My daughter is dramatic, believe me, this talk of TB or some new fangled diagnosis of asthma or whatever you people dream up won't be founded. Let's simply call her healthy so my wife...we just wanted to get on the books with you and Dr. Bonaroti that's all. My Theresa is, well, I care about her..."

His voice cracked and he drew a deep breath. Rose was unaccustomed to men tearing up and less for it to be a man who runs one of the biggest, most important mills in the country. Was there something more to Theresa's case than she'd been told? Rose backed off, giving him space.

"She is lovely. And there are ways to ease her difficulties."

He nodded still gazing at his daughter, a loving expression on his face, much like she'd seen on Henry's many times. Mr. Sebastian wiped his tears away with the heel of his palm.

Theresa coughed and shot up, eyes wide, shoulders folding in on every drawn breath. Fear swamped her face. Mr. Sebastian gently pushed Theresa on her back, telling her to calm down and breathe. Rose grabbed her stethoscope, put the buds in her ears and focused on the sounds of Theresa's heart and lungs.

Rose moved Mr. Sebastian's hands and helped Theresa to sit. She supported the girl's chest with one hand and rubbed her back with the other, hoping to show Mr. Sebastian how he might better alleviate his daughter's breathing, that reclining might not help in her case. Rose watched, trying to discern what sort of cough and hacking this was that afflicted Theresa. Listening with the stethoscope revealed wheezing, but no mucus or blood, just a dry, violent cough.

Rose's soothing touch took effect and Theresa fell back, her coughs subsiding to a few per minute. Rose pulled the second bed pillow over and stacked it on the first, resting Theresa against it.

Mr. Sebastian got up and left the room before Rose realized that's what he was doing. No matter, most men didn't stick around for nursing tutorials, couldn't manage that type of care for plenty of reasons. The fact that he had been there at all was what had surprised Rose.

Theresa smiled at Rose through her still strained breath.

"Okay, Theresa," Rose said. "Good to see you again. I'm going to listen to your heart and lungs one more time."

Rose placed the stethoscope against the pink nightgown and looked into Theresa's face. Their gazes met and Rose felt…something. Rose looked away to concentrate better.

"Yesterday was amazing. Awful, I mean," Theresa said in between deep breaths.

"Shhh, I need to get your pulse."

Rose lifted Theresa's right wrist and turned it upward to place her fingers where she could feel the thumping of Theresa's blood, and determine whether her heart was beating efficiently.

She glanced at the wrist for the blue veins that would guide her fingers then glanced back and stared. Across Theresa's wrist was a chocolate mark, the shape of Florida or one of the great lakes. It looked like…Rose drew back.

Theresa looked up quizzically.

Rose looked toward the bank of windows near the bed.

"Don't worry. My parents would have caught my cough by now if it were contagious…"

Rose lifted Theresa's hand and ran her finger around the brown shape. "Where did you get this?"

"You never saw a birthmark before?" Theresa said.

Rose traced it with her fingertip. It couldn't really be the same. She narrowed her eyes, locking on Theresa's face, trying to see...something. Theresa hacked into her hand. Rose rubbed her back for support until Theresa finished coughing then sat on the bed with the girl. Rose lifted her wrist and put her fingers over the mark yet again.

Theresa smiled through her calming breath. "What's my pulse?"

Rose dropped Theresa's hand and went back to the dresser. She had no idea what the pulse-rate was. She wrapped her stethoscope around the instruments on the dresser. "You don't have TB. That much I'm sure of. You're just...your father mentioned asthma. I think that diagnosis is correct. There are some new medicines, but, well, let me talk to Dr. Bonaroti and I'll get back to your parents."

"I think it's the smoke-line here near the zinc mill," Theresa said. "Did you see it out there? Doctor Bonaroti mentioned the awful zinc mill smoke at my initial appointment, that it might bother me." Rose stiffened and faced Theresa. "Smoke line? Every step you take is directly out of one smoke line then into the next."

Theresa's eyes were closed and she had pulled her blankets back up to her neck. She nodded, showing Rose she was listening even though clearly ready to sleep again. Rose fussed with her instruments, shifting them in and out of inconsequential groupings. "You live here, you live with smoke. It runs through us like blood. I tend to think it's the mill itself that's most dangerous."

When Rose turned back to Theresa she had fallen asleep. Rose went to the bed and lifted Theresa's hand again, looking at the mark. She drew her forefinger around it again. Perhaps it looked more like Maine. Perhaps Rose's memory had been wrong all these years. Maybe she didn't remember exactly what the birthmark looked like. It wasn't as though other babies didn't have birthmarks on their wrists.

Theresa flinched, but didn't wake.

"Well, someone finally quieted her down a bit," Mr. Sebastian said from the hall.

Rose jumped and dropped Theresa's hand.

"I haven't seen her sleep like that in a decade. You're quite the nurse."

Rose quickly placed Theresa's hand on her torso, patted it, and tucked the blankets around her body.

Mr. Sebastian joined Rose at the bed. "She's a bit of a soft soul, this one."

Rose shrugged. "When one tiny fly gets in the ointment, perhaps a wire-puller falls asleep on the job, the slag man dumps it in the wrong spot, the blast furnace cools just a smidgen too much, a fella falls from a crane because he forgets to strap himself in…and like that, in an instant, the entire operation is compromised. Of course the girl is soft. She can't breathe."

Rose looked up to find Mr. Sebastian staring at her. Rose felt exposed. Did she appear unprofessional? Had he noticed the odd way she must have been mesmerized by his daughter's wrist? She instinctively brushed her hands over her hair, and straightened her uniform. He cocked his head, watching Rose as though she were a math problem to solve.

She hoped it didn't mean her funding campaign had met its end. She waited for him to say something, to ask questions, but he simply squeezed Theresa's hand and sauntered away as though Rose were not in the room at all.

"I'll finish her sheets," Rose said to the closing door, "and change her gown then give my report to your wife. I'm sure she'll appreciate being apprised of Theresa's condition."

Rose completed her work, breathing like an asthmatic herself. Once finished she wiped her forehead with the back of her hand, staring down at Theresa. Could this girl be my daughter? Rose repeated the question silently. She readjusted her bag over her arm and looked one last time at the mark on Theresa's wrist. She shook her head and told herself it must be anxiety. She was tired. Henry had been right about her needing a day off. Maybe this was simply ordinary tension showing itself, cutting away at her sanity. For Rose to look at a patient's wrist and decide it must be the daughter she gave away so many years ago, well, that was insane.

* * *

Rose balled up the cotton sheets and placed them in the newspaper. The Sebastians would be wondering if she was pocketing the sterling silver dresser accessories if she didn't get moving. Rose shoved the mass of newspapers under her arm and raced down the staircase to the kitchen. Mrs. Sebastian was ordering a maid to help the cook and another to air out Mr. Sebastian's office.

Rose lifted her bundle toward Mrs. Sebastian. "I'll need that boiling water." Rose tried to wipe away the confusion she felt.

At the Formica kitchen table Mrs. Sebastian sat with her cigarettes, dealing cards for solitaire. "Over there. Set them by the stove."

A new surge of irritation developed inside Rose. This household should run like an army division when it came to Theresa's health.

Rose called to the maid who was helping to dry the dishes. She held up the dirty linens in her direction. "You'll need to put these directly from the papers into the water, no matter what pressing event may threaten to draw you away. Don't lay contaminated sheets on the countertop."

Mrs. Sebastian flicked her Zippo and closed her eyes, while lighting her cigarette. "Sit, Rose."

Rose hesitated. "I should make my next call."

With her foot, Mrs. Sebastian pushed one of the chairs out from under the table, offering it to Rose.

Rose was shaken from the sight of that birthmark, her mind playing tricks, and needed to leave the house. She was exhausted and wanted to forget everything. "Of course, I can sit. But I need to wash my hands." Mrs. Sebastian dragged on her skinny cigarette and gestured toward the sink.

Rose washed her hands, and sat back at the table, shifting, trying to get comfortable with the idea of lounging around instead of heading to her next job, and getting away from the house that was whittling away her composure.

Mrs. Sebastian snapped her fingers, a loud crack emanating from her exquisite hands.

"Yes, Ma'am," the maid said, and extracted a fifth of vodka and a cut glass tumbler from a cabinet. After crushing some ice she'd chipped from a chunk in the icebox, the maid splashed the vodka into the glass and set it in front of Mrs. Sebastian who threw the drink back hard and quick.

She stuck her tongue out like a child then grinned, pushing her empty glass into the air. "Rose will take one, won't you, Nurse?"

Leave, Rose thought. Get out of here. But as her mind was telling her to depart, her body was settling into the chair. Rose nodded. "Sure."

The cook laid a second tumbler with ice on the table. Rose's mouth watered as the vodka washed into the glass.

Mrs. Sebastian tamped her cigarette into a chipped Limoges saucer and her lazy gaze lifted to meet Rose's. "So? What's the girl got this time?"

Rose decided this drink wasn't the first of Mrs. Sebastian's day and threw back her shot of vodka. "Asthma. Like your husband said. Dr. Bonaroti must have been misled, he thought you said she'd been suspected of having TB."

Rose could not seem to dispel her unease, the sight of the brown birthmark stuck inside her brain. Had she seen that? Was the shape the same as she remembered?

Mrs. Sebastian drew herself up as though reinforcing her energy for what was to follow. "I suppose there is nothing we can do for asthma. Besides keeping her as inactive as possible."

Rose shook her head. She wasn't ready to argue the inactivity point—she needed to research some cases like Theresa's and discuss future treatment and protocol with Dr. Bonaroti, not to mention the money for the clinic. Focus. Yes, this was what Rose should be thinking about. The clinic. "Well, yes, for acute attacks there's epinephrine and on a regular basis we can give her Asthmador..."

"Lordy-be, no. We've tried all that. We want her *fixed*." She lit a cigarette and waved away the smoke that lifted from it. "I have a baby on the way and a twenty-year-old daughter with the wherewithal of a six year-old and I was told a nurse in Donora was so good that she could fix things so my daughter would be normal. That's you, right? Rose the nurse?"

Twenty-years-old, Rose repeated the words in her mind. Was it possible? Her gut told her it was. She needed to get as much information as she could. She drew back and held her glass up, rattling the ice to get the cook's attention. The woman splashed some vodka into Rose's glass. She sipped this one, knowing Mrs. Sebastian would not ask her to leave before she'd finished her refreshment. Rose reorganized her thoughts and leaned over the table. "What the...what did you just say about me?"

"Dr. Culvaney in Gary said Dr. Peters in Pittsburgh said Dr. Bonaroti in Donora said he'd put you in touch with us, because for lazy, coughing patients there was no one better than you at just tossing people out of bed, onto their feet and..."

Rose raised her eyebrows. Mrs. Sebastian pulled another chair over to her. She slid off her mules and rested her feet on the seat. Rose was proud that her reputation had reached all the way to Gary, Indiana and back. That alone should have been all the credentials she needed to give stout orders to the Sebastian family regarding Theresa's care whether it offended them or not.

But, Rose stopped herself from telling the woman that perhaps the root of Theresa's problem was the mother. Instead, Rose took another sip. She still needed two things from Mrs. Sebastian: funding for the clinic and access to Theresa.

Mrs. Sebastian lifted her hand, a thread of smoke curled off the cigarette and bee-lined for Rose. She resisted the urge to wave it away.

"I need to come back to gather more data." Rose popped open her bag, rifling through it. "Here, this tea should help reduce Theresa's wheezing. Just administer a cup or two every few hours."

Rose shuffled back through her bag, trying to figure out how she might ask the questions that kept her from leaving. She needed to confirm that this craziness regarding Theresa's birthmark was just that.

"Well, thank you," Mrs. Sebastian said. "I look forward to further diagnosis. And Nurse..."

"Yes?"

"I haven't made up my mind regarding the clinic. I have some concerns. I don't have time to address them right now."

"You're busy, yes." Rose forced a warm smile over her frigid mood.

Mrs. Sebastian pulled one of her feet up across her leg, rubbing her swollen ankle. She struggled to stretch past her bloated belly, trying to keep a firm grip on her foot.

"Let me help you with that," Rose said. "I'll get the fluid moving in your joints if even for a moment."

Mrs. Sebastian fell back in her seat and exhaled, tilting her cigarette in Rose's direction.

Rose bent over Mrs. Sebastian's feet, looking at the bulging skin. She felt poise return as she began to work on one ankle. She could be conversational as long as her hands were moving and she was under the cover of her nursing skill.

"You said you lived in Gary." If they never lived in Pittsburgh perhaps there was no reason for Rose to worry about Theresa any more than she would another patient. "Gary's nice."

Mrs. Sebastian's face went slack from the skill of Rose's hands, her voice dropping to a whisper. "Yes. Gary. Oh, and Pittsburgh...before and after that. That's where we got our Theresa. Mayview." Her eyes lit up. "I didn't think of it until just this moment. But I think that's why I'm hesitant to fund a medical initiative. I gave money to Mayview at the time we *got* Theresa. It didn't go well. The money was misused in my opinion. Some people are simply..." Mrs. Sebastian's voice trailed off.

Mayview. Rose felt as though she'd been sucked into a coal mine. She reached back in her memory, falling back through her past to when her baby had been born.

"Nurse?"

Rose looked up. She had stopped rubbing Mrs. Sebastian's ankle and had slumped into her seat without even realizing it.

Mrs. Sebastian twirled the cigarette into the saucer, smoothing a perfect ash-dome onto the end of it. "Don't stop. I think my feet are actually shrinking." Rose nodded and resumed the massage. This was her chance to be sure.

"My cousin," Rose said. "She was at Mayview. She worked there, I mean." Rose's words barely made it out of her mouth. "What's Theresa's birthday, again?"

Mrs. Sebastian blew the smoke out the side of her mouth before tamping the cigarette out. "Twenty years ago. Born the 12th of October."

Rose kept rubbing, digging her fingers in the space where the anklebone met the muscle beneath it.

Mrs. Sebastian lit another cigarette. "So tiny. She had rose-pink skin, perfectly set eyes, bow mouth, made for the big screen. Even as a two-hour old newborn, it was as though I were looking into the face of a great child, like I imagine Hepburn's mother must have looked at her, or Bacall's."

Rose worked her way up into the woman's calf. Mrs. Sebastian leaned to the side, resting her cheek in her hand, elbow on the table. "The social worker at the hospital put the girl in my arms and she snuggled into my chest, gurgling, that sound, it was magical."

Rose pushed and kneaded the muscle, lost in Mrs. Sebastian's words, drowning in her recollections of Theresa's first hours of life. Right or not, she felt as though Mrs. Sebastian stole those moments and held them up as hers, when they should have, when they *might* have been Rose's.

Mrs. Sebastian flicked her hand toward her other leg, directing Rose to rub it.

"It was quite an experience," Mrs. Sebastian said as Rose shifted to get a grip of the other foot. "I remember, oh yes. That's right. The social worker was a bully of sorts. She droned on and on about the young mother insisting we give the baby a saint's name of all things. She'd wanted Anastasia, can you imagine? I was partial to Nancy. Or my maiden name as her first name. But the girl, apparently, had been insistent. So we thought Theresa prettier than

Anastasia. The woman and I couldn't—ouch!" Mrs. Sebastian said.

Rose snapped her hands back.

"It's tender there!"

Rose straightened and shook out her hands, unsure if she was startled by the force she'd inflicted or by Mrs. Sebastian's words. She started to sweat again. Rose *had* made that demand twenty years before, hadn't she? *Had* she? Rose sifted through her memories of the past, peeling it back to that day, the moments after they'd injected her with a sedative. Suddenly the demand that her baby be given a saint's name was fitted into Rose's history like her bones fit into her skin. She had wanted her baby protected as she went off into the world alone.

Rose moved back to her bag, opened it, drew out another package of tea and set it on the table. She needed to regain her composure and professionalism, but felt so mystified by this information and numbed by the vodka that her only option was to leave.

Mrs. Sebastian raised her glass and shook the ice, drawing the cook's attention. "You've lost a child, haven't you, nurse?"

Rose's throat felt as though it were shrinking, as though she were the one with asthma. She pulled her gloves from her coat pocket and wiggled her fingers into them.

She couldn't meet Mrs. Sebastian's gaze. "I'll phone tomorrow with the time of my next visit." And, as Rose bolted onto the porch she could hear that Mrs. Sebastian and her minions had already collapsed into the drudgery of housekeeping conversation.

* * *

Outside Rose saw small, ghostly footprints scattered across the porch and remembered Leo had been with her that morning. Rose was too unnerved from seeing the birthmark to be angry with Leo for disappearing. Her gaze followed the footprints that trailed off the side of the wooden planks.

One of the maids poked her head out the kitchen door. "Your hat." Rose took it and adjusted it on her head.

The maid clasped her hands at her waist. "The wee-one went around the bend to the front porch. Takin' in the sights of the great zinc works, he said, to watch the cars travel below on Meldon. Not that he can see them today, no siree, not with all this fog. "

Rose nodded and went down the steps. She wended along the cement path that hugged the side of the house. Out of sight of anyone in the kitchen she stopped and fell back against the blackened brick of the hulking house. The church bells—dozens of them were ringing, and melded with the cacophony of the mills. Her head felt as if it would split open. Rose wished the moist, ugly air would kill off her pain, the sensation that someone had grabbed her heart and twisted it inside her chest. She dropped her bag to her feet and rubbed her temples hoping she didn't buckle.

Her skin tingled as she tried to line up the facts. All she could do was feel the effects of knowing nothing would be the same again. Rose wrapped her coat close to her throat. Leo's voice, his singing, came from around the corner. She opened her eyes, but her sight barely penetrated the thick fog. Were these facts about Theresa a coincidence? Had the events of the last couple of days been too unnerving?

Rose crossed herself and asked God for guidance. Was it possible? Had He brought her daughter back? She vowed to do everything to ensure Theresa's safety, whatever that meant after twenty years apart. Apart. A flutter contracted Rose's stomach, the kind she felt the first time a pregnancy quickened. She pressed her hand into her belly, trying to make it stop. It couldn't be true.

Rose needed to carry on with her day and complete the expected tasks, but her mind plunged back to the day her first daughter was born. She closed her eyes and let the images envelop her like the fog. She saw the baby's face, her eyes clenched, her mouth somehow almost shaped into a smile. As though the girl knew Rose was her mother and it didn't matter that Rose had nothing, and was an orphan, only fifteen.

"It's time. Rose," Bennett had said trying to peel Rose's hands from the baby. Rose wouldn't let go. In those last moments she memorized every inch of her; the way an abundance of hair stood on her head and flipped over at the ends, her thick curled eyelashes, her feet drawn up into her bottom, her fingers balled into fists and the birthmark, the brown amoeba-shaped splotch. She traced it with her finger as Bennett grew impatient and pulled the baby away one last time.

Rose had believed this man. He had promised to protect her, that they would have more children once he finished college, that they would have a home together. And, she ignored the feeling that if she let the baby go she was letting go of something much bigger than Bennett suggested.

She remembered the woman in a wool coat who eased the baby from Bennett's arms.

"I promise," Bennett had told Rose. "You will have all the things you want. But this baby needs a home now with parents who can give her real things right now. She'll probably have brothers and sisters close in age. She'll have everything we can't give her."

Rose reached upward, begging for the baby. He gave her to the woman and turned back to Rose and sat on the bed with her. "Let me take care of you before I try to take care of a family. No one will ever know she existed. We'll put this behind us. No one will ever have to know the shame we feel right now."

He pulled Rose toward him, smoothing her hair, loving her the way she had needed love her whole life. She couldn't speak. Bennett knew about Helen, the girl who was adopted from the orphanage. The family had returned her, beaten, her face collapsed on one side.

"I promise," Bennett said. "The baby won't be mistreated, she won't be like Helen. This is a kind family. And, we will be together."

Rose clung to Bennett, marveling at his confidence. Tears streaked her cheeks and mucus clogged her nose. But she was grateful for this hero who would change her life. Bennett would give her love more than anything.

Now, the memory chilled Rose. Her throat itched, forcing her to cough. Her glove was blackened far quicker than normally was the case. She squinted into the fog. It seemed to be getting darker, lower, with no sign of lifting. Rose leaned her head back against the brick wall, displacing her hat. She pushed it back into place.

How had she been so stupid to believe Bennett? How could she have given up her daughter? She had trusted him. Rose covered her mouth. She should have been stronger. From the moment she let go of her baby, something in Rose told her not to trust Bennett, that she was on her own and would have to take care of herself. And, here at the Sebastian's, Rose long grown up, her life changed completely, all over again.

Chapter 8

Rose edged along the wall, following the sounds of Leo on the front porch. Around the corner she found him bouncing like a ball, his hair flopping over his eye. He had removed his coat, his white shirt grayed in the two hours he'd been outside.

Rose stuck her thumb in the direction of the steps. "This way, little rabbit." She waited while Leo leapt from one riser to the next. Rose squeezed Leo's hand.

"It is ugly today, Auntie Rosie. Mama will have some words over this fog today. You know the sun shines *every day* in Wilmington. I remember it. Even when it rains, the sun peeks through the clouds." Leo wiggled his fingers near his eyes. "Lemon yellow. Not silvery like here."

Rose stopped and looked toward the mills then into the sky. The sun should have been dousing the land with its rays. By now, she should have had to shield her eyes from the brightness even if it were slightly overcast. It was as if the sun hadn't even risen that day.

The pair stomped down the sidewalk, spreading the thick soot with each step. Maybe the reason Rose tolerated Donora, even liked it was that it suited her life-long string of bad luck. Maybe poor Sara Clara had simply never suffered imperfection before and living in this dark, grey world made her feel she was missing something she was used to having—bright yellow happiness.

"It's okay, Leo. Fog'll pass then today will be like all the rest."

"That's what Mama's afraid of."

Rose felt as though she'd taken on a suit of dread, strong enough to hold an elephant above ground.

"Take my hand. I don't want you to fall," she said as they stepped onto the sidewalk that would take them to Tenth Street and back up to McKean. Rose wanted to fit some grocery shopping in between stopping at Dr. Bonaroti's and forcing her life, as much as she could, back to the normal she knew two days before.

* * *

On McKean, Rose stopped and coughed so hard it bent her forward. "We need to stop at Isaly's before we hit Doc's office so let's pick up the snail's pace, how 'bout it?"

Rose couldn't wait to get to Dr. Bonaroti's. She still would not believe Theresa was her daughter. She'd been talking herself into the idea that coincidences like this do happen—that it's possible Theresa was some other baby girl adopted on the day Rose's was born, to a Pittsburgh family who'd gone to Mayview, and had a birthmark that looked exactly like Rose remembered. The coincidental confirmation, Rose thought was in Theresa's records. She hoped it wouldn't seem strange for Rose to request Theresa's entire file when she was merely doing a follow-up exam.

If questioned, she could make a case for wanting to read the file from beginning to end since Theresa had a respiratory event when Rose was caring for her. Cathy, the receptionist, knew Rose was meticulous. Community nurses often did dig into a patient's file, writing dissertations on their visits.

Rose and Leo stopped at Sixth and McKean where she would normally see the street bursting with people, and the G.C. Murphy, grocery stores, fine clothing stores, and pharmacies would host a steady stream of noontime patrons.

But Wednesday, the fog obscured the massive glass windows that fronted brick, stone and wood plank buildings. Rose could see shocks of orange and black decorations through the murkiness, announcing the coming Halloween parade, something that always inflated Rose's and the town's spirits.

"Can't see," Leo said, covering his eyes as though shading them from scorching sun.

Rose bent down. "Jesus, Leo, it's actually clearer at your eye level. Quit trying to make a salami out of the back end of nothing. A little fog never hurt anyone."

Rose squeezed Leo's hand and continued walking south on McKean.

She silently recited her list: chipped ham, jumbo lunchmeat and Klondike ice creams. Normally she would roast a chicken on Wednesday, but Rose didn't have enough time to head to the butcher, and get to Isaly's. The thought of feeding her family lunchmeat for dinner was abominable, but that day, she was lucky to still be upright.

Inside the Isaly's, Rose's eyes flicked over her fellow patrons—Pete Scarsboro, Donna Katz, Mike Hanratty— who said hello with a raised hand or nod. They couldn't seem to stop talking about the fog long enough to utter their greetings aloud.

Some said the fog was highly unusual, and called it smog. They insisted it was as though a lid was over the valley, trapping more mill-smoke and fumes than usual. Others argued that it was no different than any other day; the air was simply still on the river and its overall calm was allowing the regular fog to hover. Nothing to worry about.

Pete Scarsboro slapped his grocery list on the glass counter for the butcher and talked over his shoulder. "The fellas at the mill in Monessen got smoke, too, but they ain't got none of this kind of fog. Fellas say it's the zinc mill."

"Yunz guys are just alarmists."

Rose jumped at the raspy voice and turned to see Meany Collins behind her.

"Tell 'em Rose, nothin' wrong with a smidge of smoke and fog. Live inside a horseshoe at the foot of mountaintops and yunz'll get a little fog in town. Stop yer bellyaching. Tell em' Rosie."

Rose smiled then noticed what he was cradling. "What the hell, Meanie? Have you lost your ever-loving mind with that sugar? *Powdered* sugar? Donuts, cookies? Sweet Christmas Eve, have you gone around the bend?" She ripped the boxes from his hands and tossed them onto the deli-counter. "Forget having your leg chopped off, you'll be dead if you eat all that. Now get on home." Rose ordered Martin the deli-man to re-shelve the items. "I'll have Johnny bring you a pound of Kielbasa and some green beans, but I don't have the time to stand here until you leave so just get on and I'll send the meat over later."

Meanie slumped.

"Don't pout!" Rose said to his back. "I just saved your life."

"Ayeya," Meanie said as he waved Rose's words from the air with a curled, leathery hand. He shuffled out of the store, mumbling.

"Ah, git off the fella's back, Rosie," Gary Adamchek's unmistakable growl came from the soda fountain counter.

She spun around.

"Dolly doom is what I've started calling yunz—you and Doc Bonaroti. Now Henry, too. If not for the ray of sunshine Johnny, the *football* star, why yunz would have nothing but dark clouds and angst at yer heels. Lucky for you, you gave birth to the golden boy of the century."

Rose froze at Henry's name. It made sense that people would have heard Henry got the hack-saw at work, but Rose had been so shaken by the events of the last day and a half that until that moment she hadn't the time to worry that people might find out why he was fired. She stalked over to the soda fountain where Adamchek sat, his meaty paws wrapped around a black coffee. I know your wife wasn't singing that tune when I eased her pain in her final days, Rose thought. She winced at the image of his wife, shriveled up, trying hard to live.

"I'll disregard your snide remarks and take a charitable view of your sorry existence since your wildly better half passed away," she said. "If Henry thought he was doing the right thing then you better believe he was. And, yes, Johnny *is* a star. Your son could be, too if you had him buckle down and apply himself. It's just hard work. Don't hold it against us." Rose had never been more irritated with her family, but she needed to defend them in public. She was grateful she actually wanted to.

He grunted while the other men at the counter looked away. "Yeah, well, don't be so high and mighty, Nursie. You think your life is so perfect. You think your Johnny is so perfect? Your little *Mag-da-lena*?" The way Adamchek said Magdalena's name ran chills up Rose's spine.

Rose was familiar with Adamchek's jealousy; this time it seemed to sting a little more.

"I have my own private nurse who happens to know your life is *not* perfect," Adamchek said.

Rose shook off the ill feeling. Adamchek was disgusting, resentful, and mean, but harmless in any real way. He was just blowing smoke.

"Private nurse, my ass."

The butcher brought Rose her grocery bag. She was grateful to have something to do with her hands.

"You leave my Rosie, alone," the butcher said. "Not an honest man or woman in town who wouldn't admit to feeling relief just at the sight of this nurse." Rose felt her insides settle though Adamchek didn't seem to realize the butcher had entered the conversation.

"Nurse Dottie's my nurse. And *you* need to keep something in mind." Adamchek scowled as he looked up at Rose from his stool. "Whatever shortfall you have after the Sebastians dole out some cash, keep in mind the community chest might not have any funds to make up the difference. The fellas who decide what to do with the money are looking to expand the mill hospital rather than funding your clinic."

Rose moved her grocery bag from one hip to the other hoping to cover up her panic at hearing that information.

Adamchek smirked. "You and Bonaroti need to learn a thing or two about what Dottie and the other mill nurses already know about the location of Donora's money tree. And that golden boy of yours, you better tell him to spend more time on the field and less in the bar tickling the ivories in the Hill District or whatever horseshit his band does there."

A crash at the back of the store startled Rose. There, on the floor, cans and boxes scattered around him, was Ian Greshecky, trying to right the display he'd knocked all to hell.

The clerk groaned and started to scold Ian. Rose waved him away, saying she'd help clean up. She raced back there, set her bags down and began to stack the cans and boxes with him. Rose hoped she'd find the right words for a boy who lost his parents as a five year-old, and the day before, his aunt.

When they were done, Rose stood, but he remained on the floor. Rose pulled him to his feet and several cans fell out of his coat, denting as they hit the ground. He was stealing, right there in front of Rose.

"Ian. You can't..." This boy knew right from wrong, but he was desperate. Isabella had been a second mother to him. Losing her must have pushed him over the edge.

She wanted to scold him, tell him that all he had to do was ask for help and she'd find a way; she wanted to smack him on the ass like she would Leo or John, but seeing him, basically orphaned twice was too close to what she had experienced. She scooped up her grocery bag and shoved it into his arms. "Take these. I'll be over—to help you get re-settled. Your uncle will shape up. I'll make him. I know—"

Rose stopped herself mid-lecture, not wanting to embarrass him further. "Just go on, I'll be there in the next day, or Miss Fanny. She'll be over by the day's end, I'm sure." He shoved the bag back at Rose, surprising her. She shoved it back and with that final movement he took off out of the store, hugging the groceries to his chest.

Rose pushed the last can back into place, leaned her head on the shelf and crossed herself, lost in what she couldn't control. She had no more room on the tab for groceries at Isaly's and no time to get to another store before she was due at the clinic. She sighed and thought of all the ways she might be able to make plain chicken broth seem like filet mignon. She'd lived on less, payday was Friday—Henry would get most of his pay for the two weeks, wouldn't he? She wouldn't be paid until the middle of November.

She took Leo's hand, ignoring his questions regarding their now missing groceries, and the sneer that rode up on Adamchek's mug.

"Don't be an asshole when you grow up, Leo. The one good thing about seeing one in person is knowing you never have to be like him."

Rose did not care that someone might call her Dolly Doom; her duties often required acknowledging truths people didn't want to. Her position might be misunderstood or underappreciated. What mattered was that she did what was right.

Leo squeezed Rose's hand and smiled up at her between skips and hops. Sometimes the truth did hurt and no one knew that more than Rose.

* * *

Rose and Leo made a quick jag up to Thompson Avenue to Dr. Bonaroti's office. He worked out of a storefront. Several families rented the rooms above the office, stuffed inside like Sunday's pigs in a blanket. Though Rose was paid through a one-time donation by the outgoing superintendent and his wife, and spent most of her time visiting homes, she worked closely with all six doctors in town. She kept a few hours each week at the clinic in Bonaroti's office, seeing patients and offering lessons for families who wanted more information than she could give in their home.

Bonaroti, the most outspoken of all the doctors, appealed to Rose. All six were kind and went about their business with steady hands, but none were as colorful and straightforward as Bonaroti despite his stirring up trouble with the mills. If he didn't do so much for the people of Donora she might have held his rabblerousing against him.

And, he had cared for Henry's Uncle Sam before he died, ensuring he received the best attention a person with few means could. After Rose and Henry had emptied their bank account in caring for Uncle Sam, Bonaroti stepped in and added to the funds. Rose would never forget that, and was forever indebted to him.

Opening the doctor's office door sent a bell tingling. The receptionist, Miss Cathy looked up and grinned, her bucked teeth hanging over her lower lip. Rose lifted her hand to say hello and Leo plopped onto his knees on one of the wooden, slatted chairs by the floor to ceiling windows. He fiddled with the strings that worked the curtain pulls. Rose smacked his bottom.

"Now you sit," she said. "I have work to do in the back. Don't cause Miss Cathy a lick of trouble." Rose should have headed up the hill, done her chores, and soothed her husband's soul that surely smarted from his firing, but she needed to file her reports. More than being committed to her responsibility, she wanted to read

Theresa's file, to ferret through the girl's medical history. She told herself it was Theresa's discomfort she wanted to reduce and she did want that, but she also knew the information in the files might alleviate her own.

Leo ran his finger down the window glass, making squeaky noises.

"Dammit, Leo," Rose brushed his hand from the glass. "Looky here." Rose knelt in the chair beside him and used her coat sleeve to wipe away his fingerprints.

As she did, she noticed a woman step partially into view, her head bent down. Another woman leaned in as though whispering in the first one's ear. Something in the hazy sight of them magnetized Rose. She strained to see more. They shifted out from behind the building, but were still obscured by the dark fog. The first woman was familiar. Rose moved closer to the glass, wiping it with her cuff. Was it? It couldn't be. Then there was that signature toss of her long hair. Hair that should have been held neatly back with a gumband, making a pretty ponytail. Rose pushed her forehead against the glass. What would *she* be doing down on Thompson? Magdalena.

"What in Gilmore cemetery hell is going on?" Rose said. She pushed away from the window to find out.

"Magdalena!" Leo yelped and scrambled ahead of Rose, heading out the door. Leo ducked in between people walking down the street, running behind the women Rose had seen together.

By the time Rose reached the spot she'd seen Magdalena and her friend standing, only Leo was there, looking as confused as she felt.

He lifted and dropped his shoulders. "It wasn't her, I guess," Leo said.

Rose turned in a circle, squinting into the fog. "You sure?" They couldn't both be mistaken.

"She woulda stopped when we called if it was, right?" Leo said.

Rose made a final rotation and stopped at the sight of Miss Ester's Dress Shop, her storefront hidden by the fog, an eerie outline of ghostlike mannequins in the window, calling Rose's attention in a way it never had before. Rose clenched her jaw. That's what Magdalena was doing down here, Rose thought. Had she already quit school?

She stuck her hand out to Leo. "This way, Leo. We're going to pay a visit to Miss Ester and set a few things straight."

Rose stepped off the curb to cross the street, but heard voices coming through the fog, panicked words, carrying on the shrill screams of someone who was seeing another in pain or danger. Rose moved toward the voices and didn't get far before she saw Nurse Dottie and Doc Bonaroti huddled on the sidewalk with Shirley Pollack.

Shirley coughed and hacked, hands on her knees. "Down at G.C. Murphy, Mr. Schmidt collapsed." Shirley grasped Bonaroti's arms and used them to straighten up.

Dr. Bonaroti balled his fists and turned Shirley away, heading back down toward McKean Avenue. "It's these blasted mills. No rational human can deny it. That zinc mill is a monster!" He poked his finger toward the zinc mill. "Rose, get our bags. I'll meet you at Murphy's. Dottie, head to the McCallister's and we'll finish our discussion later."

Rose sent Leo home with strict instructions to stay on the inside of the sidewalk and move slowly, not stopping until he was safely in the house.

She moved as quickly as possible, her own lungs a little short on breath—the air burning as her body worked harder. She teetered somewhere between a shuffle and a run. She dodged people in the daytime darkness, the streetlights barely showing through the atmosphere, their beams, impotent now.

Out of breath, Rose finally reached where Schmidt lay on the ground. His face was smog grey, as though he'd been colored with it from the inside out. He was writhing on the cement. Rose waved her hands in front of her, trying to shoo the fog away like smoke, but there was no displacing the heavy blackness.

Bonaroti knelt over Schmidt's chest, trying to keep the man from flailing around, and to assess what exactly was causing Schmidt's shortness of breath. Bonaroti put his ear at Schmidt's mouth and laid his hand on his chest.

"He's breathing, but it's shallow," Bonaroti said. "This isn't like his normal attack. He's never fallen over like this."

Rose knelt down and lifted one of Schmidt's arms over his head while Bonaroti applied pressure to his back. His breathing weakened further.

"Put him flat, put his legs over your bag," Bonaroti said. "Let me try something."

Rose followed directions, but was perplexed.

Doc put his ear to Schmidt's mouth and put his fingers on the man's neck. "He's not breathing anymore. Heart's still beating, though." Rose was astonished. He gave him several breaths right from his mouth into Schmidt's.

"Doc? That's not an accepted…"

"Look," Bonaroti said as he straightened and began to push on Schmidt's chest. "His color's coming back. Here, take his pulse. I'll give him some more air if needed."

Rose lifted Schmidt's wrist. It was splattered with white house paint, making his bluish hue even more evident.

She put her fingers in place for the pulse. "There it is. Weak, but there."

Bonaroti and Rose worked together, shifting back and forth, Rose pulling his arm up, checking his pulse and Bonaroti giving breaths. They were relentless until Schmidt's wife appeared on scene, horrified at the sight of Rose and the doctor bent over her husband. Rose realized how strange it must have looked.

Mrs. Schmidt whacked at both of them, sending Rose back on her heels, her mouth smarting from taking one of the grieved woman's blows.

Bonaroti cradled Schmidt's body, trying to keep his airway open.

Mrs. Schmidt draped herself over her husband. "He's grey! Grey as the fog!" she said.

Rose bent down, trying to pull the woman away, to comfort her while Bonaroti worked. But the woman shrugged, bellowing to leave her alone.

Chuck, the gasoline attendant, arrived on scene in a rusty blue pickup truck. With his one arm, he pulled an old door from the bed to use as a stretcher. They heaved Mr. Schmidt onto it, hoping to get him to Charleroi Hospital in time to relieve his labored breathing.

The men struggled to get the large man into the back of the truck, and Rose walked Mrs. Schmidt to the front where she would ride.

When Bonaroti hopped in the back with Schmidt, Rose closed the tailgate.

"Those damn mills are killing us all," he said.

"Don't bring the mills into this, Bonaroti." Mrs. Schmidt said. "Little Jim'll lose his job, his pension and then we'll have nothin'!"

Chuck's truck engine wouldn't turn over, the engine howling in protest.

"Rose," Dr. Bonaroti said, his words snapping with military directness. "Sebastian called. Tomorrow, head back there. Read Theresa's file, first. School them in all they need to know about caring for her. They're opposed to giving her Asthmador but I'm sure that would ease her discomfort."

Rose nodded, concerned that phone calls from the Sebastians were made so soon after her visit.

"Old man Sebastian," Bonaroti said, "was rambling some sort of nonsense. I'm not sure about what. But, he mentioned he wanted Dottie to see Theresa and I said, no, she's a mill nurse. I can't see his daughter tomorrow. Schedule's filled up already. Calls piling up like slag in Palmer Park. Go back and fix whatever problem that man has. We aren't playing musical nurses just because he has a..."

Rose leaned in to hear better, but the engine finally turned over and the truck pulled away. She lifted her hand to wave and watched as the taillights disappeared into the fog. Why had Sebastian mentioned Dottie, of all people? Rose's stomach twisted. That nurse would not replace her. Especially when it came to Theresa. Rose knew Doc trusted her and that's why he told her to read the files and follow-up the next day. Rose ran the events of the last hour through her mind again as she moved back through the fog.

Rose looked at her watch. Cathy would have left the office so Rose would head home and file her reports the next day. She hoped Mrs. Schmidt would be more grateful that her husband was alive than put off by the rescue technique Doc had used. She knew it made sense to do what Bonaroti did—they did it for babies all the time—but it was strange for family members, like Mrs. Schmidt to see someone blowing air into another person's mouth and pressing on a chest.

Rose and Bonaroti had studied James Elam's account of breathing for a polio victim in just this way. It had worked and that was good enough reason to consider employing it even though it had yet to make the medical annals as accepted practice. She was fortunate to work with such a courageous doctor and she knew together they were making a difference.

Still, Rose did not need a complaint filed against Bonaroti while they were trying to secure funds. She exhaled. She tried to remember how her day had started. It seemed as though the events that marked it were lived by someone else. Rose stopped to catch her breath after a few steps home. Her heart pounded and she felt dizzy. She grasped the railing on the stairs.

The birthmark came back to her, the memory of the tiny infant who bore one, and Theresa. Rose looked back over her shoulder. She almost turned to go back to the office to read the file. But she didn't. She started back up the steps, moving slowly, entertaining the thought that Theresa might be hers, not wanting to know for sure.

Chapter 9

Rose wiped her feet on the mat outside her home, the mindless motion soothing her. The whistle for the shift change had blown about the time Schmidt was tumbling to the sidewalk. And now, as Rose tried to block Mrs. Schmidt's screams from her mind, she could hear the chorus of housewives hollering the names of errant children who'd not yet returned for dinner. Like a strange piece of music, notes played together, though not quite fitting, Mrs. Sullivan's voice then Mrs. Gregorchek's then Mrs. Carpenetti's, then the chorus of the Westerman sisters and on it went until every child was home, eating dinner with family before the men of the house had to go to sleep to get ready for the early morning shift or leave for the all night one.

Rose unhooked her coat and hung it on the wall. She could hear Johnny's gang in the living room. Band practice. Nearly every day after football practice, they would gather at the Pavlesics, laughing through the occasional twang of a guitar, crack of the drums, and pop of a trumpet as they warmed up their instruments. In between all the chatter, Johnny's voice rose, his jovial spirit and endless stream-of-consciousness punctuating the other boys' thoughts, making them buckle over in laughter again.

Rose leaned against the wall outside the room, wishing she could capture all of the boys right there, never let them grow up, allow Johnny that kind of fun for the rest of his life with the gang he'd known since the day he was born. That wasn't possible; the other boys would start in the mill as soon as they decided they'd had enough of their senior year of high school or immediately after graduation. And these guys, talented as they were in music, had no choice but to starve as an artist or eat well as a card-carrying, union steel worker. But Johnny had choices.

The smell of chicken, potatoes and buttered green beans made her think she'd been too hard on Sara Clara. Perhaps the girl came to her senses and actually did something useful today.

Rose needed to wash up, change into a dress, and find out what the hell had happened with Magdalena that she would want to quit school. After that, she'd get down on her knees to pray that Henry had found a job.

Rose's attention was drawn to the notes of a song. The boys had actually stopped talking, Johnny had taken the liberty to shut himself up long enough to play the trumpet. That was an ongoing joke of the fellas, that they pushed him to play trumpet over piano. At least for five seconds, he wouldn't be talking incessantly.

Rose watched the boys clustered around the room. Johnny slipped and slid around the floor, moving with his trumpet as though he'd born with it attached to his body. Pierpont Jasper—the lanky colored kid never without a suit and bowtie, whose limbs looked nearly rubber, started his sax solo. Dicky Solvinsky plucked at the piano, his plump belly folding over his belt. Prunzie Schaffer rattled away on the drums and Wild Bill Rodriguez fitted his violin into the collection of bluesy sounds. Modern music, Johnny called it, not like Rose's pre-war swing.

The bluesy notes seemed to speak more than simply emit sounds. The boys' music reached right into her soul and made her want to cry. Maybe the boys were better at music than Rose had allowed. Maybe there was...no, no, no, heading down a road of music will only, surely, lead back to these mills. She reminded herself that it was her job to deny Johnny this flight of fancy—a "life" with the band. He'd regret that choice in ten years. She would not allow him to make a stupid decision, and risk everything.

Now with Henry losing his job, Johnny's future depended more than ever on securing a scholarship—on the game he'd be playing on Saturday.

How could Henry have done such a careless thing?

Rose then thought of Theresa Sebastian, and understood how Henry could have been so stupid. Rose had been stupid once, too. Her lie was long and deep and kept secret her entire marriage. Rose rubbed her temples. Too much thinking and not enough action for one day.

"Hey Mum." Johnny dashed across the room and all the fellas stopped playing. He planted a kiss on Rose's cheek. "Hey, the fellas are stayin' for dinner."

"Sure, sure. They might not want to, though."

The three boys on the couch leapt up. "We want to, Mrs. Pavlesic. Anything for a meal at your place," pudgy Tommy Tubbs said, rubbing his belly.

"But, I uh, I don't know who made dinner. I just got home." Rose felt as though the numbness that had gripped her was affecting her ability to talk. She just wanted to hide.

"We'll sweep the porch and the walkway," Pierpont said.

Rose would normally have teased Pierpont saying he and the fellas had a lot more than sweeping to do to earn one of her dinners.

"Sure, okay, fellas. Sweeping. That would be nice."

"Hey Mrs. Pavlesic, let me feel your muscles, come on, let me see that bicep."

Rose laughed at that. "Get the hell out and sweep, the only muscle I'm interested in seeing is yours pushing a broom."

She wished she could trade places with those boys, any one of them. The words of Father Tom or whatever his name was, filled her mind—forgive yourself. The boys went back to their instruments and Rose headed to get two brooms. She wanted to forgive herself, but couldn't. Now maybe with Theresa right in front of her, she could finally do that, she could tell her the truth.

Rose opened the closet door and a tumble of hats and gloves fell to the floor. Theresa had not suffered as Rose had worried. She had not had her face bashed in like her friend Helen. Rose scooped up the woolens and shoved them deeper onto the shelf. With brooms in hand, Rose headed back to the boys, listening to them play, nodding at the skill she could no longer deny. Rose told herself to let her past go. To find a sense of peace in knowing Theresa was alive and relatively well. Well enough. But, she couldn't. As much as she wanted to, she just could not.

* * *

Magdalena stood outside the bathroom door. Her bare toes furrowed into the worn rug. Her stomach contracted, releasing acid every few seconds. She pushed her hair back from her face with both hands and drew a deep breath.

She needed to talk to her mother, explain why she'd changed their plans. But could she do that?

Maybe Magdalena shouldn't. Not right then. Not when she'd just walked in the door.

Magdalena grasped her throat. Her mother was so strong, so practical. Surely she would see the sense Magdalena's plan made once she learned the whole story. Her mother would be pleased that Magdalena found someone who loved her. Like Henry loved Rose.

Tears filled her eyes. But, Magdalena did not love him. She had done something wrong and had no valid excuse. She would have to lie and sacrifice her dream of being a scientist and marry him, so her family would not be shamed. But, disappointing her mother?

Her father had seemed to know how it felt to disappoint Rose even though he didn't say how he had. Everyone in the house was afraid of Rose, but Magdalena.

Magdalena pushed open the bathroom door and forced a smile at her mother.

Rose pulled her brush and lotion from under the sink. "Hi Magdalena. Give me a minute."

Magdalena sat on the side of the tub. Rose peeled off her uniform, and stood barefoot, her white slip shifting up and down as her mother reached for soap and stretched for her shampoo bottle. Magdalena knew exactly where her mother had been that day just by looking at her slip.

The white material was pristine from the top to an inch above the hem. That last inch offered testimony to her day. Red iron-ore dust from the blast furnace and yellowish dustings over the black soot told her Rose had been near the zinc mill.

Rose bent over the sink, head drooped forward, hands clamped around the rounded sink edges.

"Mum?" Magdalena said, and felt her lips quiver.

Rose turned. Her expression looked pained then irritated. She straightened and squinted at Magdalena. "You look as though you rubbed your head all over your pillow. What the hell's going on with the histrionics, parading around town when you should be in school? Commiserating with Ester about a career in sewing?"

She wanted her mother to hold her. But, she was frozen.

Rose turned her hands palm up, water dripping from her fingertips. "What's so bad today Magdalena?"

Magdalena shook her head. She knew Rose's unspoken words. Nothing we have to deal with is as bad as what I've seen so toughen up.

Magdalena leapt up and fell forward into her mother. She felt Rose absorb her weight and steady them both. Rose gripped Magdalena's shoulders and pushed her away so she could see her face but Magdalena didn't look at her mother. She sobbed mouth open at her mother's shoulder.

Rose surrendered to the hug and she rubbed Magdalena's back. "It's just a phase. You'll get that scholarship and you'll get your confidence back. That's what's wrong, right? Just a little insecurity? Those boys giving you a hard time for taking physics again? You'll be so happy once the pressure is off and you're in college." Magdalena's face stayed plowed into Rose's body.

Just say it, Magdalena thought. Just get the words out.

"I don't have time for—"

Magdalena nearly gagged getting out the words. "I'm pregnant."

Rose stiffened and she stopped rubbing Magdalena's back.

Rose dislodged Magdalena from her body and tried to capture her gaze. "Now. What did you say?"

"I'm so, so sorry, Mum."

Magdalena saw her mother's face contort as she came to understand exactly what her daughter had said.

"Who did this? Your father will snap the S.O.B's. neck. If I don't rip his arms off first. Who did *this*?"

Rose pulled away from Magdalena. A flurry of comments and questions flew out of Rose's mouth so fast Magdalena could not answer them. She clutched at her skirt; afraid if she let go she might keel over.

Rose covered her mouth with both hands, speaking through her fingers. "We'll put the boy in jail. I'll kill him."

Magdalena straightened. Now was the time for her to claim she loved the boy she let inside her body, but not inside her heart. "I've been in love, well, for as long as I can remember…"

Rose dropped her hands and bit her lip.

"I'm seventeen, Mum. You treat Johnny like he's a grown-up and me like a baby, and oh, I love him, I do. I know you will never speak to me again. I tried, I love—"

Rose shook her head and spun the faucets on, doused her hands under the water. Magdalena watched Rose's muscles contract and relax, scrubbing the Camay over her hands, up her forearms, under her arms, as though cleaning up after a long night of working in the mill, as though she were covered in the same filth that Magdalena felt inside.

Rose scrubbed her face again. "I don't know why you would say all this, why you would want to break my heart. You loved him for as long as you can remember?" Rose bent over the sink and splashed her face, choking on the suds that streamed into her mouth. She rested her forearms on the curved porcelain, water rushing down the drain.

Magdalena breathed heavily, her thoughts muddled and tired. She'd worked so hard to make her mother's dream come true, to aspire to something other than a mill-wife. And now, she was exactly what her mother hadn't wanted.

"Mum, please. You always wanted a bigger family, more children, but you couldn't. So, I can. I will. I'll have all the kids you wanted."

Water dripped from Rose's face into the sink. "You're doing this for me?"

"Half the girls my age quit school already and will be married within two years. What does it matter if I get married now? What's wrong with me being like everyone else?"

Rose straightened and reached for a face towel. There was nothing there. "Dammit! That damn Sara Clara! Dammit, dammit." Rose blasted past Magdalena. She followed her mother to her bedroom. Wanting forgiveness. Rose had never had a weak moment in her life, but she was sure Rose could forgive her. Rose was a lot of things, but heartless, she was not.

Magdalena watched Rose dig through a clothesbasket at the end of her bed, searching for a towel. She tossed the contents of the basket until she reached the bottom, but no towels. She looked at the ceiling and collapsed to the floor, pulling the bedspread to her face.

Magdalena had never seen her mother like this. It frightened her and Magdalena began to sob, unable to catch her breath in between wails. "Please, Mum, look at me." Magdalena held her arms out to her mother.

Rose shook her head and pulled the spread from the bed and over her balled up body, rocking back and forth.

"Then yell at me," Magdalena's voice was thin. "Please say *something*, but don't ignore me. I know it's not what you wanted, that you lived a different life than me. I know you've never made a stupid decision in your life. I'm. So. So. Sorry."

Rose winced and stared at the floor, rocking.

Magdalena dropped to her knees next to her mother. "I just wanted someone to hold me. Someone who paid attention, who loved me for the way I was at every moment." Suddenly, the words seemed real to Magdalena. *Had* she been looking for something more?

Magdalena reached out to her mother, her hand shaking more and more as her mother refused to take it. It looked as if Rose had vacated her body, as though someone else was speaking through her. A meek, mumbling person, who barely pushed her words above a whisper.

"Your family wasn't enough? I wasn't good enough? The mother's always at fault," Rose said. Tears welled in her eyes but not like Magdalena imagined. Rose's quiet tears frightened Magdalena more.

"Mum, please, look at me."

"You have no idea what it's like to need someone's touch. None," Rose said. "You're a slut."

Magdalena cradled her hand against her stomach. "What did you say?"

Rose hadn't looked at Magdalena when she said the word, but there it was, branding Magdalena's heart with shame and Rose's lack of forgiveness.

174

"You betrayed your family, your upbringing, your future, yourself. You will never be the same after this."

Magdalena's throat constricted. She couldn't swallow. Her mother despised her. She'd never in her life heard of a mother calling her own daughter a slut. Not for any reason.

"You have no right to run off with some boy when you had *this* family. When you had *me*." Rose rocked, arms locked around her legs, head buried in her knees.

Magdalena shook her head. She couldn't stand Rose's reaction, the way she seemed to disengage, release Magdalena from her heart. Magdalena hadn't meant to get pregnant, to do it at all. But it had felt so good to be loved that way. Magdalena finally stopped sobbing, paralyzed by her own fears. It was as if air was entering through her skin rather than her lungs. She stared down at her mother, balled up, fragile in her terrible meanness.

Magdalena was so grateful for her father. He would make her feel better. He wasn't afraid to hold her, tell her everything would be fine. Her mother was simply not capable. Magdalena ran out of the room, looking for her father, for someone, anyone, to tell her everything would be all right.

* * *

Half an hour later, a dazed Rose still sat beside the bed, nubby spread pulled up to her chin, her knees to her chest.

She was livid at Magdalena's betrayal, the accusation, *noooo*, the *evidence* of her bad mothering now spattered over their lives like grease from a frying a pan and it wouldn't easily be wiped away. Still, the anger toward Magdalena was nothing compared to the shame, the reason she couldn't bring herself to look at Magdalena, to touch her, to comfort her.

Curled there, barely drawing breath, it wasn't her daughter whom she mentally flogged and hated to her core. It was her own pitiful self. It wasn't a failure in Magdalena's character that led to sex out of wedlock; it was a defect in Rose's, her former sins. She'd thought she'd done such a good job of raising her children. Rose grasped her hair, pulling it from her scalp, not hard enough to pull it out, but to serve as a reminder that she deserved pain. It was her lot in life.

Rose's mind reeled from her past, and she found herself reliving the time when she was utterly alone. Her bed then was a spindly, canvas cot in a cold cinder block cellar. The slow pulse of a ceiling leak tracked the night minutes as though time itself were as hobbled as she. It was in that setting that Bennett, her first love, arrived on scene, the first man who looked at her and saw a person.

His interest was all it took for her to disrobe, to remove her values and morals like an old coat. His attention dissolved her common sense, her ability to gauge a person's motives. She wanted him touching her, on top of her, in her. She could not get him far enough, long enough inside her.

Sex with Bennett had made her whole. He approached her body like fine marble, a museum sculpture he was permitted to touch. The awe in his eyes had made Rose think God was finally being good to her. Bennett explored every slope on her body; it was as though each part began its existence once he drew his strong hands over it. She finally felt herself—her existence had mattered to another living soul.

Before and after sex, Bennett and Rose spun the web of their future; his mind met hers like God himself had promised them to each other. They marveled at the smallest details; that they shook their coats off with the same brusque irritation, that they strangely buttoned their shirts from the bottom up, that they…well, it didn't matter what form stupidity took, it was that Rose had found joy and love and belonging and didn't even recognize it as stupidity until it was too late. And, somehow she passed *that* on to her daughter.

Rose pushed Magdalena from her mind and focused on Bennett, the first to show her love. At least what she thought was love. Until she knew he couldn't love anything, let alone her. Still, decades later, the image of Bennett Fayhe was as strong as the fog that had hung around all day. His face above hers, his expression near climax, whispering he loved her, convincing her he would save her from her dismal world. She wouldn't have to scrape for an ounce of affection or a moment of joy again. He was there bathing her in it.

Rose had believed him, and in the relationship that had created their baby. Theresa. Rose had thought the strands of her past and present were sealed off from one another forever.

Rose remembered Bennett's promise to share the rest of his life with her, if she gave Theresa away so they could go to school and make something of themselves before they had a family. She watched Bennett from the window, as he left the hospital, his posture relaxed as he ducked into the taxi. She saw the relief on his face, the irritating shudder that told he was never coming back.

Rose could still feel her hands on the ice-cold hospital window, a chill spreading from her palms through the rest of her, and the new, but intense sensation of love obliterating her. Somehow, Rose had passed her lapse of judgment from twenty years before, to Magdalena.

And, as Rose could barely breathe; she felt other thoughts forming in her mind. She pushed back at the memories of sex that were born before Bennett. That *ogre's* hands, the way she could see his hands on her, but she had trained her mind not to allow her heart or skin or soul to feel them. His words shifted through her mind. "You're a whore, Rose, you are my sweet slut."

Those words like grenades, exploding with the shame she'd thought she buried long ago. She could not believe she said the word, slut, aloud earlier. And now, she had called Magdalena it.

And Rose could not believe after a lifetime of forgetting what had brought on the single biggest mistake of her life, her past had returned and dashed down the halls of present time, reminding her of her irresponsibility from twenty years before, what others thought of her. What she knew to be the truth all along.

Rose choked on her own phlegm. She imagined Magdalena in her bedroom, crying, sharing Rose's tears of shame, as though they were co-conspirators in a murder, finally caught and sentenced to death in the same courtroom.

Rose had been there for Magdalena, giving her the best their limited funds could buy, showing her a woman could have everything in life if she worked at it. Most of all she gave her the opportunity to be raised by a loving, ever-present family.

The father of Magdalena's baby was still unknown to Rose, but she knew she didn't want to see the boy...wouldn't be able to be in his presence without killing him...oh, my God, she'd have to marry the man. Or be sent away. To St. Mary's in Sharpsburg? St. Paul's in Oakland? Never. Mayview? Not after Rose had spent her pregnancy and part of her nursing experience there. Surely they'd have records and they'd see that not only that Rose was a morally lapsed teen, but she'd bred one, too.

Rose wanted to comfort Magdalena, but she couldn't move, her lingering anger making it impossible for her to rise to her feet and put her daughter ahead of herself. She deserves to be alone, she thought, the abrasive image shocking Rose. How could she think that, want that for her daughter? Slut! The word kept popping into Rose's mind. She clenched her teeth; terrified she might scream it out!

Rose heard the door push over the nappy carpet then back, clicking shut. She could smell Henry. How could Rose tell him about his daughter? How could she break his heart? He would kill Magdalena.

Rose threw off the bedspread and reached under the bed, pretending to search for something. How could she explain her crying in a crumpled heap on the floor?

"Dinner's ready," Henry said settling on the floor beside her.

She foraged around the carpet for lint. Rose wiped her eyes, still peering under the bed. "It's dusty, linty under here. Dusty," Rose mumbled. She was not ready to put a stake in Henry's heart. He was a kind man, but there was a difference between being kind and dealing with your young daughter getting pregnant. He was sensitive; it would be too much for him to handle. She couldn't have the two of them falling apart.

"Just cleaning this mess," she said, steadying her voice.

Henry grabbed her at the back of her neck, gently massaging the spot where a knot had formed, throbbing like a bruise. He knew her body well, though she never again allowed herself to become enamored with someone else's affection for her.

"I'm not hungry." Rose shrugged.

He rubbed circles around her back. "Well, I think you'll have a hard time resisting this dinner. All your favorites. I even made chocolate cake."

Rose waved her hand over her shoulder, sucking back rising sobs. She couldn't speak. She plucked more lint from the matted carpet fibers, punching each piece into the palm of her hand.

Henry cupped his hand over hers, making her stop her useless work. "Everything's going to be okay. We'll make everything work out, we have a plan."

Rose froze. She must have misheard him. She narrowed her eyes at the lint in her hand.

"I mean it. We'll all be okay," Henry said.

"Of course we're okay." Rose shook her head. This couldn't be right. Magdalena would not have told Henry something like this without asking Rose to be there to support her. Magdalena may have tried to see what Henry would think if she said she wanted to quit school. But, she would not have told him this. Henry was a loving father, but he was not, he was *not* Magdalena's mother.

"What are you talking about?" Rose's thin voice was worn down with the sadness behind it.

"She's a tough girl. She can handle it."

Rose's body tightened, her skin felt as though it were gripping the bones inside her, suffocating her. "You know?"

Rose finally turned and looked Henry dead in the eye.

Henry brushed Rose's hair off her face. She shrugged his hand away.

"Whatever we decide," Henry said, "she's strong. We raised a good daughter."

Rose stared at him, suddenly hit by the reality of what Henry had said. That he knew, and was calm. Clearly he'd processed this much longer than she had. But it was what he hadn't said that hit her hard. The realization hit her. She'd ignored it for years as life trundled on productively and happily in the case of the children. She suddenly felt attacked by Henry, his relationship with Magdalena.

"You mean, *you* raised a good daughter. I wasn't home. I was working."

"She gets her strength from you," Henry said.

"Same difference. Being strong won't erase this, Henry. This is so bad in so many ways that I can't even think straight. Above all she'll rot in hell like rancid meat. This is a serious matter of her soul, her...what the hell do you mean whatever we decide? What choice do we have? Her life is over."

"Well, she could marry the fella. Or not."

"What fella? She told you who that bastard is?" Rose pounded the floor with her fist. "She couldn't find the words to fill me in on that one."

Henry spread his hands open and cocked his head.

"What? I'm too hard on her? Well, not hard enough, apparently. It's because I work? Because I feel the need to contribute to our community, to be a nurse. I wasn't home enough, those old bitties across the way always say. This is my sin as much as hers. What man? Who did this?"

Henry rubbed his mouth as he spoke some mumbled words.

"What? Tony? Tucharoni? The fella next door?"

Henry closed his eyes then met Rose's gaze, a barely perceptible nod.

Her face flamed. She covered it with her hands. "The son of a woman who can't even bring her laundry in before it rains? That boy? *That* boy?"

Henry took Rose's hands from her face then leaned back on one elbow.

"How long have you known about this?"

Henry played with the chenille knots on the spread and nodded. "Ah, Jesus Christ, Rose, does everything have to be about you? That's what's got your hair on end, isn't it? Your perfect world is crumbling because your husband is trying to do the right thing and so is your daughter. You don't want the embarrassment."

Rose couldn't have been more off-balance if he had hit her. Who did he think he was, ferreting around in her thoughts, thinking he knew anything at all about what was inside her mind, the secrets she kept.

She poked her finger through the air at him. "Don't tell me what I think or why I think it. All I've ever wanted was this family to be secure and happy."

"Can't you be as generous with us as you are with your patients? For once. Cut your own family some slack for fuck sakes."

Henry's scolding voice belied his casual posture. His tone was unfamiliar. Rose scrambled to her feet and stalked to her closet where she yanked an old dress over her head then shoved her feet into scuffed black pumps.

"Every damn thing I do in this world is for our family. *Everything*. Why don't we just start hanging our underwear on the outside lines from now on? Oh, and why not get Johnny to knock-up a few gals while we're at it. And let's see, well, we can all have a luau in hell because that's where everyone in this house is headed. Magdalena doesn't have the excuse of stupidity or alienation of affection like me—"

"What the hell are you talking about Rose?"

"Shut up, shut up, shut up!" Rose balled her fists and slammed them onto the dresser—a fit like patients she'd seen in Mayview. Who was she kidding? She shuddered like some of her bunkmates used to in the orphanage, the silent rage seeping from their bodies when no one was looking. Rose could feel her past rolling back toward her like a molten steel-filled ladle.

"Stop it." Henry said. "Nothing has been decided. Magdalena wanted your guidance. I'm sure you still have a chance to offer it if you can get past this bullshit. Whatever the hell is going on in your head. You're more than happy to help every pregnant girl and woman you stumble across in the name of community nursing. How do you think that makes your daughter feel?"

"And what about your bullshit?" Rose said. "What the *hell* would make you put our entire family in jeopardy to help one colored man out in the mill as though it would change anything if you opened your big trap."

Henry sprung to his feet. "You think I'm a failure—an ex-baseball player, a poet who keeps his writing to himself, a man in a mill doing a brainless job. But to me, being a poet and working in that mill are related and neither is brainless. Auden seems to think writers transform invisible thoughts into concrete items—words. I help make the most useful metal in the world out of slivers of the very earth we stand on. That mill is poetry in action, if you look past the obvious dirt and hardship associated with it. My life's been good in that mill, but if I overlooked this injustice—that would make me a failure. If it hadn't been thrown into my face, maybe I could have gone along with everything, but, well, it was the right thing to do. *You* do that all the time; stick up for those who need it—the world beyond yourself. I would have thought you'd be proud. My life should mean something, too."

Rose grunted. Why the hell was he always dragging Auden into everything, like the poet was there, moderating, like Auden gave a damn about their family and its problems?

"You're not a failure," she said.

"I know that."

"Do you? You ran back to Donora as fast as your feet would take you. I know you wanted to go to college but you were too scared to do it."

Henry raised his hands as though doing a monologue on stage. "Everything we fail to be—" Henry said.

"Stop quoting Auden! You sound stupid." Rose opened and slammed her underwear drawer. The conversation meandered down paths she hadn't ever explored.

"I was paraphrasing! And why don't you stop hoarding things! It makes you desperate." Henry stood, bent forward, rage ripping at his muscles, he pointed to Rose's closet. "I know what you hide in that closet. And it's not just that you hoard canned goods and whiskey. You hoard who you are, your feelings, your love. You have to control everything! Sometimes life is not yours to control."

Rose bit her bottom lip. He was wrong. She loved her family fiercely with all the affection she'd never shared with anyone. She dismissed his assessment as it being "just Henry," to being ultra-sensitive.

"Someday you'll thank me for having food stores." She was only trying to be sure that the family could survive the next time all their money went to some sick relative or broken windows or new refrigerator. The depression was barely over, the war, just seconds from being over, she was protecting them.

All these noble things, yet all she felt was dishonor. Control, her ass. Rose felt a surrendering calm hit her and her voice was steady once again. Yes, Rose controlled what she could, but it was only for the sake of everyone in that family.

"The right thing, isn't always the *right* thing, Henry," Rose said. "There are subtle differences you might not be used to navigating."

"My point exactly."

"Well, then I guess we're clear." Rose did not mean to be condescending, yes, yes, she did. He deserved it after keeping that kind of secret with their daughter. He deserved to feel bad for weaseling his way into his daughter's life, taking Rose's place, being more of a mother than she was.

"We're clear all right," Henry said. "And I am stunned that you of all people would face your daughter's situation in this way. Hiding, avoiding, punishing. Of all people. I know it's not what you planned, but why would you act like this? The entire time we've known each other…you know what Rose? Just forget it. Suffice it to say I'm deeply disappointed."

"That makes two of us." Rose jumped and covered her ears when Henry left, the door struggling over the ugly rug, finally slamming shut making it sound as though a bomb had detonated right in their own bedroom.

Henry attacked a stain at the kitchen counter although he knew the brown, whatever it had been, had sunk deep inside the veneer and would never be freed from its Formica grave. Still he had to move, to do something to mask the anger-infused, fear cocktail that swirled deep in his belly.

Behind him at the kitchen table sat Johnny and the fellas in his band. Everyone else was gone for dinner to other homes. Auntie Anna and Unk only got out of the house once a week for dinner at the Croatian Club. This time Sara Clara and Buzzy were more than happy to take them. Thankfully Magdalena was having dinner at the Tucharoni's. Rose simply needed a few minutes to pull herself together, and if Magdalena was gone, that would help. Henry pulled at the strings of Rose's apron which he'd tied around his neck, feeling as if a rock were boring into the base of his neck vertebrae.

Out of the corner of his eye he saw Rose at the doorway to the kitchen. She did it often, observing the family, just as he did. She'd told him it was because she appreciated such a loving family after her life in the orphanage. He had believed her until this afternoon. He wanted to understand her rage, and would have understood it better if she had screamed bloody murder at Magdalena, like she would have done in much lesser circumstances, but this. This unwillingness to speak to their daughter didn't make sense. It was not like Rose at all.

To the outsider, Rose appeared cold, always the calm clinician, even toward her children. People often talked behind her back, Henry had heard it himself, when drunken lips loosened up in any one of the bars in town.

But people also admired Rose, needed her when their lives were at their worst, thought she could be funny, all those things. But Henry always thought those drunken ramblers were wrong when they thought her dedication to nursing was evidence she wasn't devoted to her family. She was simply more efficient than the rest of the world, at everything she did.

And so Henry filled in her parenting gaps and coddled the children when Rose backed away for one reason or another. But now this fear had risen. Fear he didn't know his wife at all.

Henry pushed his shirtsleeves over his forearms, breaking into a sweat. He drizzled the brown juices over the top of the roast one final time then pulled it from the oven.

He turned toward the table with the roasting pan. Rose wiped her brow with the back of her hand, straightened her back then waltzed across the floor as though nothing had changed in her well-ordered life. Henry was relieved to see her pull on her cloak of normalcy. He wished he could do the same when it came to thinking of her.

Though Henry was not pleased his daughter had gotten pregnant, the revelation did not evoke disgust or hate or anger toward her. He didn't know how or why, but he had an underlying feeling that all would work out for Magdalena. And he was not the religious one. He marveled at how Rose's religion seemed to agitate her more than comfort her. Yet, there *he* was, feeling, when it came to Magdalena, as though Jesus himself had descended to support him.

Henry held up the roasting pan in Rose's direction in case she wanted to take over the meal. She looked away then sat at the table.

Henry brought the food to the table.

Pierpont elbowed Rose, grinning. "Mrs. Pavlesic, shouldn't you be doing the dishes right about now?"

Rose was slow to meet Pierpont's gaze and the boy drew back, glancing at his band mates for a clue to what was happening.

Rose must have realized she had done something odd and she pushed away from the table and did the dishes. Henry felt a stab of sorrow. A small change in Rose's behavior felt as big as the news of the pregnancy.

The meat was so tender it nearly turned to stew right on his plate. Every swallow met with tightened muscles.

Conversation worked around the table, Rose nodding occasionally to show she was paying attention. Henry knew that everyone sitting there was aware of Magdalena's situation. Strange, as smart as Rose was, as intuitive as she could be when it came to her work and the lives of the families she serviced, she clearly did not surmise she was the last to know. While Henry thought that was peculiar, he allowed an influx of relief over the matter to settle in. It would be one less thing he had to apologize for once all his lies finally surfaced.

* * *

Johnny sat at the kitchen table watching his mum pretending to scrub the dishes and his dad forcing half-chewed roast down his gullet. Johnny's eyes stung as he kept the banter bouncing around the table to avoid admitting their world was about to shift.

Damn Magdalena. Always demanding the attention. At the time he was going to give his parents the biggest news of his life. Normally it was her unusual intellectual achievements that turned her spot on earth toward the sun. This time, it was her ruined girlhood blotting him out, as usual.

And now, as he was plotting to break his mother's heart to save his life, Magdalena went ahead and ripped Rose's heart clean out of her chest. There was nothing left inside there for Johnny to break.

Johnny's stomach wrenched tight as he watched his parents avoid each other, his father with that damn hound-dog mug, his mother accidentally dropping plates and spending far too long cleaning up the broken pieces.

At least Johnny had seen his dad's hound-dog frown before. The time his father was caught in a lie. A lie only Johnny was privy to. Until the past few days anyhow. The mug was back and he hated to see his entire household whisper and clutch at scraps of secret conversation, behind Rose's back. His mother's silence scared the hell out of him. But he had to be brave. He had to be like her. It was what she taught him even if she wouldn't see it that way.

"Mum, we're headed over to the Tap Room to play tonight."

"Oh, playing in the big venues these days, are you?"

The fellas laughed around the table. His mother seemed to shed her angst as though he'd been mistaken it had been there in the first place. It shouldn't have surprised him; she did not know she was the last person to know about Magdalena.

There was no turning back now. He had to get it off his chest. Rose's gaze lifted to meet Johnny's. He took a swig from an Iron City beer bottle. That would spark her back to normal.

Rose waved Johnny over and took the beer from his hands. She chugged the entire bottle.

Johnny's friends flooded out of the kitchen, and Johnny stood there waiting for Rose to respond. She looked away. Never speechless, this one, yet there she was, mouth dead still in her head.

"You okay, Mum?"

"Sure, what's not to be okay? I've got beer, a son headed to some college on a football scholarship, a daughter headed to Pitt, what's not to be okay, Johnny boy? I mean besides all of us burning in hell and all."

He cracked a smile and glanced at his father. She thought everyone was going to hell pretty much and often they could joke about it.

"No drinking, Johnny. You're great at what you do. You have a gift from God, you *are* a gift from God. You don't need confidence in a bottle like some folks."

Henry dropped his coffee mug onto the table with a thud. Johnny watched as Rose caught his father's gaze, his tight mouth and discreet headshake, signaling something to his mother—what it was Johnny wasn't sure.

"Oh all right," Rose said, "I suppose your father's right. I certainly don't need to tell you again that you can be anything you want if you just apply yourself. But, you're too young for drinking. That Lacey boy died of drinking too much with his gang and the Tremens fella passed out at the wheel of his car. No drinking. When you've graduated from college you can have sixty beers a day for all I care. You have a big game on Saturday then dinner will be here with the Notre Dame scout."

"That it?" Johnny said.

"Of course that's not it. But that's all I'll say for now."

Johnny broke into a grin. "Seriously? That's all you'll say?" He was losing his nerve. He needed to tell his mother he would not meet with the scout, that he didn't want him coming to dinner, that she would never understand how he felt. He wanted to scream that her life is *exactly* as she wanted it. But that didn't mean she could force everyone into her mold for how the world should be.

"Let's make a deal, Rose, my dear mother," Johnny said, knowing he'd always had good results with charm more than whining.

"Now you're an Atlantic City dealer, are you?"

"Seriously. You've never really even listened to me play more than when I practice. Mr. Patrick said I'm talented.

In the real way. If you come see me play and leave without understanding truly how good I am, then I'll drop it. November 6th, I'm playing with this fella up in Pittsburgh. Louisiana Red's his name. He plays with Crit Walters. Up his house in the Hill. Right on his porch, this amazing gathering, with amazing music…"

Henry went to the sink and filled a glass with water.

His mother stiffened. Johnny was pushing her, even with her ability to act as though nothing was wrong. "Johnny," Rose said, "I'm being really patient after a really hard day and I'm telling you…"

He couldn't take it anymore. The charm would have to go. Johnny shifted his weight and grimaced. "Don't call me Johnny. My name is John. Please."

Rose forced a smile. "Johnny. John, nah, shit, I can't call you John. You're my baby, my Johnny. My boy. Sorry. You'll have to live with it. And, I just, well, I *have* heard you play. I *know* you're talented. That doesn't make it a good career choice. Certainly not playing with some guy in the Hill on his porch. Louisiana Red? On a porch…" Rose sighed then looked at Henry.

She smoothed Johnny's hair back and shook her head. "Go ahead. Go on to the Tap Room. But take that Old Granddad from the cupboard and welcome the scout to Donora tonight. Just drop it off at the hotel before you head to the Tap Room. We'll talk about next week, next week." Rose said.

Johnny bit his lip then straightened. Was she really dropping this? Small steps, his mother had always told him. "So that's it?"

"Do what I say and that'll be it." She held her finger up. "And, the fog. Watch your step out there."

Henry turned from the sink where he was scrubbing the roasting pan and glared at Rose.

Suddenly Johnny felt the need to smooth things over as he always did.

"And Dad," He said. "I wrote three poems the other day. In the style of Auden, then Blake. You were right, seeing how two guys could write about the same things so differently, really showed me a lot. It'll work for that college essay Mum's always bending my ear to write. Poetry? That'll sizzle their grey-matter, don't you say?"

He had failed to tell them the truth, what he had planned. He felt so trapped between what he wanted and his need to please his parents. He wanted the same things as his mother, he just knew he could do it in a different way. Why didn't she believe him?

Rose forced her smile, her cheeks looking like they would burst from tension. Johnny longed to see his mother's real smile.

"That'll knock their socks off for sure. You know, Mum, it will. I promise."

Henry grabbed his son and gave him a jerky hug before turning him into a headlock. "Now get out of here or you'll be up all damn night." They scrambled across the linoleum then Henry released Johnny and went back to the sink.

Johnny couldn't leave without coaxing a real smile from his mother, at least trying to.

She was staring at her hands, pushing a cuticle back with her thumbnail. When Johnny didn't move away she finally looked up at him. He gave her a cheesy grin and did a little jig to the tune of *In the Mood*.

She didn't dance with him as usual. She crooked her finger at him and he moved closer. She cocked her head to the side, looking into his eyes like she'd discovered an alien on the street then she ran her finger along his jaw line. She put her hand on his chest as though she was feeling his heartbeat.

"What, Mum?"

She shook her head and looked as though she was going to cry. Rose never cried and Johnny couldn't stand there and see it for the first time. And so he left, feeling as though he would never manage the path through life that he had chosen, but not willing to give up trying. It was not like him to quit, no matter who stood in his way. Even if the person in his road was his mother.

Chapter 10

Rose threw back three shots, while Henry had two, after they finished cleaning the kitchen in silence. Rose could play "normal," with the rest of the world. At least to keep Magdalena's pregnancy a secret, but she would not let Henry off the hook. He had ruined part of their marriage with his secrets.

After the dishes she went into the yard for air. What a joke that was. The air was fat with black, grainy smog. But still she stayed, drawn across the grass where muted light shone from the Tucharoni's windows. Softened by the fog, their house looked as though it was part of a storybook scene, and all that went on in that house was warm and loving.

Rose snuck up close to the window and rubbed a corner of one wavy pane with her finger. From the foothills, the song of the mill narrated. The flying shear, the familiar sound of steady slicing through steel, calmed her heart, as though she'd been birthed from the womb of a steel mill instead of a woman.

Through the window Rose watched Magdalena at the Tucharoni's tiny Italian-tiled kitchen table, surrounded by their many family members. They were sandwiched like chipped ham in white bread, spilling out, dropping off the sides. Mrs. Tucharoni, Tony's mother, stood behind Magdalena. What was Magdalena doing there?

Mrs. Tucharoni ran her plump fingers through Magdalena's auburn hair, while the rest of the family listened to what ever she was saying. Magdalena smiled and threw her head back in a laugh. Was Tony really the father? The Tucharoni boy?

The entire family raised their mismatched glasses in a toast and Mrs. Tucharoni kissed the top of Magdalena's head as though Magdalena had been *her* daughter for the last sixteen years. Rose bit the inside of her cheek. They looked so happy, all of them, like they actually loved one another. Being jammed in that house like kielbasa in Bob the butcher's cabinet apparently suited them.

Rose glared at Tony, hoping her gaze would burn a hole through the glass, searing the center of his forehead, dropping him on the spot. But she imagined her nursing instincts would take hold and she'd be in the kitchen, easing him back to life. She squeezed her eyes shut to the image of him on top of Magdalena. There was no scenario with Tony Tucharoni pleasant for Rose.

Magdalena should take care of the baby without him. Rose couldn't allow Magdalena to give up the baby for adoption as she had done with Theresa. If only the pregnancy could just disappear. Like those women Rose often cared for after taking home-concocted tonics, or abortions performed by certain doctors who didn't live in Donora.

Rose covered her ears as though she could block out the sound of her own horrifying thoughts. There were lots of ways to get rid of a baby. Many were unsafe, some never worked, and worse, some did. Rose knew that would not save Magdalena's soul—erasing the pregnancy. And there was no way for Magdalena to raise the baby alone. There was no way to reverse what she had done.

Magdalena was smart, but green as hell. She had no idea what she had done in having sex with that boy. The Pavlesics would be maligned forever. The next five generations would sit around kitchen tables squawking about the downfall of the house of Pavlesic. How could Henry's life have ended up like it has? For a fella who struck out Mel Ott three times, here he was just like everyone else, turning out loose daughters and aimless sons.

Henry's voice came through the fog, calling for Rose. She wandered back toward the mottled light glowing near the door. When she got close enough, Henry stepped out with her tweed coat and nurse's bag. "Bonaroti called. Skinny's down the Merry-Go-Round. Trouble breathing."

Rose turned away from Henry and he slid the coat over her arms. "Not unusual." She was relieved to have an excuse to leave for a while.

Henry brushed lint from her shoulders. "Folks are sicker by the minute. Fog's worse." Henry said.

She faced Henry and buttoned the coat-collar, wishing he'd head back into the house.

He stepped closer. "Bonaroti didn't want to take any chances."

Rose wanted her warm gloves, but wasn't about to delay leaving to get them. "Umhmm." She reached for the bag.

Henry moved it out of her grasp. "He insisted you go."

Rose nodded. She knew what Henry needed from her right then. She cleared her throat and grasped the bag handles, her hands covering his. She wanted to say all was forgiven, that there was much more for them to worry about.

They stared at each other and finally Henry released his grip on the bag. Rose settled it over her forearm and Henry stepped back. He pulled a set of knit gloves from his back pocket.

Rose pulled them on. "Thank you." She felt a twinge of affection stir.

Henry dug his hands into his pockets. "Rose."

"Henry," she said.

"Better go."

And, she did. Heading down the back hill, she thought of Skinny, her plan of action. She was sure it would be the usual type of call where he wanted a little attention more than anything else. Rose glanced back at the Tucharoni home and shook off her tormented thoughts. At least there was someone who needed her and she would not fail to be there.

* * *

The night lit up from the blast furnaces at the bottom of the hill, so powerful, not even the fog could keep the blazing shades of red under its cloak. She shuffled along, down the steps, feeling each one with her foot as though blind. The railing was moist from the dewy humidity, and seeped through her knitted gloves. She steadied herself, as though she'd never walked those steps before. Her heel caught on a crack in the cement and she fell, spinning backward and down. She grasped the metal, her nurse's bag falling off her shoulder and she dangled there, butt nearly on the next step down. She wrenched herself upward, groaning.

"Nurse Pavlesic." A voice came from a few steps above Rose. She could see just their feet stopping next to hers and felt their arms latched under her armpits, across her chest, heaving her upward. She turned and looked up into Mr. Sebastian's face. She yanked down her crooked coat that had hiked up past her waist and felt for her hat, realizing she hadn't put it on.

"Is everything all right? Theresa?" Rose said. She wheezed in the dense, heavy air, trying not to be noisy like Theresa and every respiratory case she'd dealt with the last few days. Her heart pummeled inside her chest. The words, "my daughter," kept shooting around her brain. She knew it didn't make sense, but there was no denying the connection she felt to Theresa.

Mr. Sebastian leaned down from two-steps above. "She's having her usual problems, it was rough earlier though. After you left she turned the color of summer plums."

Rose wrapped her arms around herself. "Jesus, did Dr. Bonaroti come?"

"No, no, like I said, this is all very commonplace, it comes and goes."

Rose stared, not believing what she was hearing, the casual tone. "Well, call him next time. Call *me*." Let me take care of her, Rose thought. I'm her mother, me.

"I will, Nurse." He cleared his throat then stepped down another two stairs, meeting Rose at eye-level. "I've come up here every night for the last week. Did you know that?"

Rose looked away; the odor of whiskey accompanied his words. She hoped he didn't drink as heavily as his wife seemed to. Both turned and started inching downward— their conversation as stilted as their steps. How would she have known that the man spent each of the fourteen nights he'd been in town, up on her hill?

"Magnificent view," he said. "Not tonight of course. Overlook Terrace's is much different. That's a mistake, being there, across from the zinc mill. Theresa's fragile, wheezing for years, but this is making it much worse."

"So, you've come over here to check out the real estate?"

He stared at the side of Rose's face. Her hand instinctively went to her ear, brushing her hair over the double lobe, out of habit.

He finally looked directly at Rose. "No. I've been coming here to talk to you, but I always change my mind before knocking on the door."

She didn't feel she had to be coy with Mr. Sebastian. Rose assumed his concerns with the clinic were more practical than Mrs. Sebastian's. He would want to know the money was well spent, but not be worried about whether the choice to fund the clinic would allow for fashionable dinner parties and balls with fancy people. Rose suspected that partially drove Mrs. Sebastian's decisions—the prospect of a glitzy social life with those not associated with Donora's healthcare situation.

"What? Your whole family just swoops in when the mood strikes?" Rose said. "Your wife wasn't as shy."

"No, well, like I said, I did not actually knock. But I like spontaneity, I admit it."

"Pfft. It has its place. So? How can I help you? I have to make a call down at the Merry-Go-Round. It's probably nothing, but people are particularly sick these past two days."

Sebastian and Rose hastened their pace down the stairs; he occasionally took her elbow when her foot would lose ground on a step.

"Well, I kept coming to talk to you about the clinic, but something kept me from knocking on your door. Then I met you, saw you with Theresa and I'm even less sure we're making the right decision. My wife is against spending money on the clinic—says she wants to see her money erected with brick and lined with marble walls and such."

Rose didn't have time to waste. She knew Skinny was probably mildly affected by the overbearing fog of the day, but she needed to be sure.

"Spit it out. Are you funding the clinic or not?"

He stopped and Rose stopped with him. He blew out air and crossed his arms. Rose looked down the hill to where Mr. Sebastian was staring. Rose was confused. A man in his position in the mill should not be this concerned with a small chunk of money donated to a cause that benefitted an entire town. Yank the money and be done with it or hand it over.

"It has value," he said.

Rose suddenly understood how much he loved Theresa. She realized right then that seeing Rose care for his daughter must have had an impact. He must have come to believe everyone deserved the kind of treatment his daughter did. Still, she wondered why he was gazing down the hill like the mills were his lost love.

"I know what happened with your husband," Mr. Sebastian said, clearly done with his end of the discussion of the clinic.

"It's a small town," Rose said. Her face flooded hot; relieved the fog was so thick he couldn't see her embarrassment. It wasn't any of his business, her husband losing his job for no good reason.

"He's wrong, you know."

Rose's neck tightened. She wiggled her shoulders to loosen up the tension and flipped her hair back, brushing it behind her ears. She could feel her anger growing. She had no choice but to defend Henry.

"My husband meant well. He cares. In a way different than most. We're hoping he gets his job back. Work is plentiful around here until you don't have any," Rose said.

Mr. Sebastian was staring past her again. Rose looked behind her to see what drew his attention. Nothing.

"You look familiar Rose. Have we met before the other day?"

Rose caught her balance as she stepped from the last stair onto the sidewalk that ran down Fifth Street to Meldon, and the Merry-Go-Round bar where a sick man was awaiting her arrival. She wanted to scream. Yes, he'd seen her before. Every day when he looked at his daughter he could see Rose's face. Theresa was her baby and Rose wanted her back. She'd wanted her back for twenty whole years. But, if there was one thing Rose was sure of, she never met the family who adopted her baby so many years before.

Rose tapped her foot and sniffled, trying to be calm. "No. We've never met. Any chance of Henry getting the old job back? Maybe give him a shift at the Zinc mill?"

You owe me for a lifetime with my flesh and blood, Rose thought.

"There's always a chance, but I don't know. I'll talk to his supervisor..."

Rose fixed her gaze hard on Sebastian's. What bullshit.

Rose knew men were not very observant when it came to even the most important life events and she could not imagine that he'd remember what she looked like if he had seen her the day Rose gave her daughter away. She hoped he'd finish what he started to say about Henry losing his job so she stayed silent.

"I should be satisfied that Donora has such a compassionate nurse as you—that no person, even strangers go neglected. Theresa is lucky you're here. And I'll talk to my wife about rethinking her cause. I'll tell her Nurse Shaginaw's plan may not—"

"Dottie Shaginaw? What's she got to do with it? She's never been a supporter of our clinic. Thinks all the money should funnel into the mill hospital. As if the only people who count in town are the ones turning iron into steel. As if the rest of us are useless byproduct. As if she's better than—"

Rose did not approve of her rivalry and insecurities entering into a discussion with the one man who could convince his wife to pay for the clinic. So she shut the hell up.

"Doc wants me to stop by tomorrow to check on Theresa." Rose started walking across McKean, heading to Meldon, satisfied Mr. Sebastian had no idea who she was.

"Hurry on to your patient. Your husband must be very understanding of your position in the community to have you gone most of the day and half the night."

Rose bit the inside of her cheek as she held back her words. Normally, Henry would barely register her comings and goings because he'd be resting up for his shift at the mill. The thought of Magdalena shocked her again.

Perhaps she had been gone too much. But, hell, they'd been in school. Both of them good students, good kids, what good would it do to sit around listening to the soaps all damn day, if she could get her housework done and be a nurse? Yes, she was gone day and night but she had not been negligent.

Rose nodded, not wanting to push her luck with him, and they moved down the sidewalk. The echo of their shoes reached Rose's ears, over the din of the mill, making her aware of their silence. The only things she wanted to say to him were improper; she wanted his daughter to know she was the woman who gave birth to her.

When they reached Meldon Avenue, Mr. Sebastian tipped his hat and Rose ducked under the roof that hid the door to the bar, relieved to be back in her element, ready to nurse someone back to health and feel as though she actually served a purpose.

* * *

The entrance to the Merry-Go-Round bar had a roller skate for a door handle. Skinny had screwed it into the wood when a brawl between a womanizer and a cuckold resulted in the original handle being knocked off. With a tug the door yawned open and a drape of blue cigarette smoke whooshed past her with warm heat. She fruitlessly waved the smoke away and stepped inside.

Rose hooked her coat onto the arm of one of the dilapidated coat-racks and heard it groan in protest. Across from the racks was a U-shaped bar. Eleven men sat like sculptures, only their arms moving to raise their beers to their lips. It wasn't until Mr. Bresner waved her over that any of them looked her way. Their faces drooped with drink, as though their facial features had been melted by alcohol and endless shifts in the mill. Not even their eyes managed to hold their normal shape, even blinking too big a movement to make.

"Skinny?" Rose shouted as she walked past the bar heading toward the backroom.

One bar-sitter shoved his thumb over his shoulder toward the back door Rose was already heading for.

Rose pushed through the backroom door and flicked the light switch to the right of the door. Skinny was splayed across a cot; his enormous belly rose and fell with guttural snores. Rose snatched the evening paper from his desk, spread it on the chair then lay her bag on top popping it open. She hooked the stethoscope into her ears and paced across the sloped wooden floor to Skinny. His lungs were remarkably clear for all the mucus shuffling around. Definitely upper-respiratory—that was good. As though seven moves of the stethoscope was the charm, Skinny shot up throwing Rose back on her ass.

"Jesus H. Christ!" Rose tripped over her breaths.

"Nice gams, Rosie," Skinny said. He swung his legs over the side of the cot, peering at her from his drooping posture, head bowed, breathing hard.

Rose's dress had shimmied up her thighs to her garters. She scrambled to her feet and smoothed her dress. "I don't have time for this shit," Rose said. "Bonaroti called, squawking about how you had one foot in the grave and the other on a banana peel."

"Nah-uh, he said that? That man's an alarmist." Skinny said.

"People are getting sick. Schmidt nearly died today."

"I heard." Skinny rattled off the list of mostly men who were having trouble breathing that day. Rose knew these men all had compromised health before, before, what? Rose shook her head, she knew what before was. The fog. The money made from three miles of thriving mills was a trade-off, the smoke, a sign of success and pride. Some people were weaker than others, but Rose knew a good life was better than a long one.

"Well I'm glad I'm not counting on you to mourn my almost death some day."

"You'll outlast us all, Rosie."

"Oh Christ, I hope not."

The valley was always foggy and its men were strong, the strongest of their kind. Yes, the soot was a nuisance, making three times the work that other women had on a daily basis. Yes, the men did bone-crunching work, but they were born of steel, even the ones who emigrated from other countries, even those fellas had steel in their blood, strength like no other, or they would not have found their way to a place like Donora to do work like they did. People just end up where they're supposed to be.

"What?" Skinny clapped his hands in front of Rose's face. "People end up where they're supposed to be? What in hell's half acre are yunz muttering about?"

Rose shook her head—she didn't realize she had spoken aloud her thoughts. She put the stethoscope into her ears, ordered Skinny to relax, and placed the metal face along several spots on his back. Skinny rambled about some fellas from Pittsburgh busting several bar stools earlier that day. Rose was satisfied with Skinny's pink color, but warned him to take his history seriously, to call right away if he experienced any more trouble.

"Now get on out there and have a drink, Rosie. On me. I'm great. Thought I took a heart attack, but as soon as I laid down and napped, I got back to normal."

A wall-shattering crash made Skinny and Rose leap. The storage room door had flown open. Rose thought something had exploded, and headed, cautiously that way. Skinny tried to grab her hand and pull her back, but Rose wiggled loose from his grip. Laughter and the sound of cards being shuffled drew Rose closer. Once she could see into the space, she peered at a circular table, five men, cigars in mouth, cards in hand, drinks on the table and floosies draped around the room.

Rose smoothed her hair, staring. She couldn't rip her gaze from the women—their dyed flaxen hair, beet-red lips and curve hugging clothing. She nearly overlooked one of the men.

Rose's heart thumped so hard she grabbed her chest.

Buzzy. Sitting there, cards fanned in his paws. He flipped her that patronizing grin, some vixen on his lap. Rose couldn't believe what she was seeing, her eyes focusing on who was standing behind him. Dottie Shaginaw?

"Buzzy Pavlesic!" Rose bellowed and cut across the floor to the doorway. At the threshold, she stopped short. Two other men were familiar, Mr. Adamchek, the man she had a run-in with at Isaly's that day, and Mr. Saltz, the neighbor man who abused his poor missus. The look of the third man made her recoil; that guy and two others, she'd never seen before.

They sat like fat pigs, their hands working their cards without looking down. They were too busy smirking at Rose, gambling away their incomes without a thought for their loved ones.

She felt enraged and disappointed at the same time.

Rose stepped toward the doorway, ready to rip Buzzy from his seat and drag him home to explain to Sara Clara and the rest of them what he'd been up to, but Adamchek lifted his ripped, booted foot and kicked the door shut on her nose.

Rose reached up and pounded on it, hearing a lock slide closed and laughter erupt behind it. She leaned her forehead against the door; all her dreams for a new home were disappearing on the other side of it. And Sara Clara— Rose felt instant regret for how hard she'd been on her since they'd moved north.

Was this why Sara Clara could only get out of bed every other day, was so frightened all the time? Most likely Sara Clara had no idea what Buzzy was doing, just that he wasn't where he should be. Rose pounded on the storage room door again, but no one answered and she felt the angry blood, numb her limbs.

A gruff voice called her name from the doorway. A barrel-chested, crew-cutted man appeared with forearms that told the tale of his years working up from a laborer to wire-puller, to boss in the mill. Jack Dunley shook Rose's hand and slapped her between the shoulder blades. Skinny pushed up off the cot and lumbered out the door, taking his spot behind the bar.

Rose tensed and looked back toward the door that hid Buzzy. There was no way in. It wasn't like this was the only spot in town where men were drinking and gambling away their livelihoods. Skinny wouldn't make them open it. She would deal with Buzzy later.

Jack guided her toward the bar and pulled out a stool. He patted the round seat. "Get on up there, Missy. Yunz could use a stiff one."

Rose should have left; she had too much work waiting for her, a daughter to handle, a secretive husband, and a wayward son. "Written all over my face, is it?"

"I just know the feeling, is all, I'm saying," Jack said.

Again, she thought of laundry, dusting, cleaning her instruments, Henry, John, Magdalena. "I *could* use a stiff one."

"Sometimes you just need a goddamn drink." Jack pushed his fist into the air. "Skinny, my man! Two shots, two beers. Yesterday."

Jack scratched his five o'clock shadow. Rose hated the sandpaper sound it made. It reminded her of the orphanage. She backed away.

His hands flew into the air like he was signaling a touchdown, his eyes bugging out. "Goddammit, just sit, Rose." He pushed her onto the barstool.

Jack took her bag and set it below the bar. Rose ignored the impulse to snatch it off the floor and educate him on the appropriate places and ways a nurse's bag could be set down. But, Jack slapped her on the back again, smacking her will to do the proper things right out of her. He slid onto the stool beside her and she grimaced. Skinny sent two shots and two glasses of beer careening down the bar. She needed this, to lose herself, to forget, for just a minute. That's all.

Rose tossed back the Old Granddad and followed it with sixteen ounces of Iron City. She cleared her throat and ordered a glass of water from Skinny. He slid a glass of tap water into her waiting hand. Jack lit a cigarette and offered Rose one. She declined with a wave.

Within seconds her body warmed to the alcohol and her blood fizzled inside her veins like it was coming to life for the first time. What bag on what germ-ridden floor?

"So. Yunz guys okay for money?"

Rose closed her eyes. She knew everyone would know about Henry's firing, but she forgot how quickly word would spread. Jack would definitely know, being on the inside of mill operations, and all, but still. She wasn't one to discuss money, ever.

"Money? Rose?"

Rose faced him head on, she leaned her elbow on the bar. It slid off. She righted herself and cleared her throat before putting her other hand on her hip.

"Do you talk to your fellow uppity-ups at the mill like that? Yunz this, yunz that? That how you speak when you're in the pristine white offices that somehow manage to sport fine white, wool carpets even as thick smoke swirls around the fibers, feet stomping the debris into the rug, but it still somehow stays white. You say shit like "Yunz" in those rooms?"

Jack pursed his lips and threw his hands signaling a touchdown again before turning back to the bar. "Christ Almighty, just having a little small-talk here, Rosie. Just a little fucking small talk."

"Does Sax Fifth Avenue tell Kaufmann's their business? You're being nebby like everyone else in this town. Can't a person lose her savings to her husband's poor judgment without the whole town having a take on it?"

"People yammering already?"

Rose shrugged. "Haven't actually heard anything, but I can feel the talk as though the lines of communications coursed right through my very own veins."

Rose downed her water and shifted on her stool, relaxing. She lifted her hand and signaled to Skinny who delivered another shot and beer for each of them.

She turned to face Jack. "So, is Henry done for in this town? You're a boss. Isn't there something you can do with all the power the union has these days? Management can't just fire a fella like they did Henry? Just for sticking up for another fella?"

Jack squinted at Rose. "Yer a tender-hearted soul, ain't ya?" Jack said.

"I just like to see what's right, done. That's all."

He stared at Rose as though he had no idea what she was talking about.

"Same old song and dance. People don't want to hear shit about anything that paints the mill as imperfect. Even the union." He took a gulp of his drink, wiped his mouth with the back of his hand. "Won't do us no good if the mills are shut down. We're part of the 'Arsenal of Democracy' and it's bad if a pusher is late back to his post after chatting up the nurse in the hospital while she cleaned the slag off his heel."

He scratched his forehead, shook his head. "Bonaroti called all ten fellas on city council and expects us to meet and decide to close down the mills until this fog clears. Imagine that. Millions in product and machinery down the shitter? Can't shut down a goddamn blast furnace because it's a little foggy. Has anyone seen London or San Francisco? Half the world's foggy—"

"Hold it." Rose held her hand up to Jack. "Back up to the man being late due to slag, chatting up a nurse? Henry? He was chatting up Dottie? That slag on his heel? That was no small injury. Not debilitating, but in need of looking at. I mean, Henry's a lot of things, but he's no chatterbox. You think he was chatting up Dottie instead of working? *That's* why he got fired?"

Jack's jaw fell in surprise. "Just why the hell do you *think* Henry got fired?"

"Well, sticking up for a colored fella of course." Rose saw Jack's expression. "What? That's *not* the reason?"

Jack moved his head in a figure eight like he was trying to shake the truth out of his skull. "I'm not saying a word. The past is the past, we all make mistakes, er, right? Henry's a good egg, that one…"

Rose's faculties were fully numbed; she was having trouble processing Jack's words. His mouth moved, shaping words, his eyebrows rising and falling, but nothing made sense. She kept telling herself to remember his words that she would sort through them later because something was not right.

"But I'll see what I can do for Henry," Jack said. "The rest of it? Well, come on, everyday is foggy around here. So what it's lasted all day and into the night this week? Makes it more Halloweeny. You can't buy that kind of atmosphere. Hell, if it's like this on Friday we'll have the best Halloween parade in history!" Jack threw back his shot.

Rose's mind wandered as though *it* were schlepping through the fog. What exactly *was* coming out of those mills? If the steel and coatings made in the zinc mill were strong enough to build up the entire country then maybe what the byproducts were made of weren't healthy.

And, what the hell would any of that mean for Henry? Another lie? Could there be more to the story? No, Jack was rambling, and Rose was tipsy, exhausted, blind-sided by the discovery of her first daughter and the pregnancy of her second, by Buzzy, Johnny's attitude. For once Rose pushed a problem off her shoulders instead of taking it on.

"Like you said," Rose said. "The mill put us on the map. It's a trade-off. But if one person dies, I'm gonna bang on doors with Bonaroti. People apparently think I'm a neb-nose anyhow. I mean I tell people how to wipe their asses and scrub their hands, how to save money and hide it from irresponsible husbands, what's wrong with telling people they're being poisoned by the very mill that pays their bills? I'm not saying shut 'er down, but people should be privy to the information."

"I agree with part of that," Jack said, raising his beer.

"The mills allow us to try to save my salary for a home," Rose said and meant it. "A real home—a home with forced air, where soot isn't the first thing I see when I wake or leave the house would be indescribable, don't you think?"

Jack raised his eyebrows at Rose.

"But," she said, "the mills, think of where things were twenty years ago—double, twelve-hour shifts, men dropping like flies at the age of forty. Things have changed; we get a fair shake now. But, the kids. There's so much more to the world than what's here. Somewhere there's cleanliness."

"Ah, the burden of technology and its trappings," Jack said. "Can't have the good without the bad. Would yunz leave your family? As much as I see hints of discontent in our little discussion here tonight, I know yunz are one of us, one with the mill; you understand they wouldn't hurt us; they're our little gift from God. Every material involved in making steel comes right from God's own earth."

Rose lifted her mug of beer into the air. "Gift from God!" Rose wasn't so sure about that, but she was losing her willingness to argue.

Jack joined her in the toast.

"Well, how's this for crazy" he said. "Unk's oldest pal from grade-school—Larry, uh, what's-his-face barreled through town, stopped in here on his way down to the burgh and couldn't stop chirping about your other uncle's money that's hid in yunz guy's house. So, maybe you're closer to that home of yours than you think."

Rose bent over the bar laughing so hard her cheeks hurt. Whatever Jack was drinking to make him so optimistic, she needed more of. She slapped the bar and ordered another bourbon shot. This was the third person who'd mentioned this hidden money to her in a few days. Before that, she'd heard gossip about it, but if there was anything Rose knew, it was every inch of that house and there was nothing hidden there except more dirt than was imaginable.

"Well, if you measured wealth in filth then maybe Larry's right, we're sitting on a goldmine."

Rose could tell her words were melding together like iron meeting heat, but she couldn't stop rambling. She'd never so much as breathed a smidgeon about her former life. She never wanted to, never had to once she'd left the orphanage for Mayview, until now. Out poured her stories of cold oatmeal breakfasts, meat sandwiches made from what fell onto the floor first and often, nothing but bread for dinner.

Jack's jaw went slack, his eyes bright with interest in Rose's story. "That's a tale if I ever heard one. Must love having all that family around, now. Dinner on the table every night. Hang up the nursing bag and enjoy your family."

"Nahhhh," Rose's words lost their life, and fell flat against the bar she couldn't quit staring at. "I'd die. Without nursing. It's who I am. Hen doesn't need me. The kids don't. Nursing? There's always some helpless schlep who needs an ass-wiping lesson or nine."

Jack looked into his beer. "Henry's one lucky fella to have someone who carries her weight and then some, but youthful and lovely and smart and lovely."

Rose felt the right side of her mouth pull into a half-smile. She was enjoying the conversation that felt more like commiseration. There was comfort in the fact neither would remember what they'd said. And sitting there with him, she felt a flutter of attraction.

She was too drunk to move, for good and for bad she was stuck there. Rose giggled into her beer. The booze swelled her mood and she forgot all that had been bothering her as she spun around on the barstool, feeling like she was on a carnival ride, wishing all but her nursing life would spin away like a top.

* * *

It couldn't be her.

Henry whipped his head around to see, and shook his head. What was Rose still doing there? He ducked behind the coat rack and surveyed the room. He spread a brown wool coat away from a black one that smelled of body odor and peered past the wooden pole that held the whole thing up.

Rose. Her back was to him, then her profile, spinning on the stool. She threw her head back laughing like she didn't have a care in the world, like she was being photographed for Life Magazine or some shit. She leaned over her beer, gulping it while lifting her hand to signal for another. Henry's friend Jack sat with Rose, enraptured, swimming in her hilarity.

Henry squinted through the coats. Rose was not the type to linger and socialize after a call. Buzzy had told Henry over the phone that Rose had been unable to get into the back room and he would be trapped there until she was gone. Not that he could leave, anyhow. The men who were going to break his legs didn't think it was smart to let him wander since Buzzy owed them seven hundred dollars.

Henry nearly stepped forward to spill the whole thing to Rose, to simply tell her the truth and make Buzzy, make all of them just own up to their deceit and start things over. But, Rose had been through too much that day. Did he really need to pile on more trouble? He was chicken-shit, he knew it. Maybe if Dottie hadn't been involved he could come clean, but not then, not there.

Rose laughed out loud, bending forward, nearly into Jack's lap. Her laughter was unladylike and he had loved it from the first time he heard it. When had he heard it last?

Rose straightened and hiccupped, laughing harder. Jack was enjoying her, his hard, barrel-belly quaking. Henry's stomach tightened. Not with fear or dread, but full, black jealousy. Maybe he wouldn't have felt threatened if he hadn't put such mileage between him and Rose. He'd never felt jealous.

The first time Henry met Rose she was drunk. But sweetly so. She knew who Henry was, a pitcher for the Pirates, but unlike most women—those who were awed by him—Rose was charmed, not enamored. She regaled his teammates with tales of nursing, and for the first time, the fellas weren't telling their stories of baseball glory. This chestnut-haired, long-legged, intelligent woman mesmerized them. She was an equal. And she knew it. A woman like that was the kind of woman Henry could marry.

He glanced at his watch. He needed to get to Buzzy before he was dismembered. He'd have to deal later with his envy over watching Jack share such a delightful time with Rose. He'd just have to go into the storage room through the back of the bar instead of through the front.

Henry turned and exited the bar, his breathing labored by the air. He moved slowly along the sidewalk, inching along the wall to get to the back of the building, remembering his first night with Rose—the night they married, and had sex for the first time. There was no coy, shyness on Rose's part, no "help me through this, I've never done it," act. And, when it was over, she left. Had a sandwich in the kitchen. Not with a pout and shame splashed across her face or weighing on her posture. She just had a bite then went to work.

Leaving Henry, utterly, somehow sadly in love. Rose was not a woman who thought she drew her first breath upon the arrival of her prince. No, this woman did not need anyone but herself and for Henry that was as intoxicating as a woman could be.

Henry did not have time to reminisce. Twenty years had brought problems and right then, his problem was Buzzy. Henry reached the back room door and pounded until a large man, his bloated fingers clutching a baseball, let Henry in. Henry watched as the man lobbed the ball into the air, spinning it, its autographs melting into a blur as he did.

Henry shook his head. In the cramped room of stale booze and broken souls, Henry saw once and for all, that his brother would sell anything for gambling, even the baseball Henry had gotten signed by every one of his Pittsburgh Pirate teammates. Even that.

* * *

On the way home, Henry had run into Johnny's friends. They had already dropped Johnny home because he was too drunk to play in the band that night. They'd said that instead of dropping the booze off to the scout, Johnny had drunk half of it himself. Like true friends would, the boys made sure the scout would come to dinner after the game on Saturday, but Henry wasn't sure how they'd hide the fact Johnny never delivered the expensive booze as Rose had ordered him to do.

Now even in the safety of his own house, he felt small as if he were some helpless kid. And his thought to come clean, disintegrated at the sight of Rose kneeling in prayer in their bedroom. They'd both had enough for one day. Normally he'd coax Rose out of her prayers and into bed, but that night, he just needed to be near her.

He sighed. He wished he'd had her faith. Not that he didn't believe in God, he just couldn't stomach the rigmarole of organizing the great being who gave and took life from all into a series of behaviors and chants and expectations that no one honestly ever upheld.

Still, he thought some of her religious behaviors might seep into his skin and save them both. He knelt beside her and put his elbows on the bed like hers, hands clasped, eyes closed, searching for a prayer he might recite.

He felt Rose move and when he opened his eyes and turned she was already sliding her arms around his neck, straddling him, covering him with kisses as desperate as he felt.

He grabbed her ass and pulled her into him with a clean jerk. Her head fell to the side; she smiled without opening her eyes, and pressed her pelvis into him. He dove into her neck and worked down her cleavage with his lips, his fingers working the buttons of her dress. He pushed the neckline of her dress over her shoulders and ran his hands around her back, unhooking her bra in one movement.

She wiggled out of the bra and leaned back on her hands, as if she were sunbathing. He grabbed at her, wanting every bit of her in his mouth. With one arm around her waist he lifted her off his lap, to the floor, him between her legs. He stopped kissing her long enough to unbutton the rest of her dress to the hips and pulled the whole thing over her lifted ass. He tossed the dress aside and ran his fingers down her lips as he pushed against her. She nipped his forefinger, and he pulled her underpants off.

"What do you want, Rose?"

"You, inside me."

"Nothing else?"

She shook her head and pulled him down by the shirt, kissing him so hard his bottom lip began to swell. He kept his weight off her body while she worked his belt off, his jeans, then his boxers. She grabbed him around his penis and he thought he might come right on her.

She moved her hand around his balls and back up his shaft before wrapping her legs around his waist, pulling him into her. She ran her hands over his back, latching on like he couldn't get inside far enough to fill up whatever it was she was missing.

He rolled onto his back. She perched on him, moving slowly, her hair dropped over one shoulder and their gazes connected. In that moment, Henry saw kindness, relief, and love, in Rose's face. If not for that, he might wonder if she even liked him.

Henry watched Rose come on top of him. Her pink face relaxed, and she appeared twenty years younger, the way she had the first time he met her, the day she made him love her, feeling like it was the first time he figured out a body could feel that way.

He got up on his elbows and took Rose's face in his hands, kissed her. He tasted salt on his lips. Was she crying?

He laid back down, Rose on top and she squeezed him harder, as though their connection was keeping her alive. And, they fell asleep like that. Neither one bothered to clean up. Neither one bothered to even move.

Chapter 11

Rose sat up in bed and reached across expecting to feel Henry's vacated spot. But her hand whacked warm flesh. She flopped back onto the pillow and flung her arm across her forehead as she tried to piece together the events of the last few days.

Not only wasn't Henry on the night shift, but he had no shift to work at all. She swung her feet off the bed and sat on the edge wiggling her toes. She hoped the movement might jar her empty memory and get her blood working its way back through her body. She looked toward the mirror on the wall and patted her matted hair. Her pale, sunken face disapproved of the night before.

Drunk as a skunk came to mind as she recalled the previous night, but not many details. Mostly she was struck by a heavy sense of regret. Henry stirred and rolled toward her, rubbed her lower back, massaging her tailbone. The spot that always seemed to ache.

"John came in early this morning. You were dead asleep," Henry grumbled. "Said he did speak to the Notre Dame scout."

Rose felt the weight on the bed shift and heard Henry flick open his Zippo lighter, inhaling fresh smoke. She glanced at him, remembering Johnny had gone to drop off some booze for the scout as a little "welcome to Donora," gesture.

He drew on the cigarette with one hand; his other hand cradled a yellow piece of paper, his poetry no doubt.

Rose tossed the clock onto the bed. "What's with this damn *John* business? His name is Johnny, end of story." She strained to hear the morning noises but didn't hear much. She was normally the conductor of such morning noises, but the smell of coffee was clear and present.

"Ahh, the boy's growing up is all," said Henry. "Call him John once or twice and it will be over."

"What was his answer? He's coming?"

Henry pulled Rose onto her back and looked down into her eyes. "The scout?" he said. "Of course."

Rose did not have time for fooling around, hugging or anything of the sort. She squirmed away and went to her washbasin. The water was polluted, tinged grey from multiple uses and made her pause before dousing her rag in it.

"So Johnny's coming around, eh? I knew he would. He's a good boy, did what I said, everyone's happy."

Henry looked away.

Rose shrugged, took her Camay bar and headed to the bathroom annoyed that no little night-time fairy entered her room and changed the water in her wash basin. Or a maid, a girl as Mrs. Sebastian had called her. Rose had been so worried that her first baby might have been raised in squalor by some childless woman who wanted slave labor—a little girl to do what she didn't feel like. Rose should be grateful Theresa grew up wealthy. Yet, something was wrong with the picture of Theresa's life. Something didn't fit.

In the bathroom she smacked the roof of her mouth again with her tongue, then threw water right from the faucet into her mouth. She lathered and scrubbed herself with her Camay beauty bar, and a hangover induced queasiness swept over her. She covered her mouth and examined herself in the mirror, her graying skin, and swallowed her nausea. She noticed a black speck under her forefinger nail and once the sickness died back she grabbed the Camay again.

Rose dug her nail into the Camay and moved it over the surface of the soft cake, trying to dislodge the dirt particle. As she worked the soap into her nails, Rose couldn't help her mind from wandering down different paths, to the clinic's funding, to Henry, Magdalena, Buzzy, Sara Clara, that damned to hell Dottie. All of them fought for Rose's attention, but it was Theresa she couldn't push away. If she could just read her file and see her again she would know the truth and she would know what to do next. She was Theresa's nurse after all. And as a nurse, Rose could do anything.

* * *

In the bedroom, Henry shuffled around, pulling a clean, collared shirt and casual slacks from his dresser. Rose reached behind her to hook her bra; feeling like that simple movement was too much activity after the night before. How much did she drink? She was no lightweight. She tried to recall the night's events.

Rose froze, hands still behind her.

The bar. Jack Dunley. Buzzy. Mr. Sebastian.

It all swarmed back.

She dropped her hands and covered her mouth. She couldn't put it all together, but she felt like she'd done something wrong. Had she?

"Hen, I saw Mr. Sebastian and he seemed to imply you didn't get fired for sticking up for the colored fella, that it had something to do with this fog? And then Jack Dunley, now that I'm thinking about it, he seemed to think it had more to do with Dottie...the day your foot was injured."

Henry buttoned his shirt, avoiding her.

Rose sat on the bed with her stockings and garters. She would wear her robe until it was time to put on her

219

uniform. Rose wasn't sure she wanted Henry to clarify what any of that meant. Maybe she should let it go. Be one of those women who just did enough in life to get by. But she couldn't let that happen…she couldn't keep from questioning.

"How the hell does Dottie's name keep popping into every damn conversation I have lately? The Sebastians, Doc Bonaroti, too. She doesn't know about Mag—" She stopped smoothing one stocking just before she was to lock it into place, remembering Dottie had been at the bar with Buzzy and his crew.

Henry combed his hair, parting it in the mirror. Though he didn't make eye contact with Rose she saw it in his reflection, the surprise in his eyes, the surrender.

"I didn't think I'd have to tell you why exactly I got fired," he said. "I thought I'd be back at work. Stupid in light of things."

"What the hell are you talking about? Well, which is it? Is something going on with you and Dottie or Dottie and your brother or are you just on a mission to save the less fortunate souls of Donora?"

Henry laid the comb on the dresser and sat beside her. She spilled sideways into his shoulder and then straightened, tugging the second stocking on and making a run with a jagged nail. She nearly burst into tears at the sight of the tear. She didn't even know the truth, but she didn't have to. All she knew was Henry had kept yet another thing from her and that was all that mattered.

She rubbed her temples, listening to Henry's rendition. She couldn't look at him, but she felt the bed rise when he stood. He paced as he told his story of his breakdown at work. Rose kneaded the bridge of her nose and peeked through her fingers at Henry, his hands moving for emphasis as he explained that he had lost his mind. That he had been feeling sorry for himself, with the kids headed off to college the next year, remembering all the promise his life held as a baseball player and college bound kid.

"And then, there was the colored fella standing there, being shit on by some fucking hunky and I had just met with Bonaroti and he'd filled my melon with all that bull about the impurities coming from the mills."

Rose straightened and wrapped her arms around her waist squeezing her bony midsection. Henry's face was alive as she hadn't seen it in twenty years.

Henry knelt in front of Rose, massaging her knees. "And I just went nuts. I scaled the crane like a fucking monkey, jumping around, screaming about all this injustice in the world, these big things like poison in the air and the fact the colored man was treated like vermin and really, inside all I was doing was yelling about the fact that I, the guy with all the promise, finished things up with nothing even close to his potential...then, getting down, I stepped in the wrong spot at the wrong time and some slag splashed out, onto my heel..."

Rose ran her hand through Henry's hair then patted his shoulder. She knew what Henry meant, but it was no excuse to act such a fool that you get fired. Rose wanted to tell him to toughen up because there was no room for this horseshit in their lives. Wouldn't she just love to do the same, go crazy for all the injustice in the world?

"And Dottie?"

Henry turned away and stood.

"Hen? What does any of what you just said have to do with neb-nose Dottie? Your brother was in that bar playing cards last night, with Dottie, looking over his shoulder." Rose felt her insides shifting around, as though her body knew something her mind didn't want to admit.

He sighed and sat on the bed, his back to Rose. "Nothing to worry about. Same old stuff that always has you upset with Dottie. Nothing that means anything. And Buzz left the bar. I'm sure he was gone before you were even done with your call to Skinny. It's not like you sat there all night drinking or something."

Rose flinched and stole a glance at Henry. Had someone called him and told him she was boozing it up with another man? He sure was friendly the night before and no one would have called that morning, so, he couldn't know how she'd been drinking. Even if he did, it wasn't as though she'd done anything wrong, even if she felt like she had, even if she couldn't really remember.

Rose attached the final latch from garter to stocking and dug her fingers into Henry's arm. "Dottie doesn't know anything about Magdalena, does she? She's been around an awful lot lately and I don't like her weaseling into our lives, I don't like her knowing things that aren't hers to know."

Henry held Rose's gaze. "You should worry more about drinking too much while making calls than what Dottie's up to, don't you think?"

Rose released Henry's arm and smoothed his shirt where she'd been gripping him. She nodded and as she got to the door she thought she heard Henry sigh. The kind of sigh a person let go when he realized he'd just gotten out of a mess by the skin of his teeth. So she drank too much the night before. She deserved a little drink now and then. She stopped there.

"I believe you Hen. I do." She had to. If she couldn't trust Henry, even after he kept a secret with Magdalena, whom could she trust? Rose glanced over her shoulder, catching the sight of Henry buckled over, head in hands. Was his posture that of a man who'd told a lie and another and at least a third in the hopes of making the first go away? No, it was man who needed to find a job and that would best be done without Rose coaching him all the way. She would trust Henry and focus on her responsibilities. Someone had to keep things right. And, that would have to be Rose.

* * *

Rose drummed her fingers on her forehead, giving herself a pep talk. A little headache never hurt anyone. She'd grown accustomed to Leo being with her. That day, she'd come to appreciate the mental diversion Leo afforded, his presence gently leading her from the life she could no longer control to nursing, where she seemed to be master of her universe.

She stalked into the yard then stopped, struck by the darkness, and checked her watch for the time. Was she earlier than she thought? The fog was heavy and she had to hold her wrist close to her face. She tilted it to catch a sliver of light and read the time. She was not late for work at all.

Now this *was* unusual fog. Rose coughed and snatched at the air, trying to capture a chunk of it, as though that were possible. And yet, in a way it was. She could taste the metals in her mouth, the grainy remnants of the mills. She coughed again, stuck her head inside the door, yelling to Unk and everyone who was listening that Unk should not go out that day. If she could feel the heaviness of the fog, if it could make her sputter, then it was no time for someone with health issues to gallivant around Donora.

"Ellooooooooo!" Mrs. Tucharoni's Italy-infused voice carried through the fog to Rose.

The woman must have guessed Rose came out of the house when she opened the door and a bright enough light pushed into the yard through the fog. Rose stepped quietly, hoping to disappear into the blackness without having to talk to the woman who birthed the boy who'd impregnated Rose's daughter.

But, as though Mrs. Tucharoni had headlights for eyes, she cut Rose off in the yard, waddling faster than Rose would have thought she could.

"Have to go, Mrs. Tucharoni. See you later," Rose said, and heard a string of Italian words tossed at her back as she strode away.

Too much to do. First she had to stop at the Saltz home to work on Joey's polio-stricken legs. Rose's stomach clenched at the multi-layered nursing tasks required. Henry's words came back to her—she was compassionate with her patients. She was, but she kept her distance. She had to if she wanted to continuously traipse through the guts of her neighbors' broken down lives. She returned to where Mrs. Tucharoni was standing and pointed at a sheet hanging from the clothesline.

"You don't mind if I borrow one of these, right?"

Mrs. Tucharoni raised her chin toward the sheet in agreement then grabbed Rose's arm as she reached for the sheet. Rose turned; the scent of lemon wafted from the woman's freshly washed hair.

"Sara Clara." Mrs. Tucharoni said slowly. "She have shower? Shower for Magdalena. For baby. I want to say—"

"Later," Rose knew how rude she was being, but hearing that yet another decision had been made for her, that another person was planning something for Rose's daughter without her permission, that people were talking about this as though perfectly normal, was too much for her to take. Didn't any of these people realize that each reference to this pregnancy was a knife in her spine? It was a blatant reminder that she had not been Magdalena's confidante at any stage leading up to and past her discovery her daughter was pregnant. Control of her life was an illusion.

Rose stomped away. She didn't have time for musing about things she could not change so she wrapped herself in a plan of action for her patient, Joey Saltz. It was where Rose wanted to live forever, where no one caused her trouble that she couldn't handle.

Mrs. Tucharoni called again and Rose froze. The woman couldn't see Rose, but her voice, what she had said, what was behind the words, suddenly hit Rose. She had not become the mother she thought she would. But she couldn't help it. She had no choice in the matter. She would never be like Mrs. Tucharoni, the mother who could look at a pregnant teen and think it was a good thing. Rose looked back into the fog and though she couldn't see through it, she could clearly see her life.

Work had saved her once and it would again. Rose realized she couldn't depend on Henry, or his family, or her children. She straightened her shoulders, and headed for Joey Saltz's; through fog so dark she couldn't see the curb of the sidewalk, the street lamps illuminating only an arms-length of space below them. She hadn't been the kind of mother she wanted to be. Obviously, her family thought she fell short, keeping secrets from her, and with that realization, she turned her feet, her mind, toward work.

* * *

Rose battered away on the Saltz's door. They never could hear a damn thing in that house. Finally, Rose pushed open the door and stepped inside. Onions, body odor, and a jarring farm stench greeted her. What the hell? Rose wrinkled her nose and breathed through her mouth as she walked past the broom closet. She stopped, went back and pulled open the door.

Fifty yellow chicks tumbled out the door, peeping, waddling, crapping all over each other. Rose covered her mouth.

On cue Mrs. Saltz stepped out of her bedroom and into the hall. Her teary onslaught began, arms draped around Rose's neck. Rose recoiled, holding her breath to avoid the dirty body smell.

Rose told Mrs. Saltz she couldn't keep peeps in the house, that it wasn't sanitary and her other children could still be at risk for polio even if it was almost November. Mrs. Saltz whimpered and said she thought it would help their family if they could furnish their own eggs.

Rose stepped over peeps, shoving them aside with her foot. Just because there was some data that pointed away from filth ushering polio into the body, Rose wasn't taking chances with letting patients house animals as though they were battening down on Noah's Arc. But, she needed to tend to the boy. If she stopped to get rid of the peeps, she'd never get anything done so she would have to trust Mrs. Saltz to do her part.

Rose lumbered past Mrs. Saltz, toward Joey's room. "Tell me how Joey is, and then get those peeps outside or in the cellar. Anywhere but in here."

"Joey. He's in pain, in such pain. He can not breathe."

Rose had mentioned Warm Springs, Georgia, where they could send Joey to ease his pain. It was much more effective to work his limbs in combination with the warm spring therapy, but it was expensive. Rose had enough of Mr. Saltz putting his own drinking ahead of his son. After seeing him last night at the Merry-Go-Round, Rose was sure what didn't go to drink, went down the shitter at the card game. Right along with Buzzy. Two dumb-asses, both of them on the losing end of poker more often than not.

"Listen," Rose said in a whisper. "I saw your husband last night, gambling. He must have money. If we're one day away from payday and he has enough to enter a game, then he's holding out on you. You could probably pay for—"

Mrs. Saltz grabbed Rose's arm, pulled her closer and whispered, her German accent camouflaging her words even more when she spoke quietly. Rose held her breath and leaned down.

"I've managed," Mrs. Saltz said, "to push away almost enough money to send Joey to warm spring. Before he go, I think we need iron lung. This air is thick, filled with garbage. The general manager mill man say he have nothing to say about air, but I know. I only *sound* stupid." Mrs. Saltz interjected German words when she couldn't find the right English ones.

Rose would have pulled away and dismissed her words as nonsense, but something made her listen. Had this broken, sorrowful, weepy woman actually managed such a feat as hiding money from her husband—enough to send her son to Warm Springs? Rose felt reprimanded. Not that the woman could have known that Rose's brother-in-law drained their savings repeatedly. But still, Rose always dutifully handed over most of her money to Auntie Anna. Henry had said that was what family did, when they first moved in with them fifteen years ago. Eager to be part of the big Pavlesic family, Rose had obliged.

Rose patted the woman on the shoulder. "That's something, saving that money. Really, that's really...stunning."

"Your Unk teach me how to save. Tell me where to hide in my house. Plain sight, he say."

Could it be possible that Mrs. Saltz would know where the old man had hidden his rumored money? If there really was such a thing. "Where does Unk say you should hide it?"

A croupy cough and groaning came from behind the closed door of Mrs. Saltz's bedroom. She put her finger to her lips ending the discussion and resumed her wails, disappearing into the kitchen.

Rose reached for Joey's doorknob, but didn't turn it. She wondered if Mrs. Saltz's crying was some sort of mechanism to maintain the balance or imbalance in her life. Rose heard Mr. Saltz grumbling behind the other bedroom door and it made sense. If Mrs. Saltz went too long without wailing, he'd suspect perhaps she could function, after all. Rose had trouble believing Mrs. Saltz had managed to hide away enough money for Warm Springs—but if she had, then Rose was even more puzzled. Why would Mrs. Saltz live the way she did?

More grumbling and thrashing came from Mr. Saltz's bedroom. Rose glanced over her shoulder to Mrs. Saltz by her husband's door, her hand poised on the knob. She hobbled over to Rose and waved for Rose to bend forward to whisper in her ear.

"I sorry to be the one," Mrs. Saltz said. "But a nice lady like you should know. I know women like you from Germany. Know a lot, yes. But, how you say it, not what happening right under nose?"

Rose drew back, her face contorted with confusion.

Mrs. Saltz waved Rose back.

"Mr. Pavlesic," she said in a whisper. "He there last night. Merry-Go-Round with men and poker and women. People run at mouth, like the chicks in the closet." She opened and closed her fingers to her thumb. "Chirp-chirp. Chirp. They say you know everything but what *your* husband is up to."

Rose felt her jaw drop, but she couldn't seem to close it.

"I say, *you* the nurse I want in my house. Not hoity-toity mill nurse."

Rose bit the inside of her cheek as panic flew through her. "You mean Dottie? Dottie Shaginaw?"

A clamor came from Mr. Saltz's bedroom followed by groaning. Mrs. Saltz scurried off like a rat from fire. Rose stared at the woman's back as she disappeared into the bedroom. Rose heard Mrs. Saltz's cries behind the door and her husband's angry voice ordering her to get some water, and cursing. The door opened and a teary-eyed Mrs. Saltz came out.

"Wait, Mrs. Saltz. Did your husband say if Buzzy won or lost last night?"

"Lost. But *your* Mr. Pavlesic, he there, he take care of things for his brother. I feel bad for you, for having husband who—"

Glass broke behind the Saltz's bedroom door and Mrs. Saltz cringed then re-entered the bedroom before she could finish her end of the conversation.

Rose wanted to burst into that room, tell him where he could shove his demands, and ask what the hell the missus had been talking about. Could Mrs. Saltz have been confused? Rose had been drunk the night before, but she knew Henry had been with *her*. He'd been home when she arrived, hadn't he? She thought she heard him in the bathroom and then he appeared as she was praying.

She tried to remember the timeline of the night before, once she'd begun drinking, but she couldn't. She would sit down and map it out if she had to, later, but right then she had a job to do. And if she found out Henry was up to any sort of bullshit, why she'd simply toss him in the Mon.

* * *

Rose entered Joey's room and smiled in the direction of his bed. Normally he was looking right at her, happy, alert, ready with a knock-knock joke. The kind of person Rose thought everyone should emulate. The kid had suffered a lot. Rose would take his body, and push and pull it, feeling as though she was ripping him apart and he wouldn't make a sound. Rose took a deep breath and hummed as she popped open her bag.

She crept over to his bed and sat beside him. He was sleeping, his breath choppy and more shallow than usual. She wiggled his shoulder.

"Hi," she said.

He opened his eyes and pushed himself up, his tendons in his neck stretching. He grimaced from the pain, but his cracked lips gave way to a smile.

Rose allowed him to struggle, knowing how important it was that Joey control his life. He fell back on his pillow. She fussed with the stethoscope. *Hail Mary full of grace...Hail Mary, Hail Mary...*her lips repeated the well-worn prayer, but her mind prayed something else—thanks that her children had never, ever suffered like Joey. She reminded herself that she'd have to add this to her list of sins—thanking God that her children were healthy.

A loud meow startled Rose and she spun around, bouncing the bed, making Joey suck back air.

A cat sprung onto Rose's back. She threw her shoulders back, biting her lip to keep from screaming and scaring Joey. The hairball would not let go. It dug his claws in and her skin stung. She flailed her arms, spinning around the room until she stumbled backward, landing on Joey's bed, the cat finally releasing Rose.

Rose sprang up and spun around, hands covering her mouth, not breathing, mortified that she'd just flung herself onto the bed of a pained, sick child.

But when she finally focused she saw Joey had pushed to sitting and was petting the cat, mewing at it as it mewed back. His breath was still labored, his complexion grey, but his demeanor, calm.

If this was any other person, she would have ripped the mangy cat from the patient's grip. But she let Joey nuzzle it, the purring turning her stomach, but lighting Joey's face like Christmas at the Carnegie's.

He explained that the cat wasn't his. "But he likes me. And my mum. He sits on her all day long."

Rose nodded. She knew who owned the cat, the man who slept under the Saltz's porch, behind the loose lattice. No one seemed to know he was there. Mr. Saltz would have charged him a boarder's fee no doubt. No, like Rose apparently not knowing what her husband was up to, the Saltz's did not know who lurked under their very house.

"I can't breathe, Nurse Pavlesic."

Rose jumped at the sound of Joey's voice. She cocked her head and watched him breathe. She pushed him gently backward onto the pillows, reaching around the feline.

The cat hissed as Rose pulled one of Joey's hands free. "Let's take a look, right here." Joey's forefinger scratched at the cat's neck, appearing and disappearing below the fur.

He released the cat and it leapt away.

Rose turned Joey's wrist over to take his pulse.

"Nurse?" Joey said through his sandpapery voice.

"Just breathe, Joey, just breathe."

Rose studied his wrist and began recounting his pulse.

"I watch out that there window. I see little Leo hopping about, heading to work with you, playing jacks and hopscotch and tag..."

Rose nodded and tried to focus on his pulse.

"You think I'll hop and run and play tag again some day, Nurse?" Joey's eyes watered with his strained words.

"Yes, you will." Rose's voice cracked. She wondered how she could tell this boy such a lie. It wasn't in her nature to sugarcoat anything. "Anything's possible, Joey. You just need to believe. And breathe. Just breathe."

He turned toward the window and gazed out, as though he could see beyond the fog that shrouded his normal view of their street. Rose counted his pulse yet again. After a few tries she focused and finally completed the task.

"You lost count a-gainnnnn," Joey said.

"What?"

"You lose count every time you take my pulse. You start over every time at least twice."

"Well with you chattering like you do...working around that damn *cat*, kiddo that's no surprise. Now stuff it in your sock."

"Aren't you going to trace it?"

"What?"

"My wrist. You always rub my wrist with your thumb before you lay your fingers there. I love that. It tickles."

Rose stared at Joey's wrist. She realized right then that she'd spent her entire nursing lifetime looking at people's wrists, studying the way blue veins and red capillaries sprawled across one person's and shot down another's, the way coloring might be darker or lighter in some spots, looking for her daughter, hoping someday that Florida-shaped marking would somehow appear on someone's wrist, revealing the little girl she'd given away.

"I didn't realize I did that," Rose said.

She finally focused long enough to get an accurate count.

"It's okay," Joey said.

"Hmm?"

"You losing count. I like that touch. Yer sort of mean n'at, always yelling at this person and that, but underneath it all you're a kind person. I can feel it in yer fingers when you're not yanking my limbs all to whatnot. Tell me again 'bout Sister Kenny who devised this torture. Please, your story makes me laugh."

Rose smiled then once out of Joey's sightline the grin fell away. She put her hands under his head, pulling his neck straight. The pain she planned to inflict would help him maintain a minimal level of health, but Rose believed it was worth it.

She took a deep breath, letting the exhaled air wash away her emotions, so she would be able to do her job, inflicting pain, and then come back and do it again. She couldn't let sympathy mix in her heart, let herself feel what he did. That wouldn't help Joey. She needed to be a nurse first.

She removed his sock and a rancid odor of filth smacked her. It blended with her queasy stomach and she swallowed her nausea. She grabbed the sole of his foot with one hand and pushed down on his quad with the other, bringing forth the first scream she'd ever heard Joey let out. She thought, she'd have to report his decline in health and wondered if he would have to be hospitalized; no medical facility in their right mind would attempt to place an iron lung in a rat-trap like the Saltz's.

Rose finished Joey's exercises, washed him down, dressed him in the cleanest pajamas she could find before giving him a nip of bourbon for the pain she'd caused and then pulled Mrs. Tucharoni's clean sheet from her bag and tucked it around Joey's body. Rose left the Saltz's crooked home to a chorus of screams and thuds of furniture and other items hitting the walls.

She felt an urge to go to Henry and not only thank him for the wonderful life he'd given her, but also to confess to him about her first baby, about her virginity that didn't exist when they married. But then, really, her current state of mind was best soothed by her work and a proper Church confession.

Chapter 12

Like a stopped up bowel system, the typical five minute jaunt to the church—was now stops and starts, people straining through sidewalks, pushing into bustling housewives and hurried businessmen, jostling others so often that people quit apologizing and chattering about the binding fog. They simply kept going toward their destination. This fog was not normal. Nothing was. But Rose kept making her way through the thick fog. She'd never seen it this oppressive, so debilitating. It was definitely all wrong, and Rose would meet with Bonaroti about it. This time she would listen. There must be something more she could do.

Rose reached the church, her chest tight from the stinging air. Even she, someone in perfect health, was feeling the effects of the gritty smog. She ran her tongue around her mouth and spit into the grass beside the steps. It was too dark for Rose to see if her mucus was black or clear. Just the fact she had to spit told her everything she needed to know. Maybe that day was the one that brought all her sins down around her head. Maybe God had finally decided to punish her. And he was so repulsed by her he'd punish the entire town.

Inside the church, Rose dipped her hand in the holy water font, crossed herself and noticed Father Tom sitting in the pew across from it. She hoped that meant Father Slavin was in the confessional. She headed down the aisle and saw the confessional was free.

Father Tom sat with one foot over his knee, toying with his shoelace. "So, what brings you here a mere twenty-four hours after your last confession and twelve or whatever it was since that one?"

"It's actually twenty-six hours." Rose straightened and gripped her bag handles tight, her nails digging into her palms. "*Normally*, when the confessional is empty I'd find Father Slavin in the sanctuary, dusting, polishing silver, refilling the candles, *dusting*."

Father Tom narrowed his eyes at Rose and raised his shoulders. He didn't snap back as she expected, and for a moment she stopped judging, long enough to look into the man's eyes.

"Well," Father Tom said, "I dunno much about what the general public thinks of me, but I do remember Father Slavin telling parishioners he introduced me to that I was wise. He actually used that word. As if he knew I'd need that sort of positioning when *you* came in." He clasped his hands together and pointed his forefingers at Rose as though they were a barrel of a gun. "So, have at it."

"Here?"

"God can hear us just the same right here."

Rose looked around at the empty church, and felt off-kilter. She thought she should tear out of church and offer her sins directly to God instead of through the priest. But something in Father Tom's kind face softened her, made her shuffle into the pew behind him.

She covered her eyes and rested her elbow on the back of the pew in front of her.

She started in a strained whisper. "Bless me oh Lord for I have sinned. It's been roughly twenty-six hours since my last confession. One, I drank like a steel man on payday last night. I came dangerously close to flirting. Well, I did flirt, and I liked it. Four through 100, I swore using various and sundry words including the Lord's name in vain. Atrocious thoughts for various people in my life along with my wishing certain ones might drop dead found their way into my head. Just popped in there like the devil himself."

Father Tom leaned back turning his ear directly toward Rose as though he might have missed a few words.

Rose was picking up speed. "I have deep frustration toward my husband. The frustration is *tinged* at the very least with pure hatred. He's one of the smartest men I know. But, not smart in practical ways and that gets in the way of real life. He's all up in his head," Rose wheeled her hand in a circle at the wrist, "And he's keeping secrets. That's where the hate lives. The other 'I'm too busy thinking bullshit,' just pisses me off. He's commiserating with people who cause me so much trouble and that's what makes me want to vomit. And then there's my daughter Magdalena."

Rose stopped talking and she realized all the other stuff she blurted out was just a dam holding back her real dismay. She peeked at the priest through her fingers. She didn't know why, but she trusted the man. Maybe because he would soon be gone when Slavin returned. She could unburden herself to someone who would never sit at her dinner table.

"Magdalena's pregnant. She's seventeen and pregnant. And I hate her for it. How could she do that?" Rose ground her teeth so hard they hurt.

Father Tom's face conveyed confused interest, like a scientist tackling a theoretical quandary.

Rose tightened her whisper. "I taught her and taught her and taught her. And she had the nerve to say all she wanted was to be held or loved or some shit as though her father and I hadn't done just that. I grew up in an orphanage. I know what 'needs to be held' means and that daughter of mine does not know what she was talking about. And, she didn't listen. She went about her life without a thought for me. I mean, doesn't she know the weight of her sins? That now *I* have to bear some of the sin? My soul already has a reservation at the inn in hell and I'm full up to my chin with my own misdeeds...Slut."

"You didn't call her that, did you?"

Rose shook her head slowly. "But I said the word. She thinks I did."

"Are you confessing or discussing, Rose?" Father Tom cut her off.

Rose dropped her hand from her eyes and met Father Tom's gaze.

"I want to offer my thoughts on your crises," he said, and exhaled. "But yesterday you said you didn't need that, only a penance and I don't want to throw out penance willy-nilly, so I'd like you to clarify what exactly you are confessing. Or discussing. I'm fine with that, too."

Rose bit her lip and ran her fingers into the pew's carvings that snaked and circled and ran down its back.

Rose was about to tell him where to shove it when it came to her. *This* was what Henry had been talking about. The thought hit her hard. She did hoard her pain. She did not share who she was. And she wanted to discuss this with Father Tom. For the first time in her life, she didn't move right over whatever problem there was in front of her—how could she possibly fix all that had gone wrong by saying a few Hail Marys? Maybe she could let it all out, finally. For the first time, she wanted to release all her sins and still have someone to tell her she wasn't going to rot in hell.

Sister John Ann was the one who had brought Rose so fully back to the church. In deed anyway. The woman had helped her through Bennett's leaving, and nursing school, convincing Rose that some of her failing was due to her lackadaisical spiritual life. If Rose just went back to the church, really committed to its structure and beliefs, she would live a much happier, richer, safer life. And she had. She had done everything Sister John Ann had asked, for nearly twenty years.

Father Tom tapped Rose's hand.

She straightened at Father Tom's recognition of her still sitting there, struck mute. "Oh. Yes. Yes. Um. Go on. Please."

"Six Rosaries."

"Six Rosaries?" What happened to the discussion? She thought he would take the lead. What happened to the warmth she'd just felt emanating from him, telling her she could trust him? Why couldn't he sense what she wanted?

"Six," he said.

Rose squeezed her eyes shut and gripped her bag. She wanted to scream. She needed to know the world isn't falling into a black hole, that Donora wasn't being swallowed up by fog, that her family wasn't slipping into the banks of hell. *Please.*

Rose heard Father Tom shifting in his seat and she opened her eyes.

His head was bowed and his elbow rested on the back of the pew between them, his hand was raised, palm toward her. She felt comfort from the sight of him like that—open.

He spoke with his eyes shut. "You have been redeemed by God countless times over. At this point, it's you who needs to take responsibility for your life. You're doing the right things. Every little moment doesn't have to be parsed into sins and non-sins. And, I think this—this minute attention to the sinful details of your existence—is very much rooted in something that gives you great shame and pain. Usually, those things are rooted in childhood."

His voice was calm and Rose let it wash over her. "You move a mile-a-minute. I think for you, there would be some benefit in just *being*. Go to the country, take in some nature. It's not good for people to live inside all this noise. It numbs what's important. Nature is God's way of letting us know he is here."

Rose's lips quivered thinking of her endless list of sins. He understood, somehow he did. She fitted her hand into the outline of his, heat from his skin melding with hers as his long fingers topped hers off.

"I've tried to make my whole life a work in redemption," Rose said, her voice rising and carrying into the rafters before she pushed it back into a whisper. "*Can't you see that?* Can't anyone see that? God can't. He brought on this barrage of punishment and either he's an asshole or I haven't been redeemed for shit." Rose crushed her eyes closed. Heat rushed between their hands as though God himself connected them. She could feel his compassion running into his hand to hers. She wanted to tell him everything.

"Sometimes, Rose," Father Tom said, "you just need to pray, not confess or pray *for* something or for your soul or for some specific *thing*. Sometimes you just need to ask for your own private, peace. And finally, let this go. Or tell your husband about it and free yourself. *Just let go of it.* You have been redeemed."

Rose sat with that thought. She waited to be awash in relief, to have her hair blown back by the grace of God. She remained, open to the hard evidence she'd been redeemed, the feeling of purity that she always experienced to some degree after confessing her sins. She needed to tell everything, to bleed the infection in her soul before it could be healed, but she couldn't get the words out.

Peace didn't emerge or settle in her heart. Anxiety took over and Rose felt panic shake her lingering hopefulness. She opened her eyes and looked at the Father's calm expression. Rose could not believe his words even though she wanted to.

She would feel the redemption. God didn't work in small, quiet ways. He either ripped the earth open or thrust it back together. God didn't just sprinkle a little quiet grace. Father Tom was wrong and she had wasted her time.

She snatched her hand away from Father Tom's and tore out of the pew without another word. She bolted up the aisle and her attention was drawn to a body in a pew ten rows back. Dottie Shaginaw—statue still, staring into space as though she might not notice a crazed woman racing away from a priest.

Rose's common decency was absent in the face of her dismay at the state of her soul.

"Dottie Shaginaw. I bet you have a slew of sins to purge. So, get on with it."

Dottie turned to Rose, her gaze following Rose down the aisle.

Rose looked back over her shoulder while still moving toward the exit. She watched Dottie stand, straighten her shoulders and arrange her nurse's hat.

That woman had much to confess and Rose was sure some of it, at least, had to do with Rose's family. Rose did not like her own harum-scarum demeanor, her loss of control and decorum, and did not appreciate Dottie of all people witnessing it.

For the first time in Rose's life the church was more prickly heat than soothing ointment. The air was humid and suffocating and she wondered if hell was, instead of scorching flames, a slow roasting blister.

Rose left the church, and gave a sidelong glance at the holy water and knew without a doubt she wasn't coming back.

* * *

Rose entered the doctor's office and was greeted by the receptionist, Cathy. She didn't look up when she informed Rose that Bonaroti had been called out to care for six men. "Doc's convinced it's the mills. I don't know if he's right but this fog hasn't lifted for three days. I'm starting to think he's onto something."

Rose was starting to agree with Bonaroti, too.

"He wants you to see Theresa Sebastian, first, then he'll meet you back here. He wants to have a meeting with council and the board of health."

"I don't understand."

"To shut the mills down until this smog lifts."

Rose shook her head at the notion. "No one'll ever agree to that. You shut the mills down and not only do you lose production, but the furnaces are shot. They'll never do it."

Cathy leaned across her desk and waved Rose closer like she was about to let loose a wild secret. "They might have to. Some fellas from the government—I'm talking the Feds here, no joke—are looking into this smog. Say because we sit in this valley, with the river fog, and strange weather, that there's an inversion—a temperature inversion. The heavy air usually on the bottom is on top, like a lid, holding down the smoke from the mills and all those chemicals. Says, the zinc mill's smoke is the worst and it's going to kill us all if we just sit here like—"

"That makes sense. I never, thought...but that's exactly right."

Cathy leaned forward, her eyes bugged out. "The Fed guy. Doc spoke to him on the phone for *two hours* this morning. He said they could take the mills to a dead heat if necessary. The furnaces won't crack if they do that."

"The parade's still on? The game?"

Cathy nodded.

"The folks getting sick aren't outside, right? I mean other than Schmidt the other day. It'll pass. Maybe faulty coal furnaces? It has to pass, it always does." Rose's words were thin in her own ears. Still, she felt it necessary to say them even if she didn't believe them.

"Depends who you ask," Cathy said.

"Right." Rose turned to go into the back room to read Theresa's file.

"Listen Rose," Cathy leaned on her elbows, chin on her intertwined fingers. "I have a suggestion regarding Magdalena. I know a fella. The Doc here might see his way to helping you, but I understand the need fer yunz to keep your business close to the vest n'at. But, there's a fella up in Pittsburgh who could set Magdalena up nice."

Rose shuddered.

"Rose?" Cathy's voice startled Rose. "You look like you came around the corner and smacked into the ghost of Sixth Street gate. Or like you were drinking. I wouldn't tell anyone if you decided to have the pregnancy handled like we discussed. Magdalena could go on with her life, you could go on with yours and everything would go back to normal. I mean, it's not like it would be a bad life if she married. God knows married life's been good for me. And well, your Henry is a catch. I'm babbling. But, it just seems like yunz guys have such grand plans for the kids and you're sort of charmed n'at. I'd hate to see her just, well...get married."

Rose shoved her hands in her coat pockets to hide the way they shook. Henry was a good man. He had understood Rose—seemed to know that a single caress on the shoulder or glance across the table with a reassuring wink was what she needed at a given time.

With those small gestures, Rose felt as though he had given her permission to omit information about herself, that he somehow knew she'd had layers of acts stacked up inside her like coal seams. He'd seen no reason to mine those areas of her past, knowing that to pick away at it might risk her very existence just so he could say there was nothing he didn't know about her. Maybe she'd inadvertently given him permission to keep secrets, too.

He was good, that Henry. He allowed her to work. In a real profession, not just some sort of clerk or sales girl. He understood her need to care for others. That she could not survive life using traditional marital happiness measures. Yes, of course, she was happy. There certainly hadn't been time to mope around when things happened that might make her unhappy. No she was not the moping type.

Cathy shrugged and sighed then lit a cigarette as she stood to take Rose into Dr. Bonaroti's office. She waved her hand in the direction of the doctor's desk. "That fat file, the one shaped like the backend of Mugsy Davichek. That's Theresa Sebastian's file."

Cathy patted her hair with the hand that held the cigarette and fumbled for the light switch with the other. "It's chock full of tiny handwriting and illegible stuff n'at. So, if yunz need anything Rose, if you want that fella's number in Pittsburgh you just pick up the phone."

Rose nodded. She was already in Dr. Bonaroti's chair ripping open the file. She started at the back, where she thought she might find information that would allow Rose to shape a version of Theresa's childhood in her mind.

"Natural Mother strong, healthy. Husband is deceased, but no signs of family or anything associated with being a married woman of childbearing age. A young man has visited the mother. Claims to be her brother. We suspect he is the father. Despite clearly nomadic lifestyle, the baby and mother are exceedingly healthy. Mom suffers no ill mental effects of having adopted out her offspring. Baby, exceptionally healthy."

Rose sat back and rubbed her forehead. No ill mental effects? Rose didn't remember the nurses or doctors assessing her in regard to her mental state. What would make them write that, assume that? She'd been so young and naïve that she believed they'd bought her story. Rose read every word in Theresa's file, trying to picture every inch that Theresa had grown—the numbers in black and white, Rose visualized what the quantities would have looked like on the real life baby.

It was only a couple of months before the regular doctor visits began for Theresa. *"Inconsolable." "Bruising." "Weight Loss." "Malnourished." "Mrs. Sebastian indicates that baby has rejected her, that the infant knew she wasn't her mother. Mother admitted to St. Francis for a rest."*

Chills lifted the hairs on Rose's arms. *Theresa knew I gave her away.* Rose wondered if Theresa had her own haunting soul shadow to deal with daily. In the file it was clear, Theresa missed her mother. She knew the difference, she *knew.*

Rose slid a pencil from Dr. Bonaroti's jar and tapped it on the desk blotter. What did this mean? It had been clear to Rose that Theresa was more a distraction to the Sebastians than a daughter. Maybe not Mr. Sebastian, but still, with him being a leading citizen and all, Rose could not imagine he would have the time to spend with Theresa on a normal basis.

Rose read through each page in the file, the pages getting whiter and whiter as she got nearer the top of the pile. A picture was forming in Rose's mind—Theresa's vacillation between being healthy and deathly ill, the idea that her parents didn't want her asthma to be treated in any ongoing way—a girl no one wanted to be troubled by?

In addition to the notes about Theresa's health, there were frequent citations from Mrs. Sebastian's psychiatric doctors, some seeming to characterize her as a very mentally fragile woman and others attributing her visits and "rests" as attempts to garner attention from her husband and others.

There were a few notes regarding Theresa and excessive bruising, some that indicated "hand-shaped," or "roundish in shape," but it never said how they got there—until the final page. It indicated that a doctor in Pittsburgh thought Theresa was inflicting the bruises on her own body. Rose held her breath. Doctors suggested Theresa rest at one of the health resorts in the southwest where the air was clean and dry and free of irritants associated with industrialized cities.

Rose closed the file slowly, trying to hide her anger with purposeful, quiet movements. It was a simple case of inept parenting. If Rose had been Theresa's mother, this file would not exist. She should reveal who she was, and take Theresa away from the zinc mill. Rose felt a pulsing in her head. Was the zinc mill the problem? Or was she just jealous, upset that the people who raised her flesh and blood weren't that good at it.

No, Rose thought, Theresa's problem was Theresa's weak mother and father who, well, hit her perhaps. Rose was sure Theresa didn't inflict her own bodily harm.

Rose straightened and re-straightened the files, squaring them off, turning them and then squaring them off again. She couldn't get up, yet she couldn't sit still. She wished the Sebastians hadn't been so well off. If they were poorer, they would have sought the care of a visiting nurse rather than doctor after doctor. Doctor's notes were never enhanced with descriptive details as nurses' observations would be. But, Rose thought, had the Sebastians been poor, they might not have sought any sort of care at all.

Rose pushed to standing. She drew deep breaths; all of her worried energy about the Pavlesic family was now channeled into action. She would get to Theresa, find a way to remove her from the Sebastian home. Rose could envision the history of interactions between Mr. and Mrs. Sebastian, arguing over what to do with Theresa, suggesting that they made a mistake in adopting her from an unknown woman of no means.

Well, Rose thought, they were selfish assholes, the Sebastians, for Rose had seen Theresa with her own eyes, seen what a lovely woman she'd become and if anything in that file had told Rose about the family, it was that they were the ones who were sick and all that Theresa needed was to be placed back with her true family, her birth mother—Rose.

* * *

Rose bid Cathy goodbye, ignoring her attempts to continue their discussion about Magdalena. Rose stepped into the fog and drew a breath that made her hack into her hand. She coughed violently, knowing she needed to get to her appointment at the Sebastians, fog or not. The air had grown thicker, blacker, coal dust suspended in what would have normally just been grayish fog. Rose tried to wipe it away, but merely displaced it temporarily.

She turned to head down the sidewalk when she realized the fog had hidden the fact that she was standing elbow to elbow beside someone else. She was too distracted to be polite and pushed past the person, plodding past others, doing her best not to knock into anyone else.

Rose covered her mouth as she walked in stops and starts, thinking back to the day she gave Theresa away, the way she clung to Bennett, the scent of his cologne, both comforting and repelling. She repeated Bennett's words of love and marriage; they would have ten children once he finished school.

The words had blanketed her in warmth on a cold night. While a nurse had administered a strong drug when her cramping grew too great, Rose drifted into sleep reassuring herself that she could convince Bennett she could keep their daughter while he finished college, and could handle anything to ensure they all stayed together.

When Rose awoke from the drug-induced sleep, a blurry outline of a man sat at the end of her bed. She thought it was Bennett. Had he been there all along?

Rose was not fully awake, but her body was shaking at the sight of the man. Mr. Reeve, the director of the orphanage came closer and bent over to whisper in her ear. His hand slid up her thigh, resting just below her pubic bone, squeezing her leg, fingers brushing her stitches as he did.

Rose looked to her right and left—the curtains separating her from other postpartum mothers were drawn.

"You thought you could leave the orphanage, Rose? You thought you could confide our secrets in that slick fella, Bennett, did you?"

Rose couldn't speak, but shook her head, eyes focused on Mr. Reeve, his face directly over hers. She would never have told Bennett what Mr. Reeves had been doing to her since she could first form a memory.

"Well, I set Bennett straight. Told him you were a slut, whoring around the orphanage, with everyone from the janitor to the fellas in the kitchen. Everyone but me, Rose. I can keep a secret. You will not leave me. I love you Rose. I told him that earlobe of yours was the mark of the devil, that he shouldn't bother with you anymore."

Rose touched her ear, sobbing quietly. She couldn't believe Reeve was telling the truth, but she remembered the relief on Bennett's face when he stepped into the cab, when she saw him leave the other night.

Don't blame me, Rose, for Bennett's departure. I saw him leaving your room. He was cozy with his daddy's attorney. He was on his way to Harvard. You're not even a flicker of a memory in that big brain of his."

Rose shook her head. Make this man go away. "He's coming back. We promised together. We're not giving the baby away."

"I was afraid you might decide that, Rose. You orphans often do this kind of thing." He shifted on the bed and leaned into Rose. "I told him it wasn't his. And you signed papers. I watched you and Bennett sign them. It's done, over. And he's gone."

That couldn't be right. Bennett would never believe the baby wasn't his. And he had looked her in the eye and promised he would marry her, that they would have more children.

Mr. Reeves lifted the sheets and pulled one of Rose's legs to the side, examining her like she were an animal. Rose held her breath. She knew better than to flinch away and ignite the man's anger.

"You were smart to give that bastard child away, yes, to hide the evidence, but I will not see you go. You are mine. You have been since you came to me, since we were first together."

Rose told herself not to panic, that he couldn't hurt her at the hospital where doctors and nurses were running in and out, where only flimsy fabric formed walls. But as Rose was completing that thought Reeve pushed on top of her. She gasped, squirming. She dug her nails into his arms, trying to wiggle out from under him.

This was her only chance for people outside of the orphanage to know what he was doing to her. She started to scream and he covered her mouth with one hand. Rose was weak from the sedatives, but she managed to get her teeth into his palm. He hesitated at her bold bite. Rose drew a breath then heard a thunk.

Reeve collapsed onto Rose, knocking her wind out as his full weight hit. When he didn't move, Rose shoved him over, moving out from under him. She stood, steadying herself with a metal handrail, trying to figure out what happened.

She stared at his unconscious body then focused on the person coming toward her. Sister John Ann, with a cracked water jug in her hand. Rose hyperventilated trying to stuff back her tears, her shame, the truth. The nun embraced Rose and shushed her, telling her not to fret, that she would help.

Rose didn't know what Sister John Ann understood, exactly, and the nun never forced Rose to tell her what happened. But, she decided right then she would never depend on anyone for anything again.

Sister John Ann seemed to understand that unspoken vow Rose made to herself. She did not let Rose flounder in self-pity or grow weak in bad memories. She kept Rose busy and offered her work: doing chores and learning the discipline that resuscitated Rose's very being.

At Mayview Rose began her informal, though intensive nursing education. Sister John Ann provided the opportunity for Rose to nurture her first flutter of self-respect. With every biology fact and nursing protocol she learned, Rose felt as though a piece of her broken self was fitted into the place it had always belonged. A new vision of who she was and could be was forming and it wasn't long before Rose was prepared for formal nursing school.

And as Rose moved forward with no one calling her a slut or a whore, without any man touching her body without permission, she managed to push those characterizations out of her mind. She grew stronger and more determined to succeed in all the ways that would ensure she was safe from harm.

But, unbeknownst to Rose the acts of two men were tattooed on her soul whether she allowed herself to recall the initial sting or not. She was marked in ways no one could see, in ways she'd thought had scarred over. She hadn't thought the dead wounds required further attention. Slut, whore. She had forgotten the foul names, the feelings that came with knowing that's what someone had decided she was. She'd forgotten the exact pain that came with the memories until the day she found herself uttering the same horrid sentiments to her very own Magdalena.

Rose nearly buckled over at the thought, but kept moving forward through the fog. How could she have directed such cruelty at her daughter? She would fix that, she told herself, but first she needed to solve the problem that had plagued her for over twenty years.

* * *

Rose knocked on the Sebastian's front door. The uniformed maid let Rose into the house. It smelled of a recently cleaned pine-lemon. Rose wanted to see Theresa alone. The maid protested, but Rose took the stairs two at a time, hearing the maid's voice calling for Mr. Sebastian.

Rose laid her coat outside the door on the chair that the Sebastians had placed there the first time Rose had come to examine Theresa. She rapped on the door with the back of her knuckles, a little harder and faster than she intended.

"Come in," Theresa said.

Rose entered the stale-smelling room and headed to the far side near a window looking out at the back, not directly at the mill. She raised the window a few inches to let some air in.

"You've got to open these windows, at least during shift changes, at least twice a day." Rose said. "If the maids have to dust an additional time, that's fine. That's what they're paid for, right?"

Theresa fell back on her pillows with dramatic flourish. "Oh thank you! Someone with some sense." Rose opened the next set of windows, glancing at Theresa, trying to casually assess her degree of illness versus just what her parents seemed to want her to experience. Theresa hung off the side of the bed, peering under it, foraging for something.

Rose finished opening up the room and turned, hands on hips to watch Theresa full on. Theresa ratcheted her body up, sitting on her bed, a stack of medical and social work books on her lap. Rose's heart nearly stopped at the sight of Theresa pouring over the academic texts like other twenty-year-olds studied Ladies Home Journal.

"I've been reading," Theresa said, and stopped her voice catching on asthmatic constrictions of her bronchial tubes. "Nurse, would you look at this with me? I've been reading up on my own case and ever since that visit to the Lipinski's. Well, I want to be a social worker. Or a doctor."

Rose bit the inside of her mouth, trying to fend off the torrent of emotion sweeping through her. The last time she'd seen Theresa she was like a wet rag, intellectually uninterested, and now, look at her, fully engaged in the larger world. Rose's world. She was surer than ever that Theresa would benefit if she knew who they both were.

It was like watching an alien view of herself from twenty years before. Rose bustled across the room, carried the chair with her nurse's bag, from the hall into the room and set it by the door to distract herself from her emotions. She dug through her bag, collecting her instruments and thoughts, buying time. She wanted to behave professionally in this very personal situation.

Rose turned to Theresa, blood pressure cuff and stethoscope in hand. "You're pale, grayish around the eyes, bluish. What's that tell you?" Rose said as she headed toward Theresa's bed. If Rose talked nursing, she would remain calm.

Theresa opened her mouth to talk, her face screwed up and she began to cry. Rose wanted to hold her sobbing daughter, but that wouldn't be appropriate. What would she do in a normal nursing situation?

"No crying, Theresa. Look at yourself." Rose grabbed a silver hand mirror from the dressing table and took it to the bed. "You are young and alive and aside from the asthma which I concede is problematic, you're utterly healthy you're just like—"

Rose stopped midsentence and took the mirror back to its place among other silver knick-knacks.

Theresa stared at Rose. "Like what?"

Like me. "Like an ox. You need to move more, that's all. You'll get sores on your ass if you lay there like that one more second." Rose sat beside Theresa on the bed. "Look at you. So excited now that you've found an interest in your health. You are alive at the opportunity to help someone else."

Theresa wiped her eyes, growing pinker as she became more animated. Rose moved her hand closer to Theresa's wanting to hold it. To rock her like a baby and then push her out of the nest, to see her fly like Rose knew she could.

"I had to beg mother for hours. Just to let me check these books out of the library," Theresa said. She played with her bedspread grazing Rose's fingers with hers each time she smoothed and bunched the silky material.

Theresa drew and let out a deep breath. "Mother nearly lost her mind and said a lady like me doesn't need to have a career, certainly not becoming a doctor or helping poor people. Then she said I paid for it by having another attack. I'm smart enough to be a doctor, you know. I just doubt myself once in a while."

Rose took Theresa's chin and turned her face toward her. "You have the guts, you just don't know it, yet. I have an uncle who's half dead and he only accepts help when he's so tired he's forgotten he doesn't want help from anyone. You can do anything you want. Look at you, diving into medical books and social work journals second year med students avoid like the plague. You are doctor material if I ever saw it. Now get up." Rose sprung off the bed and held her hands out to Theresa.

Theresa swung her feet over the side of the bed. Her white nightgown bunching around her knees. Her long legs were the palest Rose had ever seen. Her blue veins peeked through the skin.

Rose dragged her to her feet. "Ever been dancing?"

Theresa threw her head back and said, angrily. "No."

"Good, you have spunk." Rose led Theresa through intricate waltz steps, the girl as light as the fog on a normal day. "Here, just keep moving, I need to see how much your system can handle."

"But you said I'm healthy."

"Yes, yes, but that's me looking at you lying there dead as a doornail. Anyone's healthy under those circumstances. I need to see you imitating a living person not a dead one."

Theresa laughed, her head back. "That's really sort of rude." Rose spun her around, enjoying the girl's pluckiness, excited that there was no sign of pulmonary distress.

"I've seen your file. But there's lots missing in it." Rose wanted to ask her if she had ever been on a date, been kissed, visited New York City, had a Christmas when she got the very thing she wished for but didn't think possible. But she settled on the mundane. "Where would you like to live? What do you want out of life?" Rose said.

Theresa scrunched up her face and slowed down. "I don't know." Theresa gripped Rose's hands, her lotioned skin, like butter against Rose's. She watched the girl for distress. Nothing.

Rose felt energy surging through her; she could see it in Theresa's face, too

"I have something to tell you," Rose said. "A miracle, in a way. It was years back. You won't believe it, but—"

Out of the corner of Rose's eye she saw movement at the bedroom door, Mr. Sebastian.

Rose was confused, embarrassed, as though Sebastian had walked in on her nude. He was seeing something he shouldn't. She had let her emotions out and they took hold of her, dragged her into an unprofessional place.

Still, part of Rose wanted to declare right there who she was, to pronounce the Sebastians unfit parents; Rose could give Theresa everything she needed. But Rose knew you didn't do things like that. The news of an illegitimate baby was something to be buried.

"What sort of treatment are you offering, Nurse Pavlesic?" He looked between Rose and Theresa repeatedly, his face concerned. "I doubt I would find much hand-holding and dancing suggested in the annals of nursing care if I were inclined to look."

Rose and Theresa dropped hands.

"Matter of fact," Rose said, "you *would* find hand-holding in the literature and practical cases. And it wouldn't hurt you to do a little more of it yourself. I've read Theresa's case and...well..." Rose glanced at Theresa who was smiling, clearly not scared anymore.

I'm her mother, Rose said silently to herself.

Mr. Sebastian pulled Rose by the arm, wrenching her backward toward the door. Rose couldn't take her eyes off of Theresa, frightened this might be the last time she saw her. Sebastian's fingers tightened on Rose's arm, meeting at the bone under her bicep. She tripped over the chair that held her bag as Mr. Sebastian muscled her through the doorway.

Mr. Sebastian leaned over Rose, shoving her against the wall, his voice low enough for Theresa not to hear.

"You read her file? Just what were you going to tell her? We never told her anything regarding her birth. And there's no way that after all these years, we would happen upon the woman who gave birth to Theresa. That woman claimed to have been on her way to Boston with some hotshot playboy. That woman was glad to be rid of Theresa and we were glad to have her."

He released Rose from his grip and ran his hand through his hair.

Rose didn't know where she summoned the courage. "I read the file," she said. "You *didn't* want her. Neither did your wife. She spent all that time in the care of psychiatric doctors, you made Theresa think she was crazy and weak.

That file tells me everything I need to know." *I am her mother.* "She is so much more than you've let her be. She's in there hiding books and journals as though they were rancid, diseased objects rather than the key to opening up a world to a girl who's obviously brighter than the dickens, for the love of Jesus himself! Let her be who she is."

Mr. Sebastian grabbed Rose's things and prodded her down the hall toward the stairs.

"Did the file indicate the times I didn't sleep for days while caring for Mrs. Sebastian, when she *couldn't* sleep and the baby wouldn't either? Or how I nursed them both back to health from pneumonia? Or how I got TB and spent my days and nights away from them so to not infect either? Was there one word in those files about me?"

Rose stopped at the bottom of the stairs. She was nauseated and light-headed. She had to stay close to Theresa. She needed to care for her.

"Please let me continue her care," she said. "I will tell her there was a lapsed moment, that I'd been recently grieved by an unexpected loss, that I had a moment—"

Mr. Sebastian gripped Rose's arm again and forced her toward the door, tossing her bag and hat out onto the porch. "I'll let you know two things. First, I don't know what I witnessed in that room, what you were up to, but I'm sure you are not permitted to reveal what's in confidential files. Two, I'm not sure at all you embody the character needed to properly administer a community health clinic.

"I've been nursing for nearly two decades. I can do it in my sleep."

"Or while drunk?"

Rose drew back.

He clenched his jaw. You smell like a brewery. I smelled it last night. I wonder if you even had a patient to see at the Merry-Go-Round at all."

Rose covered her mouth. The vodka? Stale beer odor from the night before?

"Just so we're clear. I don't want to see you back here," he said. "Theresa believes we are her parents. Trust me, her birth mother was more than happy to give her up. I'm a practical man and I went to the mother to be sure she was okay with this and I didn't even have to ask. She turned to the nurse before she saw me and said. "I can breathe again," and she combed her hair as though that were her only concern.

Rose's eyes widened. She scraped through her memories for that phrasing. Had she really said that? Maybe. But... "I just meant...*she* probably meant that her diaphragm was finally relieved of the weight of a baby, not that...no, no I don't believe any mother would have said that, meant it that way. Do you realize the gift you have lying in that bed?"

Rose pushed her hair behind her ears, sweat licking her fingertips. She froze as Mr. Sebastian's gaze broke from hers and leveled on her double earlobe.

"What?" she said. "Haven't seen a person who isn't perfect before?"

Mr. Sebastian reached for Rose's ear. She stepped back.

"The problem is," he said stepping forward, narrowing his eyes at her ear. "I've seen that ear before."

Rose opened her mouth to ask him what the hell he meant. When she realized, she looked away so he couldn't see that side of her face. Rose recalled that day, the way some man had entered the room and walked nearly to the bed. Rose remembered the well-dressed fellow standing there as though he had a question to ask. But, as she put her brush down, smoothed her hair, the man was gone. The nurse chased him away. Could that have been him?

"Don't come back," Mr. Sebastian said. "Tell your husband he's done for good."

Rose turned back to him, lifting her chin. He took her shoulders and backed her through the doorway, onto the porch.

"That's right," Mr. Sebastian said. "I took up for Henry saying he was only helping his daughter. That he was desperate to help her and was late from break for that reason. He was not simply milling around the hospital with the nurses for fun. But now I see. The whole Pavlesic family has a bent toward making trouble. You can forget about that clinic of yours being funded. You are out of line and starting January, 1949 you are out of a job!"

He slammed the door on Rose making her stumble.

She'd lost Theresa again and now, it seemed, Henry's story of what he'd been up to in order to get fired had changed yet again.

Chapter 13

Rose stood dazed outside the Sebastian's home, the zinc mill grinding away across the street, sending smoke into the air. Mr. Sebastian knew who she was?

The fog had grown more tangible, grainy as though she could chew it. She was comforted by its odd weight; it would hide her from anyone she passed.

Her eyes began to tear, slapped with emotion of twenty years. She wrapped her coat tight against her, her shoulders bunched up as though she were walking into whipping wind rather than the stillness that kept the fog battened over the town.

Walking home, the fog filled her lungs, choked her, made her feel like Unk must feel every blessed day of his life. She cleared her throat repeatedly, feeling claustrophobic. She pressed on, catching her toe on this crack, her heel falling into that crevice, moving as though she were drowning in the Monongahela River.

Voices rose and spiked the fog as she passed clutches of people, made anonymous by the scratchy fog. The passersby excitedly discussed Saturday's football game, the way they were going to beat the Monongahela Wildcats to all hell.

Donora Dragons had been rated the best football team in the country a few years back and it wouldn't take much for them to garner that distinction again. And people discussing Johnny—murmurs of the scouts in town to watch and meet him—the idea that at least one more fella would be headed off to college on a scholarship.

The town, not just the person who earned the award, always shared that pride. Johnny needed to understand that. He and his success belonged to Donora as much as it did his family and John, himself. It wasn't just Rose who wanted this for her son. He'd see that some day. Many knew the gift college would bring.

Rose tripped over a bulky, soft thing in the sidewalk, surprised to discover she'd tripped over a person.

Adamchek squealed like a woman. "Don't it just paint the right damn picture that it's *you* falling over my big ass in the middle of the street."

"You, Adamchek. Fourteen thousand people in this town and all I ever see is you. Quit following me. I'm not in the mood for any of your bullshit. And, stay away from Buzzy."

The two of them scrambled to their feet using each other's bodies for leverage, grunting to be the first to regain their balance.

He smelled like garlic perogies. Rose brushed the front of her coat. "Watch it next time, Dumbo," she said.

"We'll see who the dumbo in this town is. Don't you worry." Adamchek brushed past Rose, knocking her shoulder to the side.

"Is that supposed to be a threat of some sort?" Rose wondered if his words had something to do with Buzzy, Henry?

"You just make sure your son shows up to play Saturday. He's gallivanting around town playing music to all hours. I got cash on that game, you know. Your kid will make or break more than a few fella's accounts," he said and disappeared into the fog.

She looked around wondering if anyone was close enough to have witnessed any part of the exchange, but she couldn't see another soul. She was relieved her reddened face was hidden. What the hell did he mean? She coughed into her hand as she started walking again, then stopped, the cough buckling her over at the waist. Mother of God, that fog was rotten, Rose thought.

When she got to Doc Bonaroti's office, a pair of ladies stood in the doorway, huddled and mumbling—one with an accented voice, the tired cadence familiar to Rose.

"Mrs. Lipinski?" Rose said.

"It's me."

Rose stepped closer and saw that Mrs. Lipinski was supported by Nurse Dottie Shaginaw. Rose felt a swell of anger.

"Nurse Shaginaw," Rose said.

"Hello, Nurse Pavlesic. So good to see you."

Rose unlocked the office door with her key and held it for Dottie and Mrs. Lipinski to shuffle through.

"Thank you Nurse Shaginaw. I'm sure you have many a man's life to save in the mill hospital. Maybe one of the supervisors has a head cold and needs you to assist him? I don't want to hold you up with matters of community nursing."

Rose took on Mrs. Lipinski's weight and used her foot to hook the leg of a metal chair and slide it across the floor to where she could get Mrs. Lipinski to sit. Dottie bent over her nurse's bag and shuffled through it as though she were prepared to administer care to Mrs. Lipinski. She straightened with her stethoscope in hand, affixing the ear buds in place.

"Just a scorched Achilles or two, Pavlesic. At the mill. Just a bit of advice for this man or that. You know. I'm sort of a jack-of-all-nursing-trades in the mill." Nurse Dottie put one fist on her hip and shook her stethoscope at Rose. "I'm there to help whoever needs it in whatever way he needs it. My goal is to be just like you, in the mills, instead of the neighborhood, but just like you." Dottie bent into Mrs. Lipinski and put the stethoscope into place to listen to her chest. She lifted her eyes to Rose.

Rose pulled a second chair over to them and placed her bag there.

"You do not own the community, Pavlesic. I will nurse whoever needs me. I'm there for everyone. That's just how I am."

Rose pulled out her stethoscope and felt her anger, raw as an animal's. Was Dottie taunting Rose? Was she admitting to helping Henry and Magdalena? What was she insinuating?

Rose plucked Dottie's stethoscope out of her ears and pushed the woman aside with her hip, placing her own stethoscope on Mrs. Lipinski's chest. Rose forced a smile at Mrs. Lipinski who appeared apprehensive.

"It must be something to have no life except nursing, Shaginaw. Hit the Bricks and stay the hell away from me. From my life. From my patients."

"You are awful, Rose." Nurse Dottie stalked out the door, stuffing her stethoscope into her bag as she went.

Rose felt her body relax once Dottie was gone. She pulled Mrs. Lipinski to standing and moved her into Doc's office where she stripped off her coat. The woman had a scorching fever and complained of a headache so sharp she couldn't hold her eyes open any more. Rose shut off the bright light in Doc's office and let the hall light suffice to softly illuminate her work.

Rose administered some aspirin and massaged the woman's entire head area, working around her skull, cheekbones and neck, and felt fear. Her life as she'd known it had come against a brick wall. By losing control at Theresa's home, she jeopardized the clinic's funding, and behaved like a sixteen-year-old rather than a seasoned nurse. She smoothed a frozen compress on Mrs. Lipinski's forehead and shivered with the realization that her decisions in the past few days, like the fog, were far worse than she realized.

Chapter 14

At four-thirty in the morning, Rose woke with sweat drenching the nape of her neck, heat encasing her head to toe. She felt like she had during those days after giving birth, when her body disposed of its extra fluids. She tossed and twisted now in bed, trying to find a cool part of the sheets, but Henry's body released too much heat.

Her head was cluttered with too many thoughts. What if she had lost the clinic? She considered the consequences for herself, for Bonaroti, the town. Acid burned her stomach and pushed up her esophagus. She stumbled from bed, raced down the hall to the bathroom and vomited.

The thick fear was tangible. With her life balancing on poor decisions she wasn't sure she could recover. Not if she lost the clinic funding. Her hands quivered as she washed her face and brushed her teeth with baking soda.

Anxiety sent Rose to the kitchen where she made coffee and mentally ticked through her To-Do list. But would she have anything to do? What if Mr. Sebastian had already phoned Doc Bonaroti and told him his wife was not funding the clinic and that they might as well fire Rose now? She would know when she got her assignments in a few hours. Whether her termination was imminent or not, she had work to do that morning. She had promised to make Leo a lion costume for Halloween and Sara Clara had left a note saying she had not gotten to finish it the day before so Rose would start with that.

At the kitchen table, Rose sat, sewing, quietly drinking her coffee and two shots of vodka. It soothed her, like it always had since her first drink at twelve. The initial sting was worth the numbing of pain. That was the one useful thing Mr. Reeves from the orphanage had taught her.

She smiled at the thought of Leo. He'd seen the Wizard of Oz six times and could not be swayed to put together a simple cowboy costume or pull an old sheet over his head to be a ghost. Rose couldn't get used to the idea that Leo choosing to be the lion over any of the other options meant he may identify with the weaker people in the world. She'd already dummied up the costume and fitted him in it twice. All she needed to do was stitch it and attach a ropy tail and it would be ready to go for the parade.

Rose shifted in the chair, ignoring the way her foot stuck to the linoleum. She couldn't believe she'd jeopardized her nursing career, letting go of a situation, forgetting what her job was, letting her personal problems interfere with her work.

She jabbed the lion's leg stitching it in a frenzy. She and Bonaroti should have come up with a hard source of funding the minute they got the okay to start the clinic. They shouldn't have trusted that every single wife of every single superintendent would want to contribute to their cause. She had thought her time was best spent nursing, not finding alternate funding sources. How could they have been so naïve?

She had nearly finished both legs of the costume when she noticed it was half past six and time to prepare for breakfast. She looked up from her sewing and felt dizzy from the coffee and vodka. No matter. Both would have worn off by the time she had to go to work. Screw Sebastian and what he thinks he knew about her. Screw all of them.

* * *

Magdalena couldn't sleep, and heard her mother shuffling past her room. She turned on her side and curled under her covers, pained that she had disappointed her mother. The disclosure of her pregnancy caused her to understand the term "broken hearted."

The room grew stuffy and hot as though it took on the misery she felt inside. Magdalena rolled onto her back, drawing the covers up to chin, and stuck a leg out for some cooler air. She had spent her entire life trying to please her mother and now there was no way to ever do that again.

Magdalena couldn't erase what had transpired. She had felt so alone, then excited by Tony's desire for her, and the two things together made her agree to let him have her. But she refused to admit it and give credence to her mother's words. Not that she needed to hear them from her mother to know they applied.

She was a slut. It was more than pleasurable for her—sex. There wasn't a bit of it, leading up to it, the act itself, and afterward that she hadn't liked. Nothing had been the way her friends said it would be—horrible, ugly, painful. She not only let it happen. She made it happen.

Magdalena stared at her ceiling as she had millions of times, remembering how Tony's hands felt on her breasts, thighs, how his mouth moved all over her.

She thought she would go crazy lying here now. She thought she saw blue air swirling above her bed. Had she finally turned the bend? She raised her hand and tried to grab the moving air. Was she really seeing that?

She sat up, staring at the ceiling. Was it a ghost? Of future lifelong regret, probably. She reached over, turned on the bedside light, waiting for the illusion to disappear, but instead, it picked up separate pinpricks of light, swirling them as if in dance. She covered her mouth. Science was her strong suit and she knew that when a person was seeing a smog dance recital on her bedroom ceiling, something was dreadfully wrong.

Magdalena ripped her blanket off, pushed her arms into her worn bathrobe and headed to the kitchen, tying the belt as she went.

She got there in time to see Rose throwing back a shot of booze.

"Mum? Something's really wrong. The smog's in my bedroom." Magdalena looked up at the ceiling to see if the same bluish circus act could be seen in the kitchen. "Look, the ceiling. Doc was right. This is bad."

Rose would not make eye contact and Magdalena stalked across the kitchen.

"Mum? Listen to me. Please. You have to go to that meeting today, the council meeting. You need to find out what's happening here"

"I have a job to do. I'd love to have the time to join the town blowhards, but I have patients to see, Leo's costume to sew, clothes to wash, a daughter..." Rose's words slid into each other and Magdalena could not believe she never noticed before—the degree to which her mother drank. "Mum? Can you hear me at all?" Rose pushed her sewing needle into the lion's tail and pulled it back out.

"Mum?" Magdalena said realizing how many times in life she had to ask her mother if she was paying attention. The booze in front of Rose made Magdalena feel as though she'd downed a fifth of it herself.

Magdalena felt as if her body was reaching to her very core to expel her insides and she ran to the sink and threw up. She heard Rose come up behind her. Her mother slipped one arm around her and pulled her hair back from her face. Magdalena cupped her hand, and washed out her mouth with water from the faucet. Rose knotted Magdalena's hair around itself as Magdalena wiped her mouth, hand shaking.

Magdalena turned to her mother to pull her close. But Rose stiffened. Clearly she had not yet forgiven Magdalena.

Her mother looked away, the scent of whiskey filling the air. Magdalena grimaced. If her mother would not do the talking, spread her truthful, even harsh advice, then Magdalena would do it for her. She would not cower in the face of her big strong mother.

"I guess," Magdalena said. "I should listen to Cathy at Dr. Bonaroti's office. I should just see her fella in Pittsburgh. Would that make you happy? Then we could all pretend that things are like they were before. You could go on treating the town like your family and your family like strangers. We could all just pretend we're happy. That's how you like it right? Just pretending things are the way you want them to be!" Magdalena's hands flew above her head, shaking them with every word. Words that came out before they were formed and censored in her mind.

Rose squeezed her eyes shut, "Listen, Magdalena."

Magdalena pounded on the countertop. "No! You listen. You don't have to worry about me asking for anything. I don't—"

Rose gripped Magdalena's forearm. "I am trying to—"

Magdalena ripped her arm from Rose's grasp. "I won't listen, Mum. I. Don't. Trust. You."

"What?"

"You don't have to worry, you don't have to do anything for me. I'll be out of your life...you can have your booze and your perfect son Johnny and your work. That's all you care about!"

"You don't trust *me*? I'm not the one who's been living a lie, young lady." Rose jabbed her own sternum with her forefinger.

Magdalena grasped the belt around her robe and pulled it tight, squeezing her belly with it. "You never trusted me. Or Johnny. Or Dad, or anyone living in this house." She stopped, looked up at the ceiling as if she would find her courage there. "Admit it, Mum. We're not good enough. We never will be. Not even if we follow your plans."

Magdalena turned the faucet on and off then met Rose's gaze. "I look at you, Mum. I can't help it." Magdalena swallowed hard.

Rose shrugged. "Can't help what?"

Magdalena looked at her feet then back at Rose. "Part of me hates you. So, there, you're off the hook. You don't have to fake your concern anymore."

The nausea kicked back in. Magdalena covered her mouth and ran from the kitchen, knowing she would never treat her child the way Rose had treated her. Her baby would mean something more to her than just the right thing to do.

* * *

Rose staggered back to the kitchen table, and couldn't stop her hand from trembling as she reached for the vodka and poured herself another shot. She'd stare at the full glass before throwing it back. Then another and another until the downing of the booze freed her emotions, rising and rushing through her body, streaming down her cheeks. Her body quivered with the truth that she had pushed away since her first time getting pregnant and made herself emotionally unavailable.

Her tears felt like poison, cleansing her body as they shuddered out of her. Rose knew the truth about who she was. Now Mr. Sebastian did, too. Would he tell his wife? Rose was overwhelmed with despair. The chance of Sebastian funding the clinic was gone. Rose dropped her face into her hands. Could Magdalena really hate her?

The thought was more agonizing than she could ever have imagined. Rose had spent plenty of time considering the abandonment of children by their parents, but never did she consider it the other way around. After all she'd been through in life, the idea of her children pushing her aside excoriated her, leaving her to feel like she had so many times as a child: empty, alone, and undeserving.

* * *

Nursing had saved Rose. Sitting in the kitchen, she thought back to Sister John Ann who had seen something in her and pushed her toward nursing school where Rose had remade her life. She remembered the first time a patient dying of cancer said Rose made his last days worth living. Rose had brushed his teeth, changed his IV's, shaved him, and made him presentable for his grieving family. But most of all she talked to him as though he were due for lunch at the Elks the next day. She scolded him for not sitting up straight, for grumbling when she changed his sheets.

And the man had laughed. Rose had filled his lonely moments. The patient got what he needed, but Rose got even more in return. For Rose, being a nurse gave her the chance to be needed, to care for people as though they were family. Nurses were more like family than the relatives who visited their sickly relations. Rose was one of the best at critical care, a master at hospice, whatever nursing a patient needed.

In opening herself up to nursing in that way, Rose closed off the desperate part of her that had allowed Bennett into her life and bed. Still the gap behind the newly erected barrier to her heart needed to be filled. So, before she fully embraced her religion, she sowed a row of sexual partners that would have shamed the most practiced of playboys.

Unlike when her body was forcibly taken or when her affection was stolen, when Rose chose whom to seduce, how and when, she felt power and pain in her own pleasure. She convinced herself those months of angry promiscuity had helped her reclaim a physical sense of self even if she knew it was wrong. She quickly learned it was not how she *wanted* to live and going on that way would cast her into even deeper emptiness than she'd experienced before.

By the time she met Henry, she understood what men needed to see in women they wanted to marry. Rose was only required to pretend a little bit to meet Henry's expectations. He was different. He didn't pry like other fellas. He didn't ask for history and the nauseating retelling of loves gone bad. Still, even though he admired her nursing career, she knew Henry had wanted to see at least a tiny part of her as needing him; he wanted to protect her.

So Rose let him care for her by not telling him anything about her past. Beyond revealing the fact she was orphaned, she left most of the details regarding her childhood and teen years unsaid. She guessed this allowed Henry to invent anything he wanted for her. She supposed it was his kindness and understanding that no orphan would want to retell her awful upbringing that kept him from prodding her. She'd worked to condense the gruesome portions of her early life into a forgotten seed, buried in her soul and hidden behind her nursing persona, tucked away until the last few days.

Even though Rose had managed to squash the pain and ruminations about her own abuse, she could never forget that she abandoned her baby. The birth and adoption of Theresa had haunted Rose. After her self-flagellating, sexual missteps she gathered up some pride and she kept her past from handicapping her future by enacting a well-plotted string of good works and smart choices. All that had served her well, but as the days unfolded Rose was discovering she could not deal with Magdalena or Theresa because she could not deal with herself. She understood Henry's words, now.

Her delusions of past healing were shattered and she could finally see what he meant. The way she controlled everything. It had been the only way. She nodded at the thought. She wanted the best for them, the life she hadn't had as a child. She wanted their lives to be happy and full and blessed. That's all she had tried to do for them. Rose threw back another shot. Henry? He had his secrets, too. Remembering what Mrs. Saltz had said, Rose had come to realize he was no saint either.

* * *

Henry shuffled into the kitchen, his slippers scratching over the linoleum. He grabbed Rose's shot glass from her hand and pushed it aside. "What the hell are you doing?"

Who was he to question her about anything? Rose wanted to yell at him, but she saw concern in his eyes. She couldn't help herself. She went to him and collapsed into his arms.

Henry's stubbly cheek pressed against hers before he pulled back and lifted her chin. "Are you drunk? How are you going to work if you're three shittin' sheets to the wind? Is this why you were arguing with Sebastian? Were you drunk yesterday?"

"What? How did you...No! I was not."

Sara Clara rushed into the kitchen. Rose pushed away from Henry, stumbling. Sara Clara and Henry clamped Rose under each arm and shuffled her back toward the table.

"Dammit!" Rose screeched as she wiggled out of their grip and slammed into a chair.

"This has got to stop," Henry said.

Rose rubbed her hip where they'd knocked her into the table. I know, Rose thought.

"What's got to stop, Hen? Tell me please. Buzzy's gambling? Magdalena? Johnny pushing me? Or is it

Dottie?" Rose wagged her finger at Henry. "*That* has to stop. What in hell are you doing with her? I want to know, now." She reached up and poked Henry's shoulder.

Sara Clara butted Henry out of the way and bent to Rose, handing her coffee. Rose took it and swallowed the same cold coffee she'd made hours before. She spit it back into the cup.

Henry took Sara Clara by the elbow, guiding her away from Rose.

Rose stood, weaving in front of her seat. "That's right, get outta my road, Sara Clara from the south," Rose said.

"It's okay, Sara Clara," Henry said. "I've got her. She'll be fine."

Rose grabbed his arm and gripped it tight, her nails digging into his flesh. "You've got me? As though the two of you could take care of me? As though I need it? Why don't you start telling me why Mrs. Saltz said you were at the bar with Buzzy the other night? She claims you were gambling. Are you gambling now, too?"

Henry shook his head.

"We just want to help," Sara Clara said. "We know how hard this is, with Magdalena I mean, you're under stress, we understand. Let us take care of you for a change."

Rose bent at the waist burying her head in her lap. She began retching with hiccups and laughter, talking into her legs. "You two taking care of me? That's a laugh. Why don't you take care of your philandering husband?"

Rose struggled to her feet, took the vodka bottle by its neck. "The pair of you can go screw yourselves. And make it a good one." Rose wobbled from the room, feeling self-righteous, self-pity. Rose ran their words through her mind. They were put off by her controlling nature, but none of them, not one, could handle her raw emotions. Rose knew then, she was trapped by the very persona she had created long ago.

* * *

When Rose awoke from her drunken stupor, it was still Friday, October 29th. She stretched on the bed; her jaw aching from the angle her head had been jammed into her pillow. She picked at the slobber crusted at the corner of her mouth and pushed to sitting, her muscles screaming as though she'd set her limbs in plaster. She squinted at her clock, eyes as dry as her mouth and ran her tongue around the inside of her lips trying to figure what had transpired in the hours early that morning. What the hell had she done?

She glanced at the clock. She should have finished four visits by 1:00 Friday afternoon. She shook her head, trying to rid her mind of the fog that clouded even her brain. The council meeting? Bonaroti hadn't asked her to attend, but she was going.

She scrambled to her closet and threw the door open. Inside her two uniforms hung, ironed and ready. Sara Clara had actually done something around the house besides hide in her bed.

"She's not all that bad." Henry's voice made Rose jump. She spun around. He stood in the doorway, hands in pockets. "I think you'd be pleased to see she managed to wash and iron your uniforms like you like them. Starched, even." Rose remembered that morning, the way she'd been slobbering drunk, crude and rude to Henry and Sara Clara. She didn't want to be that person.

Rose thanked him, looking at the floor.

"Bonaroti showed up here an hour ago," Henry said. "Told him you had the flu. He thought you must be dead if you didn't come out of the bedroom while he checked over Unk. He moved him to the cellar, convinced that since the fog rises, the cellar would be the safest place. We moved his chair downstairs, he's got some color back..."

Rose turned away from Henry, so ashamed that she'd compromised herself, Unk, the citizens of Donora.

"Did he mention the clinic? The, uh, the Sebastians?"

"He was holding out on me, I could tell. Gave me more questions than answers, but he definitely needs you to get around to homes. Head to the people who Hawthorne can't reach, or double up and help Hawthorne move faster. There's a lot of stress on people right now with this smog—yeah, more folks are calling it smog now. The smoke's so heavy, mixing with the fog. But first we need to discuss—"

"I need time to think about Magdalena's situation—"

"I meant your drinking, what's going on with you. I don't care about your job or the clinic or fucking Sebastian. *You* are who I care about."

Rose looked at Henry, standing there, bursting with the love he'd always been willing to give, and she became more afraid than ever that he'd discover she was unworthy of it.

"I can't. I need to get through this day and have the scout over for dinner tomorrow night. I got upset and drank too much. I need to get through this next week and then…"

"Bonaroti knows you'll be late. You have time."

Rose's shoulders hunched as she leaned into the closet. She wanted to disappear inside herself. She wanted Henry to take over her life and tell her exactly why she should forget her past, and forgive herself. She wanted to tell him all that she'd done wrong in her life, and find out if he would still love her.

But the words wouldn't come out of her mouth. Until she straightened Magdalena out, and made sure her son's future was secure, the only way she could deal with what she couldn't face was to go back to work. The only way to make Henry leave her alone was to hurt him before he hurt her.

"Why don't you go back to saving Sara Clara, Henry? She actually needs your help. I don't." Rose could feel Henry's disappointment, the hurt.

"And while you're at it," Rose said. "I want to know right now what you and Dottie Shaginaw are up to. I want you to look me in the eyes and tell me you've done nothing wrong. That I have nothing to worry about."

"You have nothing to worry about." Henry's sharp tone pierced her heart, but not deeply enough to make her stop doubting.

He ran his hand through his hair, visibly irritated. "Just forget all of this. Never mind Dottie, never mind Magdalena. Just worry about your job, Rose." She was far beyond worried about her job.

Henry's expression was resentful. "You better get in touch with Bonaroti. He wants you to go to some meeting about shutting down the mills. Claims the world, Donora, is about to end...sounds like just your thing."

Rose grabbed her uniform, knowing she should stay home and begin mending their marital fence but Bonaroti needed her, and the town. And even if that made Henry mad, it was the way their life had gone and he would get over it. She was needed and she would go.

Rose thought she could at least finish the day better than she started it. She stripped out of her house clothes, eager to slip on a uniform and with it, the person she was really meant to be.

* * *

The fog had thickened even more—it was grainy and so wet it moistened Rose's cheeks. She inched her way around town, her throat scratchy, as though inundated with strep. She could barely swallow. She stopped at one home on Thompson to get her bearings, crawling up the front steps, the chipping cement digging into her palms.

She knocked at the door waiting for someone to tell her where she was. She couldn't even see if she had passed the office. When the door didn't open, Rose turned the handle. If she just poked her head inside she could regain her bearings. When she did she accidentally turned on the lights, and saw a woman writhing on the floor. Her coat was still on, a grocery bag beside her, cans and produce scattered around. Rose ran and knelt beside her.

"Mrs. Cushon?" Rose struggled to pull the woman to a sitting position, but she was like a rag doll. Rose laid her back down, undid her coat and pulled it off. The woman's hands went right to her neck, signaling she couldn't breathe.

"Okay, Mrs. Cushon, we're going to help you. That condition of yours is acting up." Rose popped open her bag and rifled through for a syringe and adrenaline. She poked the needle into the vial and withdrew the medicine. Rose rolled up Mrs. Cushon's sleeve.

"Next time, how about you call the Doc, before it gets this bad. You know we have six docs in town, right?" Rose forced a smile and a light tone into her voice as she stretched Mrs. Cushon's skin tight and plunged the needle into her muscle. Rose locked eyes with Mrs. Cushon, soothing her panic, brushing her hair back from her face, watching as the woman's breathing normalized.

Mrs. Cushon broke her gaze and looked over Rose's shoulder. Rose turned to see her patient's son, Al, standing at the door, gaping.

"Down the cellar," Al said to her.

"What?" Rose said.

"Just came from the Dvronick's. Having a tall cool one with my buddy when his father up and drops dead right there!"

"Amos! Dead?"

Al nodded, scooping his mother into his arms, struggling to his feet. "The old man wiggled around some, hands at the neck, grey as the smog itself. That fog got 'em! Right there in front of my own eyes. So next thing, the missus comes up from the cellar, coughing a little and she enters the kitchen sees her husband and she starts the same thing, choking, hacking, can't breathe. Well, me and Stevie take and shove her back in the cellar on account of her dead husband on the kitchen floor and suddenly she breathes a little better. The air isn't as bad in the cellar."

And with that he was gone, carrying his mother to the cellar.

Rose didn't know what to make of that story. Amos had a history of respiratory issues, as did Mrs. Cushon, but the fog got him? As much as Rose didn't enjoy the foggy fall days they had in Donora, it was hardly a matter of being deadly. She needed to get to Bonaroti's office, see where he wanted her to go, file this report and get someone out to the Dvronick home to see about one live and one dead person. Rose shoved the groceries into the bag and took them to the kitchen. She looked out the window of the home and a strange shifting of light through the window caught her eye.

She pulled the curtain aside and squinted. She watched a train working through town, its stack letting out smoke but instead of billowing up and out like normal, it was as though the smoke hit a ceiling. It rose a few feet then was shoved back down, rushing to the ground like liquid.

The thought of inhaling that sickened Rose. She pulled her coat tighter around her body, buttoning it. She opened several drawers in the kitchen until she found a scrap of dusting rag to cover her mouth as she headed back out. Just in case. She couldn't ignore what she had seen and heard.

She hobbled down the sidewalk, feeling along the retaining walls that marked property lines. She could hear Al Cushon screaming out the door of the home she just left "The fog got her!" His voice rising above the darkness and ever-present sounds from the mill.

Rose stopped whomever she could along the way, marveling that although many were hampered in movement by the fog, their breathing was normal. If the fog was really "getting" people, everyone would have trouble, wouldn't they? She remembered the sight of the train's stack, the smoke, and covered her mouth with the rag. No sense taking chances.

Rose finally made it to Dr. Bonaroti's office, and injected herself with adrenaline to ease her own strained breath. She administered a shot to Cathy who promptly lit a cigarette and started her choking fit all over again.

"I can taste the smog in my cigarette!" Cathy said. She stared at the end of the lit tobacco as though it had betrayed her and stomped it out on the tile floor.

Rose rifled through the drugs, anything she might use to relieve the suffocating coughs and nausea that was gripping half the town. Cathy filled Rose in on the dozens of calls from citizens requesting a visit from the doc or Rose. She was funneling all the calls she couldn't handle to the other docs in town, but they were overwhelmed, too, out on-call. No one could keep track of which home or business a doc was visiting, because as soon as he started down the street, some random person would pull him into a house to help someone.

A man had told Cathy that the firemen were traipsing around town giving shots of oxygen. One minute Rose was convinced the fog was worse than they'd ever seen and the next second, she would be reassured that it wasn't so bad at all.

Still Friday had carried on normally for others. Even though they moved slowly they still were holding the Halloween parade on McKean as planned, the marching band and cheers from costumed children spiking the quiet. Rose moved from home to home, hearing the parade down the street and was disappointed she only finished part of Leo's costume. She hoped Sara Clara had come through or maybe just pinned the spots that needed it and the boy could go to the parade. Maybe Henry had been right. If Rose hadn't been drunk, she would have finished Leo's costume.

No matter. She wouldn't drink the next two days, just to prove she could do it.

Rose had six more homes on her list of people to see when she reached the Lynch home on McKean to find Skinny more than halfway dead, and surrounded by six gambling cronies, including Buzzy.

Rose moved quickly, attempting the breathing technique she'd admonished Bonaroti for using the other day. They first dragged Skinny to the cellar where the air should have been clearer. But her efforts at reviving Skinny weren't working. The fat man had succumbed to the fog and died. Rose found herself thinking like the others, the fog got him.

Rose tried to call Matthews, one of three funeral home directors in town. But, the line was busy. She tapped her foot thinking. Should she head to her next call or keep trying to call the undertaker? She couldn't just leave Skinny here like a lump.

"Hey Sis, Rose." Buzzy shuffled across the floor. He wouldn't meet Rose's gaze, but she could see tears in his eyes. "Skinny's, dead," he said. "I can't believe it."

Rose nodded and picked up the phone. She held the phone to her ear and waved Buzzy to her, giving him a hug.

He took the phone from her and hung it up. "There's no one on the line." His voice was flat, more adult-like. "You have to talk to me." Rose grabbed the phone back, pressing the cradle over and over. "Head over to Matthews' place. Tell him we need the wagon for Skinny." Rose held the phone between her shoulder and ear and pulled her rag from her pocket, coughing into it.

"You can cough all you want," he said, "but we need to talk. It's life or death, Rose, and I need your help."

Rose pulled the rag away from her mouth, her hand dropping to her side. Was he really going to talk about himself after what had just happened?

"That's your 'what now?' Look, I know that look."

"Look Rose," Buzzy took the phone and replaced it on its cradle. "Skinny was my friend. But, he's gone now and I made a mistake. I was going to try to go behind your back. Maybe get the cash from Auntie Anna." He looked away. "Or Henry, or well, you know how things go. And I'm..." He covered his face, his lips quivering.

"Get the hell outta here. You're not asking me for money, Buzzy Pavlesic. No way. Now? And with Skinny, his body not even cold? You're unbelievable!"

Buzzy stepped forward arms open, wanting a hug, but Rose stiffened and snatched the phone from its base, turning her back on Buzzy. She pushed the cradle down repeatedly, trying to get a free line. People were dying and this guy's asking her to help him play another round of poker.

"Rose," Buzzy's voice quivered. "They'll kill me. They'll break me limb from limb. Please. I know I screwed up before, but I'm begging you. I've never begged. Please."

Rose stopped pressing the cradle and by pure luck, the line opened and Alice the operator's voice shot through the receiver. Rose asked her to place a call to Matthews to come and pick up Skinny's body. Alice told her there were three more families who needed Rose immediately.

Rose hung up the phone and started back through the kitchen to the hall.

"Rose? Sis, please. They'll hurt me, listen to me, please."

Rose waved Buzzy off as she swept by, setting out to take care of people who deserved it, who through no fault of their own were fighting off death. Not like Buzzy, some phony guy bellowing for fake help. That kind of thing, she had no time for.

Chapter 15

Rose had worked through the night with the eight docs in town, the firemen and anyone else who could help until the fog got to them, too, and they needed to head home for rest. At nine in the morning, Doc demanded she go home for breakfast and a chance to see a few minutes of the football game that would change her son's life forever. Despite the poor quality of the air, the football game wasn't cancelled. Autumnal fog was a part of half the games they played every single year. Rose and the rest of Donora were betting that after three full days of this heavy fog, on Saturday it would be gone. And, there was an important man coming for dinner that night. That dinner was the part she could actually control.

Bonaroti understood, same as everyone in town, that football was everything to a mill town kid needing a scholarship. Rose agreed reluctantly to go home to eat, freshen up and to watch some of Johnny's game but she would only do it if she were assigned calls to families on the hill near Legion Field.

At home, she washed down her body, and hearing Henry snoring in bed, found she was still angry with him. Though it surprised her that the long night hadn't deadened her anger, she was relieved that she wouldn't have time to dwell on it. Not with what lay ahead.

Rose moved quickly, washing clothes she had forbidden Sara Clara to touch, checking the icebox for the roast that she would cook for the Notre Dame scout that night. She would stop at Humphrey's Grocer for beans later. All the while she kept putting the phone to her ear, listening for a connection to the operator to make sure someone wasn't trying to reach her.

Sometimes the phone would ring and she'd get an up update on the fog and the people it was affecting. Sometimes with the line busy, she would move to the next chore, telling herself that she would find a way to do her job, see Johnny's football game, and knock the black socks right off the scout from Notre Dame.

She heard someone on the stairs. Johnny was gathering his football uniform together.

He grumbled past her while she scrubbed the stain of one of Henry's shirts. "Okay son?" Rose said.

"Yeah, no, yeah, nothing, Mum. I thought you'd be out to work by now."

"I just got home," Rose said.

Rose thought his unusual moodiness was nerves about the game. He always played his trumpet or sax before each game to relax him and Rose thought he was headed to his room to belt out some tunes before heading up the hill to the field on Waddell. She wasn't usually home to hear him play but today her schedule had been upended and instead of just leaving, she was just arriving.

By ten o'clock in the morning, after a solid hour in the cellar, scrubbing this, rinsing that, hanging mounds of laundry, Rose hauled a basket of mending up the cellar stairs, and headed to her bedroom where she would sit and put an end to an eternal stream of holes that marred everyone's socks and stockings.

She stepped into the hall and saw the entire family, except Johnny, gathered outside the front room. She heard instruments being tuned. She expected to hear a blast of hot trumpet air or moody sax tunes, but she heard, instead, the distinct sound of a violin. It sounded as if more than one person was playing. An angry, choppy tune giving way to a smooth, rolling phase almost made Rose cry.

She shifted the basket to her hip and slumped toward her family, quietly absorbed in what was going on in the room. The music stopped, startling her then started again, the bold notes of a violin, underscored by a cello.

"Heavenly," Sara Clara whispered, standing behind Rose. "Isn't it? We thought you'd gone to work! John'll be so pleased. *I* knew you'd want to hear. I do so love when he plays that sweet violin of his. His interview is going beautifully. I just knew it would!"

Rose ignored Sara Clara, and worked her way through the clot of family members, bumping them with the basket and peered into the room. Two men sat with Johnny as he played. She looked from the musical group to Henry, Leo, Auntie and Unk, standing there, heads cocked, drawn to the music like dirt to an open wound. The notes mesmerized, full and rich, as though an entire orchestra had gathered right under their noses.

The hair on Rose's neck stood up. Why in hell, before the biggest game of John's life, was he was hosting a concert and why did everyone but Rose know about it? She glared at Henry.

But Henry's eyes were closed. He was leaning against the wall with eyes shut and a smile, as though the music was filling his soul with what Rose had removed the day before.

Leo had bent down by Rose and picked up a piece of paper that was on the floor. "Here!" he said, handing it to her

Rose read: "Do not disturb, "Scout" from Julliard to see John Simon Pavlesic." It was written in Johnny's chicken scratch. Underneath, Henry's scrawl, "Good luck son, you can do it!"

Rose looked back toward the room. She'd always been a busy woman, but how was it possible? Johnny was such an accomplished violinist and she didn't know that? He mentioned learning other instruments, but she didn't realize how serious he was. She recalled what Joey Saltz had said. Now this written exchange between father and son. Rose had been pushed aside, yet again.

Rose flushed at the betrayal. She had been working after all, not spending her days at tea parties, having her hair done up at the parlor. She would not be pushed aside again. What the hell was she waiting for? Johnny was her son and she had a right to know what was going on. Rose strutted into the living room, stopping across from Johnny in his undershirt and football pants, playing the violin.

Rose couldn't help but be taken by the way his fingertips worked the strings, the bow sliding over one string then the next as though he'd been playing the violin since leaving the womb. The brass instruments were always what he played in his band and at school.

A stumpy man played the cello. His thick arms strained his suit coat at the seams while a hat was pulled down nearly over his eyes. Johnny's music teacher, Mr. DeTurk, stood with his arms crossed watching and grinning as if he had struck a coal seam in his back yard. He raised his steepled fingers to his lips as the rest of the Pavlesics squeezed into the room, listening and watching in awe.

When the music ended Rose couldn't form words. She couldn't even form thoughts. She was as moved as if she had been witness to the miracle of the loaves and fishes. But, she was emotionally and physically tired from the last day and most of all, she felt betrayed.

She moved the clothesbasket to her other hip as Johnny shook the cello player's hand and gave a bow to his family. His face was radiant, his eyes glowing. Rose was impressed with how happy he looked. Henry slipped his arm around her shoulder and squeezed.

"That boy is good, Rose. He is not just some high school band member."

Rose bit her lip. Sure, the kid could play but that didn't *mean* anything.

Johnny took the basket and set it next to the wall and then took Rose's hand and led her across the room to the cellist who was now showing Leo how to use the bow. "Mom, this is Michael Turnbow. He's the director of strings at Julliard. And you know my teacher, Mr. DeTurk, right?"

Rose nodded and smiled and told herself to be cordial. Since when was Julliard in their college conversation? Rose shook the man's hand and then Mr. DeTurk's.

"Mr. and Mrs. Pavlesic," Mr. DeTurk said. "I know you're aware of the degree of raw talent John embodies, I know how much you want him to do what's right, get an education, set goals." He glanced at Johnny smiling. "We're so lucky this wretched fog only delayed Mr. Turnbow, but it didn't keep him away for good." He laughed and Rose wondered what in the world was so funny. "Juilliard can offer John all the polish he lacks. He belongs there and I'm so pleased to know a family like yours understands his gift."

Rose wanted to wring DeTurk's neck. He knew nothing of what she thought. She was ashamed and angry and certain music was not a solid career path. Not even with a trip to Julliard first.

She frowned at Johnny long enough for him to get the message she was not happy and then she ushered the entire bunch into the kitchen for a pre-game meal. Everyone but Johnny. He was nearly late for pre-game warm-ups and Rose didn't care if the Pope himself was sitting here listening to Johnny play, she would not allow him to be late for his game.

Rose walked Johnny to the door so he could leave for pre-game. Mr. Turnbow regaled the rest of them with stories of music in New York.

Rose didn't want to argue with Johnny. She was hurt he'd kept this secret. Another child hiding something. The hurt pulsed inside, making her want a shot of vodka.

"That was really good, that playing with Mr. Turnbow." Rose brushed his hair off his forehead. "It's a lick better than playing on some man's back porch up in the Hill. I know you love music. You've convinced me. I agree you should play in a band in the off-season, between semesters, the whole shebang. You made your point. You are good."

Johnny closed his eyes then smiled at Rose.

"But now, you go on and show 'em, Johnny, show those football scouts, what you're made of, show 'em what you want, what you can do with that arm of yours." Rose squeezed Johnny and whispered into his ear. "Everyone is town's counting on you. It's not just us."

He pulled away and grinned. "I know, Mum, I will. I'll show them."

Back in the kitchen Rose was beyond solicitous to her guests, and enjoyed hearing Mr. Turnbow say how talented her son was. They were not going to think she was a poor hostess, even one put on the spot. She would have wiped their asses if they asked her to, just to prove she wasn't a complete wretch. The cello player raved about Rose's breakfast and in his sincere delivery, Rose found herself charmed and even felt a bit guilty when he left.

When they shook hands he also handed her some paperwork in a linen, cream-colored envelope and promised that at least half of Johnny's tuition for the first year of school would be covered. Rose felt disingenuous smiling, knowing there was no way in hell Johnny would attend Julliard over Notre Dame. No way in hell.

* * *

Henry felt some solace knowing Rose didn't attend Johnny's games. Her work, housework, and fear she'd witness Johnny breaking his neck kept Rose away. So, Henry arranged for a money exchange to occur at the game. Thank the Lord for Dottie and her kind, wealthy soul. Her three thousand dollar loan would cover Buzzy's gambling debts. Luckily she'd gotten the funds together without drawing attention from her parents.

Before her hospital shift she'd give Henry the money, and he would wait for one of Fat Gordon's goons to collect it. Buzzy was in hiding, somewhere, to keep his legs and fingers intact until the money shuffle was complete. This was a plan Henry could live with. He would have to. He hated lying to Rose, but he couldn't let Buzzy be maimed or worse, even if he was a jackass.

Henry made it to the Legion Field just as the marching band was heading into the stands. Not that he could see the individual band members clearly as their black and white uniforms hid behind the fog. The robust music the band normally played while filing into the bleachers came out as more of a bleating, mooing sound, the darkened field making even the most surefooted horn-blower pay more attention to where he was stepping than to what he was playing.

Henry waited behind others to head into the bleachers and squinted, looking for Johnny. Although shocks of the football players' orange uniforms peeked through the blackened air, creating a hazy auburn glow, he couldn't identify where exactly his son stood. Henry was anxious standing there with Unk, hoping his breathing would be okay outside; the old man insisted on attending and Unk had blackmailed Henry into agreeing.

"I slaved in that mill since I was 13." He had poked at Henry's chest, his voice quavering as he was clearly trying to sound firm. "I served in the first world war, I've lived with Auntie Anna for what feels like centuries. I deserve to see my grand nephew do his family, this whole town proud."

Henry had opened his mouth to argue, but Unk put his hand up to silence Henry.

"I know that brother of yours owes a shitload of cash to that old fuck Fat Gordon. I'll blow the whole shebang to old Rosie if you don't take me with you."

Henry had sighed and plopped Unk's felt hat on his pointy noggin. He couldn't leave the man in the kitchen smoking cigarettes and listening to the roar of the crowd up the hill, crying because he couldn't be there to see his nephew play. And while Henry planned to spill everything to Rose once he got everything level and right, he was not ready to confess yet another scheme. Besides, Rose never came to the games.

"Rose'll kick my ass if you drop dead, Old Man," Henry said at the field. He patted Unk on the back after a fit of coughing. The toots and thumps of the band, the smell of popcorn and grilled hot dogs, normally invoked pleasure, but all the coughing and hacking by every person who passed, worsened his morose mood.

Henry maneuvered Unk up three rows of the bleachers, through the murky swirl of air, stepping on toes, bumping into knees and feeling his way until he found a space big enough for them.

He craned his neck to see Dottie. She wasn't the type of woman to be late for her shift. She cared for Henry, he knew that, and a lot, but she had a job to do and she wasn't about to sacrifice it for him. She was just like Rose. Except, well, except for the fact Dottie wasn't his wife.

Henry felt a hand on his shoulder, spun around to Dottie in the row behind him, smiling like an angel. She slipped a paper bag over his shoulder, and Henry reached for it clasping Dottie's hand. She slid hers out from under his, patting him as she leaned over and kissed Henry on the forehead then disappeared without a word.

Two racing heartbeats later, the bag of money inside his jacket, Henry felt another hand, a vice-grip on his shoulder. When Henry turned he was up close with an unshaven, pompadoured man, mouth opened in a snide grin, a tooth missing in front. Henry couldn't miss the whiskey on his breath. Henry reached for the bag and passed it back over his shoulder, not wanting to share even the shortest conversation with this man.

The man scrunched up his face and laughed like a hyena. Henry was glad the sounds of the football game drowned out the man's chilling cackle. With a final squeeze of Henry's shoulder, the man released him and was gone.

Henry's posture relaxed and he let out the air he'd been unconsciously holding. He rubbed his forehead, and ran his hand through his hair, waiting for his blood pressure to return to normal. The chill of committing another act of betrayal, no matter how noble, receded from his mind.

That is, until he looked down the bleachers, past Unk and down one row, and only two people away. Rose was sitting there, staring at him. Henry saw her through the fog, and could tell she was wondering what the hell Henry had been up to with the cloak and dagger act.

A roar came from the crowd, starting from down below. The fans sitting the lowest could see through the fog the best. Another roar, the fans on their feet, cheering, at something good. Henry could not see, but Rose turned away from him, overwhelmed by the people near her, tugging, cheering saying Johnny had just made a first down. Henry could hear them say Johnny was impressing the hell out of every scout.

Henry grinned, heard a man next to him congratulating him. He hadn't realized anyone had taken the seat. Mr. Sebastian. Henry almost felt a pang of compassion; the man was out of his element but clearly wanted be part of the people in town. But, then the man started chattering, bending Henry's ear about something, it was hard to hear with all the cheering but something about family secrets, the value of keeping them, and keeping your name clean and clear.

What the hell was Sebastian blabbering about? Henry wished he'd shut up because he was too preoccupied with his son's playing, Unk's coughing, and scared shitless about what his wife just witnessed to make sense of what the blowhard was trying to get across.

* * *

Johnny snaked his fingers under his earflaps and pulled at them, his leather helmet feeling as if it were shrinking. He huddled his team up tight. The fog had settled thick on the field and when a player kicked off, they lost sight of the ball in the air. The fans nearest the field could see their reaction, and informed the crowd and the information rose upward like a wave.

Johnny couldn't see through the fog to his father and Unk shoving fists into the air, hollering after each play. He did catch a glimpse of the Notre Dame scout, head bent over his notebook, glancing back and forth at the field.

Johnny blinked. If he were tipsy, he'd know he was hallucinating. But there she was. He squinted and shook his head to clear his mind. Over the years he'd tried to convince her of the benefits of coming to his football games. Where else would she have ample opportunities to use her nursing skills? But she always flinched, as though the thought of seeing her son tackled to the ground was too much to handle.

But there she was, her trademark black nurse's bag dangling from her arm. Then she was gone, climbing into the stands, vanishing into the thick fog.

Her appearance threw him. He'd planned to show the scout what he was made of—like Rose had ordered. Except what he wanted to show the scout was he had no intention of playing football in college. Johnny was sure he could bring home a win, even while downplaying his own prowess.

He reminded himself the other fellas would give their right nut to play for Notre Dame. So, when the ball was snapped, instead of Johnny putting the team on his back and barreling up the field himself, he handed off to the fellas who could use a second look by the scout. He launched a few balls downfield knowing after years of practice his guys would be there to make the catch, even in the fog, and that would spotlight them.

And, when they dropped a pass, Johnny would get the blame for making the throw in the first place. He felt proud, as though his shifting the attention onto others he would ensure that everyone got what he wanted in the end. And, he'd convinced himself that he wasn't letting anyone down in the process.

* * *

Rose had spent so much time being angry with Henry that week that when she saw Unk out in this sickly fog, she didn't have the energy to make her way up the bleachers. Besides, the crowd wouldn't allow for movement and after a few minutes of staring up at him, Rose decided Unk was doing fine, especially considering how he'd looked earlier. Rose set aside her worry about the fog, like everyone else. Sure she'd seen one man die, and heard about another. The people she'd visited the day before were sick, but each of the deaths came to people with a history of breathing issues. And, the hundreds of people at the game didn't seem affected beyond the coughing and lack of visibility. It was like any other day in Donora.

She had not really spoken to Henry since their last argument, but there he was, up two rows and over a few people, with Unk. She would not miss Johnny's big game. She'd snuck in to a couple of games over the years, but the sight of him being chased down by linebackers, their thick arms closing around his body, slamming him to the ground, was too much.

She always found an excuse not to attend a game. She knew football was simply a gateway to opportunity and she relished the day when he would be safely ensconced in a job without risk of physical harm. Football led to college and that would lead to success and career and then she'd find peace.

But this game was different. He'd promised Rose he'd show the scouts how talented he was. She knew the way Henry and the residents of Donora savored the retelling of a big game, and she was determined to have seen it with her own eyes.

As she went up the bleachers, she thought she saw a red coat through the fog, Dottie Shaginaw's, and near Henry, but that would not make sense. Nurse Dottie always worked the Saturday shift in the mill hospital.

Diamond Dottie had no reason to be at the game, even a game important to the town. Rose was squeezing herself in between Davey Steinmetz and Arnie Lyons, and glanced behind her, catching sight of a man patting Henry's shoulder then slipping up the bleachers through the thickening fog. She had tried to read Henry's expression, but the haze was too dense, and burned her eyes, blurring her vision.

By the time she refocused, she was being jostled and pulled to standing by people around her. Johnny had handed the ball off to Max Furman for a first down.

Rose vaguely knew what that meant, but didn't have time to ask; Mrs. Tripp had turned around to say she was needed down below. Rose stood to make her way down when Big Ralph stopped right in front of her.

"Maybe you can go resuscitate your husband's career, Rosie? Sebastian's up there with him right now. Maybe yunz are more connected than I thought."

Rose climbed back up where she'd come from and saw Mr. Sebastian sitting, talking intently to Henry.

Could Sebastian be telling Henry about Rose? Her past? Rose's hand flew to her ear, her two lobes. She could not believe Sebastian recognized her from so long ago, but something like that, her ear, was unmistakable.

If Henry would have looked up at that moment, he would have seen Rose staring at him, but he didn't take his attention from Sebastian. Someone jostled Rose as he pushed by, making Rose turn and start back down the bleachers. Maybe Sebastian didn't even know that was Rose's husband. No way he would tell Henry about Rose. He'd want his secret kept, too. Or would he?

Big Ralph elbowed her again as she descended. "Hey Rosie, why don't you do some first-aid, neb around a bit, tell people how to live their lives and then go on home and..." Rose didn't hear the rest of what the fat man said.

Her mind was on overload. "Ahh, stuff it, big Man," Rose said pushing by him, inching down the bleachers, between neighbors, seeing that the lower she got the thinner the fog was. People slapped her on the back with "Johnny's the best," and "Another Donora boy gonna play in the big-time," and "Johnny's gonna put us on the map like Stan Musial!" Rose smiled, thanking everyone as she passed, enjoying the fact they were talking about her kid. The one the town knew would do them proud, even if Rose was a thorn in their side.

Rose stood at the bottom of the bleachers looking for whoever supposedly needed her, but no one was there. Her line of sight was much better and she watched several plays develop into nothing. Monongahela was getting the best of Donora, with Johnny actually seeming to sabotage several of his own plays, not scrambling as she'd heard he typically did, surprising even the most seasoned lineman, Instead, he stood there, knocked to hell, the ball flying out of his hands and recovered by the other team. What the hell was he doing?

Rose glanced from the field to the scout, unable to see too much of either. But she could tell by the way the scout was bent over his notebook that he was scribbling something, grimacing and shrugging after that last fumble.

It shocked her to hear Johnny's laughter rising out of the fog. She strained to see his face, was he really laughing? She couldn't see his expression clearly, but still, she knew his laugh. Rose recalled their last words to each other "Show them what you want," she had said, "I will," he told her, and Rose knew he was doing exactly that.

Her heart beat heavy and fast. Johnny had looked her in the eye and promised. Could he have purposely spoken words that he intended differently than Rose would have taken them? Had he lied without literally speaking a lie? She pulled her bag close, hugged it into her belly, feeling betrayed by yet another child. She told herself Johnny would come through for them. It was the kind of boy he was. Wasn't he?

Dave Delrio's name was called over the loud speaker, instructed to head home. His father was ill.

"And paging nurse Pavlesic." The scratchy sound of the speaker cut off Rose's self-pitying thoughts. "Head on down there with our boy, Delrio. Doc Bonaroti says you're up."

Rose looked toward the huddle on the field, to where Johnny was giving orders to his teammates, and throwing a game. Rose was disgusted at the thought. Rose left the game, pushing back her sadness, moving toward the job she was required to do.

Chapter 16

Rose wove her way through the fog, behind the Delrio boy. Each time he passed under a streetlamp there was enough light emitted to reveal a splash of his orange uniform, but even as Rose yelled for Delrio, she knew she wouldn't catch up with him until they reached his home. The darkness forced her to move slowly, to put her hands up in front of her to be sure she didn't step off the sidewalk, and run into someone.

By the time she wound down Castner Avenue to Norman, feeling her way along the porch rail, to retaining wall to porch rail, she found fireman Bill Hawthorne and Doc Schubert were consoling the Delrio's. Rose couldn't believe another person had died.

"He's not dead," Hawthorne said. "He fell out, took a heart attack, maybe. But, we gave him some oxygen and he's hanging in there."

Mr. Matthews arrived shortly after Rose. He'd been told there was a death and had rushed there, wanting to remove the body since he happened to be so close. He was out of breath, his face, tomato-red, his hair in disarray as though he'd never brushed it. His shirt sleeves were blackened and pushed up well past his elbows, tie askew.

Matthews was a serious man who normally arrived at homes looking as though he were headed to a wedding more than to prepare a body for burial. Rose raised her eyebrows at his disheveled appearance then shoved a chair under him as he collapsed, gasping for air.

Hawthorne draped a sheet over the undertaker's head and pushed two oxygen cylinders underneath to form a makeshift oxygen tent. "Just crack the valves and we'll give him fifteen minutes. He'll be good as new," Hawthorne said.

"Asthmatics. They never fare well in the fog," Dr. Schubert said.

"He doesn't have asthma," Rose and Hawthorne said at the same time. They all stared at each other, while the Delrio family fussed over Mr. Delrio, their sobs, punctuating the thick silence. Blue smoke swirled around the room, forcing everyone to clear their throat if not outright cough and choke.

Hawthorne coughed into a balled up fist. "It's this damn fog. Yesterday at three in the afternoon we had eight hundred cubic feet of oxygen. Now? Nothing. We've borrowed from Monessen, McKeesport, Charleroi...this is more than—"

"Eleven!" Matthews yelled from under his oxygen tent.

"Pipe down, Matthews," Hawthorne said. "That O2 is worth its weight in gold right now!"

"Ah, screw it, I'm fine," Matthews said ripping the sheet off his head. Hawthorne closed the valves, and Matthews rested his hands on his knees, breathing heavy but not wheezing.

He leaned back against the chair, staring at the worried Delrio family "No disrespect meant to you folks, talking this way, but I'm shoveling up body after body all night and I get back to the funeral home after nine bodies and I find out Roberts and Calucci both have a body each. Ten A.M. and eleven bodies later, I'd say we have a problem. And it's not just because we're out of caskets."

Rose folded the sheet into a tight square. "But, no one even knows. No one said a word at the game."

Hawthorne nodded. "Every house I go to, the folks inside think they're the only ones sick. No paper on Saturday, no information. Eleanor's working the Red Cross angle, setting up some emergency aid station at the Donora Hotel. The Irondale's filled with bodies I can't

295

take. Eleanor should have oxygen, beds, and adrenaline at the aid station by late today. Something's wrong, folks, whether we admit it or not."

The silence that followed nauseated Rose as much as the fog itself. What was happening? She remembered the smoke pouring out of the train stack, but that evidence that something was very wrong in town didn't change the fact she needed to get back out there and help her neighbors.

Dan Peterson banged on the front door. He needed Rose and Hawthorne to head to his house. His father, Mr. Peterson, needed them. He was a rickety, slim fellow, always suffering from a wet, hacking cough.

Rose pushed ahead. She loved that stinky bastard and didn't want to see another dead person in Donora. If they could just get some rain, some hard winds to blow away the stagnant, filthy air. Rose was sure a good harsh downpour would cleanse Donora and reveal the steel blue sky's underbelly once again.

She and Hawthorne were about to enter the Peterson home when a wailing woman drew their attention from the opposite direction. Linda Rvsevich screeched like a rabid raccoon. It wasn't until Rose and Hawthorne dragged her into the Peterson home that Linda produced her five month-old baby from inside her trench coat.

The baby was grey and wheezing. But, before Rose managed to check the infant at all, Sonny Rvsevich appeared saying he'd procured a vehicle and was driving his wife and child to the hospital in Pittsburgh.

Rose and Hawthorne argued with them the entire way down the stairs to their car, telling them they'd have an accident in this fog. But the Rvsevich family just plodded on, set on their path.

Back inside the Peterson's, Rose found Doc Schubert treating Peterson, and she and Hawthorne threaded their way through town heading upward and around the snaking streets, going wherever they heard someone was ill.

They headed south and Rose remembered the drawing she'd seen in a textbook of a lid spanning the mountain-tops, capturing industrial smoke, pressing it back down for all in the valley to breathe. She couldn't get the image out of her mind. She thought of the football field where the people at the top of the bleachers couldn't see the field and the folks further down had a better, though still gritty view.

Rose realized then they had to get as many weakened people as possible to their cellars. It had helped Mrs. Cushon the day before and she remembered Henry saying Bonaroti suggested it for Unk, but Rose hadn't really understood its importance at the time.

Rose and Hawthorne found Mrs. Dunaway straining to breathe in her living room, her son at her side, her face blue and eyes full of fear. Hawthorne and Rose began to move the woman to the cellar, and she pushed them away, punching helplessly on Rose's chest. "You're gonna shove me in the cellar and let me die? It's easier to have me closer to the ground for burial?" Mrs. Dunaway wiggled and flopped as they carried her downstairs.

Her son stood mute then followed them down the stairs.

"Bonaroti said this was poison," he said. "But no one listened. And now, you of all people are going to just let my mother sit in her cellar and suffocate? They're piling bodies up in the Hotel, for God sakes!"

Once safely down the stairs, Hawthorne administering a shot of oxygen, Rose gripped the boy's shoulders, making eye contact. She didn't have time to explain.

"Run up stairs—grab blankets, water, chairs—anything to make it comfortable in the cellar, then you're going to sit and wait for this fog to clear. Your mother will recover her ability to breathe." Rose's voice was calm, and steady and commanding. "She's never had trouble before. Make her comfortable, play cards, distract her and you'll see. This won't last forever. But, do not let her go back upstairs."

In the cellar the woman wheezed and hacked like a clotted smoke stack, but the oxygen was lessening the duration of the coughs. Rose headed back upstairs looking over her shoulder, seeing a desperate son comforting his aching mother as they waited for something—the fog to clear, or for her to die.

Upstairs, after delivering a shot of oxygen, Hawthorne placed as many calls as the clogged lines would allow, making a list of people who needed help. Alice, the phone operator, informed him that Doc Schubert had received word the mill hospital was taking on ill citizens—and not just employees—while the Donora Hotel took morgue overflow. Caskets were nowhere to be found and Bonaroti's suggestion to leave town was much too late to heed. Rose scanned the list for patients she knew.

They waited for Alice to phone back with more details, and Hawthorne impatiently tapped his pencil on the table. "Normally thirty people die here all year, Rose. You know that. Sixteen deaths since yesterday. The caskets. We're in trouble."

Rose looked back over the list trying to discern a pattern. Were the sick people concentrated in one spot?

"You work your way up the list, I'll work my way down," Hawthorne said. Rose was relieved to see Theresa's name was absent from the paper.

"Everyone on your half of the list," Hawthorne said, "is located close to your house so you should be able to stop home for dinner with that scout. John deserves it. Can't let a little fog keep one of our own from making it to the big-time."

"John?" Rose said.

"Yeah. John, your son?" Hawthorne raised his eyebrows at Rose. "Young buck is growing up."

Rose's face crumpled into confusion. What did renaming him have to do with growing up? Truth was, Johnny was behaving like a five-year-old when it came to his future.

But, this was the way things worked in Donora——a neighbor, like Hawthorne, wanting to make sure Rose had dinner waiting for Johnny's scout. No matter the trouble, you kept on with your plan, your life. Rose pretended to study the list some more.

The game. Rose hoped Johnny had managed to refocus on the game and make the kind of plays he was known for, the kind that made a gaggle of scouts rush to have him sign on the dotted line.

"Wait," Rose said. "What about the council meeting? We should be there. We need to back up Bonaroti. The mills are going to have to shut down. If the smoke won't disperse up above—if the air is stagnant and won't release itself into the atmosphere, then we have to stop the smog at the source down below. The mills. It's the only answer. Bonaroti knew it and we all ignored him."

Hawthorne and Rose split up, went to the homes on their list, dividing it vertically instead of horizontally so they would both work on opposite sides of town, meeting on Meldon where they would speak at the meeting.

Rose moved efficiently through the names and downward through town. The intensity of care allowed her to push away her problems and toil in the isolated moments of other people's pain, one patient, one home at a time, and avoid her own.

Chapter 17

Rose did her best not to rush through patients even though she needed to get to that meeting. She finished up an exam—stomach flu rather than respiratory distress—at the Huggins home and then moved on toward Meldon Avenue where all the leading citizens of Donora were meeting with the mill's higher-ups.

She'd never seen the streets deserted on a Saturday. The hush that had settled as people hid in their homes was disconcerting. She moved past Thompson, then McKean, to Meldon. The steady hum of the mills, the flying shear and nail mill punctuating the grinding machinery, were all that seemed familiar. She thought of the ever-plodding mills, their indestructibility and the people she'd seen that day. People certainly didn't come with the same guarantee as a good blast furnace.

Rose entered the council building and was surprised to see Bonaroti was not in the meeting, but standing outside the room, looking through the small window in the door. Rose laid her bag by the wall and went onto her toes to peer through the window, too. She couldn't believe he wasn't in there. He was the chairman of the board of health.

Bonaroti shifted to make room for her. "I'm just letting them warm up before I drop the hammer. Go on home," he said. Inside the room sat over a dozen men in suits, perky hats on the table beside their pens and notebooks, each in some way connected to the mill or borough council.

Rose wasn't about to leave, especially after hearing their voices rising, claiming, fog or no fog, they couldn't shut the mills down. If they did, a man said, the furnaces would cool then crack, and they'd lose money. The cost to rebuild the cracked furnaces would mean they just start all over somewhere else, in some other town where they understood what the mills meant. If they had to shut down the mills, the town would suffer. Every business in Donora depended on the mill workers to spend their wages in their establishments.

Bonaroti picked up Rose's bag and handed it to her. "Look, it's not the official meeting. They're not gonna shut 'er down until they're sure there's no other way. They won't decide that 'til Fliss gets his ass here for the meeting tomorrow. This is just a bunch of blowhards belly-aching. Your kid's having that scout over. You have a meal to prepare."

Rose wasn't listening, too focused on what they were saying in the meeting, regarding the recent deaths. Most of the deceased had a prior respiratory issue. They didn't seem to care that thousands of residents—healthy and otherwise were ill.

They talked as if they weren't breathing the same thick air as the victims were, as though they were watching the events unfold in a movie. Rose shook her head in disbelief. The mills took precedence over everything.

To her surprise Adamchek appeared at her side, jockeying for a view through the window to the room.

"Yer son threw that game. They lost 27-7. He played like an asshole."

Rose drew back. Donora lost? Her son wasn't playing his best, but losing? She'd been so distracted by her patients, she hadn't asked who won.

Adamchek scratched his belly, scowling. "People are saying old Johnny boy threw the game to save Buzzy's legs."

Rose grabbed Adamchek's collar and pulled him toward her, Bonaroti stepping in, in vain, to intervene.

Adamchek's face went red but Rose didn't care. "Don't ever let me hear you say that again. Johnny plays hard, every time. He would never throw a game. He's a stand-up young man and there isn't a person in town that'd say otherwise. Not *anyone* who wasn't green with jealousy. Sound like anyone we know?" Rose shoved his collar back into his neck, pushing him back.

He rubbed at his neck where Rose had pushed him. "He's not who you think, Nursey."

Burgess Lewis calling Adamchek's name made them stop. The burgess gestured toward them and Adamchek entered the room leaving Rose and Bonaroti in the hall.

Bonaroti squeezed Rose's shoulder, but she didn't look at him. "No one believes that, Rose. Adamchek's just frustrated. His sister was on my list. She's struggling."

Rose was about to say she thought he deserved to have someone in his family fall ill, but held her tongue.

The chatter in the meeting room got louder and Rose looked up, surprised to see Mr. Sebastian. If he was attending the meeting he, at least, must be taking situation seriously. He had a daughter with compromised breathing. He would shut the mills down.

Bonaroti's voice startled Rose. "Go home, Rose. He pointed toward the men in the room. These assholes don't care if you're here or not. I'll be in there soon to say my part. Have dinner with the scout and wait for my next call."

Rose considered her options. Was there a way to impress the scout without her being there? Sara Clara had to make dinner anyway. Rose exhaled her frustration. What difference did it make if she was there? She could never coax the scout into believing he saw something better on that football field than he did that day.

Henry and Johnny would have to handle things. In the end Rose knew they had Johnny's interests in mind. The entire family understood what Johnny's success meant to the town. A Donoran on the rise was never forgotten. But what would any of it matter if there wasn't a town? If half the town was dead?

"I can't just walk away from my patients. I *should* be in the meeting, telling what I've seen first-hand." Rose paced. "But you're here and Sebastian. He wouldn't be here if he wasn't considering shutting down the mills."

Bonaroti shrugged and pushed his glasses up on his nose.

Rose readjusted her bag. "I'll head back into the hills. Give me your list and I'll hit everyone back up to my house. I'll make it there just in time to charm the shit out of that scout. As soon as dinner's over, I'll be back out doing what I can. Rvsevich and his wife tried to leave town with their baby. Any word on if they got out?"

Bonaroti crossed his arms. "Don't know. Too late to leave now. Visibility is next to nothing so as soon as I square things away here, I'm going to hitch up some of Genovese's old wagons to his horses and start dragging people to Palmer Park. The air's clearer over there. If we move slow, hopefully, we won't get in any accidents."

Rose squeezed Bonaroti's forearm and disappeared into the fog before she changed her mind.

* * *

Rose got back to her house in time to find out Henry and Johnny had cancelled the dinner with the scout. Rose's shoulders slumped at the news, and she dropped her bag to the floor, as though it were the fog that finally got her.

She could not even process their line of thinking. How could they let Johnny's opportunity go down the toilet? It was bad enough the team lost, and he hadn't played his best, but to leave the scout on a Saturday night with dead bodies piling up in his hotel lobby?

303

She ordered Johnny to deliver a plate of Sara Clara's home-cooked dinner, pronto, along with another fifth of Old Granddad to the scout's hotel room. Rose did not have time to discuss or argue or convince. She had to get back to her patients.

Johnny shrugged looking as if he was about to throw a fit. "I'm playing at the Pavilion in *two hours*. This Notre Dame guy isn't interested. He said so after the game. You can't push everyone to do what you want."

Rose clenched her fists, taking deep breaths, knowing she would regret later her words.

"You listen to me, I've been running all over town trying to keep people alive while you're apparently throwing a game. For what reason, exactly, is evidently up for town debate. But, we don't have time to discuss why you played like a complete jackass today. Now you do what I say and act like you give a damn about your future." Rose's voice was quaking as though it were she who had done something wrong.

Johnny's jaw clenched as he held her gaze. "I do give a damn about my future and I already showed him that."

Rose rubbed her forehead as she realized what Johnny said. She knew his mind was on that Julliard scholarship. "I understand you're a talented musician." Rose said. "But to get the hell out of this town, and this smog, you have to do something that ensures you can live somewhere else."

Rose grabbed the food and whiskey and shoved them into Johnny's hands. "Drop these off to the scout, be polite, and tell him you're damn sure you want to play for Notre Dame. Then get your ass back home. Clear?"

Johnny shoved the refreshments back toward Rose. "I can't. I sprained my ankle in the game."

She could not believe his nerve. "Call Dicky, then. He'll drive you."

Johnny balked. "It'll take forever in this fog to get to the scout. I can't be late for the gig. Responsibility, you know?"

"It's not the first fog you've driven through, Johnny. Move your ass."

He shrugged and limped into the kitchen to call Dicky. Rose fell back against the hall wall. She stared at the photos on the wall, wanting to see her Johnny smile like he was in the pictures. She told herself, this was the hard part of being a parent.

Johnny grumbled past her to wait outside for Dicky, and Rose realized Johnny was not going to offer a dance or song or joke to smooth things over. That hit Rose as hard as anything. She wanted to tell him they'd sort this out later, but she knew she hadn't been wrong to say what she did, even if the delivery of her message was harsh.

Rose sighed. She wanted Johnny to have all the right tools at his disposal, but by doing that, she'd given him his independence. Her job was to raise the boy into a self-reliant man. That was why she became a nurse. There would always be a heavy flow of people who needed her. Even if her own children didn't.

* * *

Henry returned home after dropping Unk and Auntie at a friend's house where the smog wasn't so dense. He'd walked in on the tail end of Rose and Johnny's argument and decided that the truth could not wait. He wanted to confess everything, but was scared to death of all the lies he'd told. He followed Rose into their bedroom, watching her change her uniform, readying herself to go back out to care for neighbors. She was mumbling something, distracted or avoiding him or both. He cleared his throat, ready to jerk his lies into the truths they should have been.

He had no idea where to start undoing the lies—Buzzy taking the money, Johnny's interview with Julliard, getting fired, Dottie. No, not Dottie.

"Rose." Henry's voice was thin.

At her bedside table, she pulled out a flask, unscrewed the lid and drank what was left of the vodka and shoved it back in the drawer. Hands clasped she recited a Hail Mary.

If he didn't engage her soon, she'd be out the door. Buzzy's debts paid in full, made it easier to tell Rose what happened. But the guilt was crushing.

Henry watched her tie her hair back in a bun, then release a few tendrils around her ear to distract from the double lobe.

There was no right way to start this discussion, and he blurted out his words. "You're worried about Magdalena. Me too. She's not practical. Hell, even her goddamn hairstyle is impractical. But what's happened hasn't changed anything about our family. Other than enlarging it. She's our daughter and we'll have a grandbaby. You've always wanted more children." Henry ran his hand through his hair. What was he doing? He should be confessing, not bringing up even more stressful topics.

"What I'm saying is sorry. I'm sorry for the last few days and everything." Rose's expression was a mix of confusion and irritation.

"I have to go, Henry." Rose stalked from the room.

"Are you avoiding me?"

"No. I'm working."

Henry felt that comment cut into him.

The phone blasted from the kitchen.

"Don't answer it," Henry stepped in front of Rose. "I want to tell you—"

"I can't just..." Her voice dissolved as she broke away. Henry saw her snatch the receiver off its base, listening, not responding.

She looked over her shoulder, Henry waited to hear her half of the conversation. "I'll be right there." Rose hung up the phone.

"It'll be a fast appointment." Rose said, and brushed past Henry.

"What, who?"

She didn't face him. "Theresa Sebastian."

"Oh, that's rich. The mill superintendent expects you to haul ass in this fog all the way over there to tend to his princess."

"That's enough, Henry. How could you say that? She's as important as...oh forget it." She slammed their bedroom door.

Rose was angry, but he couldn't fathom her reaction to his remark about Theresa.

He opened the door to see Rose stomping around, packing instruments that shouldn't have been in their bedroom due to hygiene rules. He could see how crazy the last few days had been for her, her hands shaking.

"Rose? What's wrong?"

The phone rang again. She shouldered past Henry to answer it.

She wound the phone cord around her finger and dragged it to her waist. "Well, no, Tish, he wouldn't be over there," she said. "Not yet. He had to drop something at the hotel—"

She pulled the phone from her ear and stared at it before placing it back on its cradle.

"The line cut out," Rose said. She hovered over the phone, hands on hips as though lecturing it or willing it to ring.

"Listen Rose—" Henry said.

The ringer blared again. Rose juggled the receiver and placed it to her ear. "Tish?"

Henry alternately puffed his cheeks and blew out the stored air. He hoped another nurse or doctor made it to the Sebastians and Rose would not have to go.

"I know he can't walk. He sprained his ankle. What difference does it make? He's in a car! Tish? What did you say? He's where?"

Rose listened.

"Did they go by way of Altoona or some shit?" Rose said, shouting, clearly having trouble hearing and transmitting information.

"He's fine. He's fine." Rose said to the phone, her voice quivering. The line went dead.

Henry stood with one hand resting high on the doorjamb.

The phone rang again.

"Tish?" Rose said, and shook her head at Henry, the line still giving her trouble. Finally Rose hung up again.

"What?" Henry said.

"The boys and Johnny were down on Meldon at the Elks. I think she said they were headed to the Witchey home. Why would Tish call to say he couldn't walk? That's why I had him go with Dicky—"

"Something's wrong. Tish wouldn't have called back if it were nothing. Not with this fog."

The phone between her ear and shoulder, Rose tried getting Tish, any operator, back on the line.

Henry marched across the floor and grabbed the phone from Rose's grip. "Let's go," Henry said.

Rose shook her head. "I have to be at the Sebastian's. Theresa needs me."

"So does Johnny. Tish might not know what's happening, but something's wrong." Henry shuddered. "Like when something in the mill's about to go awry, you feel it before it happens and by then it's too late. Every other boy in the car with Johnny has a father working a shift or sleeping one off," Henry said. "I say we go down and see what's what. I agree it can't be that bad. Nothing's ever as that bad. But you know how these boys are."

Rose hesitated. "What about Theresa?"

Henry squinted at Rose, trying to figure out her response. "You'll go there after we check on John. Tish can send someone else to the Sebastian's. You need to be there for your son."

Rose tucked her hair behind her ear then listened for another dial tone on the phone.

"Johnny's tooling around town like a jackass and I'm supposed to not go see Theresa," she said. "Why? All because he probably aggravated his ankle?"

"What?" Henry's skin prickled and it felt as though his hair were lifting off his scalp. "We're going to John, to the Witchey's and then you're going to explain to me just what the hell is going on with the Sebastians." He grabbed her arm and hauled her across the kitchen.

"Don't you tell *me* what to do, Henry Pavlesic. No one tells me what to do. I would know if something was wrong with Johnny. I would feel it in my bones. I gave *birth* to him, remember? Tish was just being nice calling—she wouldn't know if I knew my son's ankle was injured. She was being nice."

"People are dropping like flies and you think Tish calls for a friendly exchange of information?"

Rose wrenched her arm from Henry's grip and went back to the phone, tapping her toe while she waited for someone to come on the line.

Henry held up her coat and nurse's bag. "Let's go, Rose."

After they left the house, Henry followed Rose trying to talk sense into her, as she headed in the direction of Theresa's house. Then he stopped persuading. In his gut he knew something was wrong with his son and he wasn't about to let him down by chasing his wife all over town.

So, they both headed in different directions—Henry straight down to Meldon and Rose downward before turning left toward the Sebastian home.

* * *

Her eyes burning from the smog Rose pounded on the Sebastian's door, fueled by worry. No one answered and she entered the home and took the stairs by two. She could feel that Theresa's condition was worsening. She felt her daughter's decline as though it were her own.

The maid met Rose at the top of the steps and ran with her down the hall. Theresa's door was ajar and Rose saw Mr. Sebastian leaning over his daughter. He turned when Rose entered the room, his eyes wide, his lips quivering with panic. "She's purple."

Rose rushed to Theresa, popping open her bag as she did. "The mills are still cranked. Why didn't you shut those things down?"

Mr. Sebastian grimaced and retreated as though Rose hit him. Theresa inhaled hard, her back arching off the bed—just like it had been noted in her files. Rose cursed herself for not getting there sooner. Damn Henry.

Rose's breath was choppy as she rifled through her bag, her fingers slipping and sliding over syringes and medication until she located the tools for treatment.

Rose inserted the needle into the epinephrine and extracted .5 mg of the medicine. She jabbed Theresa in the arm and plunged the medicine into her body. She extracted the needle and waited to see if the stress lessened, if Theresa's body would fall back to the bed, her color return.

Rose bent over, listening for Theresa's breath, watching for her chest to rise, feeling for her pulse, the smell of camellia shampoo wafting in the air. The medicine had some affect, but something was not right. She closed her eyes and listened to determine if Theresa was breathing and her heart beating.

Nothing. No warm breath on Rose's cheek, no chest rising and falling, no sound coming from Theresa's taxed respiratory system. Rose's body clenched as she lifted Theresa's arm and attempted to get her breath circulating again.

She pulled Theresa's body upward, trying to jar the life back into her. When nothing worked, Rose grew desperate, and remembered Bonaroti using chest compressions and breathing techniques on Schmidt the other day. Rose didn't hesitate beyond that single thought. If ever there was a time to try it, it was now with Theresa.

She lifted Theresa as if she were a baby and set her on the hard floor. She blew two long, distinct breaths into Theresa's mouth, and her chest lifted and fell with each burst of Rose's air. Rose couldn't feel a pulse.

Mr. Sebastian's sobs cut through the silence.

"Shhh!" Rose snapped, before blowing another set of breaths into Theresa's body. Sebastian's face went slack; his back slumped against the window frame. Rose listened and watched again for Theresa's air, her fingers at Theresa's neck, waiting to feel blood rushing where the carotid artery fed her body with oxygenated blood.

Nothing.

She gave two more quick breaths and then felt down Theresa's breastbone feeling for a good spot to administer compressions. "Sweet Jesus, help me," Rose said, and delivered three controlled strong chest blows in succession, and then two more breaths. The sequence was repeated several times while she watched and listened for signs of life.

Nothing.

But, Rose noticed Theresa's lips grew pinker. "Sweet holy Jesus," she said again and put her weight on Theresa's chest again.

"Stop that!" Sebastian's high-pitched scream startled Rose.

She hesitated then began working again.

"That's my daughter you're hurting!" He grabbed Rose's arm and tugged her away from Theresa. Rose pulled back, wiggling out of his grip. He tripped over the rug behind Rose, giving her the chance to put her ear over Theresa's mouth and fingers at her neck, listening for breath, feeling for a pulse.

Rose's eyes filled. "Thank you, Lord," she said, and collapsed in joy on top of her daughter. Rose had breathed life right into Theresa's limp body—given her life for the second time. Mr. Sebastian crawled across the floor to them, stunned by the sight of his daughter who'd clearly stopped breathing, now alive in the arms of her nurse.

His face, drenched with sweat, as if tears were springing from his pores, reflected the awe Rose felt. Rose looked at the man and knew without a doubt, he loved his daughter.

Rose rocked Theresa, buried her face in the girl's neck then pulled away when Theresa began to heave and vomit clear fluid. Rose shushed her and turned her to her side, letting the liquid expel away from her body. Rose rubbed her back as she vomited again.

Mr. Sebastian sobbed next to them, allowing Rose to work. She rubbed Theresa's back in circular motions, comforting her. Rose watched her color fully return and when Theresa could sit, she reached past Rose for her father.

And as suddenly as Rose had discovered that the Sebastian's daughter had been her long lost baby girl, Rose realized it was not her place to tear their world apart.

Sebastian met Rose's gaze and he nodded as he reached out to his daughter, and Rose passed Theresa to him. He brushed her hair back, cradling her, whispering to her.

Rose could not tell Theresa, anyone, that she was her daughter. She'd always feared she had handed her daughter over to someone incapable of loving her like she deserved. But, Theresa's father loved her even if her mother didn't. Mr. Sebastian's affection was more than some people had.

Rose rocked back on her heels and stood, her body rubbery. She gathered her instruments keeping an eye on her patient and her father. The shrill ring of the phone in the hall reminded Rose she had more work to do. Relief surged through her, knowing she could let Theresa be, and soon, she'd be home to her own family.

The maid stuck her head in the bedroom and informed Rose she had a phone call—Tish. Rose nodded and glanced at Theresa and her father before going to take the phone call. She listened to Tish, hearing the urgency in her voice.

"Johnny's at the Witchey home. Dottie Shaginaw came upon the accident when she left her shift. She helped Henry get him there. There was nowhere else to take him. No one could get a hold of Bonaroti or you, the horse and wagon, or a car and then they realized what they'd done—just get the hell to the Witchey's, Rose. I'm sorry about this. Really sorry."

Rose's stomach turned over. "Tell me exactly what's wrong."

"Just go, Rose. Just go," Tish said and hung up the phone. Rose thought she heard the woman cry. Or was it a laugh? Rose was still unconvinced it was anything serious. It couldn't be. She jogged back to Theresa's room to get her bag. She took one last look at her daughter and Sebastian and ordered them to get to the cellar or to Palmer Park until the smog lifted. They needed to take advantage while Theresa's breathing was normal.

They needed to take advantage of everything in their life. Rose still felt hurt to see her flesh and blood living as someone else's child. But she felt satisfied Theresa's life, now, was for the best.

* * *

Rose climbed the railroad tie steps that led to the Witchey's as someone opened the front door. The light from the house illuminated the form of Dottie Shaginaw. Surprised, Rose caught her foot and fell forward catching herself, barely missed striking her forehead on the next step.

Dottie pulled her up.

"I don't need your help," Rose said.

Dottie didn't respond but kept moving with Rose into the house. In the living room, Johnny's gang sat—some with heads in hands, others fetal-positioned on the sagging couch. Johnny was not there.

"There was an accident," Dottie said, petting Rose's arm. Rose snatched it away.

"The boys in the car." Dottie's voice was calm and soft, as nurses were trained to talk. "The fog, you know. They were dropping something off at the hotel. But they were, driving, I mean and when I found them Johnny was staggering about, and another fool was driving *his* car and 'course he couldn't see squat in this fog and so I pulled Johnny out of the car's path and when I did…"

Rose could see Dottie's throat constrict so hard a vein engorged in her neck and she had to cough to get a breath. Rose gripped her nurses bag handles hard, digging her nails into her palm.

"When I pulled him back," Dottie said as she demonstrated how she hitched Johnny toward her. "He stumbled and caught his footing and then, like a switch going off, his feet left him as though he had none. They just went out. He collapsed right there, like, well, I won't insult you by spelling it out." Dottie pointed toward the hallway.

Rose shook her head, unable to fathom what the woman was saying, thinking Dottie was a worse nurse than she suspected.

"He hurt his ankle in the game," Rose said. "That's what. I mean, you said you found him after the accident and he was walking around. Was he drunk? He sleeping off a fifth or something? You called me here to deal with that?"

The harder Rose gripped the straps of her bag, the more her hands shook. What was Dottie, saying?

Dottie looked down the hall and pulled Rose with her. Rose kept babbling, her mind unwilling to piece together the evidence, as she entered the bedroom where Johnny lay. Rose stormed to the bed and screamed at him. "You get up, Johnny! You get the hell up and go home." Johnny turned his head, but didn't open his eyes. Dottie had given him a sedative. Rose ripped back the blanket over his legs and she couldn't deny it any more.

The way his legs lay. No life in them, too still. She shook her head. Jesus, God, no. Rose reached to touch his knees, to move them around and see him respond, but she stopped herself before she did. Something kept her from touching him.

Johnny can't be paralyzed. As though she had the ability to scan his body, her body slumped at the realization his back was broken, that his spinal cord must be severed. That's why they were all so panicked. She spun on Dottie. "You did this."

Dottie stepped back from Rose, shaking her head.

Rose moved closer. "You've spent your entire life trying to force your way into my family. And when you couldn't do it, you took the one thing you could. My son. What kind of nurse are you? You should have made him lay still." Rose stalked toward Dottie, nose to nose.

Henry tried to pry them apart.

"She saved John's life, Rose—" Henry said

315

"Quit calling him that! His name is Johnny!"

Henry stepped in between the women and stood in front of Rose his back to Dottie, shielding her. "The rest of the boys were unconscious, if Dottie hadn't been there, he'd be dead right now."

Rose dropped her head back and wailed before her legs gave out and she fell to her knees. Henry stepped toward her and she batted him away. Henry looked over his shoulder at Dottie, just a glance, his body shifting slightly toward her in a silent offer of support. Rose saw it all as though God dropped the information right into her brain.

"I see what's happening here." Rose looked up from the floor, eerily composed, so quiet that she scared herself.

Henry bent toward Rose, his arms open. "I knew you'd understand," Henry said. "Dottie was only helping." He brushed Rose's hair back from her face and tucked loose strands behind her ear. "Let me help you up."

Henry kissed Rose's forehead and she pulled away, crab-walking backward.

"Get out," she whispered. She pulled her legs to her body, balling up. She looked between Dottie and Henry.

"What?" Henry stepped forward, gripping Rose's shoulders. She pulled away and kicked him, catching his thigh. Dottie went to help him up. "Well that's the picture right there. The happy couple together at last."

"Rose, no," Dottie said.

"Get out. Both of you."

Rose could hear Dottie crying as she left the room. Henry stood, wide-stance, arms across his chest. His voice was tight and raspy when he told Rose he would not leave. He said she had no right to be cruel to Dottie or to him. Rose didn't challenge him. She would not make Henry leave his son. Still she noticed Henry didn't deny having a relationship with Dottie.

For Rose none of it mattered anymore. That night she cut the tie that joined her heart to Henry's as though snipping a thread from a cotton shirt. She was there, with her son, but utterly, fully alone. Neither Dottie nor Henry left that night. There was nowhere to go in the choking, wheezing fog. And Rose came to see she did not need them to leave in order to wipe them from her mind.

* * *

The hours crept past as Rose knelt at Johnny's bedside praying. She didn't have her rosary but she mimicked the process, sliding her thumb against her finger mumbling her soul's greatest pain, desperate for relief.

"It was my fault."

Rose jerked upward and turned toward the voice. Dicky stood at the door, Dottie and Henry beside him. Rose searched Dicky's body for signs of an accident. Blood, ripped clothing, anything.

"We were driving down Norman," he said. "Heading to drop off that stuff to the Notre Dame fella. Johnny said he had to do that before we went to Webster to play. Said he'd promised you."

Rose flinched. No. She felt her head shake as she looked back at her broken son.

"We were driving too fast, for the fog and all. We couldn't be late for the show. Two fellas from a record label and the Julliard guy were going to be there. And, we cut over to pick up Pierpont and twisting around, near Highland Avenue, you know how that bend is."

Rose stared, wanting to comfort Dicky, tell him it wasn't his fault, but her anger kept her where she was.

"We couldn't see a thing. The fog was thick as cement, the headlights reflecting the light right back at my face." Dicky's chin quivered and he broke down.

"John's yammering about some science concept," he said between sobs. "Why the lights did that. He wanted to walk in front of the car to guide us with the lights off. Said we'd do better to go slowly. He'd guide us. You know John and we were already late. He didn't want to blow his shot with the scout or the band."

Dicky wiped his nose with his sleeve. "So I, we…we let him do it. And another car came up, lights high and John ended up between both cars…" Henry pulled Dicky into his chest, holding him as he wailed.

Rose covered her ears, she couldn't listen, her own voice too loud in her head. *Do what I say, Johnny then get your ass back here so I can…*how had she phrased it? *Tell you exactly what to do with the rest of your life?* What had she said? But looking at Dicky, she couldn't let him shoulder this burden alone. "No, no, no, sweet Dicky. It wasn't your fault." Rose's gaze went behind Dicky, to Dottie standing at Henry's side.

Dicky pulled away from Henry, lumbered toward Rose and fell into her arms. Rose buckled under his weight, but she shushed him, smoothed his hair as if he were five. He curled onto her lap beside the bed, sobbing into her chest. She didn't want him to feel guilty, but she didn't know what to say to take away his pain.

"It wasn't your fault, Dicky. Don't think that," Rose said. She wanted to scream at them all. At Johnny for being the one to volunteer to walk in front of the car, at Dicky for being so stupid to allow him. At Dottie. At Henry. But mainly, she wanted to holler at herself.

* * *

"Johnny." Rose's lips brushed his ear. No response.

She lay her cheek on his, trying to make sense of what she was seeing. He didn't respond. She felt for his pulse. It was steady. She exhaled. He was breathing, but the sedative was doing its job.

"Neck and back," she said, her voice cracking, her head going light. Her hands shook as she touched his head, without moving his neck, but checking as best she could for blood or head trauma.

"Johnny," Rose said. She could barely fight the urge to scoop him up off the bed, to hold him. She clenched her teeth and began saying her invisible rosary, yet again.

Henry stepped in and reached for John's legs.

Rose slapped back his hands. "Don't touch him."

Henry squeezed his eyes closed.

"Go do something," she said. "Find us a way to a hospital."

Henry glared as if his gaze could strip her mind of all the events except the one that Rose had forced John out into the night to deliver the booze and food to the scout.

Hours passed as everyone took turns dialing the phone to no avail.

Rose paced beside Johnny's bed, watching to be sure he kept breathing. She hated herself for not coming here first. How could she not have sensed the danger? Had she been that angry at him for disobeying her? Nothing she could do would fix this. In her gut lay heavy regret, knowledge that Johnny's accident was her fault. And for the first time in well over a decade she realized she was not the person she had wanted to be.

Chapter 18

Sunday, October, 31, 1948

By 5:30 am Rose had fallen asleep, kneeling at Johnny's bedside. Johnny stirred and wakened her. She pushed up from kneeling, feeling as though her joints had been welded into that folded position, and noticed Henry asleep beside her. Rose patted Henry on the arm, wakening him.

"Mum?" Johnny's scratchy voice sounded. She turned and bent over, hands on knees, resisting the urge to move him or encourage him to move. Johnny tried to straighten his body.

"No, no, no, no…don't move anything, Johnny. We'll give you more sedative."

Johnny squeezed his eyes shut; his face contorted in what was clearly unbearable pain.

"Shhh, shhh, shhh. Now, Johnny Pavlesic." Rose bent her head down and gripped Johnny's hand. She began to talk to herself. He would be fine. Just because he hadn't moved his lower body all night didn't mean he couldn't. Rose would not be dolly doom, she would wait to hear what the doctors said.

"Lay still," Rose told him. "It's morning. Dicky'll run for the Doc and we'll get a truck and get you into Pittsburgh or Charleroi. Something…just don't move."

Johnny's forehead wrinkled up as his breathing quickened and grew shallow. She realized he didn't understand the extent of his injuries.

Rose tried to focus on her nursing protocols. How much sedative could he tolerate? She'd forgotten to ask Dottie what she gave him. She didn't want to overdose him. But, she couldn't process anything useful in terms of alleviating her son's pain.

A barrage of feet barreling down the hall drew Rose's attention.

Bonaroti stood in the doorway with Henry and, of all damn people, Adamchek. Why? Rose spread her hands in front of her, signaling she was ready for information.

Adamchek stepped into the room explaining he rigged his truck. Rose searched his face for some malice, for some reason for wanting to see the Pavlesic family at its worst. Instead, Rose saw concern in his eyes. She would take his offer of help, even if he had accused Johnny of throwing a game just the day before.

They quickly removed a door from the Witchey's bedroom and in smooth, balanced moves, used the bed sheets to hoist Johnny onto the door. Everyone in the house removed his belt and used them as rope extensions to strap Johnny to the makeshift stretcher.

Rose opened the front door and poked her head into the darkness, the usual mill sounds mixed with groaning tugboats. As they exited the house, Rose noticed the smog had grown even coarser since the night before, as if it contained sand. Rose moved her tongue over the roof of her mouth, feeling the moist, graininess fill her nose and lungs.

She prayed this damn air wasn't making it difficult for Johnny to breathe. She did not want him gasping for air, causing his spine more trauma. They all held a section of the makeshift stretcher and shuffled toward the steps, blindly feeling with their feet, moving down the steps to the truck. Rose and the others slid the door and Johnny onto the truck bed and they exhaled in unison, relieved it didn't look as though they'd inflicted more damage.

Rose and Henry climbed into the truck bed with Johnny. Bonaroti came around the back and closed the back hatch gently while Adamchek bent over, hands on knees, huffing.

"I'm sorry it took me so long to get here, Hen, Rose." Bonaroti met Henry's gaze then Rose's before reaching across the hatch to straighten the blanket over Johnny's legs.

"Six-thousand calls in the last few days," Bonaroti said, shaking his head. "Six-thousand sick residents. Our friends and family...yesterday's council meeting yielded nothing—" Bonaroti coughed into his hand, his glasses flopping forward on his nose.

Adamchek straightened, but didn't look at any of them. Of course he'd be defensive that Bonaroti was still harping on that. Rose glared at Adamchek, wanting to berate him for his idiocy. He was one of the people who spoke up for the mills at all times. But, Adamchek had lost his typical bravado, slumped around the side of the truck and got inside. Rose continued to stare at the back of his head through the window separating the truck bed from the cab.

Bonaroti's hand covered Rose's and he squeezed it.

"He sided with us, Rose. He wanted the mills to shut down. I sent you home before he had a chance to speak. Later I ran into him helping folks. When we got the call from Tish, well, he nearly collapsed. I thought it was his heart—all that fat finally sucking the life right out of him. Bonaroti glanced at Adamchek. "But he wasn't having a heart attack. He was suffering from empathy. Hard to believe. Insisted on finding a way to get Johnny down to Mercy Hospital. Said he'd want someone to do it if it were his son. He's barely spoken a word since."

Bonaroti shouted up to Adamchek. "Ready, head on down to Mercy." Adamchek started the engine. The truck began to pull away.

Bonaroti shouted, stabbing his finger in the direction of the mills below them. "Wait!"

Everyone turned to look, squinting into the fog.

"Well I'll be damned," Bonaroti said.

Rose got on her knees to get a better view. Henry craned to see. It was as if God had reached down from Heaven and pressed the switch to off, and the mills stopped. The great bursts of blast-oven fire fell back to the ground, and with that the endless sound of nails firing, metal being flattened, sheared and shaped stopped for the first time Rose could remember. Donora was silent instead of a cacophony of industrial sounds that had become part of their every day existence, background noise that passed for them, as quiet.

Bonaroti's mouth fell open and he pushed his glasses back up on his nose. "They did it. Took the mills to a dead heat. I'll be damned."

With that Bonaroti took off down the hill, and finally Adamchek drove them to the hospital, inching along as if they were out on a scenic drive, working through the fog. Rose and Henry talked to John, telling him stories of the day he and Magdalena were born, his first birthday, the way Magdalena and he were inseparable until fifth grade.

Gales of wind licked their faces and lifted Johnny's hair. Rose brushed it back as it blew back across his forehead. She locked on Johnny's gaze, talking, hoping they'd reach the hospital before her retelling of Johnny's life-story reached this horrid day.

* * *

Rose and Henry arrived home from the hospital a little before noon, Sunday, Halloween Day. Once their cab crossed the Donora border, the fog welcomed them like wayward children. Back inside the darkness Rose felt her environment matched her life again.

Rose, seated in the passenger seat of a taxi, churned a stew of dismay and sorrow at her son's position, anger at everyone, God included.

"Mills are still down," Henry said.

Rose looked out the window.

"Still foggy," Henry said. "Maybe it wasn't the mills."

Rose didn't want to hear a word about anything other than her son.

Rose rubbed her lower back as she shuffled out of the car. The voices of the doctors describing Johnny's injuries and his protocol for treatment played through her mind. The doctor explained that while Johnny was directing Dicky's car through the smog by walking in front of it, the second car came out of the darkness like a shot. In an attempt to get out of the way of two cars, Johnny wrenched his body at the wrong angle and Dicky hit him, compressing the spinal cord, but not severing it. The cord wasn't severed, even when Dottie Shaginaw pulled him back out of traffic. But, it appeared to be bruised. And, sometimes that was enough to ruin a fella's chance of ever walking again.

There was no way for the doctors to discern if the damage was permanent at this point. Paralyzed from the waist down. Rose straightened against the words—each one piercing her heart like nails firing into wood. She wanted to believe it wasn't true, but she had to prepare herself for the chance that it was. Eventually the words would be part of who Johnny was. Until then, Rose, herself, may as well have been paralyzed.

Henry pulled Rose close, arm around her shoulder, holding her up as they moved up the yard to the side door of their stuffy little home. She was too tired to push him away. They passed the Tucharoni's kitchen window and Rose glimpsed Mrs. Tucharoni's coal-black hair, her grave expression telling Rose she had heard about Johnny.

On the steps outside the door, Rose and Henry stopped and looked into the sky. Rose dropped her head back, and felt it hit her cheeks. Tiny pricks of water that quickly turned to drops of rain, drenching them. Rose started to choke, leaving her to wonder what exactly she was choking on.

* * *

At the kitchen table, Rose sat, head in hands, feet sticking to the linoleum floor Sara Clara hadn't cleaned. The smell of coffee filled her nose. She wished for a time when that smell alone was comforting, when she might have given a shit if the floor was clean.

Her body was tired, weighted down with anxiety, fear, worry. She couldn't sleep, and the only thing that she could do was recite her rosary, and wait for the doctors to call.

Meanwhile, the news traveled around town and up the hillsides as the smog dissolved and blew out of town with miraculous winds. The weather had shifted, and lifted the giant lid off the hillside that cupped the valley, the combination of rain and wind cleansing Donora. The air was as clear as the residents had ever seen it. But, remnants of the smog still clung to the insides of people's lungs causing calls to continue pouring through phone lines. At least people could now leave town and head to a hospital. Nearly seven thousand people were sickened over those five days; nineteen had died.

Rose was marveling at that thought when the phone rang. Magdalena picked it up, listening. Rose watched her daughter's mouth fall open and she stumbled back against the sink, bracing herself. Rose raised her eyebrows and reached her rosary-clad hand into the air, signaling for the phone to be handed over. Magdalena's eyes darted to Henry who'd come into the kitchen with Buzzy, Sara Clara and Leo, and then she looked at Rose.

Magdalena dropped the phone onto the counter and backed away. Henry dashed to pick it up.

"Hello?" Henry said. He pulled the phone from his ear and stared at it. "No one's there..."

Everyone turned their attention to Magdalena who had whitened like fine-milled flour.

"Unk died. The fog got him," Magdalena said. Her voice was thin and she began to shudder. Henry pulled her into him and guided her to the kitchen table. Rose could not get that fact through her head. Could that be true? Wasn't he safely in the Donahue's cellar? Wasn't that what they told her the night before? It couldn't be true. She couldn't have lost two lives to this fog. Thirty people a year died in Donora until that weekend. Now, Unk was number twenty. Number twenty.

The silence in the kitchen was punctuated by the sounds of coffee perking, the occasional sob, the retelling of what they'd heard from Bonaroti when he called to confirm Unk's death—his chronic illness mixed with whatever was in the killing smog was just too much for him.

Unk never did go into the Donahue's cellar declaring he would not live like a mole. He'd rather be dead! The family so wrought with pain at what had happened to Johnny, and the town, and now Unk, they silently milled around, unable to do anything else. Except for Rose who could not move, and her hand relaxed and her rosary dropped to the floor.

Magdalena lifted it from the floor, coiled the beads around her finger and settled them on the kitchen table. She went to Rose and undid the gumband and the bobby pins, releasing her mother's thick hair down her back. Magdalena started at the bottom of the strands, gently persuading the knots to unclench, giving Rose the love and attention she hadn't felt in her entire lifetime and until that moment, hadn't really known it might be Magdalena who could deliver it.

Leo crawled onto Rose's lap and nestled his head against her chest, curled up like a cat. Rose wrapped her arms around him and with the conversation of her family around her, she felt loved yet wracked with pain. She would let them care for her now. Even Rose needed to be nurtured and until she found her strength again, she would let them.

Chapter 19

Rose stirred her black coffee with vodka before adjusting her church hat on the top of her head. No point in not drinking. What would that prove? She carried the steaming mug down the hall to Johnny's bedroom, wanting to put together a care package with his jeans, fresh underwear, socks, and a sweater, the length of his stay in the hospital and rehabilitation still undetermined. He was in an induced coma; the doctors hoped his immobility would allow some of the fluid around his spine to drain.

She sipped her coffee and slid open his top-dresser drawer. Inside was the usual: underwear, socks, some baseball cards, but there were also photos of him playing in smoke-blanketed bars, somehow smiling around his trumpet mouthpiece while playing. In another, violin under his chin, he was sitting on a moonlit porch, a colored fella, presumably Louisiana Red, playing beside him.

They were having a good time. In another photo he played his violin, his band members behind him, watching as though they'd happened upon a virtuoso instead of their childhood pal, Johnny. Rose traced the photo of him playing the violin. She could hear the music in her mind, as though he was right there in the room with her, playing the way he had the morning of his game. Yet, she hadn't seen how good he was then. Not really.

She bent over the drawer, crumbling the photos in her hand. Then straightening up, smoothing the photos, suddenly desperate to keep them nice, to keep those images of her son doing the thing he obviously loved most.

For a second she felt her defenses rise. Her anger took hold, with the words why would he hide these? Reality was too heavy for her usual denial. Of course, he'd hidden the pictures. Of course, he didn't share them with her. She wouldn't have cared. She was the reason he was crippled. Tears brimmed with the realization that the crippling of Johnny Pavlesic had begun long before she forced him to deliver that crap to a damn football scout.

Her throat tightened as she tried to swallow. She slid onto his bed, and curled into a ball. She wasn't sure she could face him, face anything anymore. There was a time she thought she could strong-arm anyone or thing into her liking. But now? She knew nothing.

* * *

A knock on the front door startled Rose, and she sat up in Johnny's bed. How long had she been there? She told herself to be brave. She was the mother, act like it. She pulled the door open expecting to see Jack Dunley standing there as he had agreed to taxi Rose to the hospital while Henry and Buzzy took care of Unk's funeral arrangements.

When Rose wrenched the door over the linoleum she found that Jack Dunley had siphoned his chauffeur duties off to Father Tom. Heavy rain pelted him, his hat brim nearly buckling under the weight.

Rose groaned and slumped at the sight of the priest. She didn't have the energy to discuss or repent or play whatever game expected of a parishioner in the presence of a priest. He stood there, hat in hand, then gestured toward the black parish car that would take them both to Mercy.

Rose turned to look back into the house; Johnny's football and trumpet case lay under the coat rack. Rose thought the ball would cheer him up. No, he hated football. She'd take the trumpet. But, what was the point? What was she thinking? He wasn't even awake, he couldn't even move.

Father Tom held the door open. "Rose?"

She took a deep breath and forced her feet to move, and followed him to the car. The funeral for Unk and many others would take place the next day and she wasn't ready to say goodbye to Unk, not yet. She thought she'd rather spend her time saying hello to her son.

In the car Rose attempted several times to say the rosary, but no prayers or even the microscopic movement of the beads sliding through her fingers seemed small enough for her to achieve.

She glanced at Father Tom, waiting for him to say something, but he only sighed.

Rose's hand fell to the side, the rosary slipping out of it. "I don't like God anymore. He's my crucible. I hate him." She waited for Father Tom to launch into an argument so she could really let him have it.

But he simply nodded and drove in silence, sending Rose the distinct feeling that somehow he understood.

Tuesday, November 2, 1948

At Gilmore cemetery, Henry stood perched on the hill with hundreds of mourners. The mills were back up and running, the zinc mill below bellowing its familiar yellow plume, but the air was remarkably clean. Rain had a way of refreshing the air while muddying the crushed coal streets in Donora. The sun appeared more yellow than silvery. The sight of the yolky orb made Henry think he should have felt a rush of optimism. Instead, he simply felt wasted, like the naked cemetery hillside.

Six of the twenty dead people were buried the day before. He moved tentatively on the steep, dirt hillside, the fine dirt making Auntie Anna cling to his arm. Rose moved slowly in front of him. She shifted her weight, started to topple, and dug her heel in, trying to get her footing on the jagged rocks that jutted from the cemetery land.

Henry supported Rose from behind, pushing her back to standing. She stiffened and shrugged away. He knew she was hurting so he let it go. He never admitted to wrongdoing with Dottie, their focus was Johnny and Unk, and the rest of the town. Still, Rose felt betrayed and he wasn't about to argue.

He watched Rose gazing down the hillside to the Sebastian home and noted that smoke snaked out of each of the four chimneys. They'd been told Theresa had been doing very well since Halloween night, that Rose had saved Theresa's life, but there was something off about the story and Henry hadn't forced Rose to talk about it.

He wondered if she'd had an affair with Sebastian, the way she was absorbed by the sight of the home; something in that hulking brick home had changed Rose. Maybe it was simply the loss of the clinic. Henry was too tired, too overwhelmed himself to push for answers, to ask about it even once.

Henry had taken the message from Bonaroti for Rose, too upset about Johnny to talk. The clinic was still unfunded, for a variety of reasons. Rose turned further into herself when Henry relayed the news. Mourning her work life was just one more thing on top of Johnny's accident, the illnesses of seven thousand people in Donora, twenty deaths including Unk, and then there was Dottie.

Father Tom had delivered a moving mass and now offered a eulogy on behalf of the Pavlesics, complete with Henry's poetry. Though the priest had only been acquainted with the family for a short time he spoke as though he'd known them for their entire lives. He moved among the funerals that sprung up on that part of the cemetery hill, offering kindness and warmth to the grieving families.

But, as Henry and his family moved from Unk's internment to a neighbor's and then another's, Rose grew more agitated. It took a couple more gravesides and eulogies but she finally bolted, weaving through the clutch of funeral-goers that had gathered around Benjamin Hipler's grave-site. Rose had always been so good at that, keeping her distance, feeling compassion without drowning in her patients or neighbors mistakes, illnesses and accidents. Henry figured she simply couldn't manage that any longer.

Henry called out to Rose, straining to confine his tone to a whisper. She lost her footing, and slipped to the ground. She quickly got to her knees, but Henry could tell she was disoriented. He closed in on her, seeing that she'd focused downhill toward the zinc mill, watching it sending that yellow acid into the air as though no one had died, as though nothing were wrong.

Henry yanked Rose up by the shoulders.

"Are you all right? What..."

Rose squirmed out of his grip. "Just fine."

Sara Clara came up behind Henry and took Rose by the elbow guiding her back to the throng of mourners. "Now, you just let your family care for you the way you always—"

Rose flung Sara Clara's hand off and bolted toward the cars.

Henry caught up to her near jog, but didn't make the mistake of handling any part of her body. Sara Clara flanked her other side. Rose looked between the two of them.

"Leave me the hell alone. For five minutes."

"You may hold things close," Henry's voice heaved with his fast pace, "You may not disclose a lot about how you feel, Rose, but one thing you never are, is alone. Patients, family, neighbors, you are *never* alone."

"Really, Henry." Rose stopped short making Sara Clara and Henry spray some dirt to stop beside her. "That your latest observation? Why don't you write a poem about it, or better yet, just keep a lid on it, why don't you?"

"Now, Rose," Sara Clara said, "dear, my daddy, the mayor of Wilmington, North Carolina has graciously offered to put up scores of sick Donorans, to offer them the opportunity of fresh air. Donora's sending at least two nurses down with us. Why don't you—"

Henry thought Sara Clara was a sweet woman, but naive, poking Rose the way she was.

Rose was practically spitting her words. "Your father? The one who disowned you for marrying that 'Yankee, mill-hunky Croatian,' is that how he put it?

Sara Clara's mouth tightened and her eyes filled. She fumbled with her hanky, tracing the blue embroidery before meeting Rose's gaze.

Buzzy had come from the other direction, hauling Auntie Anna by the hand, startling the trio as he roared at them, breaking the mourning silence. He struggled under Auntie's weight, but Henry knew that had more to do with him spending Saturday evening as a punching bag for the fellas he owed beyond what Dottie had helped him pay. Buzzy had sworn that amount had covered it all.

Rose had avoided Buzzy since he'd begged her for money and Henry was sure she had enjoyed his absence. His brother's sunglasses barely hid the evidence of his stupidity.

"You be nice to my wife," Buzzy said out of breath. "I've had it with walking on egg shells around you."

"Screw you, Buzzy," Rose said. She glanced at him then back at his wife. "Why don't you and Sara Clara get the hell out or pull your weight or whatever, but don't you dare hold your lazy, gambling ass up above me."

"You don't deserve Henry," Buzzy said. He ripped his glasses off and revealed two blackened eyes, one swollen shut, scabbing over. Rose flinched but wouldn't break his gaze.

"I almost lost my legs because *he* was too scared to ask *you* for help, Miss High and Mighty. And when I asked you, you were too damn busy. I can barely see or walk and you're responsible, Rose. Hen should have left you when he had the chance. He is such a good man and this is what he has to put up with."

Rose laughed in his face. "My fault that you got the hell knocked out of you? A good man? Why don't you ask Henry about his lies and then look me in the face and say he's a good man."

Buzzy threw up his hands. "He had to take the money, Rose." Sara Clara hit Buzzy in the arm. "She means that Henry gave up college to marry her and move here. He lied to her about that twenty years ago. He told her the other day…"

"Bull," Auntie Anna, said in a whisper and drew everyone's attention like she'd rung a gong. "It's about Dottie. Right, Rose? Dottie Shaginaw helping Magdalena?"

Henry shoved his hands in his pockets and looked at the ground.

"You didn't tell her about college?" Sara Clara said.

"I didn't tell her about any of it," he said.

Rose shook her head as though clearing it. Her teeth were clenched tight, adding to the tension in her face. "Now, that baked beans are spilling all over the cemetery," she said, "why don't you spill the whole damn thing, Henry Pavlesic. Tell your adoring fans about Dottie, and I don't mean about helping Magdalena. Why don't you explain what the hell is going on between the two of you?

It's nice to know I don't have to feel guilty for despising you."

Leo came across the hill crying and Buzzy and Sara Clara pulled Auntie Anna along, and went to their boy, leaving Henry and Rose alone.

Henry wanted to reach for Rose, embrace her, but he knew that was not a smart move. "Shut the fuck up and listen Rose." He kept his hands in his pocket and kept his voice as steady as he could. "I don't like secrets and it's been eating me up for a long time to keep this from you, but I was trying to help Dottie—that was the first lie, that was the relationship you're talking about. We did have relations. But not what your thinking. Not full completion. I won't deny it. It was back when my father died and I couldn't handle his death."

Rose stepped back from Henry.

"Magdalena and Johnny were so little and colicky and I needed *you* and you left me. You went into the night with that black bag of yours to the hospital to work and you left me. Dottie stopped over to see you, but like I said, you were out. And she was having some trouble. A relationship, her parents coming down on her—we'd been friends since we were six, Rose. I just wanted to help her out."

"So what? Boo-hoo. I went to work so the logical thing to do was to fuck Dottie?"

"I was helping her and yes, having someone need me for a second was comforting. And we didn't sleep together. We only—"

"So I'm not needy enough. Hmm. That's it?"

"It just happened, Rose. We never got close again that way. When Magdalena came to me two weeks ago, I didn't know what to tell her, then I got hit with the slag in the ankle and there was Dottie, like she could read my mind or some shit and before I knew it was all coming out and she said she could help Magdalena."

Henry stepped toward Rose as a hawk swooped down behind her before lifting into the air and disappearing, making him lose his thoughts. Rose grimaced and shook her head at him.

Henry crossed his arms. "In the end, I was late back to the furnace and got fired because I blew my stack, partly angry at myself, partly for the colored fella." Henry reached for Rose. She flinched away from his touch.

Henry cleared his throat, wanting to drop to his knees and beg her to forgive him. "I was just so angry that all of this was happening and I lost all sense. I wasn't sure they'd fire me so I waited to tell you until I knew for sure."

The corner of Rose's mouth twitched and she folded her arms.

Henry thought maybe she was softening. "I know Buzzy rubs you the wrong way but I promised my father I'd watch over him and I failed at that." Henry swallowed hard, forcing his shame away. It was too late for pride.

The Johnson's dog began to howl, pulling on its chain down below, next door to the Sebastians. Rose turned toward the barking. She dropped her arms and mumbled something about the dog being made of rags. Henry put his hand on her shoulder. She shrugged it off and turned back to him once Mrs. Johnson pulled it into the house.

Henry refocused on Rose, feeling vulnerable in the line of her hard stare. "I stole money from the household to keep Buzzy alive, I knew about Johnny's interview with Julliard. I did all of it Rose. All of it. And I'm sorry. I couldn't be sorrier."

Rose looked as though each word were a bullet puncturing her skin.

She broke Henry's gaze and pushed the straps of her purse over her shoulder. When she finally looked back at him, the intensity of her expression chilled him.

She jutted out her chin. "So I *gave* you the opening to betray me repeatedly. I did this, did I?"

Henry realized he'd stupidly thought releasing the inventory of deadly lies he'd told would somehow clear things up. There would be no retrieving their relationship by simply listing his trespasses. It was time for her to help make this work.

He stepped toward her and put his hand out, but didn't touch her. "I love you Rose and I love the way you are, independent, a nurse. I love you, goddammit. But until you stop seeing yourself as perfect, and disappointed that everyone else isn't, then you're going to keep losing out."

"Really Henry? Thanks so much."

"I've been wrong. I'll take what you dole out for that. But I'm telling you for your own good, stop putting your job first. Your kids need you. I need you."

"You son of a bitch. You've ruined everything. Johnny, Magdalena, everything. Why weren't you there when I needed you? You should have gone with Johnny to deliver that booze and food to the scout. Just once I'd like my husband to fill in, without me having to tell you what to do, how to do it, or when."

Henry felt a change inside, his guilt shifting to anger. "*You're* the one who went traipsing all over town. You should've been home, making dinner for the scout. Don't blame me. *You're* the one who sent Johnny out in the fog. *You* went to the Sebastians to care for someone else's stupid kid before caring for your own. Maybe if *you* had been at the accident site instead of Dottie, you wouldn't have yanked Johnny out of traffic, bruising his spine, because you're so damn good at what you do. You are God almighty perfect."

Henry's hands flew around to punctuate his words. "Maybe if once you put your family first, instead of barking orders, your son could still walk. You chose some stranger, Theresa damn Sebastian over your own flesh and blood. Blame yourself."

Rose pushed her purse over her shoulder again, hand quaking. Henry saw Rose's eyes lose their arrogance to pain and he was sure for once his words got through.

"I did not choose a stranger over my flesh and blood," she whispered with quiet anger. "You son of a bitch." Rose fingered her purse strap at the shoulder, her face losing its anger, but taking on a different tension, despair.

Henry drew back.

Tears wet Rose's cheeks. Henry resisted wiping them away.

Rose's shoulders slumped, but she held Henry's gaze. "Theresa *is* my flesh and blood. She's my daughter."

Henry dropped his hands. "What?"

Rose glanced down the hill at the Sebastian's house then nodded slowly. "I gave her away twenty years ago. And there she was, the other day. There she was."

Henry felt as if she had belted him in the stomach.

"What the hell are you talking about?" Henry remembered her harsh reaction to Magdalena's news. Her unbalanced concern for Theresa.

Rose's body tensed as though she were trying to force back the sobs that now moved through her. Her voice was flat. "I never forgot her, the orphanage. Any of it. Any of the sinful, rotten things I've done. For the last twenty years, it has followed me around, haunting me."

He couldn't process what she was saying. "Why didn't you tell me?"

Rose laughed. "Tell you what, Henry? That I was tricked into giving my baby up by the first person I ever thought loved me?" Rose buckled forward. Henry caught her.

"Rose," he said.

"You think I believe I'm perfect? I've known exactly how imperfect I am since the day I was born. My parents gave me away to monsters." She crumpled into him. "No one even touched me except..."

Henry could feel her armor split open, her entire countenance softening in a way he'd never seen before. "Should I have told you I didn't even know who the father was? Tell you before I ever got pregnant I spent a decade being used by the director of the orphanage? That his wife didn't blink? Tell you that, Henry? You would have loved me if you knew all that, right? You might be a good man, Henry, but you're no saint. I knew it even then."

Rose cried bucking into Henry. He dragged her back toward the car, thankful that onlookers would simply believe she was crying due to Johnny's accident and Unk's death.

Henry tucked her inside the car and walked around the other side and got in, staring at Rose.

"All I ever wanted was my children to have warmth and love," she said. "I loved them best by letting you love them more. If that was wrong, I'm sorry. It was all I could do. It was all I knew how."

Henry strangled the wheel, driving way too fast for the winding, rising streets of Donora. He just wanted to drop Rose off at home and get the hell out. For the first time in his life he thought he might know how Rose felt, like all there was to do was hide, pushing away anything that might not seem to fit in his world. And for the moment, one of those things was Rose.

* * *

After the funeral, Rose pushed through the side door and removed her coat. She was met with the burnt odor of food. Had Sara Clara left the oven on? Rose mustered the energy to generate a bad thought toward Sara Clara, but she was too tired for the thought to spur the frustration that typically followed such musings.

Henry dragged behind her. They didn't walk into the house together, a couple united in love and grief, as they would have before the awful fog had infiltrated their lives. Instead, their bonds were severed; they were useless to one another.

Rose felt a sudden relief at being home, only to be replaced by the realization Johnny would never be the same, and Magdalena's life would be full of remorse whether she gave the baby away or kept it.

You need to forgive yourself. Those words startled Rose as though they'd dropped through the air. Father Tom's words. He'd said them. That's the voice she'd heard. Rose unbuttoned her coat and jammed her hat on an empty hook and noticed Johnny's coat hanging there. Johnny had forgotten it that day as he ran out of the house and into Dicky's car.

Forgive yourself.

Rose thought of poor Dicky, what he had to live with. It didn't matter if everyone else forgave you if you didn't forgive yourself. She thought of the look on Henry's face when she confessed to him the details of her past. She had no way of knowing what he thought. Of course he was shocked, she could see that. But he seemed angry on top of it. Maybe he just felt shock on top of the pain he'd already been feeling. Maybe he could still forgive her for all they'd been through, for not being good enough at mothering, at being a wife.

Forgive yourself. The voice nudged her. The soul shadow. But it wasn't Theresa anymore. It was the priest.

Rose entered the kitchen and was surprised to find Mrs. Saltz, her wide backside outlined by a tight-fitting dress that squeezed her curves rather than smoothed them over. The ties of Rose's favorite apron cinched her pudgy waist. Rose tried to slink back out of the kitchen, unnoticed, but as she backed out, it struck Rose there was no wailing or crying or theatrics.

"I hear you," Mrs. Saltz said without turning from the stove. Her arm made large circles as she stirred something in the giant stockpot. "Mail on table there." Mrs. Saltz jerked her head toward the table. "Just dropped it, that US mailman."

"Oh." Rose slid into a chair at the kitchen table, feeling as though she hadn't been off her feet in weeks. Rose was hypnotized with fatigue, and the fat woman stirring at her stove. Rose did not move but took in the once neat room, seeing from a distance the stove's backsplash was covered in oil, the countertops littered with dishes and ingredients.

Mrs. Saltz dipped a tea bag in a mug and delivered the drink to Rose.

Rose held it under her nose, smelling mint.

"I thought it might suit you," Mrs. Saltz said.

Rose sipped the tea, paging through the mail in front of her, not processing what she was seeing. It wasn't until she reached the middle of the pile that she felt a jolt. The same kind of crisp, linen envelope that Mr. Turnbow had left when he visited three days before. From Julliard.

Now, her son would never have the chance to go to Julliard, even if she approved. What would they do with a cripple? This was a kid who would spend his days rotting in a chair, keeping busy playing checkers with people who had no potential. Johnny had plenty of potential but it was as if he were now a hidden coal seam trapped inside the earth, part of the world, but not able to contribute to it. Potential wasn't worth shit.

Johnny was stuck. Worse than Rose had ever imagined possible.

She dropped her head in hands, rubbing her temples and she wondered how she would handle the path her life had taken. For the first time in decades she wasn't sure if she could go on at all.

Rose was suddenly aware of the silence in the house. She opened her eyes and met Mrs. Saltz's gaze. Rose narrowed her eyes at the woman. She could not remember ever seeing Mrs. Saltz when she hadn't been about to cry or in the midst of tears. "Why aren't you crying?"

"Because *you* are."

"I'm not crying," Rose said, placing her mug back on the table.

Mrs. Saltz pointed at her chest. "I can feel you weeping here."

Rose's eyes filled, and she wiped her teardrops.

Rose was oddly comforted by Mrs. Saltz. She had never thought of her as very capable, yet there she was. In Rose's silence, Mrs. Saltz yammered on, detailing her plans to use the money she'd socked away, to move her family, without Mr. Saltz, of course, to the warm, healing springs in Georgia.

Normally Rose would have been excited, agreeing Georgia would be far enough south that Mr. Saltz would never suspect, but she didn't have the energy. The concern was gone, as though it'd never been there. Had Rose faked her entire existence, not really caring for anyone at all? Rose listened to her heart. No, she did have concern; she just didn't have anything left to give.

Forgive yourself.

Rose pushed herself up from the table, opened the hutch door and fished out a fresh bottle of vodka. She unscrewed the lid and took a swig.

Henry entered the kitchen. Maybe he'd find a way to forgive her.

Rose turned to face him; he looked stricken, his eyes shot with hate.

Henry took a shot glass from the hutch. "Bonaroti stopped by, thinks Unk died because he lived in this town. Says he can tell a guy from the valley just by eyeballin' them. Some fella, Stadler, a chemist is up here, trying to find fluoride or fluorine, of all the damned things, in the lungs of the bodies who haven't been buried. A byproduct of the zinc mill."

Henry's voice was monotone, like he was talking in order to buy time or gauge Rose's mood. "Bonaroti said the government will be in here in a day and a half and the mills are going to have to answer for this. They should have shut things down before Sunday morning. But they kept ratcheting away, collecting their cash while good people met their demise. Including John. Goddammit. The mills are full-blast running again, people working like nothing happened."

Rose turned back to her tea and pushed the vodka across the table with the back of her hand, a silent offering to Henry. She snuck a glance at Mrs. Saltz at the stove, stirring.

Henry filled the shot glass and threw it back, not looking at Rose. "Bonaroti said you could actually do something to help people when the Feds get here, do something more than just care for people after they become ill, you could actually stop people from getting ill. Said he'll need your help over the next few weeks…interviews, surveys…"

A head nod was all Rose could muster. She was so ashamed. "Hen?" Rose said, hoping he'd understand that for once she needed to hear the words that went along with how he felt about her. She needed to hear that he understood her and loved her and forgave her, but she could not ask for it.

He looked up and when she stayed mute, he shrugged and left the house, slamming the door.

Rose jumped at the sound then sighed into her tea. No person was strong enough to force anything to happen in the world. Rose sat there for hours, parsing the combination of events that occurred in the past few days wishing she could change any one of them. She tried to say a prayer but none came to mind. Her rosary wasn't in her pocket. She looked around the kitchen for something that reminded her of her life before the accident. Nothing did.

Not even Mrs. Saltz, stirring soup, seeming like the most reasonable woman God had ever crafted. Rose smirked at the thought; there was no God.

Chapter 20

Henry had slipped out of the house when Rose had caught five minutes of sleep, and didn't come back, proving to her what she had feared her entire life.

Rumor had it he had picked up a shift at the Duquesne Works, pulling overtime every shot he had, living there with a cousin. Magdalena was living with Henry now, sharing a bedroom with three cousins, twice removed, under the age of four and was, according to neighbors who spoke loud enough in front of the house for her to overhear, doing very well.

Sara Clara, Buzzy and Leo headed down south and took the fragile Auntie Anna with them. They went with the groups of fellow Donorans who'd been invited to North Carolina to cleanse their lungs. The reports coming back were that all were responding to the clean, salty breezes. Thoughts of Johnny in a rehabilitation facility in Sewickley, Pennsylvania, accompanied Rose as she went about her day.

Her activities were no longer shaped by nursing or the immediate demands of family. Rose hid herself away from the world, safely ensconced at home. She thought of her family every minute of the day, thinking that people and families were like the nails made in the mill down below. Each gripper left marks on its nails so unique they could be used to solve crimes.

And Rose thought, families were marked that way, too. If it were possible to see inside Henry or Rose and Buzzy, Sara Clara, Magdalena or Johnny—their souls would all bear distinct gripper marks of their shared misery.

Rose didn't clean the house or bathe or even eat very much. She stayed in bed mostly, not even rain slashing at her windows made her stir. Twice a week Father Tom gave her a lift to visit Johnny.

Once in a while, she braved it and opened the front door to fetch the newspaper. She could only bring herself to read the headlines and then she couldn't focus enough to leave her gaze on the page.

The November election of Truman over Dewey had come and gone, shocking the nation as most people had gone to bed thinking Dewey won and woke to find Truman the president. The weather had returned to normal in Donora with colder winter temperatures and typical fog that didn't seem to be killing anyone as the killing smog had done just weeks before.

Rose wandered her house, always having wanted a home of her own, with her own rules, no one to mess up what she fixed up, but she never knew what that might actually feel like. Until now.

She remembered that feeling she'd had the week of the fog, the sense of being with family members yet struck how alone she felt. She hadn't realized that whatever she had been feeling that day was nothing like what she felt since everyone left. She was still angry at them, but she began to miss the opportunity to tell them she was.

Alone in the house, Rose moved Johnny's instruments, the footballs, baseball gloves, basketballs, and athletic shoes from room to room every time she noticed them. Rose fully understood her part in Johnny's accident and inflicted punishment upon herself. If Johnny could not pursue his dreams—or those Rose had for him—then she would not pursue hers either.

After Mrs. Saltz left on Tuesday, November 2nd, Rose climbed into what felt like her own death as she marveled at her lack of desire to do anything. She'd stare at the walls, letting the stinky dog Rags into the house after seeing that he belonged to the Johnsons at the funeral, pulling and tugging on his rope. She felt obligated to take him in, knowing he had a home, and owners who didn't care for him.

Rose now allowed him to press up against her, follow her around the house, and drink from a cereal bowl. In bed, she'd watch the dust settling on itself, darkening the sills. She wasn't moved to wipe anything down in the least. She enjoyed the nights when the fog swirled around her ceiling at night giving her mind something to do instead of mulling over the fact Henry was no longer sleeping beside her.

She kept waiting to get bored, to rush out of bed, determined to open her own clinic, secure funding, put her family back together, but nothing happened. On the days she didn't go to visit John, she wrapped herself in smelly sheets and laid there as though the world had clamped an invisible seal over her, squelching her desire to live.

Rose ratcheted her bedside table drawer open. The flask was empty. She went to the kitchen, found nothing. Rose clawed at her cheeks, feeling dizzy. How had she come to be a person rummaging through her own house for booze, like a common beggar?

Because. That was who she'd always been.

The closet. Her secret stash of, well, everything. She shambled back to the bedroom and went straight to her closet. She got on her knees and popped open the secret panel that hid the space in the wall where her salvation lay.

She ferreted through the cans, trying for a moment to keep things neat. But then she began tossing the cans, corn, beans, Spam, baby food, cloth diapers, bottles, where was the booze?

If she could just have one little drink she could think clearly. She hit the back wall, the space now empty of its contents, but continued to feel around, convinced she'd hidden several bottles there. She pounded on the wall with both fists.

They had to be there. She put it there herself. She fell to all fours and heaved for air. Beads of sweat formed at her hairline. She bent forward, head on her knees, disoriented. She didn't know what aspect of recent life events had her most upset. Finding and losing Theresa? Johnny's accident?

Or was it Magdalena's pregnancy, or her family or losing Henry?

Rose bucked up and screamed at the air. "Haven't I paid enough?"

A voice came from nowhere. "You have."

Rose flew to the back of the closet, startled. She calmed herself; she knew that voice. She pushed aside the dresses that hid her view. Standing outside the closet was Father Tom, carrying a bag as though he might be staying somewhere for the night.

She threw her fists into the wall. "Get out! Get out! Get out!" She hit the wall so hard it gave under her weight. She paused and hit it again, exposing another hollow space in the closet. Drywall instead of plaster in this part of the closet? Unk would not have stood for such shoddy building materials.

Father Tom joined her on the closet floor, pulled her hands into his and turned them back and forth, assessing the scrapes and bruises. Rose had expelled all the energy she might have used to push him away and shove him out the door.

"I'll be staying here until your family returns," he said.

Rose shook her head. They weren't coming back. They hated each other, why would they come back?

"Well, then, until one of your friends comes to stay."

She shook her head again.

"Well, then, see, that's the problem. I'll be your friend, then. I can't have you killing yourself. People need you

Rose. You're not the kind who can just disappear and not be missed."

Rose pulled her hands from his and balled up against the wall, her head resting on her knees. She couldn't believe the priest had casually mentioned killing herself.

"Suit yourself," Rose said. "But, I won't kill myself. Don't mind if death shows up and takes me. I'd like that, actually. To just be done with it all. And just so we're clear, I don't want you here. You can't bring God back into my life just because you want to."

He nodded and examined the hole she'd made with her fists.

"Flashlight?" he said.

"Kitchen drawer."

Father Tom tripped over the canned goods, and headed into the kitchen leaving Rose to stare at the wall. What the hell was in there? How could there be another secret place? Had she been so good at hiding things that she hadn't even realized what she'd done? Who the hell built a second hidey-hole? Had she done it and forgotten?

Father Tom returned, brandishing the flashlight and shined it into the hole. "Looks like something's here."

That didn't make sense. A person couldn't forget something like that—building a false wall for Christ sakes. Was she mentally ill instead of just a liar? Stupid? She stabbed at the wall with the butt of the flashlight, piercing the wall with each blow.

The hole grew big enough for them to tunnel their fingers into and tear hunks away. Three big sections gave way and she flashed the light into the hole again. The light bounced back, reflecting off something shiny. She reached inside. Vodka. She felt crazy, how could she forget? She unscrewed the lid and took a swig, feeling it course through every inch of her, warming, numbing, calming her like magic, the way the simple act of saying the rosary used to do.

Father Tom declined her offer for a swig.

She shook her head at the wall. "I didn't build this, you know. It had to be Unk." The master bedroom was his before Rose and Henry moved in seventeen years before.

He was a hoarder, like Rose, but not a hider. He hoarded right where everyone could see him with his jars of bolts and nails and screws. But still. Rose put the vodka aside and stuck her head in the hole, the flashlight sending a sliver of light through the space between her chin and plaster hole.

Rose's vision adjusted. More whiskey and bourbon. She pulled the bottles out and set them behind her. It wasn't long before she stared uncovering cases of beer. Iron City beer. Rose cursed him silently. Why the hell would he hide that of all things? Rose had to widen the hole to maneuver the case of beer out. It didn't feel right in her arms. Too light, but not light enough to be empties.

She lifted both sides of the case, and stared down at bottles. What the hell? She closed the box, pushing it behind her. She lifted three more cases out, shaking her head, almost smiling at Unk. He'd always been a strange man, and if he'd been rich, he'd have been deemed eccentric. But, hell, he was interesting enough that half the town thought he'd buried money in the house.

Rose dove back into the hole in the wall and rooted around. Nothing else. Just the outside wall. Nothing. She sat back on one of the cases of beer. Buried money? Why would Unk tease people so? Probably to make people spend the rest of their lives wondering. What would Rose do if she found money? Five days before she had an answer. Buy a new home, pay for everyone's school. Be secure, happy. Five days before, everything had been clear.

Rose ran her hand over the case of beer beside her and lifted the two lids that met at the center, again, grabbing.

She lifted a bottle of beer from the case and hefted it in her hand, then shook it. The lid flew off. It had been removed once, and just set back on top. It was heavy, but no liquid inside. She handed it to Father Tom and he turned it over then held the opening up to his eye before pouring it into his hand. Nothing came out even though it felt full.

Rose took it from him and poked her finger into its mouth and felt paper. She snaked her finger around and finally coaxed a piece out. Twenty-dollar bills. She could only reach so far down the neck of the bottle. She ran for her nurse's bag and found long tweezers to help her remove the money. They released the cache, bill after bill, growing, oddly, more confused than gleeful.

When she had finished, the rolled up money, along with the canned goods, and soot from inside the walls, covered Rose, the floor, Father Tom and the room she'd shared with Henry for nearly two decades.

Rose couldn't do anything. Before, she'd have leapt and danced over the find, but now the money seemed unimportant.

Father Tom crossed his legs and took a swig of vodka from Rose's bottle.

"Wow," he finally said, as he collected the money, the bills that were so used to being rolled up that he couldn't flatten them to stack. Rose watched trying to make sense of it all.

Unk had intended the money for her, that much was certain; he put her vodka with the money, knew she'd know it was for her. There was a time that finding this stockpile would have solved all her problems, but now, it didn't matter. Now, she felt sickened. Out of habit, Rose began to cross herself then stopped, waving the gesture away.

Father Tom shrugged then took another swig of vodka. "You let your religion strangle you, Rose."

Rose took the bottle from Father Tom and took a big swallow.

"I know I'm assuming a lot," he said, "by saying this, but I think you need to hear it." He took the bottle back and sipped.

Rose pulled her knees into her chest, head against the wall, listening.

"You've lost God in the ritual, the expectations, the motions. You perform for Him. What you need to do is simply see Him in your unfunded clinic, in your imperfect family, in your ugly past when you were so wronged by people you trusted. God is with you, even if you're not with Him."

Rose blew out her air and took another swig of vodka. "The Pope'll have your frock for that."

"No."

Rose let the vodka wash through her body, numbing her pain, surprised she felt comfort in simply being, in sitting with someone who cared about her soul more than she did.

* * *

She woke on the floor of her closet, surrounded by the bills, the effects of the vodka on her temples, like Irish dancers on amphetamines. She remembered Father Tom. What kind of damn priest leaves a woman drinking herself to death amid the rubble of a secret hidey-hole?

Rose pulled herself up on the doorjamb of the closet, holding a bottle of vodka. She stumbled to the door, weaving through the mess.

"Father?"

She wandered down the hallway, reached for Johnny's doorknob and turned it, but couldn't push it open.

Her hand slipped and leaning against the wall, she continued to the kitchen. She grabbed a shot glass from the cabinet and sloshed some vodka in it.

Rose heard footsteps near the side door. Father Tom came into the kitchen from the front room.

"Who was at the door?" he asked.

She glanced at the clock, and then turned to Father Tom. "Shush. Mailman. Don't move!"

Rose froze, hands in the air and held her breath. She'd been successful hiding from everyone who hadn't been avoiding her.

The mailman was persistent, pounding. Rose wished him away and heard the door crank open. She ducked under the kitchen table. Father Tom ignored her frantic gesturing to join her and headed into the hall.

Rose was relieved. He would send him away.

She heard the mailman cough. "Oh, hey there, Father Tom. Didn't know you were driving the nurse to see John, today."

What was going on? Rose held her breath. The two men walked into the kitchen. The least Father Tom could do was run interference for her.

"Couldn't fit anymore in the slot and I didn't want to drop it again," said the mailman. "Thought I should check for bodies. Just in case. Hahaha."

From under the kitchen table she saw the lower legs of the mailman and his black shoes turned toward the priest's. Finally the two bent over, staring at Rose.

"Hey, Rose. That you up under there? Here's mail. Four days' worth." He stood and flopped the envelopes onto the table.

Rose nodded. "Thanks." She could barely breathe. Normally she would have been embarrassed to be found hiding, now she was simply petrified she'd have to talk to whoever found her.

He bent back over. "You're just like my wife. I tell her to use a damn mop, but she insists on cleaning the floor on her hands and knees! I say throw a mop over it and call it a day!" He left the house, without another word.

Rose pulled herself up to the table and sat, Father Tom across from her. Was he going to shadow her forever?

"Don't you have a church to run?"

"I'm all yours," he said.

They stared at the mail, the white envelopes, nothing very interesting. Except for one, its creamy, linen threads announcing its pedigree and source. Rose did a shot of vodka and filled the glass and withdrew the letter from Julliard and ripped it open.

"Dear Mr. Pavlesic..." it went on and on, glowing about Johnny's playing, conveying a sense of uniformity that made Rose sure that every student they were interested in received the exact same letter. But, at the bottom, Mr. Turnbow had handwritten his own note. "Fine young John, we are desperately awaiting your reply. I'm at the end of the road for putting things off with Henderson—the head of admissions. Please contact ASAP as I can only fend off the dogs for another few days...sincerely, Turnbow."

Rose's hands shook. Her shoulders shuddered, tears springing from her eyes, the sadness inside her, making her feel like death was on its way. She wiped the wetness with the back of her hands. There was no point in crying. Johnny could no longer do anything. He was better than he had been, starting to walk with crutches, but she would not believe he was better until she saw him sprinting down the hallway.

"He's on his way to walking Rose," Father Tom said. "He just needs time. The doctors have been clear, he's been blessed, a miracle, a phenomena of nature. It's time you forgive yourself and love him the way you have his whole life."

Rose shook her head. "I don't deserve forgiveness."

Someone at the door startled Rose and Father Tom. Doc Bonaroti flew into the kitchen with such force that Rose didn't even have the chance to consider hiding.

"You're alive? Well, yes, of course. Rose. Father Tom, glad to see you," Bonaroti said. He glanced around the house, clearly too agitated to comment on its messiness, but definitely impacted by the sight.

Father Tom excused himself saying he would take a few minutes to walk the dog and check in at the church with Father Slavin.

Father Tom shook Bonaroti's hand and the doctor turned his attention on Rose. "I need you now," he said. "Out and about. We're having real trouble getting people to talk about the fog. I put together a force of twenty housewives—twenty and they can't get reliable information! Even the mills and the union are putting ads in the paper to get people to open up their doors. That's how much pressure there is to collect this data."

Rose shrugged.

"This is what you're good at Rose. We need your help. Please Rose, these fumes, this murder in the mills—"

Rose stared into space, thinking about the ads in the paper and what it must have taken to get the mills and union to place them. Yet, citizens still weren't talking?

"Sebastian will never fund the clinic if I help collect information that links twenty deaths and seven-thousand illnesses to his mill, now will he?" Rose said.

Bonaroti waved his hand through the air as though erasing a blackboard. "That ship has sailed. He's made it clear he wants no part of funding anything right now. The missus had her baby and is confined and they're talking about moving. There's no money with the Sebastians."

Rose flinched recalling the night she breathed life back into Theresa. She had done something well, something right for Theresa, but in doing so she put off going to her son. She could not find a way to feel comfort in saving one child when she may have contributed to the pain of another.

Bonaroti straightened his bow tie. "There's a new government agency looking into the effects of industry on the environment. People are still dying, Rose. Another twenty so far. More will succumb. And the non-killing exposure the rest of us have had? Who knows what the rest of us will face in years to come," Bonaroti said.

Rose nodded but didn't speak, numb, unable to feel moved by what the doc was saying.

Bonaroti leaned against the sink, his hair flopping over one eye. "The People. People like Unk and all the rest. Four hundred people have been evacuated to North Carolina to recover, Rose. It's staggering."

He rifled through his bag for his notebook and read from it. "Sara Clara from the South's father agreed to find spots for all of them in Wilmington. Thousands—seven thousand people in this town have received care for the effects of that smog. Some scientists are saying these fluoride emissions, worked like nerve agents. It's why we couldn't hear wheezing in people who were normally healthy. It compromised those who already had problems, yes, but even formerly healthy people were affected. We're thinking the trapped chemicals simply paralyzed their lungs."

Rose grimaced.

He squeezed Rose's shoulders and she looked away.

"I need you to help interview the residents of Donora," he said. "The nurses and doctors from Washington need interpreters for the Slavs. You could do that for them. Half the town is afraid to talk. They're acting like nothing even happened. Others are angry and exaggerating facts. I'm hearing that the mills are gearing up to blame the weather, saying this temperature inversion alone is the reason for the deaths, not the chemicals from their mills. They might go so far as to say our own coal furnaces killed us if they're pressed, but they don't want to admit it could be gasses from their mills. If you go to their houses, people will listen to you. Please. We need all the data we can get our hands on to make a strong case."

"I'm not really feeling well, Doc."

"You have to help yourself, Rose. Help the people of Donora. Help Theresa. After all these years..."

Rose stiffened.

Bonaroti exhaled his frustration. "I'm the one who blacked out your name in the file, Rose. You told me the story about the orphanage, that you began your nursing studies at Mayview, well, it didn't take much for me to figure it out."

He sat across from her at the table. Rose's mouth quivered as she tried to control her body, her thoughts, her words. He couldn't have figured it out from the file. She wanted to tell him he didn't know what he was talking about, that there was nothing she could do, but couldn't get the words out.

She looked up at him, and felt a breeze from the open side door. Father Tom yelled that he was heading to the church. Rags the dog sauntered into the kitchen, went to Rose and sat by her feet. She dropped her hand and scratched the spot where his skull met the top of his neck.

Bonaroti picked up the dog's water dish and filled it. "John's accident didn't have to happen. He's your son. Do it for him."

Rose shook her head. Getting a bunch of townspeople to discuss the killing smog wasn't going to help her son.

Rose cleared her throat, "How did you figure it out? Theresa?"

"Since the first day you came here. I talked to Sister John Ann. She didn't pull punches, that one. Your secret's safe with me, Rose. Always has been."

Rose turned toward him. "You and I have shared a secret for twenty years?"

"Seventeen or so. That's what friends do, Rose."

Rose dropped her chin. She couldn't believe someone knew she was such an awful person and never held it against her. Bonaroti had done something for her and she would have to do something for him.

She owed him that much.

Chapter 21

For the first time in a week Rose washed. The simple act of bathing lifted her spirits and loosened the cobwebs that veiled her life. Rose would not start nursing again, even if there was clinic funding, but she would follow through on her promise to Bonaroti.

On a typical foggy day, Rose set out, feeling this was one way she could repay the town that had opened their doors to her as a visiting nurse. She pushed on toward the Stewart home, though her mind kept returning to thoughts of her bed, the way she had hidden there, and wanted to be back there right now.

By collecting data for the government, she told herself, she could help ensure that the killing smog never came again. Then, her reward would be jumping back into her bed until she could muster the energy and will power to make a second set of rounds.

The Stewart home was on Sycamore. Tiny, bent Mrs. Stewart answered the door and smiled, accustomed to Rose's home-care visits for her husband's chronic bronchitis. But as soon as Rose said she was there only to interview her and to gain her help interviewing other citizens of Donora, the woman slammed the door.

Rose drew back and shuddered. Rose glanced around to see Mr. Bratchy watching her from his door. He narrowed his eyes and threw his hand into the air at her. She buttoned the collar of her coat tight and started down the sidewalk, glad the clanging mill, train, and boat chorus drowned out Mrs. Stewart's words and the slamming of the door for anyone other than Mr. Bratchy.

Rose stood at the corner staring at her list of homes to visit. She ran her finger down the names, shaking. Her breathing quickened, coming in shallow bursts. She couldn't do this. She loosened her collar. She'd had plenty of doors slammed in her face before, but everything had changed. She could not try to behave as if no one in town knew her family were frauds, that no one had heard she had failed everyone in every way she had once imagined to be successful. She wrapped her coat tight against the wind, and moved half jogging, half shuffling through the cold, back to the safety of her home.

Once inside the house, she went to the kitchen and sat having coffee with vodka mixed in, waiting for the alcohol to calm her. She couldn't sit still, but yet, wanted to hide. She went to her bed and burrowed under the covers without even removing her uniform. Her bed had once been her sanctuary, but no longer held peace or refuge.

She threw back the bedspread and reached into her pocket for the list Bonaroti had given her. She stared at it, crumpled it then smoothed it as straight as possible. She made a deal with herself to do just two homes on the list today. She wanted not to care, but something would not let her give up completely.

She redid her hair, brushed her teeth and smoothed out her uniform, telling herself she could do what was required of her. So, back out into the late morning, now clear of fog, Rose went.

At the Horvat home, Alma allowed Rose inside the door. Rose cleared her throat, but nearly left when she couldn't remember what she was supposed to say. She unfolded her paper and scanned the backside of it for the information she was supposed to convey.

Alma Horvat stared past Rose at first, giving her the impression that she agreed that talking about the events surrounding the five days of fog would benefit everyone in town including the Horvats. But, Rose wasn't far into her mechanical spiel when Mrs. Horvat threw her hands into the air.

"No, no. I thought you come to discuss baby. My baby. We don't talk about mills."

Rose's eyes widened. "Oh." Rose looked down at her paper as though there would be something there to help her through this. "I didn't know you were—"

Mrs. Horvath began shoving Rose out the door. "We can't talk. I promise not to talk about mills." Rose stepped through the doorway as the belt of her coat caught in Mrs. Horvat's closing door.

Rose opened the door and pulled back her belt, securing it around her waist. She felt the shallow breathing return and shoved the paper into her pocket, wanting to run back home. Two homes that day were plenty. But, as Rose headed back home, she began to pass some of the homes she had promised to visit, feeling a heaviness grow in her gut with every step. Rose stopped. She turned back to the Miller home and stared at it.

If she didn't do it now, she would have to do it later. She promised herself that after helping Bonaroti she never had to leave her home again if she didn't want to. But, putting off what needed to be done wouldn't make that come faster. So Rose trudged back to the Millers, talking to herself, reminding herself that she'd been yelled at, pushed out of homes and cursed at before. What difference did it make that now the insults seemed to penetrate her?

And so she went, and at the twenty-third house on her list someone actually took the time to talk to her. A burly, unshaven, unkempt man raised his hands to grasp the doorjamb, his sweat ringing his underarms. Rose cringed at the odor.

"No one's making yunz stay here, Rosie. Yunz don't like the mills, leave."

Rose pushed her shoulders back and raised her chin to make full eye contact. Part of her wanted to move away, but not because of the mills. "I know the mills afforded plenty of people a good life—"

The man leaned forward, smothering Rose with his breath. "Exactly," he said.

Rose stood tall, refusing to be intimidated. The man smirked. "Rosie, yunz and those government blowhards can get the hell out of town."

Rose took offense to being lumped in with government officials. She'd nursed nearly half the town at one time or another and seeing her as the enemy was not acceptable. "You can't just tell people to leave town because you don't like what you're hearing," Rose said.

"Then why don't yunz mind yer own beeswax and start minding yer own family. Maybe yunz daughter wouldn't be knocked up and Johnny a cripple."

Rose flinched. "Johnny's not a cripple."

The man leaned close and Rose smelled the booze, kielbasa and his perspiration all at once. "Yunz are snobby, Nurse Pavlesic and it's finally come back to bite you in the ass. Yunz ain't no better than any of us, with all that education and shit. Everything always has to be yer way, doesn't it? I don't know how your people put up with yunz."

Each word he spoke pierced Rose's heart. She'd heard a different version from her own family. But it never hit her so hard.

Three small children ran up behind the man and hugged his legs, grinning as though their father was the greatest man.

He patted one child's head. "When's the last time one of yunz guy's kids did this to you? Go on, mind yer own ass and get away from us and the mills."

Rose watched the man lift the three kids up at once, and swept them into an embrace. "We're happy. Steady checks, roast beef, mashed potatoes every night. That's good enough."

Rose backed away from the door, and walked in a daze to the sidewalk.

Rose stood there, heaving for breath. Neighbors crossed the street as soon as they saw her. News must have traveled she was attempting to coax people to be truthful about their experiences with the smog. She felt lightheaded, dizzy. Black and silver dots formed in front of her eyes. She rubbed her temples. She would not let herself pass out.

A voice inside her head. Forgive yourself.

She clasped her hands over her ears. "Shut up!" She looked at the house she'd just left, the crumbling stoop, the rotting eaves and rafters, such disrepair. Inside the doorway, she could still see the man with his children, their laughter reaching Rose's ears. Even though the house was shabby, the home was alive with love. The opposite of Rose's.

And, she realized for the first time, she'd neglected the children who lived with her for seventeen years for the one that'd only lived inside her for nine months. Rose understood exactly what she needed to do to make her life whole.

She could do it. She'd been a nurse, stitched enough flesh to know that even the deadliest wounds can heal.

A family was the same, Rose told herself heading back home. Surely she could make amends. And not like she did in the past. She would do it a new way.

When Rose reached the side door of her home she could hear an argument between the Saltz's. The cries escalated to screams. Rose dashed across the street to find Mr. Saltz dragging Mrs. Saltz down the block by the hair.

Rose could see her scalp pulling from her skull. Rose yelled for him to stop, and took Mr. Saltz by the shoulders and hit him in the kneecaps with her foot, throwing him off balance and he dropped onto his back.

Rose kicked the man until he let go of Mrs. Saltz's hair. "If you ever touch her again, Mr. Saltz, I swear to God I will kill you. Understand? I will kill you."

He struggled to his feet and Rose thought he would rail on her. But he stumbled away, as much from being drunk as from being shocked.

In Mrs. Saltz's kitchen, Rose examined her. Remarkably, the woman was no longer crying. She was shaken, but mostly, she was disappointed her husband had discovered the money she'd hidden for Joey's warm springs therapy, money that would get them away from him.

Mrs. Saltz shook her head in disbelief, "That man been in washroom only five times in twenty-two years. Of course, I think money is safe in laundry box." She raised her hand and let it fall back into her lap. "One time he decides he need detergent to wash himself in face. Stupid Kraut. Don't even know what soap is."

She winced as Rose dabbed at her bloody cheek. "But money now gone. Kaput. He drink it. Then he tell me he find it. He show me it gone. He no believe my lie about money, say it was gift for him, for us, for a house. He know better."

Mrs. Saltz shifted her feet. "All these people die, my boy he lay helpless in bed with the polio. In God's sweet name, is this the way life should be?"

Rose felt the weight of Mrs. Saltz's words, the sensation of a woman who'd given up hope.

"You have to leave," Rose told her. "You have to do something for the sake of your children."

Mrs. Saltz shrugged. "Do what? You think I have place to go? Go where? Beach like your Sara Clara from South always tell me? What I do there? Sell sea shells to sea gulls?"

Rose went to the sink and ran the tap, a corner of a towel under the water. She returned to Mrs. Saltz and wiped dirt from her chin and neck.

"Yes. That's exactly what you do, Mrs. Saltz."

With Mrs. Saltz cleaned up, Rose left the house. The police had called saying they had Mr. Saltz in jail for at least one night for public drunkenness and resisting arrest. They agreed to keep him as long as possible and Rose knew she might be able to help. She left the Saltz's hearing Mrs. Saltz laughing at Rose's suggestion to move away with her children. Like that would ever happen, she had said.

Rose crossed the street to her home and thought of the money she'd found in the house. She considered turning back and telling Mrs. Saltz that she had the answer to her problems. But she couldn't. Deciding to give Mrs. Saltz the money, and put her on a train that night seemed like an easy one, but too much planning was needed. Joey couldn't travel like a healthy child. There were so many reasons not to give Mrs. Saltz money.

Rose's heels clomped across the front porch, drawing her attention to how alone she was now that it were only she who made any noise at the house. Rose entered the house, shedding her coat and bag right onto the floor near the door. Rose certainly did not want the money to go down the throat of Mr. Saltz. She stripped off her uniform as she headed to her bed. Nothing good would come of Rose giving Mrs. Saltz the money.

Rose pulled the bedspread over her head and curled into a ball. Exhaustion from having been active that day had settled in and Rose knew she could not properly decide how to help Mrs. Saltz right then. She crossed herself, but did not pray. Instead she hoped that somehow she would wake and find solutions for all that had happened.

Chapter 22

After her shower Rose put on the only clean clothes in the house—Magdalena's fitted sweater and wool slacks and toweled off her hair as best she could. She decided to wear it down hoping it might dry before seeing her son. She ran into Johnny's bedroom and grabbed his football. Maybe he would want it. Maybe he didn't hate football as much as he claimed.

She tucked it under her arm and stopped as she passed Johnny's bed. The crumbled photo she'd found in his drawer was on the floor, peeking out from under the hem of the bedspread. She stared at it from the doorway, tossing the football up and down in one hand. She ran to the side-door and punted the football out the door, watching it roll out of sight.

She grabbed her purse, the letter from Julliard and Johnny's trumpet. She stood by the door waiting for Father Tom.

She tapped her foot as she rehearsed what she would say to her son. When she got to the part where she'd talk to him about his trumpet and the letter she realized the letter was in regard to his violin playing. Or was it strings in general? She ran back into the house and grabbed his violin and guitar. Father Tom pulled up to the house and she wrenched open the door, instruments under her arms.

Father Tom bustled from his car to help.

"Rose Pavlesic you look like you're twenty dressed like that. Not that it matters, but something's different. Care to discuss it?"

Rose didn't answer and they tucked the instruments into the back seat of the car. She rolled down her window and stuck her arm outside, feeling the air hit her skin. She wasn't ready to talk about it yet.

Father Tom put the car in gear. "One change at a time," he said, winking at Rose.

Rose relaxed back against the seat and thought for the first time in forever that things just might find their way to right. And, for once she didn't pretend to know what exactly right was.

* * *

The sharp antiseptic smell of the rehabilitation hospital was familiar and made Rose comfortable. She could do this. She could.

Rose and Father Tom followed a nurse to Johnny's room. The doctors on morning rounds were huddled around his bed. A nurse's aide had Johnny's foot in his hands, pulling his leg up and out to stretch his atrophied legs. Johnny screamed, his face in pain. The doctors were discussing the bruising in Johnny's spinal column. Finally, the swelling was going down, and the nerves were once again sending messages of pain to his brain and making him scream. This was good news to Rose, from a clinical perspective—his incomplete spinal injury had a chance of being reversed. There was a good chance he would walk. He would be his old self.

Rose's eyes filled and she thought back to when he was born. Unlike Magdalena who was a quiet mouse Johnny never stopped screaming, as if he didn't belong in his own skin. Then, at age one, he changed into the good-natured boy he'd been since. Rose instantly remembered the helplessness she'd felt at not being able to take away his pain or comfort him.

Rose squeezed the envelope from Julliard and glanced at her feet, at the collection of instruments she brought from the house. How could she have been so stupid? He wasn't ready for this.

Johnny's voice cut through her silence. "Mum?"

She went to him, telling herself to treat him like a patient, distance herself so she could be helpful to him instead of a blubbering mother who could do nothing but see the worst in his future.

They held each other and Rose pulled away. The doctors had left and the aide was discussing something with Father Tom in the corner of the room.

Johnny pried her hand open and took the envelope from her hand. "What's this?"

He opened it and read the letter, tracing the words Turnbow had written with his forefinger.

Rose had never felt so unsure. "Johnny, um, well, John. My sweet John."

"John, is it?" he grinned at her coyly. "All I needed was to break my neck to get you to come around, huh?"

Rose took his hand and kissed it.

"I will never forgive myself for what happened. I'm sorry for not listening to you. I'm sorry for, well, the fact I couldn't even call you John."

"You don't have to do this, Mum. I know you want me to still go to college...well Dad said that, but then added you checked with Pitt and they could delay my acceptance, I could be a trainer for the football team, not that we have the money to pay for it without a scholarship anyway...I mean, Mum?"

Rose filled a paper cup with water and drank it down. How did Henry know? He wasn't even living with Rose let alone speaking to her. She turned toward Father Tom who glanced away and slipped out of the room. Damn small town. Secrets weren't even safe with the priest.

She pulled a chair up beside the bed. John folded the letter in his lap. "You don't have to do this because you feel guilty."

Rose felt her shudder from her toes to her scalp. Was she doing it again? She did feel guilty, but she was not acting out of guilt. She was acting the way she should have all along—by doing what was right, right for him, not her.

Rose plunked herself down in the chair, elbows on legs, chin on fists. She wanted to be very sure of what she was doing. She would not hurt her son again.

She looked at him, but he stared at the ceiling. "I am..." she said, and cleared her throat, then fumbled with a paper cup and the pitcher of water again. She barely got the water down. "I am so sorry for what happened, John."

"It wasn't your fault."

Rose gave him a look. "No, I mean before the accident. When I look back now," she said, her voice hoarse, even with the water. "I can't believe how much I didn't see. I forced you to...it wasn't as though you weren't a gifted football player or capable of college, but I didn't listen, I looked right past who you were. I was just so scared to let you be."

"You just did what worked for you, Mum. I forgave you. I just don't want to think about the future. Any of it, college, music, anything."

Rose's hand shook as she picked up the letter and smoothed it back out on the blanket.

"I know what you're doing," John said.

"What?"

"You're trying to get me to look at the letter and tell you to contact that man, but it won't matter. I'm only worth half a scholarship this year, next year I could earn a full, but how the hell can I live in a New York walkup with a wheelchair?" John's mouth spread wide as he tried to force back the tears. He sobbed twice and then took several deep breaths, cleansing away the tears.

Rose hesitated. She didn't want to hold him so tight she'd hurt his spine. She didn't want to hold him so tight that he might think she thought he was weak. But that, she thought, was her old thinking. That was her being afraid someone might know she was weak. She bolted up and grabbed him to her, shushing him. He latched on to her.

"You're going to do great, John. Anything you want to be, you can do. It doesn't matter that you're in this bed, it doesn't matter what I thought you should do. You can do whatever you set your mind to and I will do whatever I can to make it happen. Your way, though. Not mine. You will walk again and you will play your music at Julliard."

John coughed and laid back. Rose dried his tears with a napkin. He took deep breaths and his eyes lit up, glassy but cheerful. Rose held his face in her hands, seeing him differently than she ever had.

"They told me how brave you were," John said.

Rose met his gaze. "What?"

She let go of his face, feeling exposed.

"With everything that's happened. Everyone who walks in here tells me how brave you were with it all. How much they miss you in the clinic, in the homes, how much Dad and Magdalena…"

"What? Who?"

"Everyone, Mum. Nurses and doctors…neighbors, Dicky."

Did people really think that about her?

"We're not talking about me, John. It's you who …" Rose realized she sounded just like her usual lecturing self. She desperately wanted to leave the hospital knowing she wasn't who she used to be.

She should learn to accept gratitude from others.

"That means a lot," said Rose. "But it's you, I need to know you're all right. You're the brave one. You're the one who is great. Just as you are."

"No, I'm sorry, mum. We lied to you. We didn't want you upset, but Dad and I, we see now how you were protecting us and we were protecting you and now it's all torn apart."

John's chin dropped to his chest and his shoulders heaved. Rose bent into him, holding him.

Rose wanted to offer her usual platitudes; words she hadn't realized were platitudes until they stopped carrying weight. She owed him enough to finally tell the truth, to see the truth, to understand she couldn't control other people.

"I don't know what's going to happen with our family." She took his hands. "I wish I could say it would all work out for sure, but, well, I honestly don't know."

John's eyes filled and Rose felt their sting, the truth squeeze tight.

"But, I do know this, John Pavlesic. You are going to have a good life. The way you want. And I will be there to help you in whatever way I can, if you want me to."

Rose squeezed him into her body so hard he gasped.

He laughed and squeezed her back. "You're gonna bruise another vertebra if you keep that up, Mum."

Rose released him, both laughing, their eyes watery, the love between them palpable, comforting and powerful.

John's face grew serious as their laughter died down. He cleared his throat and pressed down on the bed with his fists to sit up straighter. "There's something I need to make sure you understand, Mum."

Rose shifted her weight and wiped a tear from his cheek.

"I didn't want to go to Notre Dame," he said. "I didn't care if I set the world on fire that day at the game. But I did not throw the game."

"No, no, of course not," Rose said. "You don't—"

"It's that I'm too much like you. Much as I wanted to play like I didn't care, I played hard. I tried not to, but I couldn't. That's how I know I'll be all right. You know what I mean? I'm like you."

"Oh John. I know. I do," Rose said hugging him again, inhaling the smell of his hair.

An orderly knocked on the door and entered. "I need to get Mr. Pavlesic down to therapy." Rose squeezed John again and gently laid him back down. She wiped the wetness from his face. Were they her tears or his?

Rose stood and helped the orderly get John into a wheelchair.

The man wheeled John around the instrument cases that littered the floor. She started picking them up. "I'll take those, Johnny, John, I mean. I shouldn't have..."

John grasped the doorjamb on the way through it, stopping the orderly from moving.

"Leave 'em, Mum. This place could use some good blues. And Johnny's fine, you can call me whatever you want. A name's just a word. No matter what you call me, I know I'm Johnny in your heart. What does it matter what label comes out of your mouth? You're my mum."

Rose nodded and waved to the back of John's head. Relief rushed through her when she saw that he so easily moved from being upset to heading to rehabilitation as though it were the most normal thing he could be doing.

She shuddered, slumped onto the bed and squeezed her eyes shut, fighting back tears, replaying his words. Her son was like her, he had said. He saw her as strong even though she no longer saw herself that way. She sighed and crossed herself, opening her eyes. She stared at the floor where the instruments sat. She swallowed her remorse, if John could be strong enough to move on, if he endowed her with that virtue then she'd find a way to get her strength back. To make the way he saw her true again. Somehow she would.

Chapter 23

Rose found her perspective permanently altered. Her conversation with John had renewed her, lightened her burden. She began cleaning house again, but her work was tinged with joy rather than resentment or duty. She fell back into the typical patterns of washing on Monday, ironing on Tuesday, dusting twice a day, every day. She even decided she might take in boarders if her family didn't return soon. So, in thinking someone would be living with her in the near future, she needed to redd-up the house. She started in Sara Clara's room.

Rose dug out the pink putty that they used to lift the soot from the walls and headed down the hall. She kneaded the soft clump in her hand and pushed open the door, not knowing how messy it might be. It was spotless; no clothing was strewn around, but the room felt stale. She opened the windows and turned to the wall across the way. There she saw very clearly a message from Sara Clara. The day Rose asked her to putty the walls during the week of the fog. Sara Clara said she hadn't started, but she did.

Right in her own room, she used the putty to remove some soot, and did so in a way that formed the words, "I Hate You," right on the wall. Rose laughed. She imagined Sara Clara in her mood, working the pink putty around the wall in the shape of letters, probably never thinking she wouldn't end up puttying the rest of the room, which would have camouflaged her sentiment, never imagining that Rose would ever see it. Rose ran her finger down the letters. She wasn't sure if Sara Clara had directed that at her, Buzzy, or the town of Donora, but any of them could have been her target, Rose thought.

She squeezed the putty in her hand and stopped laughing. Or was this exactly what Sara Clara had wanted; she wanted Rose to see it. Rose shrugged. It wasn't a surprise, Rose hadn't been as nice to her as she should have. And, so, Rose puttied every inch of the bedroom walls, her fingers working the soft pink glob against the plaster, absorbing the black, bringing a concrete accomplishment at the day's end.

She repaired cracks in the walls and ceiling, sanding, giving it a fresh coat of paint, She waxed the kitchen floor and scrubbed the windows with vinegar. Even between choking on the strong odor, she felt heartened thinking of the Saltz family safely tucked away in Warm Springs, Georgia. Rose had taken pride in helping Mrs. Saltz forge a new path through life with the money Rose gave her. Rose knew the decision was right and was sure that finding the cash just when Mrs. Saltz needed it so badly, meant that a large portion of it must have been intended for her.

Rose found solace in the simple act of caring for her surroundings. Still, she was lonely living by herself. Father Tom had been ordered to another parish to relieve another elderly priest and it surprised her how much she missed their talks.

Though Rose could not find it in herself to believe in God again, she returned to the religious habits that had structured her spiritual life before: daily mass, novenas, confession three times a week, and the hope that with her actions, God would somehow show up in her life. Father Tom's words kept her company when it was just her and Rags in the home.

Her indifference frightened her, her disinclination to contact Henry and Magdalena, her failure to invite them or her in-laws back into their home. They would return when they were ready to accept her as she was. If truth were told, she was afraid to ask them back. She couldn't handle them saying no. All it would take to decimate her new found strength was one blow from the people she loved. Living with ambiguity was better than being certain she was not worth loving anymore.

Rose had come to understand that perhaps it was better for a woman to focus on her family. Magdalena would not have the same regrets as Rose did, no, she would have her child with her from the first breath the baby drew.

Rose was enjoying a mid-morning break, sorting through the mail when she came across a letter that had been delivered from Henry. Rose's hands shook as she opened the envelope. She pulled out the flowered stationary then shoved it back in, unwilling to read that Henry was formally breaking up the family.

Rose sipped her coffee, opened the coal bill, and tapped the note from Henry on the tabletop. Rose told herself that he would not have used such cheerful stationery to report that he'd given up on their life together. Hell, he wouldn't have written at all, Rose told herself, tapping the edge of the note causing one corner to fold over.

Rose took the last sip of coffee and slid the note to the center of the table. She would save the news for later, for when she could accept what was in the note, no matter what the news might be.

Back at her windows, Rose thought of the note in the kitchen, her worry about what its contents would tell her, that she could not risk losing her daughter even if Henry was finished with Rose. With a circular motion, then up and down, and across, Rose created gleaming windows, offering a view of a sunny, spring afternoon. The beauty of cleanliness and sunshine could not displace her need to make things right with Magdalena and Henry. No matter what the letter might say.

She went back to the kitchen, ripped the note out of the envelope, feeling an ache for Henry in her belly. She closed her eyes worried he might never see her the way he used to. He would not forgive her. Henry was a kind man, but she understood people couldn't always put their intellect ahead of their heart. Rose had learned that the hard way.

She opened her eyes and stared down at the note she'd smudged.

> *Rose,*
> *I saw you opened an account at Mellon Bank. I'm adding to the funds.*
> *Henry*

She turned it over and back. That was it? Rose exhaled, relieved there was no finality to it. She actually attributed positive connotations to it. It was decidedly good news, she thought, feeling as though there was still a connection between them, odd, as it might have been.

Rose went back to her windows, grateful Henry had chosen to write instead of dropping in to see her. She ran her hand over her hair and looked at her palm. Not as clean as it normally was when Henry had last seen her. Despite her making progress in conducting surveys around town for Bonaroti and the government, getting residents to speak with her, Rose felt a shadow of her former self. She did not want Henry to see her that way.

Even though Rose renewed her housekeeping with vigor, taking care of herself was another matter. The simple act of removing her clothing was off-putting. Full bathing seemed too much of an effort and sometimes four days would pass before she'd break down and get under the water.

Rose was managing on behalf of Doc Bonaroti quite well. It was once she stopped moving at home, when the cleaning was done, the organizing finished, that she was left with only her thoughts and the reflection of her broken heart in the mirror of her soul. She began to realize that no matter what she did to structure her days, constructing a skeleton was not enough to have her life reborn. She was missing too much of what really mattered. But even as Rose came to realize that, she could not bring herself to make the remaining changes that would have given her a full existence.

Rose was finishing up wiping down the countertops when someone knocked at the door. Rose contemplated hiding under the kitchen table, but fought the urge to get on the floor, her head tucked into her knees. She glanced at the clock. Probably the mailman.

She opened the door to Dottie standing there, her tiny hands gloved in the palest blue leather, clenching and unclenching at her side. She rocked on the balls of her feet and settled back.

Rose swallowed hard. With all the progress she made in dealing with her own part in her ripped open world, she had not come far in how she thought about Henry and Dottie. She still seethed at the thought of their bodies joined in the most intimate of ways. Rose looked at her feet, desperate to find a classy way to tell Dottie to get the hell off her stoop.

She squeezed her eyes shut. She couldn't talk to the woman whose mouth had probably covered every square inch of Henry's body. Rose backed into the doorway, closing the door as she did.

Dottie's hand shot out, keeping the door open.

Rose crossed her arms. "What Dottie? Is there something else of my life you'd like?" Rose spun around and gestured to the room as though offering a product for sale.

Dottie stepped into the home and shoved the door closed with the usual screech.

Rose couldn't believe the woman's gall. "Bet you never have a squeaky door at chez Shaginaw?" Rose said. Resentment stung her.

Dottie's posture softened, her chin dropped and she looked away in what appeared to be genuine shame. "I just wanted to set the record straight Rose. That's all."

"Like I said, take what you want, Dottie. As you can see, besides the crusty old mutt over there, I don't have a thing left that you might covet."

Dottie put her hand up to stop Rose from speaking. "You were right. What you said the night of Johnny's accident."

"John," Rose said. "He goes by, John, these days."

"I know."

Of course she did, Rose thought. "You know, Dottie, a few weeks ago I wouldn't have granted you ten seconds of the same air I was breathing." Rose ran her hand through her greasy hair and stuck out her chest, "But I'm not so fragile anymore. I give you thirty seconds. Because I'm all sugar and goodness, now. I've changed."

Dottie raised her gaze to Rose. "That night of John's accident. You were right. I did, I do, want what you have, Rose. What you and Henry have—"

"Had," Rose said. What good was some stupid confession after all that had happened?

Dottie nodded. "It's true, I found some relief in being with Henry. Just that once."

Rose exhaled her exasperation. "I don't want a rehash of your sexual exploits, Dottie. You have doting parents, a pristine home, the best nursing job in town, a slew of friends and admirers. Isn't that enough?" Rose shrugged. "You were the one who caused John's cord," Rose said, slapping her hand over her mouth. Husband-poacher or not, Dottie was the reason John was still alive.

Dottie straightened her back and stepped forward. "Listen to me. That night when the kids were babies, sixteen years ago, I went to your house to speak with *you*. I needed a friend. Someone I could trust."

Rose broke Dottie's gaze.

"I was going to run away, leave my home, my parents, everything, I was so ashamed. They didn't approve of the person I loved. I was devastated, and vulnerable and needy, and when I got to your place, there was Henry."

Dottie stepped into Rose's sightline, forcing her to make eye contact. "Henry was like I'd never seen him, so open, so needy. And we just, well, I needed to see if…well, if I wasn't attracted to Henry, I knew I wouldn't be attracted to any man. If not Henry. Then no man."

"Boo-hoo, You diddled Henry and found out no other man would do. I'm supposed to cry because you're a spinster?"

"Listen, Rose. For once, shut the hell up and listen."

Rose crossed her arms, raising her eyebrows at being ordered to shut up.

Dottie looked at the floor then lifted her gaze to meet Rose's. "I'm not attracted to men, Rose. The relationship my parents disapproved of was with another woman."

Rose looked toward the wall, then at her shuffling feet. What did Dottie say?

Dottie pointed to her heart. "I knew it here. But I had to prove it to myself. And, yes, from the time I was six, a part of me loved Henry. My God, what's not to love? But, I was desperate that night. Well, Henry and I kissed and touched, and yes, got undressed, but we couldn't do it Rose. He couldn't. Because of you. I couldn't because of…"

Rose tapped her toe. She didn't believe a word.

"Lois Hampton." Dottie blurted the name and crossed her arms. "We've been together forever. Not living together as you know. She wants to, thinks no one will blink at a couple of gals living together, like sisters. But my parents know the truth. They caught us that night." Dottie sighed. "That's why I went to your house, to talk to you but Henry was there, just waiting to help prove to me that I was normal."

Dottie's eyes filled. "That night, I just needed someone to tell me I didn't have horns and a tail. And Henry was there. And you weren't. And you're right. I do want what you have Rose."

Rose stepped back from Dottie, trying to appear as though nothing she was hearing made any difference at all.

Dottie lifted her hand to Rose. "I want children, a family, the house. But believe me when I say, I never wanted any of that with Henry. I know that doesn't change what we did."

Rose glanced at Dottie's outstretched hand and ignored it.

Dottie re-crossed her arms. "I wanted you to know, I never meant to hurt you or your marriage. When it came to giving advice about Magdalena, I told Henry to talk to you. That was it."

Rose opened her mouth but couldn't say what she thought. There had been rumors for years regarding Dottie's preferences. Some called it off-center or queer. But Rose never gave it much credence. Rose looked into Dottie's face and was moved by her sincerity, her anguish.

Dottie wiped her brow with the back of her hand. "I've always been amazed Rose, how you live your life. You ignored people talking nonsense about your career. You were always content with the people who love your nursing care, your family. You don't give a hoot who put you down, you simply trusted they'd come around, when you have to care for them or their family. I admire you, Rose. You're brave. And so, yes, to have what you have, I couldn't put a dollar amount on it if I tried."

Rose felt overwhelmed, covered her mouth and turned to leave. Three steps down the hall, she stopped. She couldn't do it anymore. She put her hands on her hips and turned back to Dottie who was already headed out the door.

"Wait," Rose said.

Dottie came back inside.

Rose didn't know what to make, exactly, of what Dottie had just told her, but she knew no one would lie about such things. Rose knew if Dottie admitted to loving women, if she risked confiding in the person who hated her more than anyone in the world, then she must be telling the truth. And for Rose, that was stunning. Such courage. Putting the truth out there like that. She decided it was that, the truth, not an act of desperation that was driving Dottie.

Dottie took another step forward. "Rose?"

Rose resisted the urge to run again. She stepped toward Dottie, fingers laced at her waist.

"Thank you." Rose said, and shrugged.

Dottie smiled and stepped halfway out the door. "You're welcome, Rose."

And the two nodded at each other, sharing a moment, a pause in acrimony that felt like friendship, a moment of grace Rose needed more than ever.

Chapter 24

Rose had just bedded down a roast, half of which she was planning to slice and share with Donora's needy folks, when the side-door squealed open, startling her. She inched across the kitchen floor, wondering who might be entering without permission. She poked her head into the hallway and saw the back end of Buzzy, moving through the door, struggling with luggage.

Leo peeked over the mound of suitcases at Rose, jumping up and down.

She could not believe they were here. She ran down the hall and pulled Leo over the luggage. He latched his legs around her laughing. Rose smoothed his hair as he snuggled his head into her shoulder.

Buzzy smiled, nervously glancing from Sara Clara to the luggage and back at Rose. Sara Clara removed her hat and Buzzy cleared a path through the luggage for her to walk. Rose shifted Leo to her hip and moved toward Buzzy, hugging him, then Sara Clara, holding her so tight that she choked in Rose's embrace.

Rose pulled back and pinched Leo's cheek before setting him down. She opened her arms to Buzzy and Sara Clara. "Look at you. You're here."

Buzzy and Sara Clara passed a glance between them and Leo shoved a starfish up at Rose. She squatted down to his level and ran her finger over the hardened spikes, turning it back and forth.

"I've never seen one of these in person," Rose said.

"I'll take you there this summer when you come visit Auntie Anna. She said you could have hers for now and that you better get down there and visit her. You can find one yourself then."

Rose bit her lip, her eyes brimming with tears.

Buzzy and Sara Clara hung back, clutching their luggage as if waiting for Rose to attack.

Rose tousled Leo's hair and sent him to the kitchen to pour some waters for everyone. She wrenched her in-laws' bags out of their hands. "Let me take those." Buzzy and Sara Clara appeared bewildered as if they landed in a foreign country instead of the home they used to share.

"Well, I don't have all day for this kind of rubbish," Rose said. "Come on in and tell me how you've been. I've, well…I've been working with the Feds to survey people about the fog. And see, here." Rose slid the suitcases further inside with her foot and closed the door to reveal a poster size piece of butcher paper behind it. "See, I recreated the map I had of Donora and I've plotted where all the folks died during the fog. I've mapped out who got sick. I've listed the pertinent symptoms reported by everyone, according to their address. Fifty more people died in the month after the fog. Did you know that? So, I mapped their homes as well. You won't believe—"

Buzzy poked at the map where Unk's name marked where he had died. Rose saw sadness creep into his expression. His gaze slid over the map, taking in the information Rose had recorded.

"We believe it, Rose. We saw Bonaroti when we stopped to fill up the tank. He told us how you've gotten folks to talk, to tell the truth. He doesn't think the report will see the light of day because of the mills being so powerful and all and you know, politics. Well, I don't need to tell you. But, he said, you're his miracle. A living, breathing gift to the town."

KATHLEEN SHOOP

Rose looked at her feet and picked up two suitcases, touched by Buzzy's sincerity that for once didn't feel like manipulative flattery or biting sarcasm. She told herself not to hold back. "I've missed you so much," Rose said.

Sara Clara pulled off her gloves and wiped away tears.

Rose dropped the suitcases and went to her sister-in-law, folding her into her arms. You're my family. You're mine and I'm yours, Rose thought.

She squeezed her eyes shut. "It wasn't the same without you." Rose felt strange to utter those words and odder still to feel them. "It wasn't right. Not even with all I've done gathering data for the surveys. That feels good, to be effective again. But, really, for the first time, it didn't matter the same way. Even knowing it's important work."

Rose held her grip for another few seconds before releasing Sara Clara and laughing. "So that's it? You guys got your tongues taken out when you were down south or something?" It was then Buzzy pulled a clump of money from his coat pocket and held it out.

He'd stumbled upon an Alcoholics Anonymous chapter in North Carolina and though he'd just made it part way through the steps, he was back home to make amends.

"Well, I'll be damned," Rose said, taking the money. "I'll be damned." She pulled him into a hug that he couldn't squirm out of. She thought of the money she'd given to Mrs. Saltz to move, and that in giving it away, she had made room for something better.

Sara Clara's father had paid Buzzy to work while in North Carolina, and he promised Rose to refill the coffers even if it was a little at a time. She studied him as he spoke; looking for telltale signs he was playing her for a fool. But in the same way Rose had seen sincerity in Dottie she saw it in Buzzy's gaze, too.

* * *

Four weeks later, Rose and Sara Clara were working together in the kitchen. Rose was back at her stove, scrambling eggs while percolating coffee and cooking up the bacon and sausage. Sara Clara scurried around the house, readying for the job at Isaly's she now had as a part-time cashier. Leo was still asleep. The door squealed open and Buzzy returned from working at the mill, exactly 7:20. He kissed Rose's cheek, making her feel Henry's absence more than she had in months.

Buzzy yammered on about mill gossip, informing Rose of one family's needs or another. He reported what Rose already knew; many residents were still unwilling to talk about the fog and the mills.

Rose appreciated Buzzy's verbal serenade. He never really expected her to respond with more than a nod or umhum and it allowed her time to think of Magdalena and John, without the yearning it brought. She didn't fully trust Buzzy, but she saw that he had changed in a way that couldn't be denied.

The door screeched open and Dottie appeared, black bag dangling, arms laden with files. Rose scrambled to relieve Dottie of the paperwork, hoisted it onto the kitchen table, and thanked her.

"I've gone over everything and it looks good. I think we're ready to start this thing up," Dottie said as she headed back toward the doorway.

Buzzy looked at Rose and then toward the doorway.

Rose bolted after Dottie.

"It's the most generous gift, Dottie. Thank you. Now we don't have to worry about begging for clinic money, well you know what this means."

Dottie nodded turning back to open the door.

"Wait. Breakfast." Rose said. "Stay for some eggs and bacon. Please."

Dottie paused and then turned.

Rose walked over to Dottie and took her hand. "You're my friend. And friends always stay for a meal."

A small smile appeared on Dottie's face and she nodded. Then as Rose prepared the rest of breakfast, she relaxed as she heard Buzzy and Sara Clara treat Dottie as though she were family, as though they understood that she should have been all along.

For her entire life, Rose alienated herself from the other women in town. Oh, she'd nurse them in the most intimate of circumstances, but her nursing was her shield, too busy to have tea or lunch, to have even one friend. And now there was Dottie, Father Tom, and she'd come to realize, Bonaroti. Every woman needed a friend. A spouse could only do so much. Rose could see that her friendship meant something to Dottie, too. For the first time, Rose thought she just might actually be able to *be* a friend.

* * *

Rose made good on her promise not to manage anyone's life and while it made her visits with John enjoyable, she ached not knowing what his future would hold. Henry used a portion of the money they had saved for Magdalena's college—he'd spent it on something. Rose wasn't sure for what, but he never consulted her on it, just spent the money. But Rose kept her mouth shut. She'd learned to pick her arguments.

She felt good; she didn't have to manage anyone but herself.

Rose went about her now normal routine. She checked in on those needing home health care and mapped out which homes she still needed to visit to interview about the fog. And, she would stop at Mellon Bank on the corner of McKean and Fifth and check in on the accounts she'd opened for the children and Henry.

Buzzy had told her that Henry would come to town to deposit money in the account. Rose would then check up on what he'd done, feeling as though somehow they were talking to one another through the bank transactions—him depositing, her checking up on the funds. In March Rose noticed he'd withdrawn several hundred dollars and Buzzy informed her he was using the money for going to college as he had once dreamed of doing.

Rose felt compelled to meet Henry face to face, but was not confident to call him on the phone and order a meeting and was too fragile to request one. So, she planned to run into him the next time he came Donora to deposit money.

Rose had dawdled inside the bank much longer than was normal, even making small talk with people she didn't like very much. Finally realizing Henry was not coming, she left the bank and ran smack into Pierpont who was tacking paper onto the telephone pole right outside the bank.

"Hey, Mrs. Pavlesic. It's been awhile! You got to catch a glimpse of this." He shoved a paper into her hands and then nearly skipped down the sidewalk tacking up the papers on every surface he could. When Rose couldn't see him anymore, she looked at the paper he'd pushed into her hand. There in black print was an announcement that the band, *Johnny and the Slag Heap*, was to perform at the Galaxy in two weeks.

There was a photo of the fellas playing, blurry as it was—the printing must have been cheap—she could make out the forms of each boy as easy as if they had been standing in front of her. There, in the front was her Johnny, trumpet to his lips, smiling around it as he always did, leaning awkwardly against the piano, clearly up and about, but not yet the man he had been.

Rose felt like she was socked in the belly. She bent over, tears flowing that her son had not listened to her and was living the life he was destined for, rather than the one she'd constructed for him.

A tap on her back made her straighten. She wiped her tears then turned to see Magdalena standing there.

"Mum?"

Rose felt her throat tighten. She straightened her hat, overcome by the sight of her daughter's bulging belly. Henry's arm was slung over Magdalena's shoulder making Rose feel alienated from them further. She did not know what to say with them both there. Where would she start?

"You're crying," Henry said.

Rose shook her head and wiped her eyes.

"Is it John?" Magdalena said.

Rose shook her head. "Oh, Jesus, who's crying? Not old me, you know better than that." Rose had never hesitated in showing Magdalena affection or withholding it, but right then, knowing all she wanted to do was hold her daughter, she was for the first time, not sure she should.

As though Magdalena could read Rose's thoughts, she broke away from Henry and stepped toward Rose, making the first move back into her life.

Rose had never felt such a precious hug. She inhaled Magdalena's freshly shampooed hair and opened her eyes to see Henry open his arms and take both women into them, holding tight. Months earlier, a public gesture like this would have put her in the grave, but now she didn't care if they looked foolish. Her family was back with her and that was all that mattered.

Chapter 25

It was like old times; Henry and Buzzy, Sara Clara and Leo huddled around the breakfast table, swapping news. Magdalena waddled into the room, still in her bathrobe.

Rose watched her daughter, warmed by the sweet glow of her pregnant daughter. She no longer allowed herself to linger in regret, thinking that Magdalena's life might not be perfect in the way she hoped it would. Rose crossed herself so thankful she and Henry had returned regularly to make deposits in their bank account, that she could stage her running into them on McKean. Rose kissed Magdalena's cheek, the sound of her daughter saying her name filling her with love.

Magdalena ran her hand over her pregnant belly. "I want to talk to you about the baby."

"Let's go to the bedroom for privacy," Rose said.

"No, I'll say what I have to with everyone here. No secrets."

Rose and Henry's eyes met before she glanced at Buzzy and Sara Clara. Rose locked gazes with Magdalena.

"I want to go to University of Pittsburgh," Magdalena said.

"You're about to be a mother."

"I know. But, that doesn't mean I can't go to school. I know I made my bed and now I have to lie in it. But I was wondering. What if I went to college and you help raise the baby? I mean, when I think of who it is I want to be, it's someone like you, Mum. And I can't do that alone, with a baby."

Rose set the spatula down on the counter and looked to Henry then back to Magdalena.

Buzzy lowered his paper, but was remarkably speechless on the matter. Sara Clara stirred sugar into her tea.

"What," Rose said. "Like the Murphy kid who thinks his grandmother's his mother? And his real mother walks around town with her "real" children and everyone knows it, but the boy who knows something is amiss but not what?"

Rose sat beside Henry and took a sip of his coffee. "That poor kid's mixed up and I think you could trace his confusion directly back to that one error in judgment." Rose cocked her head. "And I know a lot about errors in judgment."

"I don't mean that, Mum. I'll study while the baby naps."

"What makes you think the Tucharoni boy will agree to all of this?"

"We've already discussed it. He'll live here, too."

Rose thought of the upcoming wedding ceremony Father Tom would preside over in just a few days. "I don't know if it's possible to do what you want."

"Yes you do. I do, too. Sara Clara does." Magdalena motioned to Sara Clara who nodded back.

"Sara Clara's going to watch the baby while I'm at class and you're working. I know people will talk, Mum. They'll talk any which way you slice this up. I was meant to do this, be a scientist. And, I can do both—be a mom and be educated. "

Henry sipped his coffee. "I don't know. I understand you want to do this, but it's just not done. Women have a hard enough time in college, to have to..."

Rose shook her head. She worried it would be too hard for Magdalena, too.

Magdalena tapped her foot and lifted her chin. "Even if you say no, I'm telling you right now, I'm going to college. I'll find a way. I'm going."

Henry reached across the table and took Rose's hand.

Magdalena covered her parents' hands with hers. "You see Mum, who you are, is part of me. I know I can handle this because everything you've taught me. I can do this because of you. And, isn't that what you wanted in the first place?"

Rose looked at Henry and the others.

"We'll all help, Rose," Buzzy said over his paper.

Rose cleared her throat, swallowing her reaction to Buzzy's sincerity. "If this is going to work," Rose said, "with my nursing and the mill shifts and Leo, we'll all have to pitch in. And the only way to do that is to stay in this house."

Magdalena let out a squeal and crushed Rose in a hug. Rose squeezed back as her daughter patted the back of her head and smoothed her hair, like a mother would a child, and in that small gesture, Rose felt loved.

* * *

Rose pulled her stockings and underwear from her drawer and began to dress for work. Henry came into the bedroom, but averted his gaze from Rose's naked body. A month had gone by since Henry and Magdalena returned home and neither Rose nor Henry had discussed their marriage, the lies, the way each had treated the other.

Rose rehearsed the conversation repeatedly. She and Henry would sit holding hands, looking at each other dead-on, calmly discussing their mistakes instead screaming them out the way they had at the cemetery. Now that she understood what had happened with Dottie, she needed to apologize. They both knew the facts of their pasts, but Rose wasn't sure he understood that she hadn't meant to lie so much. She forgave Henry for his lies, for pushing her aside. But, still she could not bring herself to tell him how she felt as the events of that week in October had unfolded, how it felt to lose her family, her work, herself.

He went to the bedside table and wound the clock. Rose stepped into her underpants, garter belt and hooked her bra. Henry fussed with the drawer where he kept his cigarettes.

"There's a new pack in the kitchen," Rose said.

Henry turned. Rose met his gaze in the mirror.

"Nah. I quit smoking. Figured if it was unhealthy to breathe in the smoke from the mills then inhaling smoke from flaming tobacco directly into my lungs wasn't too bright."

"Oh," Rose said. "That makes good sense."

She pulled her underwear drawer back open and lifted a small green book from underneath her stockings. She handed it to Henry and sat beside him on the bed. While he turned the book back and forth, she rolled on one stocking and snapped the suspenders to the stocking.

Henry patted her leg. "What's this?"

Rose lifted her other leg and rolled on the second stocking. "Look inside."

She attached the stocking and put her slip on while Henry cracked open the book. She smiled as his eyes registered what he was holding.

She went to the closet and took a uniform from its hanger, slipping it over her head.

When she turned to face her husband, he was already there, taking her into an embrace.

"Where did you ever get that?"

Rose drew back and ran her hand down his stubbly face. "I have my ways. You like it?"

He nodded. "It's amazing. Is it real?"

"What, you think I forged the inscription from the great W.H. Auden?"

"Did you read it?"

Rose laid her head on Henry's shoulder and latched her arms around him, feeling protected and content. "Why yes, instead of documenting the country's worst industrial disaster I sat on my ass and read a little Auden."

Henry laughed and squeezed Rose harder into his chest. "It's just incredible."

"I'm glad it suits you."

"Rose." Henry pushed Rose away and looked into her eyes.

"Henry," she glanced away.

He took her chin and lifted it so she had to look directly at him.

"I love you," he said.

Rose smiled and moved Henry's hand from her chin, nestling back into his chest. "I love you, too, Hen. I love you more than I can ever fully say."

Henry pulled back again. "What do you say we move out? They're building these new homes. They're sturdy, small brick houses. We'll have enough money to build—"

"Shush." Rose put her finger to Henry's lips and shook her head. "We're home. Just like this, here, like this." Rose shrugged. "And, so we'll stay."

Henry nodded. "I sort of feel like this is new. All of it. Us."

Rose slipped on her shoes and began to tie her hair into a bun. "New. Yeah, me too. I like that thought."

And so Rose headed into her day knowing that although she would never know exactly what might happen next in her life, she could live like that. She was finally becoming the person she had pretended to be all along.

More Notes...

I've written a companion piece that goes with *After the Fog* for those who are interested in learning more about Donora, its people, the historical five days of fog, and post-war America. For those who need just a bit more information regarding what was "real" in this novel, here are some notes:

1. Dr. Bonaroti tells Buzzy and Sara Clara that he doesn't believe the report the federal employees are writing will see the light of day. A report did come out and is referenced in the resource section. However, the surveys that were conducted and other data collected are lost in some cases and in others it's reported that US Steel will not release information they collected, even decades after the incident.

2. While residents were proud of their mills and the tonnage they churned out, Dr. Charles Stacey was clear about the fact that "Parents realized their kids should go to college if possible. In the years of 1944 and 1945 nineteen football players went to college. Playing sports was the ticket into something better."

3. Donora was nationally known as "Home of the Champions." The town was considered part of the "Arsenal of Democracy." The phrase is attributed to FDR and was widely used to garner support to ready for the possibility of war. The phrase is also said to have first been used by others

before it became well known in FDR's famous speech and beyond.

4. Although Harry Loftus related a story to me about the way he guided a car through the fog by walking with it, no real person that we know of was injured in that way as the character of Johnny was in *After the Fog*.

5. The character of Dr. Bonaroti is very, very loosely based on information available to me about Dr. Rongaus—the chairman of the board of health in Donora. Dr. Rongaus crusaded against the pollution emitted from the mills and fought to have them shut down during the smog. "Murder in the Mills," was reported to be his characterization of the situation during the deadly week. Interviews with Donora residents reveal Dr. Rongaus was direct, generous, and extremely well regarded by fellow citizens, but he did not worry about offending people if he believed in a cause. Other than drawing from the obvious, well-known aspects related to the actions of Dr. Rongaus during the fog, the character of Dr. Bonaroti is fiction.

6. The Zinc Mill in Donora closed a few years after the five days of deadly fog, but there is disagreement regarding whether the closure was a result of fog/smog fallout or the result of technology making the decades old zinc works obsolete.

7. In researching for this book, I found references to women's groups and wealthy individuals who funded visiting nurse clinics in the

Pittsburgh area—that was where the idea came from for the funding issue in *After the Fog*. There was a women's club in Donora that offered "baby clinics" up until WWII. The Donora Historical Society has a few photos of well-dressed women gathered at meetings, perhaps offering new, young, poorer mothers postnatal advice. Brian Charlton indicated the club would host baby contests as well, but the clinics do not appear to have offered medical care in the way we think of clinics today.

8. Brian Charlton indicated that Donora did have a Community Chest that helped people during the depression and operated up until WWII. A priest from St. Phillips also ran a welfare fund that faded out by WWII.

9. The deadly smog events in Donora helped push the Clean Air Act of 1955 into being. Donora's Smog Museum tagline is "Clear Air Started Here."

10. Visiting nurses were well established fixtures in Allegheny county and Pittsburgh, but did not come to Washington county until a few years after "the fog." Donora did have nurses working in the mill hospital. Interviews with Donora residents reveal that those nurses were exceptionally generous with their time and expertise, helping fellow citizens when asked. I found some references to nurses who were conducting "clinics," in the schools, but there aren't details pertaining to who they were or where they were based. Many babies were still delivered in their homes in 1948. None of the nurses depicted

in *After the Fog* are based on any specific person from Donora.

11. While many think of mothers working outside the home as a 1970's/80's development, I have spoken to women who did so well before that. Two of those ladies were my grandmothers. My Grandma Jane Arthur (a west coast gal) was a teacher who put herself through college during the depression. My Grandma Rose Jacobs (who lived in the mill-town of Etna) provided the anecdote that inspired the situation that had the character of Mrs. Sebastian visiting Rose's home in order to help her decide whether to fund the clinic. When my grandmother applied for work at Bell Telephone, someone visited her home to be sure her son (my dad) and their home would be adequately cared for if she were to work for them. Like many people in post-war America, I had the Pavlesics live with extended family under the same roof and split chores, including the care of children during the day. Finally, the name Rose is taken from my gram, and yes, the real Rose is straightforward, a bit harsh, no-nonsense, and the hardest worker you could ever hope to hire. However, the only element of the fictional Rose's backstory that is directly related to my grandmother is fact that both were orphaned (my gram and her siblings lived with relatives, not in an orphanage). Any other details related to Rose Pavlesic's personal journey and the resemblance of any other family members to any characters in the book is completely coincidental.

Book Club Guide

1. Discuss the way Rose's upbringing and the traumas she experienced colored the way she plotted her life and expected others to live. How were Rose's defense mechanisms effective or not?

2. How would you characterize Rose's relationships with Henry, Unk, Magdalena, Johnny, and others in the story?

3. What do you imagine the next phase of the Pavlesic family's life will look like?

4. Discuss Rose's ability to connect with patients of all walks of life, but her difficulty in being "intimate" with those closest to her.

5. How did religion influence Rose?

6. How is the Pavlesic family similar to yours?

7. Discuss the setting of Donora. How is it like places you've known?

8. Discuss the role of a community/public health nurse and how you see them fitting into society.

9. How was the way the citizens of Donora were reluctant to discuss the five days of fog with the survey-takers surprising to you?

10. Discuss the way people become so accustomed to a certain standard of living that they don't recognize danger. For example, explore the fact that the football game and the parade went on as planned, with many people adamantly sure the fog was no worse those days than any other.

Resources

The characters, their actions, plotlines and personal journeys in *After the Fog* are fiction. I used the facts related to the documented timeline of the darkening fog/smog and the types of illnesses that were reflected in reports of the disaster as obstacles for the characters. I also used the odd back and forth between some people understanding the fog was different than normal and others not thinking the five days were unique at all until the weekend was over. In addition, I found that some sources disagree with certain aspects of what the days were like and who was to blame.

In other words there were conflicting reports on the fog and its impact on the citizens of Donora so I had to make artistic decisions when I chose to include or ignore certain elements pertaining to the five days of Donora smog. Brian Charlton offers an in-depth presentation of the fog events along with the myths and facts that have shaped the recollections of those who witnessed and reported on the killing smog. He can be reached through the Donora Historical Society—Donorasmog.com.

Interviews about Donora, life in the late 40's, and making steel:

- Dr. Charles Stacey

- Brian Charlton

- Dave Lonich

- Mr. and Mrs. Harry Loftus

- Various attendees at 2008 Smog Museum opening and commemoration of 1948 smog disaster

- Rose Jacobs

- Jane Arthur

- Robert H. Kaltenhauser

Books, Articles, and Reports:

- *When Smoke Ran Like Water: Tales of Environmental Deception and the Battle Against Pollution*, Devra Davis (2002)

- *The Fluoride Deception*, Christopher Bryson (2004)

- *Talking Steel Towns: The Men and Women of America's Steel Valley*, Ellie Wymard (2007)

- *Community Health Association: Nursing Technique* (1930)

- The Public Health Nurse Quarterly, Pittsburgh, PA (1931)

- *Nursing Manual: Public Health Nursing Association of Pittsburgh*, PA (1941)

- The Second Five-Year Report on Poliomyelitis in Allegheny County 1945-1949, Inclusive, Wilton H. Robinson, M.D.

- "Investigation of the Smog Incident in Donora, PA, and Vicinity," James G. Townsend, MD, FAPHA, presented at American School Health Association and the Engineering, Epidemiology, Industrial Hygiene, and School Health Sections of the APHA, October 28, 1949

- Deathmap—www.calu.edu/business-community/teaching...donora-digital-collection/_files/deathmap_s.jpg

- Travel with a Beveridge—scottbeveridge.blogspot.com

- The New Yorker Digital edition—Annals of Medicine: "The Fog," Berton Roueche (1950)

- "Chats with a Public Health Nurse," Elizabeth H. Roth, Public Health Nursing Association of Pittsburgh—date unknown

- "For the Care of the Sick," McKees Rocks Gazette, author unknown, October 1919

- The Public Health Disparities Geocoding Project Monograph (Reference to Herman Biggs' quote on public health—Monthly Bulletin, NYC Health Department—1911) http://www.hsph.harvard.edu/thegeocodingproject/webpage/monograph/introduction.htm

- "Donora Smog of 1948," Barry Gilbert, EPAalumni.org, April 29, 2009

- "Splendid Achievement of the Community Nurse, Great Asset to Health of Entire District," Homestead (Leader?), October 6, 1919

- "20 Died. The Gov't. Took Lead. In 1948, a Killer Fog Spurred Air Cleanup," Jeff Gammage, Philadelphia Inquirer, October 28, 1998

- "Think You Know: It Takes 1,200 Kinds for the Many uses of Nails," William P. Vogel, Jr., Popular Science, December, 1947

- "Ethnographic Survey for Steel Industry Heritage Corporation," Washington County, PA, Cynthia Kerchmar (1992)

- *Everyday Fashions of the Forties: As Pictured in Sears Catalogs*, JoAnne Olian, ed. (1992)

- *The Age of Anxiety*, WH Auden (1947)

Acknowledgments

Thank you to Dr. Charles Stacey for your guided tours, insider/eye-witness views and kindness in helping usher *After the Fog* into the light of day. There isn't a corner or crevice of Donora that doesn't hold volumes of history and isn't immensely interesting. Thank you for discussing the practical complexities of trying to illustrate the conflict between parents who were so proud of their work and town, yet wanted so much for their children to go away to college and have a life outside the mills. Also thanks for helping me illuminate the conflict that existed for the sickened people and their desire to keep the mills running, afraid to lose what they worked so hard to gain.

Thanks to Brian Charlton—your expertise, knowledge about Donora's past, historical accuracy pointers and the ability to let fiction sit inside a non-fiction event was a fabulous gift to bestow upon me. Thanks also for the use of all the photos and maps of Donora and for insight into its various people and mill-works. The Smog Museum is a powerful testimony to an influential tragedy and a great town.

Mrs. and Mr. Harry Loftus—thank you for the valuable memories and time you shared with me. Your insights into the "five days of fog," mill politics and steel production were paramount in creating this novel. Your stories inspired mine—I feel like Kramer on Seinfeld when I say, thanks for the use of your "I walked in front of the car to guide it through the fog," tale and so many others.

Thanks to my mom for collecting volumes of nursing reports, handwritten/typed accounts of what community/public health nurses did for a living. What a treasure they are to see. I hope I brought to life the incredible work those women did in a way that honors them. And, thank you for giving me the idea of looking into Donora in the first place. Thanks to my dad for EVERYTHING!

To Rose Jacobs who has regaled me with mill-town and family lore for as long as I've been alive. Thanks for explaining the complex circumstance of being "well-off" in post-war America, but still on the cusp of losing your savings with one bad accident, one lost job, one necessary, large purchase, how having a good meal was good living, not at all what we think of good living today. You would have been an impeccable scientist—attention to detail and relentless hard work live in everything you do. Thanks for all that you've instilled in me. You taught me it doesn't matter what your education level is, make the most of it and aim to be the best you can at what you do.

For Jane Arthur—the other side of the impressive grandma coin! You taught me that there's no good reason to be under-educated, not even the Great Depression. If there's a certain job you want, you find a way to get the skills to do it! You put yourself through college, earned a scholarship and finished at a time it was unusual for women to do so. You were an amazing teacher and an inspiration. The next book's for you!

To my sister, Beth—thanks for the epidemiological analysis of *After the Fog* and for always finding humor in Pittsburgh people. Thanks, too, for your honesty...I know when you finally say something is good that it actually is.

To Lisa—as usual, I need to thank you for walking this entire book from an idea all the way through publication. I know the last thing you have time for is reading another scene let alone the entire book—yet you do it anyway. Those selfless acts are immeasurable.

Thanks so much, Catherine Coulter, your feedback and endless author talk has made publishing so much better. Your time, expertise, and endless gestures that demonstrate your enthusiasm for this work are valued beyond any expression offered here. I appreciate everything you've done!

To Jan and Bob Shoop for so generously giving my book to everyone who would take it. Thank you for your kind words about the work I did and for inviting me to a Kerr Memorial Museum Book Club meeting to discuss *The Last Letter*. I appreciate it so much.

Thanks to Barbara DeSantis—your editing insights were perfect. How could I not see the problem with the birthmark scene? And Magdalena's revelation and…and…and…on and on…Thank you!

To Julie Metz and Monica Gurevich—your covers are beautiful and I'm so fortunate to have your work envelop mine!

Thank you, Martha Alderson, your gentle plot consultations helped shape this book.

Sue McClafferty—your guidance and suggestions are forged into every word of *After the Fog*.

Crystal Patriarche—thank you for all the promotional work—you certainly helped push *The Last Letter* out of my friend bubble and into Kindle Bestsellerdom! Thanks for your fabulous work on *After the Fog*.

Kim Cecere—thank you also for your PR work! I'm so lucky to have you working with me.

Stephanie Elliot, my first editor—thank you for all the heartfelt recommendations and generous marketing you did for *The Last Letter*. I learned so much from you and you always left me laughing.

To Melissa Foster and World Literary Café. Thank you for bringing me into the world of social networking. I still stink at it, but it's great to have people like you cheering me on. Melissa, your enthusiasm and kindness are stunning and I value our friendship so much.

Madhu Wangu—thank you for your insights into Rose and her life...I still chuckle at your feedback regarding naked Unk.

Cindy Closkey and everyone at Big Big Design. Your website work is beautiful and functional—I wish my entire life worked like Kshoop.com!

MJ Rose—You are so giving with all that you know about writing, marketing and promotion. I couldn't have sold so well without you. Thank you for your sharp honesty...it's a little painful, but it's priceless.

Thanks to Steve Windwalker at kindlenationdaily.com—Those kindle ads are gold! Worth every penny and more. Your advice and sense of humor made my foray into self-publishing as profitable as I dreamed it could be.

Catherine Coulter, Michele Harden, Jen Muir, Gwen Sullivan, Mary Kay Pronio, Megan Farrell, Emily Markel, and Gretchen Kurzawa—thank you for endless reading, plotting, feedback, support, celebrating and pushing the book to everyone you know. Your excitement has made the success meaningful. I'm so glad to call you all my friends.

Thanks to Tony Harden for hauling a stash of *The Last Letter* along with golf clubs and lacrosse gear and passing the books out to all who wanted to read!

Mike Kurzawa—thanks to you for tracking down the official weather condition report for the Month of October 1948 in Donora, PA. I might still be looking for it if you hadn't found it!

To Amanda Allis—thank you for reading a draft of *After the Fog* and for being enthusiastic about both books. Your insights helped a ton and the updates on friends reading *The Last Letter* were precious to me.

Thanks to Jen Gold—your creativity inspires me.

Thank you Linda Adzima! Your encouragement and love of Rose was just what I needed!

To Maura, thank you for buying *The Last Letter* for everyone you thought would read it! I appreciate that so much. Next up: *Parking Lot 13: Essays and Stories* including: *When Your Extended Family Can't Get Where They're Supposed to be Going, How to Exit a Police Cruiser as Though You do it Everyday,* and *Deliver the Heimlich or Answer the Phone? Knowing When to Do Which.* That's for Bob.

To Wendy Curtis—you have been such a fantastic reader over the years. Thank you for bringing my work to your book club—that meant the world to me.

For Sara Claire Bulger for having a sense of humor about my using a derivation of your name for "Sara Clara from the South." You are nothing like her, but somehow the name fit!

Marcia Lehman—my first fan! I'll never forget your email saying how interested you were in reading *The Last Letter* and then the email saying how much you loved it. Thank you. The way you spread the word about the book was a true gift I can never repay.

Thanks to my family—in-laws and blood—you have all simply floored me with the way you've helped me with writing and pushing my work. I am humbled by your love. Thanks to all the children in the family...you are what makes life good.

Thanks to the teachers, administrators and students at MACS—the world is better because of all of you. Thanks for sharing your lives and classrooms with me—I truly learn something new every time I'm there. Go Pitt! That's for you, Mr. Scoumis. Next year's our year...

To the following book clubs, organizations, and businesses—I thank you for your interest and for having me talk about my work or carry it in your local store. It's an unbelievable experience to hear your thoughts, to have conversations that bring characters and events from the books to life as though their fictional world somehow matters:

Food, Friends, and Books Book Club

Kerr Memorial Museum Book Club

Anne Buechli's Book Club

Goldenrods Book Club

Shaler-North Hills Library

Oakmont Carnegie Library

DAR—KushKushKee Trail Chapter

The Cooper-Siegel Community Library, Fox Chapel, Friday morning Book Club

Mystery Lovers Bookshop—Oakmont, PA

Mae's Hallmark—Oakmont, PA

If I've forgotten anyone please remind me! I'll correct the omission with the next book. I am so lucky to have so many people with expertise and enthusiasm who see the value in my work and who work so hard to tell others about it. Thank you!

For Beth and Jake—you astound me every day. Jake, your writing and movies are horrifically fantastic and Beth your stories are beautiful and clever.

Bill, thank you for all the rest of the stuff that isn't mentioned here! I appreciate every single thing you do.

CPSIA information can be obtained at www.ICGtesting.com
Printed in the USA
LVOW06s1403291213

367302LV00005B/445/P